# THE LEGACY OF CAIN

# WILKIE COLLINS

## THE LEGACY OF CAIN

SUTTON PUBLISHING

First published in 1888

First published in this edition in the United Kingdom in 1993 by
Alan Sutton Publishing Limited, an imprint of Sutton Publishing Limited
Phoenix Mill · Thrupp · Stroud · Gloucestershire · GL5 2BU

Reprinted 1995, 1998

Copyright © in this edition
Sutton Publishing Limited, 1995

All rights reserved. No part of this publication may be reproduced, stored in a retrieval
system, or transmitted, in any form or by any means, electronic, mechanical, photocopying,
recording or otherwise, without the prior permission of the publisher and copyright holder.

British Library Cataloguing in Publication Data

A catalogue record for this book is available from the British Library

ISBN 0 7509 0453 4

*Cover picture: detail from* Mother and child *by Edward Robert Hughes (1851–1917) (Chris Beetles
Ltd, London; photograph, Bridgeman Art Library, London).*

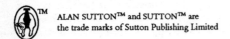 ALAN SUTTON™ and SUTTON™ are
the trade marks of Sutton Publishing Limited

Typeset in 9/10 Bembo.
Typesetting and origination by
Sutton Publishing Limited.
Printed in Great Britain by
The Guernsey Press Company Limited,
Guernsey, Channel Islands.

# BIOGRAPHICAL INTRODUCTION

WILLIAM WILKIE COLLINS was born in Marylebone on 8 January 1824. He died sixty-five years later in Wimpole Street, little more than three blocks away, and lived most of his life in that central part of London. Yet from that narrow base he managed to live as colourful a life as any other Victorian and wrote some of the most gripping novels of the nineteenth century. He is still regarded as 'the father of the detective story' and 'the novelist who invented sensation'. He himself put it more modestly. He was, he said, just a simple story teller.

Such stories, however, included *The Moonstone* and *The Woman in White*. His first published novel, *Antonina*, appeared in 1851, and his last, *Blind Love*, had to be finished by an old friend, Walter Besant, in 1889. In the intervening years Collins wrote over thirty novels and collections of stories, as well as a biography of his father William Collins. The manuscript of the first novel he actually wrote, though it was turned down by every publisher he approached and vanished for nearly 150 years, finally surfaced in New York in 1990. Entitled *Iolani; Or Tahiti as it Was*, its somewhat belated publication is now planned. Collins himself was remarkably frank about that early failure. 'My youthful imagination ran riot among the noble savages, in scenes which caused the respectable British publisher [actually Chapman and Hall] to declare that it was impossible to put his name on the title page of such a novel'.

It was during the writing of that first, unsuccessful, novel that Collins' parents first became fully aware that all their assumptions about 'Willy's future' (as he was known in the family) were quite wrong. His father, William Collins, already an RA, with a string of wealthy clients, including the late George IV, was a leading landscape artist and had readily assumed that both sons (Charles Allston Collins was two years younger than Wilkie) would also take up painting. William's own father, another William, was a picture dealer and Harriet, Wilkie Collins' mother, came from a family of painters. Both Constable and Linnell were close friends of the family as the boys grew up in Hampstead, and sketching became second nature to them both.

Yet it was the written word and a good story well told that tugged at Wilkie Collins. He later described how at his second school at Highbury, where he was a boarder, he was regularly bullied at night by the head boy. 'You will go to sleep, Collins', he was apparently told, 'when you have told me a story'. Quite an incentive. 'It was this brute who first awakened in me, his poor little victim, a power of which but for him I might never have been aware. . . . When I left school I continued story telling for my own pleasure'.

The occasions when he could do so were varied indeed. His school days were remarkably interrupted by his father's decision to take the family to Italy for two years, an extended visit that gave Collins not only visual stimuli but provided the background for what would be his first published novel, *Antonina*. It was also in Italy that, according to Dickens, Collins experienced his 'first love adventure'. As Dickens explained the affair to his sister-in-law later, it 'had proceeded, if I may be allowed the expression, to the utmost extremities'. Collins was thirteen at the time. Perhaps more important, for his writing if not his character, it was probably in Italy that his attraction to the visual began to seek an alternative outlet to painting, and where the embryo writer began to emerge from the family of artists.

When, a few years later, his father was considering whether Wilkie should be entered at art school, prior to applying to the Royal Academy, it was already clear that his interests lay elsewhere. One idea was that he should go to Oxford, before entering the Church. But William was eventually persuaded that a spell in a tea merchant's office would at least provide Wilkie with a more secure income than the desultory writing that seemed to attract him. It did not last, though since the office in the Strand was near all the publishers it at least allowed him to trail round them with his articles in spare moments. He had his first short story, *The Last Stage Coachman*, published under his name in *The Illuminated Magazine* at this time. His father's next initiative was to arrange for Wilkie to enter Lincoln's Inn and to read for the Bar, again on the assumption that it might provide a better source of income than writing. It was to be one of William's last family concerns, for he died the following year, in 1847.

Collins managed to sustain his legal studies, or at least his necessary attendances, sufficiently over the next few years to be finally called to the Bar in 1851. It may not have been a particularly attractive calling, in his eyes, but it was later to serve its purpose. Eight of his novels have lawyers as prominent characters and the drawing up of wills was crucial to several of his later plots, including *The Woman in White*. When his father died, Collins, though still ostensibly studying for the Bar, had reached the third chapter of the second volume of *Antonina*, and had already read the bulk of the first volume to his father. Thereafter he immediately laid the novel aside and took up the preparations for a memoir of his father. It was thus a biographical work, *The Life of William Collins*, and not a novel that in 1848 became his first published work and established his name in the publishing world.

With the death of William Collins his family, though saddened by his suffering, were soon showing a new kind of independence. His love for them had never been in doubt, but William had early acquired a streak of moral rectitude which over the years irritated his friends and restricted his family. Wilkie had probably felt the heavy hand more than his brother Charles, but had chosen to ride the storms when they occurred, while pursuing his personal inclinations as best he could. Once the memoirs were completed, Harriet and her two sons settled down in an imposing house overlooking Regents Park, where she was happy to play host to her sons' younger friends from the artistic and literary worlds. It was here that Wilkie came under the wing of Charles Dickens and his brother befriended John Millais, William Holman-Hunt and other Pre-Raphaelites.

It was in this period that Wilkie Collins extended the range of his writing, providing leading articles for *The Leader*, short stories and essays for *Bentley's Miscellany*, a travel book about Cornwall entitled *Rambles Beyond Railways*, as well as dramatic criticisms and a short play. Charles Dickens had already enticed him to participate in the private theatricals he was developing and within eighteen months Wilkie had performed, in a small part, at a Dickens-directed charity performance in the presence of Queen Victoria. It was a short step from this to a joint production of Wilkie's first play, *The Lighthouse*, and a later commercial production at the Olympic Theatre. Soon they were co-operating on Dickens' journal *Household Words* and, with Wilkie in the lead, nicely egged on by Dickens, sharing colourful entertainments and distractions together in London and Paris.

It was a time when Collins began to write the kind of novels that were always to be identified with him, combining well-constructed plots with strong characters, beginning with *Basil* in the early fifties, followed by *Hide and Seek*, *After Dark* (short stories) and *The Dead Secret*, and culminating in *The Woman in White* in 1860. It was also the time when he met the two women – Caroline Graves and Martha Rudd – who were to weave in and out of his life for the next thirty years.

Caroline Graves appeared first, dramatically if Collins himself is to be believed, in much the same way as the mysterious lady in St John's Wood at the outset of *The Woman in White*. The story goes that the woman in distress gave a piercing scream one moonlit night as Wilkie and his brother were accompanying John Millais back to his lodgings. Millais simply exclaimed 'What a lovely woman'. Wilkie followed her into the darkness and later told them that she was a lady of good birth who had fallen into the clutches of a man who was threatening her life.

An element of truth perhaps, but it was tinged with Collins' undoubted storytelling ability. We now know that Caroline came from a humble family in the west country, had been married young, had a child and had been left a widow. It was not long before Collins was sharing lodgings with her, even answering letters openly from the various addresses they occupied in and  around Marylebone. He even put her down as his wife, quite inaccurately, in the Census of 1861. He shared his triumphs with her, from *The Woman in White* onwards, but in spite of  her obvious wishes, he was determined not to marry her.

These were the years of Collins' best-known novels. *The Woman in White* was followed by *Armadale* (for which he received the then record sum of £5,000 before a word had been written), *No Name* and *The Moonstone*. It was the preparation of *Armadale* and the writing of *The Moonstone*, however, that were to produce such dramatic upheavals in his private life and, to some extent, account for what many critics have detected as a relative falling off in his narrative power as a novelist.

His search for background for *Armadale* took him to the Norfolk Broads and to the small coastal village of Winterton. There, or nearby, he met Martha Rudd, the nineteen-year-old daughter of a large, though poor, family. Her parents and relations have been traced (their graves are still in the local churchyard), but the timing of Martha's move to be closer to Collins in London remains obscure. What we do know is that only a few years later, when Collins was writing instalments of *The Moonstone*, already laid low by an acute attack of rheumatic gout and grieving over the death of his mother, Caroline decided to leave him and to marry a much younger man. Dickens felt that she had tried to bluff Collins into marriage and had failed. It could also have been Martha's appearance in London that proved to be the last straw.

Collins was devastated and finished *The Moonstone* in a haze of pain and with increasing doses of laudanum. It was a habit he was to follow for the rest of his life, his intake of opium eventually reaching remarkable levels, with inevitable repercussions on his writing ability. The domestic drama, however, was not yet over. Within nine months of Caroline's marriage, Martha, living in lodgings in Bolsover Street, was to bear Collins his first child; within another two years Caroline had left her husband and returned to Collins in Gloucester Place, and Martha was pregnant with his second child.

And so it continued for the rest of his life, with Caroline once more established in Gloucester Place, though probably as housekeeper and hostess rather than mistress, and Martha and his 'morganatic' family (eventually two girls and a boy: Marian, Harriet and William Charles) not far away. When he visited Martha he became William Dawson, Barrister-at-Law, and she was known as Mrs Dawson. His male friends readily accepted these arrangements, though their wives were rarely, if ever, invited to Gloucester Place or, later, Wimpole Street.

His two families, basically Caroline's grandchildren and Martha's children, happily mingled together on holiday in Ramsgate and even occasionally in Gloucester Place, but Martha and Caroline never met. It was against this domestic background, with a host of literary and theatrical friends, that he pursued the last decade and a half of his life, completing some of his more socially conscious novels, such as *Heart and Science*, as well as his more recognizable suspense novels, like *Poor Miss Finch, The Haunted Hotel, The New Magdalen, The Black Robe,* and *Jezebel's Daughter.*

He died in Wimpole Street in September 1889, and was buried at Kensal Green Cemetery. Caroline was eventually buried with him and Martha continued to tend the grave until she left London. She died in Southend in 1919. The gold locket Wilkie gave Martha in 1868, marking the death of his mother, is still in the possession of my wife, Faith, their great-granddaughter.

WILLIAM M. CLARKE

*Further Reading*

Ashley, R., *Wilkie Collins*, London, 1952.
Clarke, William M., *The Secret Life of Wilkie Collins*, London, 1988.
Peters, Catherine, *The King of Inventors: A Life of Wilkie Collins*, London, 1991.
Robinson, Kenneth, *Wilkie Collins*, London, 1951 & 1974.

# FIRST PERIOD: 1858–1859

## *EVENTS IN THE PRISON, RELATED BY THE GOVERNOR*

### CHAPTER I

#### THE GOVERNOR EXPLAINS

At the request of a person who has claims on me that I must not disown, I consent to look back through a long interval of years, and to describe events which took place within the walls of an English prison during the earlier period of my appointment as Governor.

Viewing my task by the light which later experience casts on it, I think I shall act wisely by exercising some control over the freedom of my pen.

I propose to pass over in silence the name of the town in which is situated the prison once confided to my care. I shall observe a similar discretion in alluding to individuals – some dead, some living, at the present time.

Being obliged to write of a woman who deservedly suffered the extreme penalty of the law, I think she will be sufficiently identified if I call her The Prisoner. Of the four persons present on the evening before her execution, three may be distinguished one from the other by allusion to their vocations in life. I here introduce them as The Chaplain, The Minister, and The Doctor. The fourth was a young woman. *She* has no claim on my consideration; and, when she is mentioned, her name may appear. If these reserves excite suspicion, I declare beforehand that they influence in no way the sense of responsibility which commands an honest man to speak the truth.

## CHAPTER II

### THE MURDERESS ASKS QUESTIONS

The first of the events which I must now relate was the conviction of The Prisoner for the murder of her husband.

They had lived together in matrimony for little more than two years. The husband, a gentleman by birth and education, had mortally offended his relations by marrying a woman in an inferior rank of life. He was fast declining into a state of poverty, through his own reckless extravagance, at the time when he met with his death at his wife's hand.

Without attempting to excuse him, he deserved, to my mind, some tribute of regret. It is not to be denied that he was profligate in hid habits and violent in his temper. But it is equally true that he was affectionate in the domestic circle, and, when moved by wisely-applied remonstrance, sincerely penitent for sins committed under temptation that overpowered him, If his wife had killed him in a fit of jealous rage – under provocation, be it remembered, which the witnesses proved – she might have been convicted of manslaughter, and might have received a light sentence. But the evidence so undeniably revealed deliberate and merciless premedetation, that the only defence attempted by her counsel was madness, and the only alternative left to a righteous jury was a verdict which condemned the woman to death. Those mischievous members of the community, whose topsy-turvy sympathies feel for the living criminal and forget the dead victim, attempted to save her by means of highflown petitions and comtemptible correspondence in the newspapers. But the Judge held firm; and the Home Secretary held firm. They were entirely right; and the public were scandalously wrong.

Our Chaplain endeavoured to offer the consolations of religion to the condemned wretch. She refused to accept his ministrations in language which filled him with grief and horror.

On the evening before the execution, the reverend gentleman laid on my table his own written report of a conversation which had passed between the Prisoner and himself.

'I see some hope, sir,' he said, 'of inclining the heart of this woman to religious belief, before it is too late. Will you read my report, and say if you agree with me?'

I read it, of course. It was called 'A Memorandum,' and was thus written:

'At his last interview with the Prisoner, the Chaplain asked her if she had ever entered a place of public worship. She replied that she had occasionally attended the services at a Congregational Church in this town; attracted by the reputation of the Minister as a preacher. "He entirely failed to make a Christian of me," she said; "but I was struck by his eloquence. Besides, he interested me personally – he was a fine man."

'In the dreadful situation in which the woman was placed, such language as this shocked the Chaplain; he appealed in vain to the Prisoner's sense of propriety. "You don't understand women," she answered. "The greatest saint of my sex that ever lived likes to look at a preacher as well as to hear him. If he is an agreeable man, he has all the greater effect on her. This preacher's voice told me he was kind-hearted; and I had only to look at his beautiful eyes to see that he was trustworthy and true."

'It was useless to repeat a protest which had already failed. Recklessly and flippantly as she had described it, an impression had been produced on her. It occurred to the Chaplain that he might at least make the attempt to turn this result to her own religious advantage. He asked whether she would receive the Minister, if the reverend gentleman came to the prison. "That will depend," she said, "on whether you answer some questions which I want to put to you first." The Chaplain consented; provided always that he could reply with propriety to what she asked of him. Her first question only related to himself.

'She said: "The women who watch me tell me that you are a widower, and have a family of children. Is that true?"

'The Chaplain answered that it was quite true.

'She alluded next to a report, current in the town, that the Minister had resigned the pastorate. Being personally acquainted with him, the Chaplain was able to inform her that his resignation had not yet been accepted. On hearing this, she seemed to gather confidence. Her next inquiries succeeded each other rapidly, as follows:

'"Is my handsome preacher married?"

'"Yes."

'"Has he got any children?"

'"He has never had any children."

'"How long has he been married?"

'"As well as I know, about seven or eight years."

'"What sort of woman is his wife?"

'"A lady universally respected."

'"I don't care whether she is respected or not. Is she kind?"

'"Certainly!"

'"Is her husband well off?"

'"He has a sufficient income."

'After that reply, the Prisoner's curiosity appeared to be satisfied. She said, "Bring your friend the preacher to me, if you like" – and there it ended.

'What her object could have been in putting these questions, it seems to be impossible to guess. Having accurately reported all that took place, the Chaplain declares, with heartfelt regret, that he can exert no religious influence over this obdurate woman. He leaves it to the Governor to decide whether the Minister of the Congregational Church may not succeed, where the Chaplain of the Gaol has failed. Herein is the one last hope of saving the soul of the Prisoner, now under sentence of death!'

In those serious words the Memorandum ended.

Although not personally acquainted with the Minister I had heard of him, on all sides, as an excellent man. In the emergency that confronted us he had, as it seemed to me, his own sacred right to enter the prison; assuming that he was willing to accept, what I myself felt to be, a very serious responsibility. The first necessity was to discover whether we might hope to obtain his services. With my full approval the Chaplain left me, to state the circumstances to his reverend colleague.

## CHAPTER III

### THE CHILD APPEARS

During my friend's absence, my attention was claimed by a sad incident – not unforeseen.

It is, I suppose, generally known that near relatives are admitted to take their leave of criminals condemned to death. In the case of the Prisoner now waiting for execution, no person applied to the authorities for permission to see her. I myself inquired if she had any relations living, and if she would like to see them. She answered: 'None that I care to see, or that care to see me – except the nearest relation of all.'

In those last words the miserable creature alluded to her only child, a little girl (an infant, I should say), who had passed her first year's birthday by a few months. The farewell interview was to take place on the mother's last evening on earth; and the child was now brought into my rooms, in charge of her nurse.

I had seldom seen a brighter or prettier little girl. She was just able to walk alone, and to enjoy the first delight of moving from one place to another. Quite of her own accord she came to me, attracted I dare say by the glitter of my watch-chain. Helping her to climb on my knee, I showed the wonders of the watch, and held it to her ear. At that past time, death had taken my good wife from me; my two boys were away at Harrow School; my domestic life was the life of a lonely man. Whether I was reminded of the bygone days when my sons were infants on my knee, listening to the ticking of my watch – or whether the friendless position of the poor little creature, who had lost one parent and was soon to lose the other by a violent death, moved me in depths of pity not easily reached in my later experience – I am not able to say. This only I know: my heart ached for the child while she was laughing and listening; and something fell from me on the watch which I don't deny might have been a tear. A few of the toys, mostly broken now, which my two children used to play with are still in my possession; kept, like my poor wife's favourite jewels, for old remembrance' sake. These I took from their repository when the attraction of my watch showed signs of failing. The child pounced on them with her chubby hands, and screamed with pleasure. And the hangman was waiting for her mother – and, more horrid still, the mother deserved it!

My duty required me to let the Prisoner know that her little daughter had arrived. Did that heart of iron melt at last? It might have been so, or it might not; the message sent back kept her secret. All that it said to me was: 'Let the child wait till I send for her.'

The Minister had consented to help us. On his arrival at the prison, I received him privately in my study.

I had only to look at his face – pitiably pale and agitated – to see that he was a sensitive man, not always able to control his nerves on occasions which tried his moral courage. A kind, I might almost say a noble face, and a voice unaffectedly persuasive, at once prepossessed me in his favour. The few words of welcome that I spoke were intended to compose him. They failed to produce the impression on which I had counted.

'My experience,' he said, 'has included many melancholy duties, and has tried my composure in many terrible scenes; but I have never yet found myself in the presence of an unrepentant criminal, sentenced to death – and that criminal a woman and a mother. I own, sir, that I am shaken by the prospect before me.'

I suggested that he should wait awhile, in the hope that time and quiet might help him. He thanked me, and refused.

'If I have any knowledge of myself,' he said, 'terrors of anticipation lose their hold when I am face to face with a serious call on me. The longer I remain here, the less worthy I shall appear of the trust that has been placed in me – the trust which, please God, I mean to deserve.'

My own observation of human nature told me that this was wisely said. I led the way at once to the cell.

## CHAPTER IV

### THE MINISTER SAYS YES

The Prisoner was seated on her bed, quietly talking with the woman appointed to watch her. When she rose to receive us, I saw the Minister start. The face that confronted him would, in my opinion, have taken any man by surprise, if he had first happened to see it within the walls of a prison.

Visitors to the picture-galleries of Italy, growing weary of Holy Families in endless succession, observe that the idea of the Madonna, among the rank and file of Italian Painters, is limited to one changeless and familiar type. I can hardly hope to be believed when I say that the personal appearance of the murderess recalled the type. She presented the delicate light hair, the quiet eyes, the finely-shaped lower features, and the correctly oval form of face, repeated in hundreds on hundreds of the conventional works of Art to which I have ventured to allude. To those who doubt me, I can only declare that what I have here written is undisguised and absolute truth. Let me add that daily observation of all classes of criminals, extending over many years, has considerably diminished my faith in physiognomy as a safe guide to the discovery of character. Nervous trepidation looks like guilt. Guilt, firmly sustained by insensibility, looks like innocence. One of the vilest wretches ever placed under my charge won the sympathies (while he was waiting for his trial) of every person who saw him, including even the persons employed in the prison. Only the other day, ladies and gentlemen coming to visit me passed a body of men at work on the road. Judges of physiognomy among them were horrified at the criminal atrocity betrayed in every face that they noticed. They condoled with me on the near neighbourhood of so many convicts to my official place of residence. I looked out of the window, and saw a group of honest labourers (whose only crime was poverty) employed by the parish!

Having instructed the female warder to leave the room – but to take care that she waited within call – I looked again at the Minister.

Confronted by the serious responsibility that he had undertaken, he justified what he had said to me. Still pale, still distressed, he was now nevertheless master of himself. I turned to the door to leave him alone with the Prisoner. She called me back.

'Before this gentleman tries to convert me,' she said, 'I want you to wait here and be a witness.'

Finding that we were both willing to comply with this request, she addressed herself directly to the Minister.

'Suppose I promise to listen to your exhortations,' she began, 'what do you promise to do for me in return?'

The voice in which she spoke to him was steady and clear; a marked contrast to the tremulous earnestness with which he answered her.

'I promise to urge you to repentance and the confession of your crime. I promise to implore the divine blessing on me in the effort to save your poor guilty soul.'

She looked at him, and listened to him, as if he was speaking to her in an unknown tongue, and went on with what she had to say as quietly as ever.

'When I am hanged to-morrow, suppose I die without confessing, without repenting – are you one of those who believe I shall be doomed to eternal punishment in another life?'

'I believe in the mercy of God.'

'Answer my question, if you please. Is an impenitent sinner eternally punished? Do you believe that?'

'My Bible leaves me no other alternative.'

She paused for awhile, evidently considering with special attention what she was about to say next.

'As a religious man,' she resumed, 'would you be willing to make some sacrifice, rather than let a fellow-creature go – after a disgraceful death – to everlasting torment?'

'I know of no sacrifice in my power,' he said fervently, 'to which I would not rather submit, than let you die in the present dreadful state of your mind.'

The Prisoner turned to me. 'Is the person who watches me waiting outside?'

'Yes.'

'Will you be so kind as to call her in? I have a message for her.'

It was plain that she had been leading the way to the delivery of that message, whatever it might be, in all that she had said up to the present time. So far my poor powers of penetration helped me, and no farther.

The warder appeared, and received her message. 'Tell the woman who has come here with my little girl that I want to see the child.'

Taken completely by surprise, I signed to the attendant to wait for further instructions.

In a moment more, I had sufficiently recovered myself to see the impropriety of permitting any obstacle to interpose between the Minister and his errand of mercy. I gently reminded the Prisoner that she would have a later opportunity of seeing her child. 'Your first duty,' I told her, 'is to hear and to take to heart what the clergyman has to say to you.'

For the second time I attempted to leave the cell. For the second time this impenetrable woman called me back.

'Take the parson away with you,' she said. 'I refuse to listen to him.'

The patient Minister yielded, and appealed to me to follow his example. I reluctantly sanctioned the delivery of the message.

After a brief interval the child was brought to us, tired and sleepy. For a while the nurse roused her by setting her on her feet. She happened to notice the Minister first. Her bright eyes rested on him, gravely wondering. He kissed her, and, after a momentary hesitation, gave her to her mother. The horror of the situation over-powered him: he turned his face away from us. I understood what he felt; he almost overthrew my own self-command.

The Prisoner spoke to the nurse in no friendly tone: 'You can go.'

The nurse turned to me, ostentatiously ignoring the words that had been addressed to her. 'Am I to go, sir, or to stay?' I suggested that she should return to the waiting-room. She returned at once, in silence. The Prisoner looked after her as she went out, with such an expression of hatred in her eyes that the Minister noticed it.

'What has that person done to offend you?' he asked.

'She is the last person in the whole world whom I should have chosen to take care of my child, if the power of choosing had been mine. But I have been in prison, without a living creature to represent me or to take my part. No more of that; my troubles will be over in a few hours more. I want you to look at my little girl, whose troubles are all to come. Do you call her pretty? Do you feel interested in her?'

The sorrow and pity in his face answered for him.

Quietly sleeping, the poor baby rested on her mother's bosom. Was the heart of the murderess softened by the divine influence of maternal love? The hands that held the child trembled a little. For the first time, it seemed to cost her an effort to compose herself, before she could speak to the Minister again.

'When I die to-morrow,' she said, 'I leave my child helpless and friendless – disgraced by her mother's shameful death. The workhouse may take her – or a charitable asylum may take her.' She paused; a first tinge of colour rose on her pale face; she broke into an outburst of rage. 'Think of *my* daughter being brought up by charity! She may suffer poverty, she may be treated with contempt, she may be employed by brutal people in menial work. I can't endure it; it maddens me. If she is not saved from that wretched fate, I shall die despairing, I shall die cursing——'

The Minister sternly stopped her before she could say the next word. To my astonishment she appeared to be humbled, to be even ashamed: she asked his pardon: 'Forgive me; I won't forget myself again. They tell me you have no children of your own. Is that a sorrow to you and your wife?'

Her altered tone touched him. He answered sadly and kindly: 'It is the one sorrow of our lives.'

The purpose which she had been keeping in view from the moment when the Minister entered her cell was no mystery now. Ought I to have interfered? Let me confess a weakness, unworthy perhaps of my office. I was so sorry for the child – I hesitated.

My silence encouraged the mother. She advanced to the Minister with the sleeping infant in her arms.

'I dare say you have sometimes thought of adopting a child?' she said. 'Perhaps you can guess now what I had in my mind, when I asked if you would consent to a sacrifice? Will you take this wretched innocent little creature home with you?' She lost her self-possession once more. 'A motherless creature to-morrow,' she burst out. 'Think of that.'

God knows how I still shrunk from it! But there was no alternative now; I was bound to remember my duty to the excellent man, whose critical position at that moment was, in some degree at least, due to my hesitation in asserting my authority. Could I allow the Prisoner to presume on his compassionate nature, and to hurry him into a decision which, in his calmer moments, he might find reason to regret? I spoke to *him*. Does the man live who – having to say what I had to say – could have spoken to the doomed mother?

'I am sorry to have allowed this to go on,' I said. 'In justice to yourself, sir, don't answer!'

She turned on me with a look of fury.

'He shall answer,' she cried.

I saw, or thought I saw, signs of yielding in his face. 'Take time,' I persisted – 'take time to consider before you decide.'

She stepped up to me.

'Take time?' she repeated. 'Are you inhuman enough to talk of time, in my presence?'

She laid the sleeping child on her bed, and fell on her knees before the Minister: 'I promise to hear your exhortations – I promise to do all a woman can to believe and repent. Oh, I know myself! My heart, once hardened, is a heart that no human creature can touch. The one way to my better nature — if I have a better nature — is through that poor babe. Save her from the workhouse! Don't let them make a pauper of her!' She sank prostrate at his feet, and beat her hands in frenzy on the floor. 'You want to save my guilty soul,' she reminded him furiously. 'There's but one way of doing it. Save my child!'

He raised her. Her fierce tearless eyes questioned his face in a mute expectation dreadful to see. Suddenly, a foretaste of death — the death that was so near now! — struck her with a shivering fit: her head dropped on the Minister's shoulder. Other men might have shrunk from the contact of it. That true Christian let it rest.

Under the maddening sting of suspense, her sinking energies rallied for an instant. In a whisper, she was just able to put the supreme question to him.

'Yes? or No?'

He answered: 'Yes.'

A faint breath of relief, just audible in the silence, told me that she had heard him. It was her last effort. He laid her, insensible, on the bed, by the side of her sleeping child. 'Look at them,' was all he said to me; 'how could I refuse?'


## CHAPTER V

### MISS CHANCE ASSERTS HERSELF

The services of our medical officer were required, in order to hasten the recovery of the Prisoner's senses.

When the Doctor and I left the cell together, she was composed, and ready (in the performance of her promise) to listen to the exhortations of the Minister. The sleeping child was left undisturbed, by the mother's desire. If the Minister felt tempted to regret what he had done, *there* was the artless influence which would check him! As we stepped into the corridor, I gave the female warder her instructions to remain on the watch, and to return to her post when she saw the Minister come out.

In the meantime, my companion had walked on a little way.

Possessed of ability and experience within the limits of his profession, he was in other respects a man with a crotchety mind; bold to the verge of recklessness in the expression of his opinion; and possessed of a command of language that carried everything before it. Let me add that he was just and merciful in his intercourse with others, and I shall have summed him up fairly enough. When I joined him, he seemed to be absorbed in reflection.

'Thinking of the Prisoner?' I said.

'Thinking of what is going on, at this moment, in the condemned cell,' he answered, 'and wondering if any good will come of it.'

I was not without hope of a good result, and I said so.

The Doctor disagreed with me. 'I don't believe in that woman's penitence,' he remarked; 'and I look upon the parson as a poor weak creature. What is to become of the child?'

There was no reason for concealing from one of my colleagues the benevolent decision, on the part of the good Minister, of which I had been a witness. The Doctor listened to me with the first appearance of downright astonishment that I had ever observed in his face. When I had done, he made an extraordinary reply:

'Governor, I retract what I said of the parson just now. He is one of the boldest men that ever stepped into a pulpit.'

Was the Doctor in earnest? Strongly in earnest; there could be no doubt of it. Before I could ask him what he meant, he was called away to a patient on the other side of the prison. When we parted at the door of my room, I made it a request that my medical friend would return to me and explain what he had just said.

'Considering that you are the governor of a prison,' he replied, 'you are a singularly rash man. If I come back, how do you know I shall not bore you?'

'My rashness runs the risk of that,' I rejoined.

'Tell me something, before I allow you to run your risk,' he said. 'Are you one of those people who think that the tempers of children are formed by the accidental influences which happen to be about them? Or do you agree with me that the tempers of children are inherited from their parents?'

The Doctor (as I concluded) was still strongly impressed by the Minister's resolution to adopt a child, whose wicked mother had committed the most atrocious of all crimes. Was some serious foreboding in secret possession of his mind? My curiosity to hear him was now increased tenfold. I replied without hesitation:

'I agree with you.'

He looked at me with his sense of humour twinkling in his eyes. 'Do you know I rather expected that answer?' he said slyly. 'All right. I'll come back.'

Left by myself, I took up the day's newspaper.

My attention wandered; my thoughts were in the cell with the Minister and the Prisoner. How would it end? Sometimes, I took refuge in my own more hopeful view. These idle reflections were agreeably interrupted by the appearance of my friend, the Chaplain.

'You are always welcome,' I said; 'and doubly welcome just now. I am feeling a little worried and anxious.'

'And you are naturally,' the Chaplain added, 'not at all disposed to receive a stranger?'

'Is the stranger a friend of yours?' I asked.

'Oh no! Having occasion, just now, to go into the waiting-room, I found a young woman there, who asked me if she could see you. She thinks you have forgotten her, and she is tired of waiting. I merely undertook, of course, to mention what she had said to me.'

The nurse having been in this way recalled to my memory, I felt some little interest in seeing her, after what had passed in the cell. In plainer words, I was desirous of judging for myself whether she deserved the hostile feeling which the Prisoner had shown towards her. I thanked the Chaplain before he left me, and gave the servant the necessary instructions. When she entered the room, I looked at the woman attentively for the first time.

Youth and a fine complexion, a well-made figure and a natural grace of movement – these were her personal attractions, so far as I could see. Her defects were, to my mind, equally noticeable. Under a heavy forehead, her piercing eyes looked out at persons and things with an expression which was not to my taste. Her large mouth – another defect, in my opinion – would have been recommended to mercy, in the estimation of many men, by her magnificent teeth; white, well shaped, cruelly regular. Believers in physiognomy might perhaps have seen the betrayal of an obstinate nature in the lengthy firmness of her chin. While I am trying to describe her, let me not forget her dress. A woman's dress is the mirror in which we may see the reflection of a woman's nature. Bearing in mind the melancholy and impressive circumstances under which she had brought the child to the prison, the gaiety of colour in her gown and her bonnet implied either a total want of feeling, or a total want of tact. As to her position in life, let me confess that I felt, after a closer examination, at a loss to determine it. She was certainly not a lady. The Prisoner had spoken of her as if she was a domestic servant who had forfeited her right to consideration and respect. And she had entered the prison, as a nurse might have entered it, in charge of a child. I did what we all do when we are not clever enough to find the answer to a riddle – I gave it up.

'What can I do for you?' I asked.

'Perhaps you can tell me,' she answered, 'how much longer I am to be kept waiting in this prison.'

'The decision,' I reminded her, 'doesn't depend on me.'

'Then who *does* it depend on?'

The Minister had undoubtedly acquired the sole right of deciding. It was for him to say whether this woman should, or should not, remain in attendance on the child whom he had adopted. In the meanwhile, the feeling of distrust which was gaining on my mind warned me to remember the value of reserve in holding intercourse with a stranger.

She seemed to be irritated by my silence. 'If the decision doesn't rest with you,' she asked, 'why did you tell me to stay in the waiting-room?'

'You brought the little girl into the prison,' I said; 'Was it not natural to suppose that your mistress might want you——'

'Stop, sir!'

I had evidently given offence; I stopped directly.

'No person on the face of the earth,' she declared loftily, 'has ever had the right to call herself my mistress. Of my own free will, sir, I took charge of the child.'

'Because you are fond of her?' I suggested.

'I hate her.'

It was unwise on my part – I protested. 'Hate a baby, little more than a year old!' I said.

'*Her* baby!'

She said it with the air of a woman who had produced an unanswerable reason. 'I am accountable to nobody,' she went on. 'If I consented to trouble myself with the child, it was in remembrance of my friendship – notice, if you please, that I say friendship – with the unhappy father.'

Putting together what I had just heard, and what I had seen in the cell, I drew the right conclusion at last. The woman, whose position in life had been thus far an impenetrable mystery to me, now stood revealed as one, among other objects of the Prisoner's jealousy, during her disastrous married life. A serious doubt occurred to me as to the authority under which the husband's mistress might be acting, after the husband's death. I instantly put it to the test.

'Do I understand you to assert any claim to the child?' I asked.

'Claim?' she repeated. 'I know no more of the child than you do. I heard for the first time that such a creature was in existence, when her murdered father sent for me in his dying moments. At his entreaty I promised to take care of her, while her vile mother was out of the house and in the hands of the law. My promise has been performed. If I am expected (having brought her to the prison) to take her away again, understand this: I am under no obligation (even if I could afford it) to burden myself with that child; I shall hand her over to the workhouse authorities.'

I forgot myself once more – I lost my temper.

'Leave the room!' I said. 'Your unworthy hands will not touch the poor baby again. She is provided for.'

'I don't believe you!' the wretch burst out. 'Who has taken the child?'

A quiet voice answered: '*I* have taken her.'

We both looked round and saw the Minister standing in the open doorway, with the child in his arms. The ordeal that he had gone through in the condemned cell was visible in his face; he looked miserably haggard and broken. I was eager to know if his merciful interest in the Prisoner had purified her guilty soul – but at the same time I was afraid, after what he had but too plainly suffered, to ask him to enter into details.

'Only one word,' I said. 'Are your anxieties at rest?'

'God's mercy has helped me,' he answered. 'I have not spoken in vain. She believes; she repents; she has confessed the crime.'

After handing the written and signed confession to me, he approached the venomous creature, still lingering in the room to hear what passed between us. Before I could stop him, he spoke to her, under a natural impression that he was addressing the Prisoner's servant.

'I am afraid you will be disappointed,' he said, 'when I tell you that your services will no longer be required. I have reasons for placing the child under the care of a nurse of my own choosing.'

She listened with an evil smile.

'I know who furnished you with your reasons,' she answered. 'Apologies are quite needless, so far as I am concerned. If you had proposed to me to look after the new member of your family there, I should have felt it my duty to myself to have refused. I am not a nurse – I am an independent single lady. I see by your dress that you are a clergyman; allow me to present myself as a mark of respect to your cloth. I am Miss Elizabeth Chance. May I ask the favour of your name?'

Too weary and too preoccupied to notice the insolence of her manner, the Minister mentioned his name. 'I am anxious,' he said, 'to know if the child has been baptized. Perhaps you can enlighten me?'

Still insolent, Miss Elizabeth Chance shook her head carelessly. 'I never heard — and, to tell you the truth, I never cared to hear — whether she was christened or not. Call her by what name you like, I can tell you this — you will find your adopted daughter a heavy handful.'

The Minister turned to me. 'What does she mean?'

'I will try to tell you,' Miss Chance interposed. 'Being a clergyman, you know who Deborah was? Very well. I am Deborah now; and *I* prophesy.' She pointed to the child. 'Remember what I say, reverend sir! You will find the tigress-cub take after its mother.'

With those parting words, she favoured us with a low curtsey, and left the room.

## CHAPTER VI

### THE DOCTOR DOUBTS

The Minister looked at me in an absent manner; his attention seemed to have been wandering. 'What was it Miss Chance said?' he asked.

Before I could speak, a friend's voice at the door interrupted us. The Doctor, returning to me as he had promised, answered the Minister's question in these words:

'I must have passed the person you mention, sir, as I was coming in here; and I heard her say: "You will find the tigress-cub take after its mother." If she had known how to put her meaning into good English, Miss Chance — that is the name you mentioned, I think — might have told you that the vices of the parents are inherited by the children. And the one particular parent she had in her mind,' the Doctor continued, gently patting the child's cheek, 'was no doubt the mother of this unfortunate little creature — who may, or may not, live to show you that she comes of a bad stock and inherits a wicked nature.'

I was on the point of protesting against my friend's interpretation, when the Minister stopped me.

'Let me thank you, sir, for your explanation,' he said to the Doctor. As soon as my mind is free, I will reflect on what you have said. Forgive me, Mr Governor,' he went on, 'if I leave you, now that I have placed the Prisoner's confession in your hands. It has been an effort to me to say the little I have said, since I first entered this room. I can think of nothing but that unhappy criminal, and the death that she must die to-morrow.'

'Does she wish you to be present?' I asked.

'She positively forbids it. "After what you have done for me," she said, "the least I can do in return is to prevent your being needlessly distressed." She took leave of me; she kissed the little girl for the last time – oh, don't ask me to tell you about it! I shall break down if I try. Come, my darling!' He kissed the child tenderly, and took her away with him.

'That man is a strange compound of strength and weakness,' the Doctor remarked. 'Did you notice his face, just now? Nine men out of ten, suffering as he suffered, would have failed to control themselves. Such resolution as his *may* conquer the difficulties that are in store for him yet.'

It was a trial of my temper to hear my clever colleague justifying, in this way, the ignorant prediction of an insolent woman.

'There are exceptions to all rules,' I insisted. 'And why are the virtues of the parents not just as likely to descend to the children as the vices? There was a fund of good, I can tell you, in that poor baby's father – though I don't deny that he was a profligate man. And even the horrible mother – as you heard just now – has virtue enough left in her to feel grateful to the man who has taken care of her child. These are facts; you can't dispute them.'

The Doctor took out his pipe. 'Do you mind my smoking?' he asked. 'Tobacco helps me to arrange my ideas.'

I gave him the means of arranging his ideas; that is to say, I gave him the match-box. He blew some preliminary clouds of smoke – and then he answered me:

'For twenty years past, my friend, I have been studying the question of hereditary transmission of qualities; and I have found vices and diseases descending more frequently to children than virtue and health. I don't stop to ask why: there is no end to that sort of curiosity. What I have observed is what I tell you; no more and no less. You will say this is a horribly discouraging result of experience, for it tends to show that children come into the world at a disadvantage on the day of their birth. Of course they do. Children are born deformed; children are born deaf, dumb, or blind; children are born with the seeds in them of deadly diseases. Who can account for the cruelties of creation? Why are we endowed with life – only to end in death? And does it ever strike you, when you are cutting your mutton at dinner, and your cat is catching its mouse, and your spider is suffocating its fly, that we are all, big and little together, born to one certain inheritance – the privilege of eating each other?'

'Very sad,' I admitted. 'But it will all be set right in another world.'

'Are you quite sure of that?' the Doctor asked.

'Quite sure, thank God! And it would be better for you if you felt about it as I do.'

'We won't dispute, my dear Governor. I don't scoff at comforting hopes; I don't deny the existence of occasional compensations. But I do see, nevertheless, that Evil has got the upper hand among us, on this curious little planet. Judging by my observation and experience, that ill-fated baby's chance of inheriting the virtues of her parents is not to be compared with her chances of inheriting their vices; especially if she happens to take after her mother. *There*, the virtue is not conspicuous, and the vice is one enormous fact. When I think of the growth of that poisonous hereditary taint, which may come with time – when I think of passions let loose and temptations lying in ambush – I see the smooth surface of the Minister's domestic life with dangers lurking under it which make me shake in my shoes. God! what a life I should lead, if I happened to be in his place, some years hence. Suppose I said or did something (in the just exercise of my parental authority) which offended my adopted daughter. What figure would rise from the dead in my memory, when the girl bounced out of the room in a rage? The image of her mother would be the image I should see. I should remember what her mother did when *she* was provoked; I should lock my bedroom-door, in my own house, at night. I should come down to breakfast with suspicions in my cup of tea, if I discovered that my adopted daughter had poured it out. Oh, yes; it's quite true that I might be doing the girl a cruel injustice all the time; but how am I to be sure of that? I am only sure that her mother was hanged for one of the most merciless murders committed in our time. Pass the match-box. My pipe's out, and my confession of faith has come to an end.'

It was useless to dispute with a man who possessed his command of language. At the same time, there was a bright side to the poor Minister's prospects which the Doctor had failed to see. It was barely possible that I might succeed in putting my positive friend in the wrong. I tried the experiment, at any rate.

'You seem to have forgotten,' I reminded him, 'that the child will have every advantage that education can offer to her, and will be accustomed from her earliest years to restraining and purifying influences, in a clergyman's household.'

Now that he was enjoying the fumes of tobacco, the Doctor was as placid and sweet-tempered as a man could be.

'Quite true,' he said.

'Do you doubt the influence of religion?' I asked sternly.

He answered sweetly: 'Not at all.'

'Or the influence of kindness?'

'Oh dear, no!'

'Or the force of example?'

'I wouldn't deny it for the world.'

I had not expected this extraordinary docility. The Doctor had got the upper hand of me again – a state of things that I might have found it hard to endure, but for a call of duty which put an end to our sitting. One of the female warders appeared with a message from the condemned cell. The Prisoner wished to see the Governor and the Medical Officer.

'Is she ill?' the Doctor inquired.

'No sir.'

'Hysterical? or agitated, perhaps?'

'As easy and composed, sir, as a person can be.'

We set forth together for the condemned cell.

# CHAPTER VII

## THE MURDERESS CONSULTS THE AUTHORITIES

There was a considerate side to my friend's character, which showed itself when the warder had left us.

He was especially anxious to be careful of what he said to a woman in the Prisoner's terrible situation; especially in the event of her having been really subjected to the influence of religious belief. On the Minister's own authority, I declared that there was every reason to adopt this conclusion; and in support of what I had said I showed him the confession. It only contained a few lines, acknowledging that she had committed the murder, and that she deserved her sentence. 'From the planning of the crime to the commission of the crime, I was in my right senses throughout. I knew what I was doing.' With that remarkable disavowal of the defence set up by her advocate, the confession ended.

My colleague read the paper, and handed it back to me without making any remark. I asked if he suspected the Prisoner of feigning conversion to please the Minister.

'She shall not discover it,' he answered gravely, 'if I do.'

It would not be true to say that the Doctor's obstinacy had shaken my belief in the good result of the Minister's interference. I may, however, acknowledge that I felt some misgivings, which were not dispelled when I found myself in the presence of the Prisoner.

I had expected to see her employed in reading the Bible. The good book was closed and was not even placed within her reach. The occupation to which she was devoting herself astonished and repelled me.

Some carelessness on the part of the attendant had left on the table the writing materials that had been needed for her confession. She was using them now – when death on the scaffold was literally within a few hours of her – to sketch a portrait of the female warder, who was on the watch! The Doctor and I looked at each other; and now the sincerity of her repentance was something that I began to question too.

She laid down the pen, and proceeded quietly to explain herself.

'Even the little time that is left to me proves to be a weary time to get through,' she said. 'I am making a last use of the talent for drawing and catching a likeness, which has been one of my gifts since I was a girl. You look as if you didn't approve of such employment as this for a woman who is going to be hanged. Well, sir, I have no doubt you are right.' She paused, and tore up the portrait. 'If I have misbehaved myself,' she resumed, 'I make amends. To find you in an indulgent frame of mind is of importance to me just now. I have a favour to ask of you. May the warder leave the cell for a few minutes?'

Giving the woman permission to withdraw for a while, I waited with some anxiety to hear what the Prisoner wanted of me.

'I have something to say to you,' she proceeded, 'on the subject of executions. The face of a person who is going to be hanged is hidden, as I have been told, by a white cap drawn over it. Is that true?'

How another man might have felt, in my place, I cannot, of course, say. To my mind, such a question – on *her* lips – was too shocking to be answered in words. I bowed.

'And the body is buried,' she went on, 'in the prison?'

I could remain silent no longer. 'Is there no human feeling left in you?' I burst out. 'What do these horrid questions mean?'

'Don't be angry with me, sir; you shall hear directly. I want to know first if I am to be buried in the prison?'

I replied as before, by a bow.

'Now,' she said, 'I may tell you what I mean. In the autumn of last year I was taken to see some wax-works. Portraits of criminals were among them. There was one portrait——' She hesitated; her infernal self-possession failed her at last. The colour left her face; she was no longer able to look at me firmly. 'There was one portrait,' she resumed, 'that had been taken after the execution. The face was so hideous; it was swollen to such a size in its frightful deformity – oh, sir, don't let me be seen in that state, even by the strangers who bury me! Use your influence – forbid them to take the cap off my face when I am dead – order them to bury me in it, and I swear to you I'll meet death to-morrow as coolly as the boldest man that ever mounted the scaffold!' Before I could stop her, she seized me by the hand, and wrung it with a furious power that left the mark of her grasp on me, in a bruise, for days afterwards. 'Will you do it?' she cried. 'You're an honourable man; you will keep your word. Give me your promise!'

I gave her my promise.

The relief to her tortured spirit expressed itself horribly in a burst of frantic laughter. 'I can't help it,' she gasped; 'I'm so happy.'

My enemies said of me, when I got my appointment, that I was too excitable a man to be governor of a prison. Perhaps they were not altogether wrong. Anyhow, the quick-witted Doctor saw some change in me, which I was not aware of myself. He took my arm, and led me out of the cell. 'Leave her to me,' he whispered. 'The fine edge of my nerves was worn off long ago in the hospital.'

When we met again, I asked what had passed between the Prisoner and himself.

'I gave her time to recover,' he told me; 'and, except that she looked a little paler than usual, there was no trace left of the frenzy that you remember. "I ought to apologize for troubling you," she said; "but it is perhaps natural that I should think, now and then, of what is to happen to me to-morrow morning. As a medical man, you will be able to enlighten me. Is death by hanging a painful death?" She had put it so politely that I felt bound to answer her. "If the neck happens to be broken," I said, "hanging is a sudden death; fright and pain (if there is any pain) are both over in an instant. As to the other form of death which is also possible (I mean death by suffociation), I must own as an honest man that I know no more about it than you do." After considering a little, she made a sensible remark, and followed it by an embarrassing request. "A great deal," she said, "must depend on the executioner. I am not afraid of death, Doctor. Why should I be? My anxiety about my little girl is set at rest; I have nothing left to live for. But I don't like pain. Would you mind telling the executioner to be careful? Or would it be better if I spoke to him myself?" I said I thought it would come with a better grace from herself. She understood me directly; and we dropped the subject. Are you surprised at her coolness, after your experience of her?'

I confessed that I was surprised.

'Think a little,' the Doctor said. 'The one sensitive place in that woman's nature is the place occupied by her self-esteem.'

I objected to this that she had shown fondness for her child.

My friend disposed of the objection with his customary readiness.

'The maternal instinct,' he said. 'A cat is fond of her kittens; a cow is fond of her calf. No, sir, the one cause of that outbreak of passion which so shocked you – a genuine outbreak, beyond all doubt – is to be found in the vanity of a fine feminine creature, overpowered by a horror of looking hideous, even after her death. Do you know I rather like that woman?'

'Is it possible that you are in earnest?' I asked.

'I know as well as you do,' he answered, 'that this is neither a time nor a place for jesting. The fact is, the Prisoner carries out an idea of mine. It is my positive conviction that the worst murders – I mean murders deliberately planned – are committed by persons absolutely deficient in that part of the moral organization which *feels*. The night before they are hanged they sleep. On their last morning they eat a breakfast. Incapable of realizing the horror of murder, they are incapable of realizing the horror of death. Do you remember the last murderer who was hanged here – a gentleman's coachman who killed his wife? He had but two anxieties while he was waiting for execution. One was to get his allowance of beer doubled, and the other was to be hanged in his coachman's livery. No! no! these wretches are all alike; they are human creatures born with the temperaments of tigers. Take my word for it, we need feel no anxiety about to-morrow. The Prisoner will face the crowd round the scaffold with composure; and the people will say, "She died game."'

## CHAPTER VIII

### THE MINISTER SAYS GOOD-BYE

The Capital Punishment of the Prisoner is in no respect connected with my purpose in writing the present narrative. Neither do I desire to darken these pages by describing in detail an act of righteous retribution which must present, by the nature of it, a scene of horror. For these reasons I ask to be excused, if I limit what I must needs say of the execution within the compass of a few words – and pass on.

The one self-possessed person among us was the miserable woman who suffered the penalty of death.

Not very discreetly, as I think, the Chaplain asked her if she had truly repented. She answered: 'I have confessed the crime, sir. What more do you want?' To my mind – still hesitating between the view that believes with the Minister, and the view that doubts with the Doctor – this reply leaves a way open to hope of her salvation. Her last words to me, as she mounted the steps of the scaffold, were: 'Remember your promise.' It was easy for me to be true to my word. At that bygone time, no difficulties were placed in my way by such precautions as are now observed in the conduct of executions within the walls of the prison. From the time of her death to the time of her burial, no living creature saw her face. She rests, veiled in her prison grave.

Let me now turn to living interests, and to scenes removed from the thunder-clouds of crime.

\*     \*     \*     \*     \*

On the next day I received a visit from the Minister.

His first words entreated me not to allude to the terrible event of the previous day. 'I cannot escape thinking of it,' he said, 'but I may avoid speaking of it.' This seemed to me to be the misplaced confidence of a weak man in the refuge of silence. By way of changing the subject, I spoke of the child. There would be serious difficulties to contend with (as I ventured to suggest), if he remained in the town, and allowed his new responsibilities to become the subject of public talk.

His reply to this agreeably surprised me. There were no difficulties to be feared.

The state of his wife's health had obliged him (acting under medical advice) to try the influence of her native air. An interval of some months might elapse before the good effect of the change had sufficiently declared itself; and a return to the peculiar climate of the town might bring on a relapse. There had consequently been no alternative but to resign his charge. Only on that day the resignation had been accepted – with expressions of regret sincerely reciprocated by himself. He proposed to leave the town immediately; and one of the objects of his visit was to bid me good-bye.

'The next place I live in,' he said, 'will be more than a hundred miles away. At that distance I may hope to keep events concealed which must be known only to ourselves. So far as I can see, there are no risks of discovery lurking in this place. My servants (only two in number) have both been born here, and have both told my wife that they have no wish to go away. As to the person who introduced herself to me by the name of Miss Chance, she was traced to the railway-station yesterday afternoon, and took her ticket for London.'

I congratulated the Minister on the good fortune which had befriended him, so far.

'You will understand how carefully I have provided against being deceived,' he continued, 'when I tell you what my plans are. The persons among whom my future lot is cast – and the child herself, of course – must never suspect that the new member of my family is other than my own daughter. This is deceit, I admit; but it is deceit that injures no one. I hope you see the necessity for it, as I do.'

There could be no doubt of the necessity.

If the child was described as adopted, there would be curiosity about the circumstances, and inquiries relating to the parents. Prevaricating replies lead to suspicion, and suspicion to discovery. But for the wise course which the Minister had decided on taking, the poor child's life might have been darkened by the horror of the mother's crime, and the infamy of the mother's death.

Having quieted my friend's needless scruples by this perfectly sincere expression of opinion, I ventured to approach the central figure in his domestic circle, by means of a question relating to his wife. How had that lady received the unfortunate little creature, for whose appearance on the home-scene she must have been entirely unprepared?

The Minister's manner showed some embarrassment; he prefaced what he had to tell me with praises of his wife, equally creditable no doubt to both of them. The beauty of the child, the pretty ways of the child, he said, fascinated the admirable woman at first sight. It was not to be denied that she had felt, and had expressed, misgivings on being informed of the circumstances under which the Minister's act of mercy had been performed. But her mind was too well balanced to incline to this state of feeling, when her husband had addressed her in defence of his conduct. She then understood that the true merit of a good action consisted in patiently facing the sacrifices involved. Her interest in the new daughter being, in this way, ennobled by a sense of Christian duty, there had been no further difference of opinion between the married pair.

I listened to this plausible explanation with interest, but at the same time, with doubts of the lasting nature of the lady's submission to circumstances; suggested, perhaps, by the constraint in the Minister's manner. It was well for both of us when we changed the subject. He reminded me of the discouraging view which the Doctor had taken of the prospect before him.

'I will not attempt to decide whether your friend is right or wrong,' he said. 'Trusting as I do, in the mercy of God, I look hopefully to a future time when all that is brightest and best in the nature of my adopted child will be developed under my fostering care. If evil tendencies show themselves, my reliance will be confidently placed on pious example, on religious instruction, and, above all, on intercession by prayer. Repeat to your friend,' he concluded, 'what you have just heard me say. Let him ask himself if he could confront the uncertain future with my cheerful submission and my steadfast hope.'

He entrusted me with that message, and gave me his hand. So we parted.

I agreed with him, I admired him; but my faith seemed to want sustaining power, as compared with his faith. On his own showing (as it appeared to me), there would be two forces in a state of conflict in the child's nature as she grew up – inherited evil against inculcated good. Try as I might, I failed to feel the Minister's comforting conviction as to which of the two would win.

## CHAPTER IX

### THE GOVERNOR RECEIVES A VISIT

A few days after the good man had left us, I met with a serious accident, caused by a false step on the stone stairs of the prison.

The long illness which followed this misfortune, and my removal afterwards (in the interests of my recovery) to a milder climate than the climate of England, obliged me to confide the duties of governor of the prison to a representative. I was absent from my post for rather more than a year. During this interval no news reached me from my reverend friend.

Having returned to the duties of my office, I thought of writing to the Minister. While the proposed letter was still in contemplation, I was informed that a lady wished to see me. She sent in her card. My visitor proved to be the Minister's wife.

I observed her with no ordinary attention when she entered the room.

Her dress was simple; her scanty light hair, so far as I could see it under her bonnet, was dressed with taste. The paleness of her lips, and the faded colour in her face, suggested that she was certainly not in good health. Two peculiarities struck me in her personal appearance. I never remembered having seen any other person with such a singularly narrow and slanting forehead as this lady presented; and I was impressed, not at all agreeably, by the flashing shifting expression in her eyes. On the other hand, let me own that I was powerfully attracted and interested by the beauty of her voice. Its fine variety of compass, and its musical resonance of tone, fell with such enchantment on the ear, that I should have liked to put a book of poetry into her hand, and to have heard her read it in summer-time, accompanied by the music of a rocky stream.

The object of her visit – so far as she explained it at the outset – appeared to be to offer her congratulations on my recovery, and to tell me that her husband had assumed the charge of a church, in a large town not far from her birthplace.

Even those commonplace words were made interesting by her delicious voice. But however sensitive to sweet sounds a man may be, there are limits to his capacity for deceiving himself – especially when he happens to be enlightened by experience of humanity within the walls of a prison. I had, it may be remembered, already doubted the lady's good temper, judging from her husband's over-wrought description of her virtues. Her eyes looked at me furtively; and her manner, gracefully self-possessed as it was, suggested that she had something of a delicate, or disagreeable nature to say to me, and that she was at a loss how to approach the subject so as to produce the right impression on my mind at the outset. There was a momentary silence between us. For the sake of saying something, I asked how she and the Minister liked their new place of residence.

'Our new place of residence,' she answered, 'has been made interesting by a very unexpected event – an event (how shall I describe it?) which has increased our happiness and enlarged our family circle.'

There she stopped; expecting me, as I fancied, to guess what she meant. A woman, and that woman a mother, might have fulfilled her anticipations. A man, and that man not listening attentively, was simply puzzled.

'Pray excuse my stupidity,' I said; 'I don't quite understand you.'

The lady's temper looked at me out of the lady's shifting eyes, and hid itself again in a moment. She set herself right in my estimation by taking the whole blame of our little misunderstanding on her own innocent shoulders.

'I ought to have spoken more plainly,' she said. 'Let me try what I can do now. After many years of disappointment in my married life, it has pleased Providence to bestow on me the happiness – the inexpressible happiness – of being a mother. My baby is a sweet little girl; and my one regret is that I cannot nurse her myself.'

My languid interest in the Minister's wife was not stimulated by the announcement of this domestic event.

I felt no wish to see the 'sweet little girl'; I was not even reminded of another example of long-deferred maternity, which had occurred within the limits of my own family circle. All my sympathies attached themselves to the sad little figure of the adopted child. I remembered the poor baby on my knee, enchanted by the ticking of my watch – I thought of her, peacefully and prettily asleep under the horrid shelter of the condemned cell – and it is hardly too much to say that my heart was heavy, when I compared her prospects with the prospects of her baby-rival. Kind as he was, conscientious as he was, could the Minister be expected to admit to an equal share in his love the child endeared to him as a father, and the child who merely reminded him of an act of mercy? As for his wife, it seemed the merest waste of time to put her state of feeling (placed between the two children) to the test of inquiry. I tried the useless experiment, nevertheless.

'It is pleasant to think,' I began, 'that your other daughter——'

She interrupted me, with the utmost gentleness: 'Do you mean the child that my husband was foolish enough to adopt?'

'Say rather fortunate enough to adopt,' I persisted. 'As your own little girl grows up, she will want a playfellow. And she will find a playfellow in that other child, whom the good Minister has taken for his own.'

'No, my dear sir – not if I can prevent it.'

The contrast between the cruelty of her intention, and the musical beauty of the voice which politely expressed it in those words, really startled me. I was at a loss how to answer her, at the very time when I ought to have been most ready to speak.

'You must surely understand,' she went on, 'that we don't want another person's child, now we have a little darling of our own?'

'Does your husband agree with you in that view?' I asked.

'Oh dear, no! He said what you said just now, and (oddly enough) almost in the same words. But I don't at all despair of persuading him to change his mind – and you can help me.'

She made that audacious assertion with such an appearance of feeling perfectly sure of me, that my politeness gave way under the strain laid on it. 'What do you mean?' I asked sharply.

Not in the least impressed by my change of manner, she took from the pocket of her dress a printed paper. 'You will find what I mean there,' she replied – and put the paper into my hand.

It was an appeal to the charitable public, occasioned by the enlargement of an orphan-asylum, with which I had been connected for many years. What she meant was plain enough now. I said nothing; I only looked at her.

Pleased to find that I was clever enough to guess what she meant, on this occasion, the Minister's wife informed me that the circumstances were all in our favour. She still persisted in taking me into partnership – the circumstances were in *our* favour.

'In two years more,' she explained, 'the child of that detestable creature who was hanged – do you know, I cannot even look at the little wretch without thinking of the gallows? – will be old enough (with your interest to help us) to be received into the asylum. What a relief it will be to get rid of that child! And how hard I shall work at canvassing for subscribers' votes! Your name will be a tower of strength when I use it as a reference. Pardon me – you are not looking so pleasantly as usual. Do you see some obstacles in our way?'

'I see two obstacles.'

'What can they possibly be?'

For the second time, my politeness gave way under the strain laid on it. 'You know perfectly well,' I said, 'what one of the obstacles is.'

'Am I to understand that you contemplate any serious resistance on the part of my husband?'

'Certainly!'

She was unaffectedly amused by my simplicity.

'Are you a single man?' she asked.

'I am a widower.'

'Then your experience ought to tell you that I know every weak point in the Minister's character. I can tell him, on your authority, that the hateful child will be placed in competent and kindly hands – and I have my own sweet baby to plead for me. With these advantages in my favour, do you actually suppose I can fail to make *my* way of thinking *his* way of thinking? You must have forgotten your own married life! Suppose we go on to the second of your two obstacles. I hope it will be better worth considering than the first.'

'The second obstacle will not disappoint you,' I answered; 'I am the obstacle, this time.'

'You refuse to help me?'

'Positively.'

'Perhaps reflection may alter your resolution?'

'Reflection will do nothing of the kind.'

'You are rude, sir!'

'In speaking to you, madam, I have no alternative but to speak plainly.'

She rose. Her shifting eyes, for once, looked at me steadily.

'What sort of enemy have I made of you?' she asked. 'A passive enemy who is content with refusing to help me? Or an active enemy who will write to my husband?'

'It depends entirely,' I told her, 'on what your husband does. If he questions me about you, I shall tell him the truth.'

'And if not?'

'In that case, I shall hope to forget that you ever favoured me with a visit.'

In making this reply I was guiltless of any malicious intention. What evil interpretation she placed on my words it was impossible for me to say; I can only declare that some intolerable sense of injury hurried her into an outbreak of rage. Her voice, strained for the first time, lost its tuneful beauty of tone.

'Come and see us in two years' time,' she burst out – 'and discover the orphan of the gallows in our house if you can! If your Asylum won't take her, some other Charity will. Ha, Mr Governor, I deserve my disappointment! I ought to have remembered that you are only a gaoler after all. And what is a gaoler? Proverbially a brute. Do you hear that? A brute!'

Her strength suddenly failed her. She dropped back into the chair from which she had risen, with a faint cry of pain. A ghastly pallor stole over her face. There was wine on the sideboard; I filled a glass. She refused to take it. At that time in the day, the Doctor's duties required his attendance in the prison. I instantly sent for him. After a moment's look at her, he took the wine out of my hand, and held the glass to her lips.

'Drink it,' he said. She still refused. 'Drink it,' he reiterated, 'or you will die.'

That frightened her; she drank the wine. The Doctor waited for a while with his fingers on her pulse. 'She will do now,' he said.

'Can I go?' she asked.

'Go wherever you please, madam – so long as you don't go upstairs in a hurry.'

She smiled: 'I understand you, sir – and thank you for your advice.'

I asked the Doctor, when we were alone, what made him tell her not to go upstairs in a hurry.

'What I felt,' he answered, 'when I had my fingers on her pulse. You heard her say that she understood me.'

'Yes; but I don't know what she meant.'

'She meant, probably, that her own Doctor had warned her as I did.'

'Something seriously wrong with her health?'

'Yes.'

'What is it?'

'Heart.'

# CHAPTER X

## MISS CHANCE REAPPEARS

A week had passed, since the Minister's wife had left me, when I received a letter from the Minister himself.

After surprising me, as he innocently supposed, by announcing the birth of his child, he mentioned some circumstances connected with that event, which I now heard for the first time.

'Within an easy journey of the populous scene of my present labours,' he wrote, 'there is a secluded country village called Low Lanes. The rector of the place is my wife's brother. Before the birth of our infant, he had asked his sister to stay for a while at his house; and the doctor thought she might safely be allowed to accept the invitation. Through some error in the customary calculations, as I suppose, the child was born unexpectedly at the rectory; and the ceremony of baptism was performed at the church, under circumstances which I am not able to relate within the limits of a letter. Let me only say that I allude to this incident without any sectarian bitterness of feeling – for I am no enemy to the Church of England. You have no idea what treasures of virtue and treasures of beauty, maternity has revealed in my wife's sweet nature. Other mothers, in her proud position, might find their love cooling towards the poor child whom we have adopted. But my household is irradiated by the presence of an angel, who gives an equal share in her affections to the two little ones alike.'

In this semi-hysterical style of writing, the poor man unconsciously told me how cunningly and how cruelly his wife was deceiving him.

I longed to exhibit that wicked woman in her true character – but what could I do? She must have been so favoured by circumstances as to be able to account for her absence from home, without exciting the slightest suspicion of the journey which she had really taken. If I declared in my reply to the Minister's letter that I had received her in my rooms, and if I repeated the conversation that had taken place, what would the result be? She would find an easy refuge in positive denial of the truth – and, in that case, which of us would her infatuated husband believe?

The one part of the letter which I read with some satisfaction was the end of it.

I was here informed that the Minister's plans for concealing the parentage of his adopted daughter had proved to be entirely successful. The members of the new domestic household believed the two children to be infant-sisters. Neither was there any danger of the adopted child being identified (as the oldest child of the two) by consultation of the registers.

Before he left our town, the Minister had seen for himself that no baptismal name had been added, after the birth of the daughter of the murderess had been registered, and that no entry of baptism existed in the registers kept in places of worship. He drew the inference – in all probability a true inference, considering the characters of the parents – that the child had never been baptized; and he performed the ceremony privately, abstaining, for obvious reasons, from adding her Christian name to the imperfect register of her birth. 'I am not aware,' he wrote, 'whether I have, or have not, committed an offence against the Law. In any case, I may hope to have made atonement by obedience to the Gospel.'

Six weeks passed, and I heard from my reverend friend once more.

His second letter presented a marked contrast to the first. It was written in sorrow and anxiety, to inform me of an alarming change for the worse in his wife's health. I showed the letter to my medical colleague. After reading it he predicted the event that might be expected, in two words: – Sudden death.

On the next occasion when I heard from the Minister, the Doctor's grim reply proved to be a prophecy fulfilled.

When we address expressions of condolence to bereaved friends, the principles of popular hypocrisy sanction indiscriminate lying as a duty which we owe to the dead – no matter what their lives may have been – because they are dead. Within my own little sphere, I have always been silent, when I could not offer to afflicted persons expressions of sympathy which I honestly felt. To have condoled with the Minister on the loss that he had sustained by the death of a woman, self-betrayed to me as shamelessly deceitful, and pitilessly determined to reach her own cruel ends, would have been to degrade myself by telling a deliberate lie. I expressed in my answer all that an honest man naturally feels, when he is writing to a friend in distress; carefully abstaining from any allusion to the memory of his wife, or to the place which her death had left vacant in his household. My letter, I am sorry to say, disappointed and offended him. He wrote to me no more, until years had passed, and time had exerted its influence in producing a more indulgent frame of mind. These letters of a later date have been preserved, and will probably be used, at the right time, for purposes of explanation with which I may be connected in the future.

*    *    *    *    *

The correspondent whom I had now lost was succeeded by a gentleman entirely unknown to me.

Those reasons which induced me to conceal the names of persons, while I was relating events in the prison, do not apply to correspondence with a stranger writing from another place. I may, therefore, mention that Mr Dunboyne, of Fairmount, on the west coast of Ireland, was the writer of the letter now addressed to me. He proved, to my surprise, to be one of the relations, whom the Prisoner under sentence of death had not cared to see, when I offered her the opportunity of saying farewell. Mr Dunboyne was a brother-in-law of the murderess. He had married her sister.

His wife, he informed me, had died in child-birth, leaving him but one consolation – a boy, who already recalled all that was brightest and best in his lost mother. The father was naturally anxious that the son should never become acquainted with the disgrace that had befallen the family.

The letter then proceeded in these terms:

'I heard yesterday, for the first time, by means of an old newspaper-cutting sent to me by a friend, that the miserable woman who suffered the ignominy of public execution has left an infant child. Can you tell me what has become of the orphan? If this little girl is, as I fear, not well provided for, I only do what my wife would have done if she had lived, by offering to make the child's welfare my especial care. I am willing to place her in an establishment well known to me, in which she will be kindly treated, well educated, and fitted to earn her own living honourably in later life.

'If you feel some surprise at finding that my good intentions towards this ill-fated niece of mine do not go to the length of receiving her as a member of my own family, I beg to submit some considerations which may perhaps weigh with you as they have weighed with me.

'In the first place, there is at least a possibility – however carefully I might try to conceal it – that the child's parentage would sooner or later be discovered. In the second place (and assuming that the parentage had been successfully concealed), if this girl and my boy grew up together, there is another possibility to be reckoned with: they might become attached to each other. Does the father live who would allow his son ignorantly to marry the daughter of a convicted murderess? I should have no alternative but to part them cruelly by revealing the truth.'

The letter ended with some complimentary expressions addressed to myself. And the question was: how ought I to answer it?

My correspondent had strongly impressed me in his favour; I could not doubt that he was an honourable man. But the interest of the Minister in keeping his own benevolent action secure from the risk of discovery – increased as that interest was by the filial relations of the two children towards him, now publicly established – had, as I could not doubt, the paramount claim on me. The absolutely safe course to take was to admit no one, friend or stranger, to our confidence. I replied, expressing sincere admiration of Mr Dunboyne's motives, and merely informing him that the child was already provided for.

After that, I heard no more of the Irish gentleman.

It is perhaps hardly necessary to add that I kept the Minister in ignorance of my correspondence with Mr Dunboyne. I was too well acquainted with my friend's sensitive and self-tormenting nature to let him know that a relative of the murderess was living, and was aware that she had left a child.

A last event remains to be related, before I close these pages.

During the year of which I am now writing, our Chaplain added one more to the many examples that I have seen of his generous readiness to serve his friends. He had arranged to devote his annual leave of absence to a tour among the English Lakes, when he received a letter from a clergyman resident in London, whom he had known from the time when they had been schoolfellows. This old friend wrote under circumstances of the severest domestic distress, which made it absolutely necessary that he should leave London for a while. Having failed to find a representative who could relieve him of his clerical duties, he applied to the Chaplain to recommend a clergyman who might be in a position to help him. My excellent colleague gave up his holiday-plans without hesitation, and went to London himself.

On his return, I asked if he had seen anything of some acquaintances of his and mine, who were then visitors to the metropolis. He smiled significantly when he answered me.

'I have a card to deliver from an acquaintance whom you have not mentioned,' he said; 'and I rather think it will astonish you.'

It simply puzzled me. When he gave me the card, this is what I found printed on it:

'MRS TENBRUGGEN (OF SOUTH BEVELAND).'

'Well?' said the Chaplain.

'Well,' I answered; 'I never even heard of Mrs Tenbruggen, of South Beveland. Who is she?'

'I married the lady to a foreign gentleman, only last week, at my friend's church,' the Chaplain replied. 'Perhaps you may remember her maiden name?'

He mentioned the name of the dangerous creature who had first presented herself to me, in charge of the Prisoner's child – otherwise Miss Elizabeth Chance. The reappearance of this woman on the scene – although she was only represented by

her card – caused me a feeling of vague uneasiness, so
contemptibly superstitious in its nature, that I now remember it
with shame. I asked a stupid question:

'How did it happen?'

'In the ordinary course of such things,' my friend said. 'They
were married by license, in their parish church. The
bridegroom was a fine tall man, with a bold eye and a dashing
manner. The bride and I recognized each other directly. When
Miss Chance had become Mrs Tenbruggen, she took me aside,
and gave me her card. "Ask the Governor to accept it," she
said, "in remembrance of the time when he took me for a
nursemaid. Tell him I am married to a Dutch gentleman of
high family. If he ever comes to Holland, we shall be glad to see
him in our residence at South Beveland." There is her message
to you, repeated word for word.'

'I am glad she is going to live out of England.'

'Why? Surely you have no reason to fear her?'

'None whatever.'

'You are thinking perhaps of somebody else?'

I was thinking of the Minister; but it seemed to be safest not
to say so.

My pen is laid aside, and my many pages of writing have been
sent to their destination. What I undertook to do, is now done.
To take a metaphor from the stage – the curtain falls here on
the Governor and the Prison.

# SECOND PERIOD: 1875

## *THE GIRLS AND THE JOURNALS*

### CHAPTER XI

We both said good-night, and went up to our room with a new object in view. By our father's advice we had resolved on keeping diaries, for the first time in our lives, and had pledged ourselves to begin before we went to bed.

Slowly and silently and lazily, my sister sauntered to her end of the room, and seated herself at her writing-table. On the desk lay a nicely bound book, full of blank pages. The word 'Journal' was printed on it in gold letters, and there was fitted to the covers a bright brass lock and key. A second journal, exactly similar in every respect to the first, was placed on the writing-table at my end of the room. I opened my book. The sight of the blank leaves irritated me; they were so smooth, so spotless, so entirely ready to do *their* duty. I took too deep a dip of ink, and began the first entry in my diary by making a blot. This was discouraging. I got up, and looked out of the window.

'Helena!'

My sister's voice could hardly have addressed me in a more weary tone, if her pen had been at work all night, relating domestic events. 'Well!' I said. 'What is it?'

'Have you done already?' she asked.

I showed her the blot. My sister Eunice (the strangest as well as the dearest of girls) always blurts out what she has in her mind at the time. She fixed her eyes gravely on my spoilt page, and said: 'That comforts me.' I crossed the room, and looked at her book. She had not even summoned energy enough to make a blot. 'What will Papa think of us,' she said, 'if we don't begin to-night?'

'Why not begin,' I suggested, 'by writing down what he said, when he gave us our journals? Those wise words of advice will be in their proper place on the first page of the new books.'

Not at all a demonstrative girl naturally; not ready with her tears, not liberal with her caresses, not fluent in her talk, Eunice was affected by my proposal in a manner wonderful to see. She suddenly developed into an excitable person – I declare she kissed me. 'Oh,' she burst out, 'how clever you are! The very thing to write about; I'll do it directly.'

She really did it directly; without once stopping to consider, without once waiting to ask my advice. Line after line, I heard her noisy pen hurrying to the bottom of a first page, and getting three-parts of the way towards the end of a second page, before she closed her diary. I reminded her that she had not turned the key in the lock which was intended to keep her writing private.

'It's not worthwhile,' she answered. 'Anybody who cares to do it may read what I write. Good-night.'

The singular change which I had noticed in her began to disappear, when she set about her preparations for bed. I noticed the old easy indolent movements again, and that regular and deliberate method of brushing her hair, which I can never contemplate without feeling a stupefying influence that has helped me to many a delicious night's sleep. She said her prayers in her favourite corner of the room, and laid her head on the pillow with the luxurious little sigh which announces that she is falling asleep. This reappearance of her usual habits was really a relief to me. Eunice in a state of excitement is Eunice exhibiting an unnatural spectacle.

The next thing I did was to take the liberty which she had already sanctioned – I mean the liberty of reading what she had written. Here it is, copied exactly:

'I am not half so fond of anybody as I am of Papa. He is always kind, he is always right. I love him, I love him, I love him.

'But this is not how I meant to begin. I must tell how he talked to us; I wish he was here to tell it himself.

'He said to me: "You are getting lazier than ever, Eunice." He said to Helena: "You are feeling the influence of Eunice's example." He said to both of us: "You are too ready, my dear children, to sit with your hands on your laps, looking at nothing and thinking of nothing; I want to try a new way of employing your leisure time."

'He opened a parcel on the table. He made each of us a present of a beautiful book, called "Journal". He said: "When you have nothing to do, my dears, in the evening, employ yourselves in keeping a diary of the events of the day. It will be a useful record in many ways, and a good moral discipline for young girls." Helena said: "Oh, thank you!" I said the same, but not so cheerfully.

'The truth is, I feel out of spirits now if I think of Papa; I am not easy in my mind about him. When he is very much interested, there is a quivering in his face which I don't remember in past times. He seems to have got older and thinner, all of a sudden. He shouts (which he never used to do) when he threatens sinners at sermon-time. Being in dreadful earnest about our souls, he is of course obliged to speak of the devil; but he never used to hit the harmless pulpit cushion with his fist as he does now. Nobody seems to have seen these things but me; and now I have noticed them what ought I to do? I don't know; I am certain of nothing, except what I have put in at the top of page one: – I love him, I love him, I love him.'

*    *    *    *    *

There this very curious entry ended. It was easy enough to discover the influence which had made my slow-minded sister so ready with her memory and her pen – so ready, in short, to do anything and everything, provided her heart was in it, and her father was in it.

But Eunice is wrong, let me tell her, in what she says of myself.

I, too, have seen the sad change in my father; but I happen to know that he dislikes having it spoken of at home, and I have kept my painful discoveries to myself. Unhappily, the best medical advice is beyond our reach. The one really competent doctor in this place is known to be an infidel. But for that shocking obstacle I might have persuaded my father to see him. As for the other two doctors whom he has consulted, at different times, one talked about suppressed gout, and the other told him to take a year's holiday and enjoy himself on the Continent.

The clock has just struck twelve. I have been writing and copying till my eyes are heavy, and I want to follow Eunice's example and sleep as soundly as she does. We have made a strange beginning of this journalizing experiment. I wonder how long it will go on, and what will come of it.


## SECOND DAY


I begin to be afraid that I am stupid – no; that is not a nice word to use – let me say, as simple as dear Eunice. A diary means a record of the events of the day; and not one of the events of yesterday appears in my sister's journal or in mine. Well, it is easy to set that mistake right. Our lives are so dull (but I would not say so in my father's hearing, for the world) that the record of one day will be much the same as the record of another.

After family prayers and breakfast I suffer my customary persecution at the hands of the cook. That is to say, I am obliged, being the housekeeper, to order what we have to eat. Oh, how I hate inventing dinners! and how I admire the enviable slowness of mind and laziness of body which have saved Eunice from undertaking the worries of housekeeping in her turn! She can go and work in her garden, while I am racking my invention to discover variety in dishes without over-stepping the limits of economy. I suppose I may confess it privately to myself – how sorry I am not to have been born a man!

My next employment leads me to my father's study, to write under his dictation. I don't complain of this; it flatters my pride to feel that I am helping so great a man. At the same time, I do notice that here, again, Eunice's little defects have relieved her of another responsibility. She can neither keep dictated words in her memory, nor has she ever been able to learn how to put in her stops.

After the dictation. I have an hour's time left for practising music. My sister comes in from the garden, with her pencil and paint-box, and practises drawing. Then we go out for a walk – a delightful walk, if my father goes too. He has something always new to tell us, suggested by what we pass on the way. Then, dinner-time comes – not always a pleasant part of the day to me. Sometimes I hear paternal complaints (always gentle complaints) of my housekeeping; sometimes my sister (I won't say my greedy sister) tells me I have not given her enough to eat. Poor father! Dear Eunice!

Dinner having reached its end, we stroll in the garden when the weather in fine. When it rains, we make flannel petticoats for poor old women. What a horrid thing old age is to look at! To be ugly, to be helpless, to be miserably unfit for all the pleasures of life – I hope I shall not live to be an old woman. What would my father say if he saw this? For his sake, to say nothing of my own feelings, I shall do well if I make it a custom to use the lock of my journal.

Our next occupation is to join the Scripture class for girls, and to help the teacher. This is a good discipline for Eunice's temper, and – oh, I don't deny it! – for my temper too. I may long to box the ears of the whole class, but it is my duty to keep a smiling face and to be a model of patience. From the Scripture class we sometimes go to my father's lecture. At other times, we may amuse ourselves as well as we can till the tea is ready. After tea we read books which instruct us, poetry and novels being forbidden. When we are tired of the books we talk. When supper is over, we have prayers again, and we go to bed. There is our day. Oh, dear me! there is our day.

*　　*　　*　　*　　*

And how has Eunice succeeded in her second attempt at keeping a diary? Here is what she has written. It has one merit that nobody can deny – it is soon read:

'I hope Papa will excuse me; I have nothing to write about to-day.'

Over and over again, I have tried to point out to my sister the absurdity of calling her father by the infantine nick-name of Papa. I have reminded her that she is (in years, at least) no longer a child. 'Why don't you call him father, as I do?' I asked only the other day.

She made an absurd reply: 'I used to call him Papa when I was a little girl.'

'That,' I reminded her, 'doesn't justify you in calling him Papa now.'

And she actually answered: 'Yes, it does.' What a strange state of mind! And what a charming girl, in spite of her mind!


## THIRD DAY


The morning post has brought with it a promise of some little variety in our lives – or, to speak more correctly, in the life of my sister.

Our new and nice friends, the Staveleys, have written to invite Eunice to pay them a visit at their house in London. I don't complain of being left at home. It would be unfilial indeed if we both of us forsook our father; and last year it was my turn to receive the first invitation, and to enjoy the change of scene. The Staveleys are excellent people – strictly pious members of the Methodist Connexion – and exceedingly kind to my sister and me. But it was just as well for my moral welfare that I ended my visit to our friends when I did. With my fondness for music, I felt the temptation of the Evil One trying me, when I saw placards in the street announcing that the Italian Opera was open. I had no wish to be a witness of the shameful and sinful dancing which goes on (I am told) at the opera; but I did feel my principles shaken when I thought of the wonderful singers and the entrancing music. And this, when I knew what an atmosphere of wickedness people breathe who enter a theatre! I reflect with horror on what *might* have happened if I had remained a little longer in London.

Helping Eunice to pack up, I put her journal into the box.

'You will find something to write about now,' I told her. 'While I record everything that happens at home, you will keep your diary of all that you do in London, and when you come back we will show each other what we have written.' My sister is a dear creature. 'I don't feel sure of being able to do it,' she answered; 'but I promise to try.' Good Eunice!

## CHAPTER XII

### EUNICE'S DIARY

The air of London feels very heavy. There is a nasty smell of smoke in London. There are too many people in London. They seem to be mostly people in a hurry. The head of a country girl, when she goes into the streets, turns giddy – I suppose through not being used to the noise.

I do hope that it is London that has just put me out of temper. Otherwise, it must be I myself who am ill-tempered. I have not yet been one whole day in the Staveleys' house, and they have offended me already. I don't want Helena to hear of this from other people, and then to ask me why I concealed it from her. We are to read each other's journals when we are both at home again. Let her see what I have to say for myself here.

There are seven Staveleys in all: Mr and Mrs (two); three young Masters (five); two young Misses (seven). An eldest Miss and the second young Master are the only ones at home at the present time.

Mr, Mrs, and Miss kissed me when I arrived. Young Master only shook hands. He looked as if he would have liked to kiss me too. Why shouldn't he? It wouldn't have mattered. I don't myself like kissing. What is the use of it? Where is the pleasure of it?

Mrs was so glad to see me; she took hold of me by both

hands. She said: 'My dear child, you are improving. You were wretchedly thin when I saw you last. Now you are almost as well developed as your sister. I think you are prettier than your sister.' Mr didn't agree to that. He and his wife began to dispute about me before my face. I do call that an aggravating thing to endure.

Mr said: 'She hasn't got her sister's pretty grey eyes.'

Mrs said: 'She has got pretty brown eyes, which are just as good.'

Mr said: 'You can't compare her complexion with Helena's.'

Mrs said: 'I like Eunice's pale complexion. So delicate.'

Young Miss struck in: 'I admire Helena's hair – light brown.'

Young Master took his turn: 'I prefer Eunice's hair – dark brown.'

Mr opened his great big mouth, and asked a question: 'Which of you two sisters is the oldest? I forget.'

Mrs answered for me: 'Helena is the oldest; she told us so when she was here last.'

I really could *not* stand that. 'You must be mistaken,' I burst out.

'Certainly not, my dear.'

'Then Helena was mistaken.' I was unwilling to say of my sister that she had been deceiving them, though it did seem only too likely.

Mr and Mrs looked at each other. Mrs said: 'You seem to be very positive, Eunice. Surely, Helena ought to know.'

I said: 'Helena knows a good deal; but she doesn't know which of us is the oldest of the two.'

Mr put in another question: 'Do *you* know?'

'No more than Helena does.'

Mrs said: 'Don't you keep birthdays?'

I said: 'Yes; we keep both our birthdays on the same day.'

'On what day?'

'The first day of the New Year.'

Mr tried again: 'You can't possibly be twins?'

'I don't know.'

'Perhaps Helena knows?'

'Not she!'

Mrs took the next question out of her husband's mouth: 'Come, come, my dear! you must know how old you are.'

'Yes; I do know that. I'm eighteen.'

'And how old is Helena?'

'Helena's eighteen.'

Mrs turned round to Mr: 'Do you hear that!'

Mr said: 'I shall write to her father, and ask what it means.'

I said: 'Papa will only tell you what he told us – years ago.'

'What did your father say?'

'He said he had added our two ages together, and he meant to divide the product between us. It's so long since, I don't remember what the product was then. But I'll tell you what the product is now. Our two ages come to thirty-six. Half thirty-six is eighteen. I get one half, and Helena gets the other. When we ask what it means, and when friends ask what it means, Papa has got the same answer for everybody. "I have my reasons." That's all he says – and that's all I say.'

I had no intention of making Mr angry, but he did get angry. He left off speaking to me by my Christian name; he called me by my surname. He said: 'Let me tell you, Miss Gracedieu, it is not becoming in a young lady to mystify her elders.'

I had heard that it was respectful in a young lady to call an old gentleman, Sir, and to say, If you please. I took care to be respectful now. 'If you please, sir, write to Papa. You will find that I have spoken the truth.'

A woman opened the door, and said to Mrs Staveley: 'Dinner, Ma'am.' That stopped this nasty exhibition of our tempers. We had a very good dinner.

★     ★     ★     ★     ★

The next day I wrote to Helena, asking her what she had really said to the Staveleys about her age and mine, and telling her what I had said. I found it too great a trial of my patience to wait till she could see what I had written about the dispute in my journal. The days, since then, have passed, and I have been too lazy and stupid to keep my diary.

To-day, it is different. My head is like a dark room with the light let into it. I remember things; I think I can go on again.

We have religious exercises in this house, morning and evening, just as we do at home. (Not to be compared with Papa's religious exercises.) Two days ago his answer came to Mr Staveley's house. He did just what I had expected – said I had spoken truly, and disappointed the family by asking to be excused if he refrained from entering into explanations. Mr said: 'Very odd;' and Mrs agreed with him. Young Miss is not quite as friendly now, as she was at first. And young Master was impudent enough to ask me if 'I had got religion'. To conclude the list of my worries, I received an angry answer from Helena. 'Nobody but a simpleton,' she wrote, 'would have contradicted me as you did. Who but you could have failed to see that Papa's strange objection to let it be known which of us is the elder makes us ridiculous before other people? My presence of mind prevented that. You ought to have been grateful, and held your tongue.' Perhaps Helena is right – but I don't feel it so.

On Sunday, we went to chapel twice. We also had a sermon read at home, and a cold dinner. In the evening, a hot dispute on religion between Mr Staveley and his son. I don't blame them. After being pious all day long on Sunday, I have myself felt my piety give way towards evening.

There is something pleasant in prospect for to-morrow. All London is going just now to the exhibition of pictures. We are going with all London.

*       *       *       *       *

I don't know what is the matter with me to-night. I have positively been to bed, without going to sleep! After tossing and twisting and trying all sorts of positions, I am so angry with myself that I have got up again. Rather than do nothing, I have opened my ink-bottle and I mean to go on with my journal.

Now I think of it, it seems likely that the exhibition of works of art may have upset me.

I found a dreadfully large number of pictures, matched by a dreadfully large number of people to look at them. It is not

possible for me to write about what I saw: there was too much
of it. Besides, the show disappointed me. I would rather write
about a disagreement (oh, dear, another dispute!) I had with
Mrs Staveley. The cause of it was a famous artist; not himself,
but his works. He exhibited four pictures – what they call
figure subjects. Mrs Staveley had a pencil. At every one of the
great man's four pictures, she made a big mark of admiration on
her catalogue. At the fourth one, she spoke to me: 'Perfectly
beautiful, Eunice, isn't it?'

I said I didn't know. She said: 'You strange girl, what do you
mean by that?'

It would have been rude not to have given the best answer I
could find. I said: 'I never saw the flesh of any person's face like
the flesh in the faces which that man paints. He reminds me of
wax-work. Why does he paint the same waxy flesh in all four
of his pictures? I don't see the same coloured flesh in all the
faces about us.' Mrs Staveley held up her hand, by way of
stopping me. She said: 'Don't speak so loud, Eunice; you are
only exposing your own ignorance.'

A voice behind us joined in. The voice said: 'Excuse me, Mrs
Staveley, if I expose *my* ignorance. I entirely agree with the
young lady.'

I felt grateful to the person who took my part, just when I
was at a loss what to say for myself, and I looked round. The
person was a young gentleman.

He wore a beautiful blue frock-coat, buttoned up. I like a
frock-coat to be buttoned up. He had light-coloured trousers
and grey gloves and a pretty cane. I like light-coloured trousers
and grey gloves and a pretty cane. What colour his eyes were is
more than I can say; I only know they made me hot when they
looked at me. Not that I mind being made hot; it is surely
better than being made cold. He and Mrs Staveley shook hands.

They seemed to be old friends. I wished I had been an old
friend – not for any bad reason, I hope. I only wanted to shake
hands, too. What Mrs Staveley said to him escaped me
somehow. I think the picture escaped me also; I don't
remember noticing anything except the young gentleman,
especially when he took off his hat to me. He looked at me

twice before he went away. I got hot again. I said to Mrs
Staveley: 'Who is he?'

She laughed at me. I said again: 'Who is he?' She said: 'He is
young Mr Dunboyne.' I said: 'Does he live in London?' She
laughed again. I said again: 'Does he live in London?' She said:
'He is here for a holiday; he lives with his father at Fairmount,
in Ireland.'

Young Mr Dunboyne – here for a holiday – lives with his
father at Fairmount in Ireland. I have said that to myself fifty
times over. And here it is, saying itself for the fifty-first time in
my Journal. I must indeed be a simpleton, as Helena says. I had
better go to bed again.


## CHAPTER XIII

### EUNICE'S DIARY

Not long before I left home, I heard one of our two servants
telling the other about a person who had been 'bewitched'. Are
you bewitched when you don't understand your own self? That
has been my curious case, since I returned from the picture-
show. This morning I took my drawing material out of my
box, and tried to make a portrait of young Mr Dunboyne from
recollection. I succeeded pretty well with his frock-coat and
cane: but, try as I might, his face was beyond me. I have never
drawn anything so badly since I was a little girl; I almost felt
ready to cry. What a fool I am!

This morning I received a letter from Papa – it was in reply
to a letter that I had written to him – so kind, so beautifully
expressed, so like himself, that I felt inclined to send him a
confession of the strange state of feeling that has come over me,
and to ask him to comfort and advise me. On second thoughts I
was afraid to do it. Afraid of Papa! I am farther away from
understanding myself than ever.

Mr Dunboyne paid us a visit in the afternoon. Fortunately,
before we went out.

I thought I would have a good look at him; so as to know his face better than I had known it yet. Another disappointment was in store for me. Without intending it, I am sure, he did what no other young man has ever done – he made me feel confused. Instead of looking at him, I sat with my head down, and listened to his talk. His voice – this is high praise – reminded me of Papa's voice. It seemed to persuade me as Papa persuades his congregation. I felt quite at ease again. When he went away, we shook hands. He gave my hand a little squeeze. I gave him back the squeeze – without knowing why. When he was gone, I wished I had not done it – without knowing why, either.

I heard his Christian name for the first time, to-day. Mrs Staveley said to me: 'We are going to have a dinner-party. Shall I ask Philip Dunboyne?' I said to Mrs Staveley: 'Oh, do!'

She is an old woman; her eyes are dim. At times, she can look mischievous. She looked at me mischievously, now. I wished I had not been so eager to have Mr Dunboyne asked to dinner. A fear has come to me that I may have degraded myself. My spirits are depressed. This, as Papa tells us in his sermons, is a miserable world. I am sorry I accepted the Staveleys' invitation. I am sorry I went to see the pictures. When that young man comes to dinner, I shall say I have got a headache, and shall stop upstairs by myself. I don't think I like his Christian name. I hate London. I hate everybody.

What I wrote up above, yesterday, is nonsense. I think his Christian name is perfect. I like London. I love everybody.

He came to dinner to-day. I sat next to him. How beautiful a dress-coat is, and a white cravat! We talked. He wanted to know what my Christian name was. I was so pleased when I found he was one of the few people who like it. His hair curls naturally. In colour, it is something between my hair and Helena's. He wears his beard. How manly! It curls naturally, like his hair; it smells deliciously of some perfume which is new to me. He has white hands; his nails look as if he polished them; I should like to polish my nails if I knew how. Whatever I said, he agreed with me; I felt satisfied with my own conversation, for the first time in my life. Helena won't find me a simpleton when I go home. What exquisite things dinner-parties are!

My sister told me (when we said good-bye) to be particular in writing down my true opinions of the Staveleys. Helena wishes to compare what she thinks of them with what I think of them.

My opinion of Mr Staveley is – I don't like him. My opinion of Miss Staveley is – I can't endure her. As for Master Staveley, my clever sister will understand that *he* is beneath notice. But, oh, what a wonderful woman Mrs Staveley is! We went out together, after luncheon to-day, for a walk in Kensington Gardens. Never have I heard any conversation to compare with Mrs Staveley's. Helena shall enjoy it here, at second hand. I am quite changed in two things. First: I think more of myself than I ever did before. Second: writing is no longer a difficulty to me. I could fill a hundred journals, without once stopping to think.

Mrs Staveley began nicely: 'I suppose, Eunice, you have often been told that you have a good figure, and that you walk well?'

I said: 'Helena thinks my figure is better than my face. But do I really walk well? Nobody ever told me that.'

She answered: 'Philip Dunboyne thinks so. He said to me, "I resist the temptation because I might be wanting in respect if I gave way to it. But I should like to follow her when she goes out – merely for the pleasure of seeing her walk."'

I stood stock-still. I said nothing. When you are as proud as a peacock (which never happened to me before), I find you can't move and can't talk. You can only enjoy yourself.

Kind Mrs Staveley had more things to tell me. She said: 'I am interested in Philip. I lived near Fairmount in the time before I was married; and in those days he was a child. I want him to marry a charming girl, and be happy.'

What made me think directly of Miss Staveley? What made me mad to know if she was the charming girl? I was bold enough to ask the question. Mrs Staveley turned to me with that mischievous look which I have noticed already. I felt as if I had been running at the top of my speed, and had not got my breath again, yet.

But this good motherly friend set me at my ease. She explained herself: 'Philip is not much liked, poor fellow, in our house. My husband considers him to be weak and vain and fickle. And my daugher agrees with her father. There are times when she is barely civil to Philip. He is too good-natured to complain, but *I* see it. Tell me, my dear, do you like Philip?'

'Of course I do!' Out it came in those words, before I could stop it. Was there something unbecoming to a young lady in saying what I had just said? Mrs Staveley seemed to be more amused than angry with me. She took my arm kindly, and led me along with her. 'My dear, you are as clear as crystal, and as true as steel. You are a favourite of mine already.'

What a delightful woman! as I said just now. I asked if she really liked me as well as she liked my sister.

She said: 'Better.'

I didn't expect that, and didn't want it. Helena is my superior. She is prettier than I am, cleverer than I am, better worth liking than I am. Mrs Staveley shifted the talk back to Philip. I ought to have said Mr Philip. No I won't; I shall call him Philip. If I had a heart of stone, I should feel interested in him, after what Mrs Staveley has told me.

Such a sad story, in some respects. Mother dead; no brothers or sisters. Only the father left; he lives a dismal life on a lonely stormy coast. Not a severe old gentleman, for all that. His reasons for taking to retirement are reasons (so Mrs Staveley says) which nobody knows. He buries himself among his books, in an immense library; and he appears to like it. His son has not been brought up, like other young men, at school and college. He is a great scholar, educated at home by his father. To hear this account of his learning depressed me. It seemed to put such a distance between us. I asked Mrs Staveley if he thought me ignorant. As long as I live I shall remember the reply: 'He thinks you charming.'

Any other girl would have been satisfied with this. I am the miserable creature who is always making mistakes. My stupid curiosity spoilt the charm of Mrs Staveley's conversation. And yet it seemed to be a harmless question; I only said I should like to know what profession Philip belonged to.

Mrs Staveley answered: 'No profession.'

I foolishly put a wrong meaning on this. I said: 'Is he idle?'

Mrs Staveley laughed. 'My dear, he is an only son – and his father is a rich man.'

That stopped me – at last.

We have enough to live on in comfort at home – no more. Papa has told us himself that he is not (and can never hope to be) a rich man. This is not the worst of it. Last year, he refused to marry a young couple, both belonging to our congregation. This was very unlike his usual kind self. Helena and I asked him for his reasons. They were reasons that did not take long to give. The young gentleman's father was a rich man. He had forbidden his son to marry a sweet girl – because she had no fortune.

I have no fortune. And Philip's father is a rich man.

The best thing I can do is to wipe my pen, and shut up my Journal, and go home by the next train.

$$\star \quad \star \quad \star \quad \star \quad \star$$

I have a great mind to burn my Journal. It tells me that I had better not think of Philip any more.

On second thoughts, I won't destroy my Journal; I will only put it away. If I live to be an old woman, it may amuse me to open my book again, and see how foolish the poor wretch was when she was young.

What is this aching pain in my heart?

I don't remember it at any other time in my life. Is it trouble? How can I tell? – I have had so little trouble. It must be many years since I was wretched enough to cry. I don't even understand why I am crying now. My last sorrow, so far as I can remember, was the toothache. Other girls' mothers comfort them when they are wretched. If my mother had lived – it's useless to think about that. We lost her, while I and my sister were too young to understand our misfortune.

I wish I had never seen Philip.

This seems an ungrateful wish. Seeing him at the picture-show was a new enjoyment. Sitting next to him at dinner was a happiness that I don't recollect feeling, even when Papa has been most sweet and kind to me. I ought to be ashamed of myself to confess this. Shall I write to my sister? But how should she know what is that matter with me, when I don't know it myself? Besides Helena is angry; she wrote unkindly to me when she answered my last letter.

There is a dreadful loneliness in this great house at night. I had better say my prayers, and try to sleep. If it doesn't make me feel happier, it will prevent me spoiling my Journal by dropping tears on it.

★    ★    ★    ★    ★

What an evening of evenings this has been! Last night it was crying that kept me awake. To-night I can't sleep for joy.

Philip called on us again to-day. He brought with him tickets for the performance of an Oratorio. Sacred music is not forbidden music among our people. Mrs Staveley and Miss Staveley went to the concert with us. Philip and I sat next to each other.

My sister is a musician – I am nothing. That sounds bitter; but I don't mean it so. All I mean is, that I like simple little songs, which I can sing to myself by remembering the tune. There, my musical enjoyment ends. When voices and instruments burst out together by hundreds, I feel bewildered. I also get attacked by fidgets. This last misfortune is sure to overtake me when choruses are being performed. The unfortunate people employed are made to keep singing the same words, over and over again, till I find it a perfect misery to listen to them. The choruses were unendurable in the performance to-night. This is one of them: 'Here we are all alone in the wilderness – alone in the wilderness – in the wilderness, alone, alone, alone – here we are in the wilderness – alone in the wilderness – all alone in the wilderness,' and so on, till I felt inclined to call for the learned person who writes Oratorios, and beg him to give the poor music a more generous allowance of words.

Whenever I looked at Philip, I found him looking at me.

Perhaps he saw from the first that the music was wearying music to my ignorant ears. With his usual delicacy he said nothing for some time. But when he caught me yawning (though I did my best to hide it, for it looked like being ungrateful for the tickets), then he could restrain himself no longer. He whispered in my ear:

'You are getting tired of this. And so am I.'

'I am trying to like it,' I whispered back.

'Don't try,' he answered. 'Let's talk.'

He meant, of course, talk in whispers. We were a good deal annoyed – especially when the characters were all alone in the wilderness – by bursts of singing and playing which interrupted us at the most interesting moments. Philip persevered with a manly firmness. What could I do but follow his example – at a distance?

He said: 'Is it really true that your visit to Mrs Staveley is coming to an end?'

I answered: 'It comes to an end the day after to-morrow.'

'Are you sorry to be leaving your friends in London?'

What I might have said if he had made that inquiry a day earlier, when I was the most miserable creature living, I would rather not try to guess. Being quite happy as things were, I could honestly tell him I was sorry.

'You can't possibly be as sorry as I am, Eunice. May I call you by your pretty name?'

'Yes, if you please.'

'Eunice!'

'Yes.'

'You will leave a blank in my life when you go away——'

There another chorus stopped him, just as I was eager for more. It was such a delightfully new sensation to hear a young gentleman telling me that I had left a blank in his life. The next change in the Oratorio brought up a young lady, singing alone. Some people behind us grumbled at the smallness of her voice. We thought her voice perfect. It seemed to lend itself so nicely to our whispers.

He said: 'Will you help me to think of you while you are away? I want to imagine what your life is at home. Do you live in a town or in the country?'

I told him the name of our town. When we give a person information, I have always heard that we ought to make it complete. So I mentioned our address in the town. But I was troubled by a doubt. Perhaps he preferred the country. Being anxious about this, I said: 'Would you rather have heard that I live in the country?'

'Live where you may, Eunice, the place will be a favourite place of mine. Besides, your town is famous. It has a public attraction which brings visitors to it.'

I made another of those mistakes which no sensible girl, in my position, would have committed. I asked if he alluded to our new market-place.

He set me right in the sweetest manner: 'I alluded to a building hundreds of years older than your market-place – your beautiful cathedral.'

Fancy my not having thought of the cathedral! This is what comes of being a Congregationalist. If I had belonged to the Church of England, I should have forgotten the market-place, and remembered the cathedral. Not that I want to belong to the Church of England. Papa's church is good enough for me.

The song sung by the lady with the small voice was so pretty that the audience encored it. Didn't Philip and I help them! With the sweetest smiles the lady sang it all over again. The people behind us left the concert.

He said: 'Do you know, I take the greatest interest in cathedrals. I propose to enjoy the privilege and pleasure of seeing *your* cathedral early next week.'

I had only to look at him to see that I was the cathedral. It was no surprise to hear next that he thought of 'paying his respects to Mr Gracedieu.' He begged me to tell him what sort of reception he might hope to meet with when he called at our house. I got so excited in doing justice to Papa, that I quite forgot to whisper when the next question came. Philip wanted to know if Mr Gracedieu disliked strangers. When I answered 'Oh dear, no!' I said it out loud, so that the people heard me. Cruel, cruel people! They all turned round and stared. One hideous old woman actually said, 'Silence!' Miss Staveley looked disgusted. Even kind Mrs Staveley lifted her eyebrows in astonishment.

Philip, dear Philip, protected and composed me.

He held my hand devotedly till the end of the performance. When he put us into the carriage, I was last. He whispered in my ear: 'Expect me next week.' Miss Staveley might be as ill-natured as she pleased, on the way home. It didn't matter what she said. The Eunice of yesterday might have been mortified and offended. The Eunice of to-day was indifferent to the sharpest things that could be said to her.

    ★  ★  ★  ★  ★

All through yesterday's delightful evening, I never once thought of Philip's father. When I woke this morning, I remembered that old Mr Dunboyne was a rich man. I could eat no breakfast for thinking of the poor girl who was not allowed to marry her young gentleman, because she had no money.

Mrs Staveley waited to speak to me till the rest of them had left us together I had expected her to notice that I looked dull and dismal. No! her cleverness got at my secret in quite another way.

She said: 'How do you feel after the concert? You must be hard to please indeed if you were not satisfied with the accompaniments last night.'

'The accompaniments of the Oratorio?'

'No, my dear. The accompaniments of Philip.'

I suppose I ought to have laughed. In my miserable state of mind, it was not to be done. I said: 'I hope Mr Dunboyne's father will not hear how kind he was to me.'

Mrs Staveley asked why.

My bitterness overflowed at my tongue. I said: 'Because Papa is a poor man.'

'And Philip's Papa is a rich man,' says Mrs Staveley, putting my own thought into words for me. 'Where do you get these ideas, Eunice? Surely, you are not allowed to read novels?'

'Oh no!'

'And you have certainly never seen a play?'

'Never.'

'Clear your head, child, of the nonesense that has got into it –

I can't think how. Rich Mr Dunboyne has taught his heir to despise the base act of marrying for money. He knows that Philip will meet young ladies at my house; and he has written to me on the subject of his son's choice of a wife. "Let Philip find good principles, good temper, and good looks; and I promise beforehand to find the money." There is what he says. Are you satisfied with Philip's father, now?'

I jumped up in a state of ecstasy. Just as I had thrown my arms round Mrs Staveley's neck, the servant came in with a letter, and handed it to me.

Helena had written again, on this last day of my visit. Her letter was full of instructions for buying things that she wants, before I leave London. I read on quietly enough until I came to the postscript. The effect of it on me may be told in two words: I screamed. Mrs Staveley was naturally alarmed. 'Bad news?' she asked. Being quite unable to offer an opinion, I read the postscript out loud, and left her to judge for herself.

This was Helena's news from home:

'I must prepare you for a surprise, before your return. You will find a strange lady established at home. Don't suppose there is any prospect of her bidding us good-bye, if we only wait long enough. She is already (with father's full approval) as much a member of the family as we are. You shall form your own unbiased opinion of her, Eunice. For the present, I say no more.'

I asked Mrs Staveley what she thought of my news from home. She said: 'Your father approves of the lady, my dear. I suppose it's good news.'

But Mrs Staveley did not look as if she believed in the good news, for all that.

## CHAPTER XIV

### HELENA'S DIARY

To-day I went as usual to the Scripture-class for girls. It was harder work than ever, teaching without Eunice to help me. Indeed, I felt lonely all day without my sister. When I got home, I rather hoped that some friend might have come to see us, and have been asked to stay to tea. The housemaid opened the door to me. I asked Maria if anybody had called.

'Yes, Miss; a lady, to see the master.'

'A stranger?'

'Never saw her before, Miss, in all my life.'

I put no more questions. Many ladies visit my father. They call it consulting the Minister. He advises them in their troubles, and guides them in their religious difficulties, and so on. They come and go in a sort of secrecy. So far as I know, they are mostly old maids, and they waste the Minister's time.

When my father came in to tea, I began to feel some curiosity about the lady who had called on him. Visitors of that sort, in general, never appear to dwell on his mind after they have gone away; he sees too many of them, and is too well accustomed to what they have to say. On this particular evening, however, I perceived appearances that set me thinking; he looked worried and anxious.

'Has anything happened, father, to vex you?' I said.

'Yes.'

'Is the lady concerned in it?'

'What lady, my dear?'

'The lady who called on you while I was out.'

'Who told you she had called on me?'

'I asked Maria——'

'That will do , Helena, for the present.'

He drank his tea and went back to his study, instead of staying awhile, and talking pleasantly as usual. My respect submitted to his want of confidence in me; but my curiosity was in a state of revolt. I sent for Maria, and proceeded to make my own discoveries, with this result:

No other person had called at the house. Nothing had happened, except the visit of the mysterious lady. 'She looked between young and old. And, oh dear me, she was certainly not pretty. Not dressed nicely, to my mind; but they do say dress is a matter of taste.'

Try as I might, I could get no more than that out of our stupid young housemaid.

Later in the evening, the cook had occasion to consult me about supper. This was a person possessing the advantages of age and experience. I asked if she had seen the lady. The cook's reply promised something new: 'I can't say I saw the lady; but I heard her.'

'Do you mean that you heard her speaking?'

'No, Miss – crying.'

'Where was she crying?'

'In the master's study.'

'How did you come to hear her?'

'Am I to understand, Miss, that you suspect me of listening?'

Is a lie told by a look as bad as a lie told by words? I looked shocked at the bare idea of suspecting a respectable person of listening. The cook's sense of honour was satisfied; she readily explained herself: 'I was passing the door, Miss, on my way upstairs.'

Here my discoveries came to an end. It was certainly possible that an afflicted member of my father's congregation might have called on him to be comforted. But he sees plenty of afflicted ladies, without looking worried and anxious after they leave him. Still suspecting something out of the ordinary course of events, I waited hopefully for our next meeting at supper-time. Nothing came of it. My father left me by myself again, when the meal was over. He is always courteous to his daughters; and he made an apology: 'Excuse me, Helena, I want to think.'

*     *     *     *     *

I went to bed in a vile humour, and slept badly; wondering, in the long wakeful hours, what new rebuff I should meet with on the next day.

At breakfast this morning I was agreeably surprised. No signs of anxiety showed themselves in my father's face. Instead of retiring to his study when we rose from the table, he proposed taking a turn in the garden: 'You are looking pale, Helena, and you will be the better for a little fresh air. Besides, I have something to say to you.'

Excitement, I am sure, is good for young women. I saw in his face, I heard in his last words, that the mystery of the lady was at last to be revealed. The sensation of languor and fatigue which follows a disturbed night left me directly.

My father gave me his arm, and we walked slowly up and down the lawn.

'When that lady called on me yesterday,' he began, 'you wanted to know who she was, and you were surprised and disappointed when I refused to gratify your curiosity. My silence was not a selfish silence, Helena. I was thinking of you and your sister; and I was at a loss how to act for the best. You shall hear why my children were in my mind, presently. I must tell you first that I have arrived at a decision; I hope and believe on reasonable grounds. Ask me any questions you please; my silence will be no longer an obstacle in your way.'

This was so very encouraging that I said at once: 'I should like to know who the lady is.'

'The lady is related to me,' he answered. 'We are cousins.'

Here was a disclosure that I had not anticipated. In the little that I have seen of the world, I have observed that cousins – when they happen to be brought together under interesting circumstances – can remember their relationship, and forget their relationship, just as it suits them. 'Is your cousin a married lady?' I ventured to inquire.

'No.'

Short as it was, that reply might perhaps mean more than appeared on the surface. The cook had heard the lady crying. What sort of tender agitation was answerable for those tears? Was it possibly, barely possible, that Eunice and I might go to bed, one night, a widower's daughters, and wake up the next day to discover a step-mother?'

'Have I or my sister ever seen the lady?' I asked.

'Never. She has been living abroad; and I have not seen her myself since we were both young people.'

My excellent innocent father! Not the faintest idea of what I had been thinking of was in his mind. Little did he suspect how welcome was the relief that he had afforded to his daughter's wicked doubts of him. But he had not said a word yet about his cousin's personal appearance. There might be remains of good looks which the housemaid was too stupid to discover.

'After the long interval that has passed since you met,' I said, 'I suppose she has become an old woman?'

'No, my dear. Let us say, a middle-aged woman.'

'Perhaps she is still an attractive person?'

He smiled. 'I am afraid, Helena, that would never have been a very accurate description of her.'

I now knew all that I wanted to know about this alarming person, excepting one last morsel of information.

'We have been talking about the lady for some time,' I said; 'and you have not yet told me her name.'

Father looked a little embarrassed. 'It's not a very pretty name,' he answered. 'My cousin, my unfortunate cousin, is – Miss Jillgall.'

I burst out with such a loud 'OH!' that he laughed.

I caught the infection, and laughed louder still. Bless Miss Jillgall! The interview promised to become an easy one for both of us, thanks to her name. I was in good spirits, and I made no attempt to restrain them. 'The next time Miss Jillgall honours you with a visit,' I said, 'you must give me an opportunity of being presented to her.'

He made a strange reply: 'You may find your opportunity, Helena, sooner than you anticipate.'

Did this mean that she was going to call again in a day or two? I am afraid I spoke flippantly. I said: 'Oh, father, another lady fascinated by the popular preacher?'

The garden chairs were near us. He signed to me gravely to be seated by his side, and said to himself: 'This is my fault.'

'What is your fault?' I asked.

'I have left you in ignorance, my dear, of my cousin's sad story. It is soon told; and, if it checks your merriment, it will make amends by deserving your sympathy. I was indebted to her father, when I was a boy, for acts of kindness which I can never forget. He was twice married. The death of his first wife left him with one child – once my playfellow; now the lady whose visit has excited your curiosity. His second wife was a Belgian. She persuaded him to sell his busines in London, and to invest the money in a partnership with a brother of hers, established as a sugar-refiner at Antwerp. The little daughter accompanied her father to Belgium. Are you attending to me, Helena?'

I was waiting for the interesting part of the story, and was wondering when he would get to it.

'As time went on,' he resumed, 'the new partner found that the value of the business at Antwerp had been greatly overrated. After a long struggle with adverse circumstances, he decided on withdrawing from the partnership before the whole of his capital was lost in a failing commercial speculation. The end of it was that he retired, with his daughter, to a small town in East Flanders the wreck of his property having left him an income of no more than two hundred pounds a year.'

I showed my father that I was attending to him now, by inquiring what had become of the Belgian wife. Those nervous quiverings, which Eunice has mentioned in her diary, began to appear in his face.

'It is too shameful a story,' he said, 'to be told to a young girl. The marriage was dissolved by law; and the wife was the person to blame. I am sure, Helena, you don't wish to hear any more of *this* part of the story.'

I did wish. But I saw that he expected me to say No – so I said it.

'The father and daughter,' he went on, 'never so much as thought of returning to their own country. They were too poor to live comfortably in England. In Belgium their income was sufficient for their wants. On the father's death, the daughter remained in the town. She had friends there, and friends nowhere else; and she might have lived abroad to the end of her days, but for a calamity to which we are all liable. A long and serious illness completely prostrated her. Skilled medical attendance, costing large sums of money for the doctors' travelling expenses, was imperatively required. Experienced nurses, summoned from a distant hospital, were in attendance night and day. Luxuries, far beyond the reach of her little income, were absolutely required to support her wasted strength at the time of her tedious recovery. In one word, her resources were sadly diminished, when the poor creature had paid her debts, and had regained her hold on life. At that time, she unhappily met with the man who has ruined her.'

It was getting interesting at last. 'Ruined her?' I repeated. 'Do you mean that he robbed her?'

'That, Helena, is exactly what I mean – and many a helpless woman has been robbed in the same way. The man of whom I am now speaking was a lawyer in a large practice. He bore an excellent character, and was highly respected for his exemplary life. My cousin (not at all a discreet person, I am bound to admit) was induced to consult him on her pecuniary affairs. He expressed the most generous sympathy – offered to employ her little capital in his business – and pledged himself to pay her double the interest for her money, which she had been in the habit of receiving from the sound investment chosen by her father.'

'And of course he got the money, and never paid the interest?' Eager to hear the end, I interrupted the story in those inconsiderate words. My father's answer quietly reproved me.

'He paid the interest regularly as long as he lived.'

'And what happened, when he died?'

'He died a bankrupt; the secret profligacy of his life was at last exposed. Nothing, actually nothing, was left for his creditors. The unfortunate creature, whose ugly name has amused you, must get help somewhere, or must go to the workhouse.'

If I had been in a state of mind to attend to trifles, this would have explained the reason why the cook had heard Miss Jillgall crying. But the prospect before me – the unendurable prospect of having a strange woman in the house – had showed itself too plainly to be mistaken. I could think of nothing else. With infinite difficulty I assumed a momentary appearance of composure, and suggested that Miss Jillgall's foreign friends might have done something to help her.

My father defended her foreign friends. 'My dear, they were poor people, and did all they could afford to do. But for their kindness, my cousin might not have been able to return to England.'

'And to cast herself on your mercy,' I added, 'in the character of a helpless woman.'

'No, Helena! Not to cast herself on my mercy – but to find my house open to her, as her father's house was open to me in the bygone times. I am her only surviving relative; and, while I live, she shall not be a helpless woman.'

I began to wish that I had not spoken out so plainly. My father's sweet temper – I do so sincerely wish I had inherited it! – made the kindest allowances for me.

'I understand the momentary bitterness of feeling that has escaped you,' he said; 'I may almost say that I expected it. My only hesitation in this matter has been caused by my sense of what I owe to my children. It was putting your endurance, and your sister's endurance, to a trial to expect you to receive a stranger (and that stranger not a young girl like yourselves) as one of the household living with you in the closest intimacy of family life. The consideration which has decided me does justice, I hope, to you and Eunice, as well as to myself. I think that some allowance is due from my daughters to the father who has always made loving allowance for *them*. Am I wrong in believing that my good children have not forgotten this, and have only waited for the occasion to feel the pleasure of rewarding me?'

It was beautifully put. There was but one thing to be done – I kissed him. And there was but one thing to be said. I asked at what time we might expect to receive Miss Jillgall.

'She is staying, Helena, at a small hotel in the town. I have already sent to say that we are waiting to see her. Perhaps you will look at the spare bedroom?'

'It shall be got ready, father, directly.'

I ran into the house; I rushed upstairs into the room that is Eunice's and mine; I locked the door, and then I gave way to my rage, before it stifled me. I stamped on the floor, I clenched my fists, I cast myself on the bed, I reviled that hateful woman by every hard word that I could throw at her. Oh, the luxury of it! the luxury of it!

Cold water and my hairbrush soon made me fit to be seen again.

As for the spare room, it looked a great deal too comfortable for an incubus from foreign parts. The one improvement that I could have made, if a friend of mine had been expected, was suggested by the window-curtains. I was looking at a torn place in one of them, and determined to leave it unrepaired, when I felt an arm slipped round my waist from behind. A voice, so close that it tickled my neck, said: 'Dear girl, what friends we shall be!' I turned round, and confronted Miss Jillgall.

## CHAPTER XV

### HELENA'S DIARY

If I am not a good girl, where is a good girl to be found? This is in Eunice's style. It sometimes amuses me to mimic my simple sister.

I have just torn three pages out of my diary, in deference to the expression of my father's wishes. He took the first opportunity which his cousin permitted him to enjoy of speaking to me privately; and his object was to caution me against hastily relying on first impressions of anybody – especially of Miss Jillgall. 'Wait for a day or two,' he said; 'and then form your estimate of the new member of our household.'

The stormy state of my temper had passed away, and had left my atmosphere calm again. I could feel that I had received good advice; but unluckily it reached me too late.

I had formed my estimate of Miss Jillgall, and had put it in writing for my own satisfaction, at least an hour before my father found himself at liberty to speak to me. I don't agree with him in distrusting first impressions; and I had proposed to put my opinion to the test, by referring to what I had written about his cousin at a later time. However, after what he had said to me, I felt bound in filial duty to take the pages out of my book, and to let two days pass before I presumed to enjoy the luxury of hating Miss Jillgall.

On one thing I am determined: Eunice shall not form a hasty opinion, either. She shall undergo the same severe discipline of self-restraint to which her sister is obliged to submit. Let us be just, as somebody says, before we are generous. No more for to-day.

$$\star \quad \star \quad \star \quad \star \quad \star$$

I open my diary again – after the prescribed interval has elapsed. The first impression produced on me by the new member of our household remains entirely unchanged.

Have I already made the remark that, when one removes a page from a book, it does not necessarily follow that one destroys the page afterwards? or did I leave this to be inferred? In either case, my course of proceeding was the same. I ordered some paste to be made. Then I unlocked a drawer, and found my poor ill-used leaves, and put them back in my Journal. An act of justice done to one's self.

My father has often told me that he revises his writings on religious subjects. I may harmlessly imitate that good example, by revising my restored entry. It is now a sufficiently remarkable performance to be distinguished by a title. Let me call it:

*Impressions of Miss Jillgall*

My first impression was a strong one – it was produced by the state of this lady's breath. In other words, I was obliged to let her kiss me. It is a duty to be considerate towards human infirmity. I will only say that I thought I should have fainted.

My second impression draws a portrait, and produces a stiking likeness.

Figure, little and lean – hair of a dirty drab colour which we see in string – small light grey eyes, sly and restless, and deeply sunk in the head – prominent cheek-bones, and a florid complexion – an inquisitive nose, turning up at the end – a large mouth and a servile smile – raw-looking hands, decorated with black mittens – a misfitting white jacket and a limp skirt – manners familiar – temper clevery hidden – voice too irritating to be mentioned. Whose portrait is this? It is the portrait of Miss Jillgall, taken in words.

Her true character is not easy to discover; I suspect that it will only show itself little by little. That she is a born meddler in other people's affairs, I think I can see already. I also found out that she trusted to flattery as her first experiment on myself.

'You charming girl,' she began, 'your bright face encourages me to ask a favour. Pray make me useful! The one aspiration of my life is to be useful. Unless you employ me in that way, I have no right to intrude myself into your family circle. Yes, yes, I know that your father has opened his house and his heart to me. But I dare not found any claim – your name is Helena, isn't it? Dear Helena, I dare not found any claim on what I owe to your father's kindness.'

'Why not?' I inquired.

'Because your father is not a man——'

I was rude enough to interrupt her: 'What is he, then?'

'An angel,' Miss Jillgall answered solemnly. 'A destitute earthly creature like me must not look up as high as your father. I might be dazzled.'

This was rather more than I could endure patiently. 'Let us try,' I suggested, 'if we can't understand each other, at starting.'

Miss Jillgall's little eyes twinkled in their bony caverns. 'The very thing I was going to propose!' she burst out.

'Very well,' I went on; 'then, let me tell you plainly that flattery is not relished in this house.'

'Flattery?' She put her hand to her head as she repeated the word, and looked quite bewildered. 'Dear Helena, I have lived all my life in East Flanders, and my own language is occasionally strange to me. Can you tell me what flattery is in Flemish?'

'I don't understand Flemish.'

'How very provoking! You don't understand Flemish, and I don't understand Flattery. I should so like to know what it means. Ah, I see books in this lovely room. Is there a dictionary among them?' She darted to the bookcase, and discovered a dictionary. 'Now I shall understand Flattery,' she remarked – 'and then we shall understand each other. Oh, let me find it for myself!' She ran her raw red finger along the alphabetical headings at the top of each page. '"FAD." That won't do. "FIE." Farther on still. "FLE." Too far the other way. "FLA." Here we are! "Flattery: False praise. Commendations bestowed for the purpose of gaining favour and influence." Oh, Helena, how cruel of you!' She dropped the book, and sank into a chair – the picture, if such a thing can be, of a broken-hearted old maid.

I should most assuredly have taken the opportunity of leaving her to her own devices, if I had been free to act as I pleased. But my interests as a daughter forbade me to make an enemy of my father's cousin, on the first day when she had entered the house. I made an apology, very neatly expressed.

She jumped up – let me do her justice; Miss Jillgall is as nimble as a monkey – and (Faugh!) she kissed me for the second time. If I had been a man, I am afraid I should have called for that deadly poison (we are all temperance people in this house) known by the name of Brandy.

'If you will make me love you,' Miss Jillgall explained, 'you must expect to be kissed. Dear girl, let us go back to my poor little petition. Oh, do make me useful! There are so many things I can do: you will find me a treasure in the house. I write a good hand; I understand polishing furniture; I can dress hair (look at my own hair); I play and sing a little when people want to be amused; I can mix a salad and knit stockings – who is this?' The cook came in, at the moment, to consult me; I introduced her. 'And oh,' cried Miss Jillgall in ecstasy, 'I can cook! Do, please, let me see the kitchen.'

The cook's face turned red. She had come to me to make a confession; and she had not (as she afterwards said) bargained for the presence of a stranger. For the first time in her life she took the liberty of whispering to me: 'I must ask you, Miss, to let me send up the cauliflower plain boiled; I don't understand the directions in the book for doing it in the foreign way.'

Miss Jillgall's ears – perhaps because they are so large – possess a quickness of hearing, quite unparalleled in my experience. Not one word of the cook's whispered confession had escaped her.

'Here,' she declared, 'is an opportunity of making myself useful! What is the cook's name? Hannah? Take me downstairs, Hannah, and I'll show you how to do the cauliflower in the foreign way. She seems to hesitate. Is it possible that she doesn't believe me? Listen, Hannah, and judge for yourself if I am deceiving you. Have you boiled the cauliflower? Very well; this is what you must do next. Take four ounces of grated cheese, two ounces of best butter, the yolks of four eggs, a little bit of glaze, lemon-juice, nutmeg – dear, dear, how black she looks! What have I said to offend her?'

The cook passed over the lady who had presumed to instruct her, as if no such person had been present, and addressed herself to me; 'If I am to be interfered with in my own kitchen, Miss, I will ask you to suit yourself at a month's notice.'

Miss Jillgall wrung her hands in despair.

'I meant so kindly,' she said; 'and I seem to have made mischief. With the best intentions, Helena, I have set you and your servant at variance. I really didn't know you had such a temper. Hannah,' she declared, following the cook to the door. 'I'm sure there's nothing I am not ready to do to make it up with you. Perhaps you have not got the cheese downstairs? I'm ready to go out and buy it for you. I could show you how to keep eggs sweet and fresh for weeks together. Your gown doesn't fit very well; I shall be glad to improve it, if you will leave it out for me after you have gone to bed. There!' cried Miss Jillgall, as the cook majestically left the room, without even looking at her, 'I have done my best to make it up, and you see how my advances are received. What more could I have done? I really ask you, dear, as a friend, what more *could* I have done?'

I had it on the tip of my tongue to say; 'The cook doesn't ask you to buy cheese for her, or to teach her how to keep eggs, or to improve the fit of her gown; all she wants is to have her kitchen to herself.' But here again it was necessary to remember that this odious person was my father's guest.

'Pray don't distress yourself,' I began; 'I am sure you are not to blame, Miss Jillgall——'

'Oh, don't!'

'Don't – what?'

'Don't call me Miss Jillgall. I call you Helena. Call me Selina.'

I had really not supposed it possible that she could be more unendurable than ever. When she mentioned her Christian name, she succeeded nevertheless in producing that result. In the whole list of women's names, is there anyone to be found so absolutely sickening as 'Selina'? I forced myself to pronounce it; I made another neatly-expressed apology; I said English servants were so very peculiar. Selina was more than satisfied; she was quite delighted.

'Is that it, indeed? An explanation was all I wanted. How good of you! And now tell me – is there no chance, in the house or out of the house, of my making myself useful? Oh, what's that? Do I see a chance? I do! I do!'

Miss Jillgall's eyes are more than mortal. At one time, they are microscopes. At another time, they are telescopes. She discovered (right across the room) the torn place in the window-curtain. In an instant, she snatched a dirty little leather case out of her pocket, threaded her needle, and began darning the curtain. She sang over her work. 'My heart is light, my will is free——' I can repeat no more of it. When I heard her singing voice, I became reckless of consequences and ran out of the room with my hands over my ears.

## CHAPTER XVI

### HELENA'S DIARY

When I reached the foot of the stairs, my father called me into his study.

I found him at his writing-table, with such a heap of torn-up paper in his waste-basket that it overflowed on to the floor. He explained to me that he had been destroying a large accumulation of old letters, and had ended (when his employment began to grow wearisome) in examining his correspondence rather carelessly. The result was that he had torn up a letter, and a copy of the reply, which ought to have been set aside as worthy of preservation. After collecting the fragments, he had heaped them on the table. If I could contrive to put them together again on fair sheets of paper, and fasten them in their right places with gum, I should be doing him a service, at a time when he was too busy to set his mistake right for himself.

Here was the best excuse that I could desire for keeping out of Miss Jillgall's way. I cheerfully set to work on the restoration of the letters, while my father went on with his writing.

Having put the fragments together – excepting a few gaps caused by morsels that had been lost – I was unwilling to fasten them down with gum, until I could feel sure of not having made any mistakes; especially in regard to some of the lost words which I had been obliged to restore by guess-work. So I copied the letters, and submitted them, in the first place, to my father's approval.

He praised me in the prettiest manner for the care that I had taken. But, when he began, after some hesitation to read my copy, I noticed a change. The smile left his face, and the nervous quiverings showed themselves again.

'Quite right, my child,' he said, in low sad tones.

On returning to my side of the table, I expected to see him resume his writing. He crossed the room to the window, and stood (with his back to me) looking out.

When I had first discovered the sense of the letters, they failed to interest me. A tiresome woman, presuming on the kindness of a good-natured man to beg a favour which she had no right to ask, and receiving a refusal which she had richly deserved, was no remarkable event in my experience as my father's secretary and copyist. But the change in his face, while he read the correspondence, altered my opinion of the letters. There was more in them evidently than I had discovered. I kept my manuscript copy – here it is:

'*From Miss Elizabeth Chance to the Revd Abel Gracedieu*

(Date of year, 1859. Date of month, missing.)

'DEAR SIR,
'You have, I hope, not quite forgotten the interesting conversation that we had last year in the Governor's rooms. I am afraid I spoke a little flippantly at the time; but I am sure you will believe me when I say that this was out of no want of respect to yourself. My pecuniary position being far from prosperous, I am endeavouring to obtain the vacant situation of housekeeper in a public institution, the prospectus of which I enclose. You will see it is a rule of the place that a candidate must be a single woman (which I am), and must be recommended by a clergyman. You are the only reverend gentleman whom it is my good fortune to know, and the thing is of course a mere formality. Pray excuse this application, and oblige me by acting as my reference.
'Sincerely yours,
'ELIZABETH CHANCE

'P.S. – Please address: Miss E. Chance, Poste Restante, St Martin's-le-Grand, London.'

'*From the Revd Abel Gracedieu to Miss Chance*

(Copy)
'MADAM,
'The brief conversation to which your letter alludes, took place at an accidental meeting between us. I then saw you for the first time, and I have not seen you since. It is impossible for me to assert the claim of a perfect stranger, like yourself, to fill a situation of trust. I must beg to decline acting as your reference.
'Your obedient servant,
'ABEL GRACEDIEU.'

\*      \*      \*      \*      \*

My father was still at the window.

In that idle position he could hardly complain of me for interrupting him, if I ventured to talk about the letters which I had put together. If my curiosity displeased him, he had only to say so, and there would be an end to any allusions of mine to the subject. My first idea was to join him at the window. On reflection, and still perceiving that he kept his back turned on me, I thought it might be more prudent to remain at the table.

'This Miss Chance seems to be an impudent person?' I said.

'Yes.'

'Was she a young woman, when you met with her?'

'Yes.'

'What sort of a woman to look at? Ugly?'

'No.'

Here were three answers which Eunice herself would have been quick enough to interpret as three warnings to say no more. I felt a little hurt by his keeping his back turned on me. At the same time, and naturally, I think, I found my interest in Miss Chance (I don't say my friendly interest) considerably increased by my father's unusually rude behaviour. I was also animated by an irresistible desire to make him turn round and look at me.

'Miss Chance's letter was written many years ago,' I resumed. 'I wonder what has become of her since she wrote to you.'

'I know nothing about her.'

'Not even whether she is alive or dead?'

'Not even that. What do these questions mean, Helena?'

'Nothing, father.'

I declare he looked as if he suspected me!

'Why don't you speak out?' he said. 'Have I ever taught you to conceal your thoughts? Have I ever been a hard father, who discouraged you when you wished to confide in him? What are you thinking about? Do *you* know anything of this woman?'

'Oh, father, what a question! I never even heard of her till I put the torn letters together. I begin to wish you had not asked me to do it.'

'So do I. It never struck me that you would feel such

extraordinary – I had almost said, such vulgar – curiosity about a worthless letter.'

This roused my temper. When a young lady is told that she is vulgar, if she has any self-conceit – I mean self-respect – she feels insulted. I said something sharp in my turn. It was in the way of argument. I do not know how it may be with other young persons, I never reason so well myself as when I am angry.

'You call it a worthless letter,' I said, 'and yet you think it worth preserving.'

'Have you nothing more to say to me than that?' he asked.

'Nothing more,' I answered.

He changed again. After having looked unaccountably angry, he now looked unaccountably relieved.

'I will soon satisfy you,' he said, 'that I have a good reason for preserving a worthless letter. Miss Chance, my dear, is not a woman to be trusted. If she saw her advantage in making a bad use of my reply, I am afraid she would not hesitate to do it. Even if she is no longer living, I don't know into what vile hands my letter may not have fallen, or how it might be falsified for some wicked purpose. Do you see now how a correspondence may become accidentally important, though it is of no value in itself?'

I could say 'Yes' to this with a safe conscience.

But there were some perplexities still left in my mind.

It seemed strange that Miss Chance should (apparently) have submitted to the severity of my father's reply. 'I should have thought,' I said to him, 'that she would have sent you another impudent letter – or perhaps have insisted on seeing you, and using her tongue instead of her pen.'

'She could do neither the one nor the other, Helena. Miss Chance will never find out my address again; I have taken good care of that.'

He spoke in a loud voice, with a flushed face – as if it was quite a triumph to have prevented this woman from discovering his address. What reason could he have for being so anxious to keep her away from him? Could I venture to conclude that there was a mystery in the life of a man so blameless, so truly pious? It shocked one even to think it.

There was a silence between us, to which the housemaid offered a welcome interruption. Dinner was ready.

He kissed me before we left the room. 'One word more, Helena,' he said, 'and I have done. Let there be no more talk between us about Elizabeth Chance.'

## CHAPTER XVII

### HELENA'S DIARY

Miss Jillgall joined us at the dinner-table, in a state of excitement, carrying a book in her hand.

I am inclined, on reflection, to suspect that she is quite clever enough to have discovered that I hate her – and that many of the aggravating things she says and does are assumed, out of retaliation, for the purpose of making me angry. That ugly face is a double face, or I am much mistaken.

To return to the dinner-table, Miss Jillgall addressed herself, with an air of playful penitence, to my father.

'Dear cousin, I hope I have not done wrong. Helena left me all by myself. When I had finished darning the curtain, I really didn't know what to do. So I opened all the bedroom doors upstairs and looked into the rooms. In the big room with two beds – oh, I am so ashamed – I found this book. Please look at the first page.'

My father looked at the title-page: – 'Doctor Watts's Hymns. Well, Selina, what is there to be ashamed of in this?'

'Oh, no! no! It's the wrong page. Do look at the other page – the one that comes first before that one.'

My patient father turned to the blank page.

'Ah,' he said quietly, 'my other daughter's name is written in it – the daughter whom you have not seen. Well?'

Miss Jillgall clasped her hands distractedly. 'It's my ignorance I'm so ashamed of. Dear cousin, forgive me, enlighten me. I don't know how to pronounce your other daughter's name. Do you call her Euneece?'

The dinner was getting cold. I was provoked into saying: 'No, we don't.'

She had evidently not forgiven me for leaving her by herself. 'Pardon me, Helena, when I want information I don't apply to you; I sit, as it were, at the feet of your learned father. Dear cousin, is it——'

Even my father declined to wait for his dinner any longer. 'Pronounce it as you like, Selina. Here we say Eunice – with the accent on the "i" and with the final "e" sounded: Eu-ni-see. Let me give you some soup.'

Miss Jillgall groaned. 'Oh, how difficult it seems to be! Quite beyond my poor brains! I shall ask the dear girl's leave to call her Euneece. What very strong soup! Isn't it rather a waste of meat? Give me a little more, please.'

I discovered another of Miss Jillgall's peculiarities. Her appetite was enormous, and her ways were greedy. You heard her eat her soup. She devoured the food on her plate with her eyes before she put it into her mouth; and she criticized our English cookery in the most impudent manner, under pretence of asking humbly how it was done. There was, however, some temporary compensation for this. We had less of her talk while she was eating her dinner.

With the removal of the cloth, she recovered the use of her tongue; and she hit on the one subject of all others which proves to be the sorest trial to my father's patience.

'And now, dear cousin, let us talk of your other daughter, our absent Euneece. I do so long to see her. When is she coming back?'

'In a few days more.'

'How glad I am! And, do tell me – which is she? Your oldest girl or your youngest?'

'Neither the one nor the other, Selina.'

'Oh, my head! my head! This is even worse than the accent on the "i" and the final "e". Stop! I am cleverer than I thought I was. You mean that the girls are twins. Are they both so exactly like each other that I shan't know which is which? What fun!'

When the subject of our ages was unluckily started at Mrs

Staveley's, I had slipped out of the difficulty easily by assuming the character of the eldest sister – an example of ready tact which my dear stupid Eunice doesn't understand. In my father's presence, it is needless to say that I kept silence, and left it to him. I was sorry to be obliged to do this. Owing to his sad state of health, he is easily irritated – especially by inquisitive strangers.

'I must leave you,' he answered, without taking the slightest notice of what Miss Jillgall had said to him. 'My work is waiting for me.'

She stopped him on his way to the door. 'Oh, tell me – can't I help you?'

'Thank you; no.'

'Well – but tell me one thing. Am I right about the twins?'

'You are wrong.'

Miss Jillgall's demonstrative hands flew up into the air again, and expressed the climax of astonishment by quivering over her head. 'This is positively maddening,' she declared. 'What does it mean?'

'Take my advice, cousin. Don't attempt to find out what it means.'

He left the room. Miss Jillgall appealed to me. I imitated my father's wise brevity of expression: 'Sorry to disappoint you, Selina; I know no more about it than you do. Come upstairs.'

Every step of the way up to the drawing-room was marked by a protest or an inquiry. Did I expect her to believe that I couldn't say which of us was the elder of the two? that I didn't really know what my father's motive was for this extraordinary mystification? that my sister and I had submitted to be robbed, as it were, of our own ages, and had not insisted on discovering which of us had come into the world first? that our friends had not put an end to this sort of thing by comparing us personally, and discovering which was the elder sister by investigation of our faces? To all this I replied: First, that I did certainly expect her to believe whatever I might say. Secondly, that what she was pleased to call the 'mystification' had begun when we were both children; that habit had made it familiar to us in the course of years; and, above all, that we were too fond of our good father to ask for explanations which we knew by experience would distress him. Thirdly, that friends did try to discover, by personal examination, which was the elder sister, and differed perpetually in their conclusions; also that we had amused ourselves by trying the same experiment before our looking-glasses, and that Eunice thought Helena was the oldest, and Helena thought Eunice was the oldest. Fourthly (and finally), that the Reverend Mr Gracedieu's cousin had better drop the subject, unless she was bent on making her presence in the house unendurable to the Reverend Mr Gracedieu himself.

I write it with a sense of humiliation; Miss Jillgall listened attentively to all I had to say – and then took me completely by surprise. The inquisitive, meddlesome, restless, impudent woman suddenly transformed herself into a perfect model of amiability and decorum. She actually said she agreed with me, and was much obliged for my good advice.

A stupid young woman, in my place, would have discovered that this was not natural, and that Miss Jillgall was presenting herself to me in disguise, to reach some secret end of her own. I am not a stupid young woman; I ought to have had at my service penetration enough to see through and through cousin Selina. Well! cousin Selina was an impenetrable mystery to me.

The one thing to be done was to watch her. I was at least sly enough to take up a book, and pretend to be reading it. How contemptible!

She looked round the room, and discovered our pretty writing-table; a present to my father from his congregation. After a little consideration, she sat down to write a letter.

'When does the post go out?' she asked.

I mentioned the hour; and she began her letter. Before she could have written more than the first two or three lines, she turned round on her seat, and began talking to me.

'Do you like writing letters, my dear?'

'Yes – but then I have not many letters to write.'

'Only a few friends, Helena, but those few worthy to be loved? My own case exactly. Has your father told you of my troubles? Ah, I am glad of that. It spares me the sad necessity of confessing what I have suffered. Oh, how good my friends, my new friends, were to me in that dull little Belgian town! One of them was generosity personified – ah, she had suffered, too! A vile husband who had deceived and deserted her. Oh, the men! When she heard of the loss of my little fortune, that noble creature got up a subscription for me, and went round herself to collect. Think of what I owe to her! Ought I to let another day pass without writing to my benefactress? Am I not bound in gratitude to make her happy in the knowledge of *my* happiness – I mean the refuge opened to me in this hospitable house?'

She twisted herself back again to the writing-table, and went on with her letter.

I have not attempted to conceal my stupidity. Let me now record a partial recovery of my intelligence.

It was not to be denied that Miss Jillgall had discovered a good reason for writing to her friend; but I was at a loss to understand why she should have been so anxious to mention the reason. Was it possible – after the talk which had passed between us – that she had something mischievous to say in the letter, relating to my father or to me? Was she afraid I might suspect this? And had she been so communicative for the purpose of leading my suspicions astray? These were vague guesses; but, try as I might, I could arrive at no clearer view of what was passing in Miss Jillgall's mind. What would I not have given to be able to look over her shoulder, without discovery!

She finished her letter, and put the address, and closed the envelope. Then she turned round towards me again.

'Have you got a foreign postage-stamp, dear?'

If I could look at nothing else, I was resolved to look at her envelope. It was only necessary to go to the study, and to apply to my father. I returned with the foreign stamp, and I stuck it on the envelope with my own hand.

There was nothing to interest *me* in the addresss, as I ought to have foreseen, if I had not been too much excited for the exercise of a little common sense. Miss Jillgall's wonderful friend was only remarkable by her ugly foreign name – MRS TENBRUGGEN.

# CHAPTER XVIII

### EUNICE'S DIARY

Here I am, writing my history of myself, once more, by my own bedside. Some unexpected events have happened while I have been away. One of them is the absence of my sister.

Helena has left home on a visit to a northern town by the seaside. She is staying in the house of a minister (one of Papa's friends), and is occupying a position of dignity in which I should certainly lose my head. The minister and his wife and daughters propose to set up a Girls' Scripture Class, on the plan devised by Papa; and they are at a loss, poor helpless people, to know how to begin. Helena has volunteered to set the thing going. And there she is now, advising everybody, governing everybody, encouraging everybody – issuing directions, finding fault, rewarding merit – oh, dear, let me put it all in one word, and say: thoroughly enjoying herself.

Another event has happened, relating to Papa. It so distressed me that I even forgot to think of Philip – for a little while.

Travelling by railway (I suppose because I am not used to it) gives me the headache. When I got to our station here, I thought it would do me more good to walk home than to ride in the noisy omnibus. Half-way between the railway and the town, I met one of the doctors. He is a member of our congregation; and he it was who recommended Papa, some time since, to give up his work as a minister and take a long holiday in foreign parts.

'I am glad to have met with you,' the doctor said. 'Your sister, I find, is away on a visit; and I want to speak to one of you about your father.'

It seemed that he had been observing Papa, in chapel, from what he called his own medical point of view. He did not conceal from me that he had drawn conclusions which made him feel uneasy. 'It may be anxiety,' he said, 'or it may be overwork. In either case, your father is in a state of nervous derangement, which is likely to lead to serious results – unless he takes the advice that I gave him when he last consulted me.

There must be no more hesitation about it. Be careful not to irritate him – but remember that he *must* rest. You and your sister have some influence over him; he won't listen to me.'

Poor dear Papa! I did see a change in him for the worse – though I had only been away for so short a time.

When I put my arms round his neck, and kissed him, he turned pale, and then flushed up suddenly; the tears came into his eyes. Oh, it was hard to follow the doctor's advice, and not to cry too; but I succeeded in controlling myself. I sat on his knee, and made him tell me all that I have written here about Helena. This led to our talking next of the new lady, who is to live with us as a member of the family. I began to feel less uneasy at the prospect of being introduced to this stranger, when I heard that she was Papa's cousin. And when he mentioned her name, and saw how it amused me, his poor worn face brightened into a smile. 'Go and find her,' he said, 'and introduce yourself. I want to hear, Eunice, if you and my cousin are likely to get on well together.'

The servants told me that Miss Jillgall was in the garden.

I searched here, there, and everywhere, and failed to find her. The place was so quiet, it looked so deliciously pure and bright, after smoky dreary London, that I sat down at the further end of the garden, and let my mind take me back to Philip. What was he doing at that moment, while I was thinking of him? Perhaps he was in the company of other young ladies, who drew all his thoughts away to themselves? Or perhaps he was writing to his father in Ireland, and saying something kindly and prettily about me? Or perhaps he was looking forward, as anxiously as I do, to our meeting next week.

I have had my plans, and I have changed my plans.

On the railway journey, I thought I would tell Papa at once of the new happiness which seems to have put a new life into me. It would have been delightful to make my confession to that first and best and dearest of friends; but my meeting with the doctor spoilt it all. After what he had said to me, I discovered a risk. If I ventured to tell Papa that my heart was set on a young gentleman who was a stranger to him, could I be sure that he would receive my confession favourably? There was a chance that it might irritate him – and the fault would then be mine of doing what I had been warned to avoid. It might be safer in every way to wait until Philip paid his visit, and he and Papa had been introduced to each other. Could Helena herself have arrived at a wiser conclusion? I declare I felt proud of my own discretion.

In this enjoyable frame of mind, I was disturbed by a woman's voice. The tone was a tone of distress, and the words reached my ears from the end of the garden: 'Please, Miss, let me in.'

A shrubbery marks the limit of our little bit of pleasure-ground. On the other side of it, there is a cottage standing on the edge of the common. The most good-natured woman in the world lives here. She is our laundress – married to a stupid young fellow named Molly, and blest with a plump baby as sweet-tempered as herself. Thinking it likely that the piteous voice which had disturbed me might be the voice of Mrs Molly, I was astonished to hear her appealing to anybody (perhaps to me?) to 'let her in'. So I passed through the shrubbery, wondering whether the gate had been locked during my absence in London. No; it was as easy to open as ever.

The cottage door was not closed.

I saw our amiable laundress in the passage, on her knees, trying to open an inner door which seemed to be locked. She had her eye at the keyhole; and, once again, she called out: 'Please, Miss, let me in.' I waited to see if the door would be opened – nothing happened. I waited again, to hear if some person inside would answer – nobody spoke. But somebody, or something made a sound of splashing water on the other side of the door.

I showed myself, and asked what was the matter.

Mrs Molly looked at me helplessly. She said: 'Miss Eunice, it's the baby.'

'What has the baby done?' I inquired.

Mrs Molly got on her feet, and whispered in my ear: 'You know he's a fine child?'

'Yes.'

'Well, Miss, he's bewitched a lady.'

'What lady?'

'Miss Jillgall.'

The very person I had been trying to find! I asked where she was.

The laundress pointed dolefully to the locked door: 'In there.'

'And where is your baby?'

The poor woman still pointed to the door: 'I'm beginning to doubt, Miss, whether it *is* my baby.'

'Nonsense, Mrs Molly. If it isn't yours, whose baby can it be?'

'Miss Jillgall's.'

Her puzzled face made this singular reply more funny still. The splashing of water on the other side of the door began again. 'What is Miss Jillgall doing now?' I said.

'Washing the baby, Miss. A week ago, she came in here, one morning; very pleasant and kind, I must own. She found me putting on the baby's things. She says: "What a cherub!" which I took as a compliment. She says: "I shall call again to-morrow." She called again so early that she found the baby in his crib. "You be a good soul," she says, "and go about your work, and leave the child to me." I says: "Yes, Miss, but please to wait till I've made him fit to be seen." She says: "That's just what I mean to do myself." I stared; and I think any other person would have done the same in my place. "If there's one thing more than another I enjoy," she says, "it's making myself useful. Mrs Molly I've taken a fancy to your boy-baby," she says, "and I mean to make myself useful to *him*." If you will believe it, Miss Jillgall has only let me have one opportunity of putting my own child tidy. She was late this morning, and I got my chance, and had the boy on my lap, drying him – when in she burst like a blast of wind, and snatched the baby away from me. "This is your nasty temper," she says; "I declare I'm ashamed of you!" And there she is, with the door locked against me, washing the child all over again herself. Twice I've knocked, and asked her to let me in, and can't even get an answer. They do say there's luck in odd numbers; suppose I try again?' Mrs Molly knocked, and the proverb proved to be true; she got an answer from Miss Jillgall at last: 'If you don't be quiet and go away, you shan't have the baby back at all.' Who could help it? – I burst out laughing. Miss Jillgall (as I supposed from the tone of her voice) took severe notice of this act of impropriety. 'Who's that laughing?' she called out; 'give yourself a name.' I gave my name. The door was instantly thrown open with a bang. Papa's cousin appeared, in a dishevelled state, with splashes of soap and water all over her. She held the child in one arm, and she threw the other arm round my neck. 'Dearest Euneece, I have been longing to see you. How do you like Our baby?'

To the curious story of my introduction to Miss Jillgall, I ought perhaps to add that I have got to be friends with her already. I am the friend of anybody who amuses me. What will Helena say when she reads this?

# CHAPTER XIX

### EUNICE'S DIARY

When people are interested in some event that is coming, do they find the dull days, passed in waiting for it, days which they are not able to remember when they look back? This is my unfortunate case. Night after night, I have gone to bed without so much as opening my Journal. There was nothing worth writing about, nothing that I could recollect, until the postman came to-day. I ran downstairs, when I heard his ring at the bell, and stopped Maria on her way to the study. There, among Papa's usual handful of letters, was a letter for me.

'Dear Miss Eunice

        *      *      *      *      *

  'Yours ever truly.'

I quote the passages in Philip's letter which most deeply interested me – I am his dear Miss; and he is mine ever truly. The other part of the letter told me that he had been detained in London, and he lamented it. At the end was a delightful announcement that he was coming to me by the afternoon train. I ran upstairs to see how I looked in the glass.

My first feeling was regret. For the thousandth time, I was obliged to acknowledge that I was not as pretty as Helena. But this passed off. A cheering reflection occurred to me. Philip would not have found, in my sister's face, what seems to have interested him in my face. Besides, there is my figure.

The pity of it is that I am so ignorant about some things. If I had been allowed to read novels, I might (judging by what Papa said against them in one of his sermons) have felt sure of my own attractions; I might even have understood what Philip really thought of me. However, my mind was quite unexpectedly set at ease on the subject of my figure. The manner in which it happened was so amusing – at least, so amusing to me – that I cannot resist mentioning it.

My sister and I are forbidden to read newspapers, as well as novels. But the teachers at the Girls' Scripture Class are too old to be treated in this way. When the morning lessons were over, one of them was reading the newspaper to the other, in the empty schoolroom; I being in the passage outside, putting on my cloak.

It was a report of 'an application made to the magistrates by the lady of his worship the Mayor'. Hearing this, I stopped to listen. The lady of his worship (what a funny way of describing a man's wife!) is reported to be a little too fond of notoriety, and to like hearing the sound of her own voice on public occasions. But this is only my writing; I had better get back to the report. 'In her address to the magistrates, the Mayoress stated that she had seen a disgusting photograph in the shop window of a stationer, lately established in the town. She desired to bring this person within reach of the law, and to have all his copies of the shameless photograph destroyed. The usher of the court was thereupon sent to purchase the photograph.' – On second thoughts, I prefer going back to my own writing again; it is so uninteresting to copy other people's writing. Two of the magistrates were doing justice. They looked at the photograph – and what did it represent? The famous statue called the Venus de Medici! One of the magistrates took this discovery indignantly. He was shocked at the gross ignorance which could call the classic ideal of beauty and grace a disgusting work. The other one made polite allowances. He thought the lady was much to be pitied; she was evidently the innocent victim of a neglected education. Mrs Mayor left the court in a rage, telling the justices she knew where to get law. 'I shall expose Venus,' she said, 'to the Lord Chancellor.'

When the Scripture Class had broken up for the day, duty ought to have taken me home. Curiosity led me astray – I mean, led me to the stationer's window.

There I found our two teachers, absorbed in the photograph; having got to the shop first by a short cut. They seemed to think I had taken a liberty when I joined them. 'We are here,' they were careful to explain, 'to get a lesson in the ideal of beauty and grace.' There was quite a little crowd of townsfolk collected before the window. Some of them giggled; and some of them wondered whether it was taken from the life. For my own part, gratitude to Venus obliges me to own that she effected a great improvement in the state of my mind. She encouraged me. If that funny little creature – with no waist, and oh, such uncertain legs! – represented the ideal of beauty and grace, I had reason indeed to be satisfied with my own figure, and to think it quite possible that my sweetheart's favourable opinion of me was not ill-bestowed.

I was at the bedroom window when the time approached for Philip's arrival.

Quite at the far end of the road, I discovered him. He was on foot; he walked like a King. Not that I ever saw a King, but I have my ideal. Ah, what a smile he gave me, when I made him look up by waving my handkerchief out of the window! 'Ask for Papa,' I whispered as he ascended the house-steps.

The next thing to do was to wait, as patiently as I could, to be sent for downstairs. Maria came to me in a state of excitement. 'Oh, Miss, what a handsome young gentleman, and how beautifully dressed! Is he——?' Instead of finishing what she had to say, she looked at me with a sly smile. I looked at her with a sly smile. We were certainly a couple of fools. But, dear me, how happy sometimes a fool can be!

My enjoyment of that delightful time was checked when I went into the drawing-room.

I had expected to see Papa's face made beautiful by his winning smile. He was not only serious; he actually seemed to be ill at ease when he looked at me. At the same time, I saw nothing to make me conclude that Philip had produced an unfavourable impression. The truth is, we were all three on our best behaviour, and we showed it. Philip had brought with him a letter from Mrs Staveley, introducing him to Papa. We spoke of the Staveleys, of the weather, of the Cathedral – and then there seemed to be nothing more left to talk about.

In the silence that followed – what a dreadful thing silence is! – Papa was sent for to see somebody who had called on business. He made his excuses in his sweetest manner, but still seriously. When he and Philip had shaken hands, would he leave us together? No; he waited. Poor Philip had no choice but to take leave of me. Papa then went out by the door that led into his study, and I was left alone.

Can any words say how wretched I felt?

I had hoped so much from that first meeting – and where were my hopes now? A profane wish that I had never been born was finding its way into my mind, when the door of the room was opened softly, from the side of the passage. Maria, dear Maria, the best friend I have, peeped in. She whispered: 'Go into the garden, Miss, and you will find somebody there who is dying to see you. Mind you let him out by the shrubbery gate.' I squeezed her hand; I asked if she had tried the shrubbery gate with a sweetheart of her own. 'Hundreds of times, Miss.'

Was it wrong for me to go to Philip in the garden? Oh, there is no end to objections! Perhaps I did it *because* it was wrong. Perhaps I had been kept on my best behaviour too long for human endurance.

How sadly disappointed he looked! And how rashly he had placed himself just where he could be seen from the back windows! I took his arm and led him to the end of the garden.

There, we were out of the reach of inquisitive eyes; and there we sat down together, under the big mulberry tree.

'Oh, Eunice, your father doesn't like me!'

Those were his first words. In justice to Papa (and a little for my own sake too) I told him he was quite wrong. I said: 'Trust my father's goodness, trust his kindness, as I do.'

He made no reply. His silence was sufficiently expressive; he looked at me fondly.

I may be wrong, but fond looks surely require an acknowledgement of some kind? Is a young woman guilty of boldness who only follows her impulses? I slipped my hand into his hand. Philip seemed to like it. We returned to our conversation.

He began: 'Tell me, dear, is Mr Gracedieu always as serious as he is to-day?'

'Oh no!'

'When he takes exercise, does he ride? or does he walk?'

'Papa always walks.'

'By himself?'

'Sometimes by himself. Sometimes with me. Do you want to meet him when he goes out?'

'Yes.'

'When he is out with me?'

'No. When he is out by himself.'

Was it possible to tell me more plainly that I was not wanted? I did my best to express indignation by snatching my hand away from him. He was completely taken by surprise.

'Eunice! don't you understand me?'

I was as stupid and as disagreeable as I could possibly be: 'No; I don't!'

'Then let me help you,' he said, with a patience which I had not deserved.

Up to that moment I had been leaning against the back of a garden chair. Something else now got between me and my chair. It stole round my waist – it held me gently – it strengthened its hold – it improved my temper – it made me fit to understand him. All done by what? Only an arm!

Philip went on:

'I want to ask your father to do me the greatest of all favours
– and there is no time to lose. Every day, I expect to get a letter
which may recall me to Ireland.'

My heart sank at this horrid prospect; and in some mysterious
way my head must have felt it too. I mean that I found my head
resting on his shoulder. He went on:

'How am I to get my opportunity of speaking to Mr
Gracedieu? I mustn't call on him again as soon as to-morrow or
the next day. But I might meet him, out walking alone, if you
will tell me how to do it. A note to my hotel is all I want.
Don't tremble, my sweet. If you are not present at the time, do
you see any objection to my owning to your father that I love
you?'

I felt his delicate consideration for me – I did indeed feel it
gratefully. If he only spoke first, how well I should get on with
Papa afterwards! The prospect before me was exquisitely
encouraging. I agreed with Philip in everything; and I waited
(how eagerly was only known to myself) to hear what he would
say to me next. He prophesied next:

'When I have told your father that I love you, he will expect
me to tell him something else. Can you guess what it is?'

If I had not been confused, perhaps I might have found the
answer to this. As it was, I left him to reply to himself. He did
it, in words which I shall remember as long as I live.

'Dearest Eunice, when your father has heard my confession,
he will suspect that there is another confession to follow it – he
will want to know if you love me. My angel, will my hopes be
your hopes too, when I answer him?'

What there was in this to make my heart beat so violently
that I felt as if I was being stifled, is more than I can tell. He
leaned so close to me, so tenderly, so delightfully close, that our
faces nearly touched. He whispered: 'Say you love me, in a
kiss!'

His lips touched my lips, pressed them, dwelt on them – oh,
how can I tell of it! Some new enchantment of feeling ran
deliciously through and through me. I forgot my own self; I
only knew of one person in the world. He was master of my
lips; he was master of my heart. When he whispered, 'Kiss me,'

I kissed. What a moment it was! A faintness stole over me; I felt
as if I was going to die some exquisite death; I laid myself back
away from him – I was not able to speak. There was no need
for it; my thoughts and his thoughts were one – he knew that I
was quite overcome; he saw that he must leave me to recover
myself alone. I pointed to the shrubbery gate. We took one
long last look at each other for that day; the trees hid him; I was
left by myself.


# CHAPTER XX

### EUNICE'S DIARY

How long a time passed before my composure came back to
me, I cannot remember now. It seemed as if I was waiting
through some interval of my life that was a mystery to myself. I
was content to wait, and feel the light evening air in the garden
wafting happiness over me. And all this had come from a kiss! I
can call the time to mind when I used to wonder why people
made such a fuss about kissing.

I had been indebted to Maria for my first taste of Paradise. I
was recalled by Maria to the world that I had been accustomed
to live in; the world that was beginning to fade away in my
memory already. She had been sent to the garden in search of
me; and she had a word of advice to offer, after noticing my face
when I stepped out of the shadow of the tree: 'Try to look more
like yourself, Miss, before you let them see you at the tea-table.'

Papa and Miss Jillgall were sitting together talking, when I
opened the door. They left off when they saw me; and I
supposed, quite correctly as it turned out, that I had been one
of the subjects in their course of conversation. My poor father
seemed to be sadly anxious and out of sorts. Miss Jillgall, if I had
been in the humour to enjoy it, would have been more
amusing than ever. One of her funny little eyes persisted in
winking at me; and her heavy foot had something to say to my

foot, under the table, which meant a great deal perhaps, but which only succeeded in hurting me.

My father left us; and Miss Jillgall explained herself.

'I know, dearest Euneece, that we have only been acquainted for a day or two, and that I ought not perhaps to have expected you to confide in me so soon. Can I trust you not to betray me if I set an example of confidence? Ah, I see I can trust you! And, my dear, I do so enjoy telling secrets to a friend. Hush! Your father, your excellent father, has been talking to me about young Mr Dunboyne.'

She provokingly stopped there. I entreated her to go on. She invited me to sit on her knee. 'I want to whisper,' she said. It was too ridiculous – but I did it. Miss Jillgall's whisper told me serious news.

'The minister has some reason, Euneece, for disapproving of Mr Dunboyne; but, mind this, I don't think he has a bad opinion of the young man himself. He is going to return Mr Dunboyne's call. Oh, I do so hate formality; I really can't go on talking of Mr Dunboyne. Tell me his Christian name. Ah, what a noble name! How I long to be useful to him! To-morrow, my dear, after the one o'clock dinner, your Papa will call on Philip, at his hotel. I hope he won't be out, just at the wrong time.'

I resolved to prevent that unlucky accident by writing to Philip. If Miss Jillgall would have allowed it, I should have begun my letter at once. But she had more to say; and she was stronger than I was, and still kept me on her knee.

'It all looks bright enough so far, doesn't it, dear sister? Will you let me be your second sister? I do so love you, Euneece. Thank you! thank you! But the gloomy side of the picture is to come next. The minister – no! now I am your sister I must call him Papa; it makes me feel so young again! Well, then, Papa has asked me to be your companion whenever you go out. "Euneece is too young and too attractive to be walking about this great town (in Helena's absence) by herself." That was how he put it. Slyly enough, if one may say so of so good a man. And he used your sister (didn't he?) as a kind of excuse. I wish your sister was as nice as you are. However, the point is, why am I to be your companion? Because, dear child, you and your young gentleman are not to make appointments and to meet each other alone. Oh, yes – that's it! Your father is quite willing to return Philip's call; he proposes (as a matter of civility to Mrs Staveley) to ask Philip to dinner; but, mark my words, he doesn't mean to let Philip have you for his wife.'

I jumped off her lap; it was horrible to hear her. 'Oh,' I said, '*can* you be right about it?'

Miss Jillgall jumped up too. She has foreign ways of shrugging her shoulders and making signs with her hands. On this occasion she laid both hands on the upper part of her dress, just below her throat, and mysteriously shook her head.

'When my views are directed by my affections,' she assured me, 'I never see wrong. My bosom is my strong point.'

She has no bosom, poor soul – but I understood what she meant. It failed to have any soothing effect on my feelings. I felt aggrieved and angry and puzzled, all in one. Miss Jillgall stood looking at me, with her hands still on the place where her bosom was supposed to be. She made my temper hotter than ever.

'I mean to marry Philip,' I said.

'Certainly, my dear Euneece. But please don't be so fierce about it.'

'If my father does really object to my marriage,' I went on, 'it must be because he dislikes Philip. There can be no other reason.'

'Oh, yes, dear – there can.'

'What is the reason, then?'

'That, my sweet girl, is one of the things that we have got to find out.'

★   ★   ★   ★   ★

The post of this morning brought a letter from my sister. We were to expect her return by the next day's train. This was good news. Philip and I might stand in need of clever Helena's help, and we might be sure of getting it now.

In writing to Philip, I had asked him to let me hear how Papa and he had got on at the hotel.

I won't say how often I consulted my watch, or how often I looked out of the window for a man with a letter in his hand. It will be better to get on at once to the discouraging end of it, when the report of the interview reached me at last. Twice, Philip had attempted to ask for my hand in marriage – and twice my father had 'deliberately, obstinately' (Philip's own words) changed the subject. Even this was not all. As if he was determined to show that Miss Jillgall was perfectly right, and I perfectly wrong, Papa (civil to Philip as long as he did not talk of Me) had asked him to dine with us, and Philip had accepted the invitation!

What were we to think of it? What were we to do?

I wrote back to my dear love (so cruelly used) to tell him that Helena was expected to return on the next day, and that her opinion would be of the greatest value to both of us. In a postscript I mentioned the hour at which we were going to the station to meet my sister. When I say 'we', I mean Miss Jillgall as well as myself.

★    ★    ★    ★    ★

We found him waiting for us at the railway. I am afraid he resented Papa's incomprehensible resolution not to give him a hearing. He was silent and sullen. I could not conceal that to see this state of feeling distressed me. He showed how truly he deserved to be loved – he begged my pardon, and be became his own sweet self again directly. I am more determined to marry him than ever.

When the train entered the station, all the carriages were full. I went one way, thinking I had seen Helena. Miss Jillgall went the other way, under the same impression. Philip was a little way behind me

Not seeing my sister, I had just turned back, when a young man jumped out of a carriage, opposite Philip, and recognized and shook hands with him. I was just near enough to hear the stranger say, 'Look at the girl in our carriage.' Philip looked. 'What a charming creature!' he said, and then checked himself for fear the young lady should hear him. She had just handed her travelling bag and wraps to a porter, and was getting out. Philip politely offered his hand to help her. She looked my way. The charming creature of my sweetheart's admiration was, to my infinite amusement, Helena herself.

## CHAPTER XXI

### HELENA'S DIARY

The day of my return marks an occasion which I am not likely to forget. Hours have passed since I came home – and my agitation still forbids the thought of repose.

As I sit at my desk I see Eunice in bed, sleeping peacefully, except when she is murmuring enjoyment in some happy dream. To what end has my sister been advancing blindfold, and (who knows?) dragging me with her, since that disastrous visit to our friends in London? Strange that there should be a leaven of superstition in *my* nature! Strange that I should feel fear of something – I hardly know what!

I have met somewhere (perhaps in my historical reading) with the expression: 'A chain of events'. Was I at the beginning of that chain, when I entered the railway carriage on my journey home?

Among the other passengers there was a young gentleman, accompanied by a lady who proved to be his sister. They were both well-bred people. The brother evidently admired me, and did his best to make himself agreeable. Time passed quickly in pleasant talk, and my vanity was flattered – and that was all.

My fellow-travellers were going on to London. When the train reached our station the young lady sent her brother to buy some fruit, which she saw in the window of the refreshment-room. The first man whom he encountered on the platform was one of his friends, to whom he said something which I failed to hear. When I handed my travelling bag and my wraps to the porter, and showed myself at the carriage door, I heard the friend say: 'What a charming creature!' Having nothing to conceal in a journal which I protect by a lock, I may own that the stranger's personal appearance struck me, and that what I felt this time was not flattered vanity, but gratified pride. He was young, he was remarkably handsome, he was a distinguished looking man.

All this happened in one moment. In the moment that followed, I found myself in Eunice's arms. That odious person, Miss Jillgall, insisted on embracing me next. And then I was conscious of an indescribable feeling of surprise. Eunice presented the distinguished-looking gentleman to me as a friend of hers – Mr Philip Dunboyne.

'I had the honour of meeting your sister,' he said, 'in London, at Mr Staveley's house.' He went on to speak easily and gracefully of the journey I had taken, and of his friend who had been my fellow-traveller; and he attended us to the railway omnibus before he took his leave. I observed that Eunice had something to say to him confidentially, before they parted. This was another example of my sister's childish character; she is instantly familiar with new acquaintances, if she happens to like them. I anticipated some amusement from hearing how she had contrived to establish confidential relations with a highly-cultivated man like Mr Dunboyne. But, while Miss Jillgall was with us, it was just as well to keep within the limits of common-place conversation.

Before we got out of the omnibus I had, however, observed one undesirable result of my absence from home. Eunice and Miss Jillgall – the latter having, no doubt, finely flattered the former – appeared to have taken a strong liking to each other.

Two curious circumstances also caught my attention. I saw a change to, what I call self-assertion, in my sister's manner; something seemed to have raised her in her own estimation. Then, again, Miss Jillgall was not like her customary self. She had delightful moments of silence; and when Eunice asked how I liked Mr Dunboyne, she listened to my reply with an appearance of interest in her ugly face, which was quite a new revelation to my experience of my father's cousin.

These little discoveries (after what I had already observed at the railway-station) ought perhaps to have prepared me for what was to come, when my sister and I were alone in our room. But Eunice, whether she meant to do it or not, baffled my customary penetration. She looked as if she had plenty of news to tell me – with some obstacle in the way of doing it, which appeared to amuse instead of annoy her. If there is one thing more than another that I hate, it is being puzzled. I asked at once if anything remarkable had happened during Eunice's visit to London.

She smiled mischievously. 'I have got a delicious surprise for you, my dear; and I do so enjoy prolonging it. Tell me, Helena, what did you propose we should both do when we found ourselves at home again?'

My memory was at fault. Eunice's good spirits became absolutely boisterous. She called out: 'Catch!' and tossed her journal into my hands, across the whole length of the room. 'We were to read each other's diaries,' she said. 'There is mine to begin with.'

Innocent of any suspicion of the true state of affairs, I began the reading of Eunice's journal.

If I had not seen the familiar handwriting, nothing would have induced me to believe that a girl brought up in a pious household, the well-beloved daughter of a distinguished Congregational Minister, could have written that shameless record of passions unknown to young ladies in respectable English life. What to say, what to do, when I had closed the book, was more than I felt myself equal to decide. My wretched sister spared me the anxiety which I might otherwise have felt. It was she who first opened her lips, after the silence that had fallen on us while I was reading. These were literally the words that she said:

'My darling, why don't you congratulate me?'

No argument could have persuaded me, as this persuaded me, that all sisterly remonstrance on my part would be completely thrown away.

'My dear Eunice,' I said, 'let me beg you to excuse me. I am waiting——'

There she interrupted me – and, ho, in what an impudent manner! She took my chin between her finger and thumb, and lifted my downcast face, and looked at me with an appearance of eager expectation which I was quite at a loss to understand.

'You have been away from home, too,' she said. 'Do I see in this serious face some astonishing news waiting to overpower me? Have *you* found a sweetheart? Are *you* engaged to be married?'

I only put her hand away from me, and advised her to return to her chair. This perfectly harmless proceeding seemed absolutely to frighten her.

'Oh, my dear,' she burst out, 'surely you are not jealous of me?'

There was but one possible reply to this: I laughed at it. Is Eunice's head turned? She kissed me!

'Now you laugh,' she said, 'I begin to understand you again; I ought to have known that you are superior to jealousy. But, do tell me, would it be so very wonderful if other girls found something to envy in my good luck? Just think of it! Such a handsome man, such an agreeable man, such a clever man, such a rich man – and, not the least of his merits, by-the-bye, a man who admires You. Come! if you won't congratulate me, congratulate yourself on having such a brother-in-law in prospect!'

Her head *was* turned. I drew the poor soul's attention compassionately to what I had said a moment since.

'Pardon me, dear, for reminding you that I have not yet refused to offer my congratulations. I only told you I was waiting.'

'For what?'

'Waiting, of course, to hear what my father thinks of your wonderful good luck.'

This explanation, offered with the kindest intentions, produced another change in my very variable sister. I had extinguished her good spirits as I might have extinguished a light. She sat down by me, and sighed in the saddest manner. The heart must be hard indeed which can resist the distress of a person who is dear to us. I put my arm round her; she was becoming once more the Eunice whom I so dearly loved.

'My poor child,' I said, 'don't distress yourself by speaking of it; I understand. Your father objects to your marrying Mr Dunboyne.'

She shook her head. 'I can't exactly say, Helena, that Papa does that. He only behaves very strangely.'

'Am I indiscreet, dear, if I ask in what way father's behaviour has surprised you?'

She was quite willing to enlighten me. It was a simple little story which, to my mind, sufficiently explained the strange behaviour that had puzzled my unfortunate sister.

There could indeed be no doubt that my father considered Eunice far too childish in character, as yet, to undertake the duties of matrimony. But, with his customary delicacy, and dread of causing distress to others, he had deferred the disagreeable duty of communicating his opinion to Mr Dunboyne. The adverse decision must, however, be sooner or later announced; and he had arranged to inflict disappointment, as tenderly as might be, at his own table.

Considerately leaving Eunice in the enjoyment of any vain hopes which she may have founded on the event of the dinner-party, I passed the evening until supper-time came in the study with my father

Our talk was mainly devoted to the worthy people with whom I had been staying, and whose new schools I had helped to found. Not a word was said relating to my sister, or to Mr Dunboyne. Poor father looked so sadly weary and ill that I ventured, after what the doctor had said to Eunice, to hint at the value of rest and change of scene to an overworked man. Oh, dear me, he frowned, and waved the subject away from him impatiently, with a wan pale hand.

After supper, I made an unpleasant discovery.

Not having completely finished the unpacking of my boxes, I left Miss Jillgall and Eunice in the drawing-room, and went upstairs. In half an hour I returned, and found the room empty. What had become of them? It was a fine moonlight night; I stepped into the back drawing-room, and looked out of the window. There they were, walking arm-in-arm with their heads close together, deep in talk. With my knowledge of Miss Jillgall, I call this a bad sign.

An odd thought has just come to me. I wonder what might have happened, if I had been visiting at Mrs Staveley's, instead of Eunice, and if Mr Dunboyne had seen me first.

Absurd! If I was not too tired to do anything more, those last lines should be scratched out.

## CHAPTER XXII

### EUNICE'S DIARY

I said so to Miss Jillgall, and I say it again here. Nothing will induce me to think ill of Helena.

My sister is a good deal tired, and a little out of temper after the railway journey. This is exactly what happened to me when I went to London. I attribute her refusal to let me read her journal, after she had read mine, entirely to the disagreeable consequences of travelling by railway. Miss Jillgall accounted for it otherwise, in her own funny manner: 'My sweet child, your sister's diary is full of abuse of poor me.' I humoured the joke: 'Dearest Selina, keep a diary of your own, and fill it with abuse of my sister.' This seemed to be a droll saying at the time. But it doesn't look particularly amusing, now it is written down. We had ginger wine at supper, to celebrate Helena's return. Although I only drank one glass, I dare say it may have got into my head.

However that may be, when the lovely moonlight tempted us into the garden, there was an end to our jokes. We had something to talk about which still dwells disagreeably on my mind.

Miss Jillgall began it.

'If I trust you, dearest Eunice, with my own precious secrets, shall I never, never, never live to repent it?'

I told my good little friend that she might depend on me, provided her secrets did no harm to any person whom I loved.

She clasped her hands and looked up at the moon — I can only suppose that her sentiments overpowered her. She said, very prettily, that her heart and my heart beat together in heavenly harmony. It is needless to add that this satisfied me.

Miss Jillgall's generous confidence in my discretion was, I am afraid, not rewarded as it ought to have been. I found her tiresome at first.

She spoke of an excellent friend (a lady), who had helped her, at the time when she lost her little fortune, by raising a subscription privately to pay the expenses of her return to England. Her friend's name – not very attractive to English ears – was Mrs Tenbruggen; they had first become acquainted under interesting circumstances. Miss Jillgall happened to mention that my father was her only living relative; and it turned out that Mrs Tenbruggen was familiar with his name, and reverenced his fame as a preacher. When he had generously received his poor helpless cousin under his own roof, Miss Jillgall's gratitude and sense of duty impelled her to write, and tell Mrs Tenbruggen how happy she was as a member of our family.

Let me confess that I began to listen more attentively when the narrative reached this point.

'I drew a little picture of our domestic circle here,' Miss Jillgall said, describing her letter; 'and I mentioned the mystery in which Mr Gracedieu conceals the ages of you two dear girls. Mrs Tenbruggen – shall we shorten her ugly name, and call her Mrs T.? Very well – Mrs T. is a remarkably clever woman, and I looked for interesting results, if she would give her opinion of the mysterious circumstances mentioned in my letter.'

By this time, I was all eagerness to hear more.

'Has she written to you?' I asked.

Miss Jillgall looked at me affectionately, and took the reply out of her pocket.

'Listen, Euneece; and you shall hear her own words. Thus she writes:

'"Your letter, dear Selina, especially interests me by what it says about the *two* Miss Gracedieus." – Look, dear; she underlines the word Two. Why, I can't explain. Can you? Ah, I thought not. Well, let us get back to the letter. My accomplished friend continues in these terms:

'"I can understand the surprise which you have felt at the

strange course taken by their father, as a means of concealing the difference which there must be in the ages of these young ladies. Many years since, I happened to discover a romantic incident in the life of your popular preacher, which he has his reasons, as I suspect, for keeping strictly to himself. If I may venture on a bold guess, I should say that any person who could discover which was the oldest of the two daughters, would be also likely to discover the true nature of the romance in Mr Gracedieu's life." – Isn't that very remarkable, Euneece? You don't seem to see it – you funny child! Pray pay particular attention to what comes next. These are the closing sentences in my friend's letter:

"'If you find anything new to tell me which relates to this interesting subject, direct your letter as before – provided you write within a week from the present time. Afterwards, my letters will be received by the English physician whose card I enclose. You will be pleased to hear that my professional interests call me to London at the earliest moment that I can spare." – There, dear child, the letter comes to an end. I dare say you wonder what Mrs T. means, when she alludes to her professional interests?'

No: I was not wondering about anything. It hurt me to hear of a strange woman exercising her ingenuity in guessing at mysteries in Papa's life.

But Miss Jillgall was too eagerly bent on setting forth the merits of her friend to notice this. I now heard that Mrs T.'s marriage had turned out badly, and that she had been reduced to earn her own bread. Her manner of doing this was something quite new to me. She went about, from one place to another, curing people of all sorts of painful maladies, by a way she had of rubbing them with her hands. In Belgium she was called a 'Masseuse'. When I asked what this meant in English, I was told, 'Medical Rubber', and that the fame of Mrs T.'s wonderful cures had reached some of the medical newspapers published in London.

After listening (I must say for myself) very patiently, I was bold enough to own that my interest in what I had just heard was not quite so plain to me as I could have wished it to be.

Miss Jillgall looked shocked at my stupidity. She reminded me that there was a mystery in Mrs Tenbruggen's letter, and a mystery in Papa's strange conduct towards Philip. 'Put two and two together, darling,' she said; 'and, one of these days, they may make four.'

If this meant anything, it meant that the reason which made Papa keep Helena's age and my age unknown to everybody but himself, was also the reason why he seemed to be so strangely unwilling to let me be Philip's wife. I really could not endure to take such a view of it as that, and begged Miss Jillgall to drop the subject. She was as kind as ever.

'With all my heart, dear. But don't deceive yourself – the subject will turn up again when we least expect it.'

## CHAPTER XXIII

### EUNICE'S DIARY

Only two days now, before we give our little dinner-party, and Philip finds his opportunity of speaking to Papa. Oh, how I wish that day had come and gone!

I try not to take gloomy views of things; but I am not quite so happy as I had expected to be when my dear was in the same town with me. If Papa had encouraged him to call again, we might have had some precious time to ourselves. As it is, we can only meet in the different show-places in the town – with Helena on one side, and Miss Jillgall on the other, to take care of us. I do call it cruel not to let two young people love each other, without setting third persons to watch them. If I was Queen of England, I would have pretty private bowers made for lovers, in the summer, and nice warm little rooms to hold two, in the winter. Why not? What harm could come of it, I should like to know?

The cathedral is the place of meeting which we find most convenient, under the circumstances. There are delightful nooks and corners about this celebrated building, in which lovers can lag behind. If we had been in Papa's chapel I should have hesitated to turn it to such a profane use as this; the cathedral doesn't so much matter.

Shall I own that I felt my inferiority to Helena a little keenly? She could tell Philip so many things that I should have liked to tell him first. My clever sister taught him how to pronounce the name of the bishop who began building the cathedral; she led him over the crypt, and told him how old it was. He was interested in the crypt; he talked to Helena (not to me) of his ambition to write a work on cathedral architecture in England; he made a rough little sketch in his book of our famous tomb of some King. Helena knew the late royal personage's name, and Philip showed his sketch to her before he showed it to me. How can I blame him, when I stood there the picture of stupidity, trying to recollect something that I might tell him, if it was only the Dean's name? Helena might have whispered it to me, I think. She remembered it, not I – and mentioned it to Philip, of course. I kept close by him all the time, and now and then he gave me a look which raised my spirits. He might have given me something better than that – I mean a kiss – when we had left the cathedral, and were by ourselves for a moment in a corner of the Dean's garden. But he missed the opportunity. Perhaps he was afraid of the Dean himself coming that way, and happening to see us. However, I am far from thinking the worse of Philip. I gave his arm a little squeeze – and that was better than nothing.

★    ★    ★    ★    ★

He and I took a walk along the bank of the river to-day; my sister and Miss Jillgall looking after us as usual.

On our way through the town, Helena stopped to give an order at a shop. She asked us to wait for her. That best of good creatures, Miss Jillgall, whispered in my ear: 'Go on by yourselves, and leave me to wait for her.' Philip interpreted this act of kindness in a manner which would have vexed me, if I had not understood that it was one of his jokes. He said to me: 'Miss Jillgall sees a chance of annoying your sister, and enjoys the prospect.'

Well, away we went together; it was just what I wanted; it gave me an opportunity of saying something to Philip, between ourselves.

I could now beg of him, in his interests and mine, to make the best of himself when he came to dinner. Clever people, I told him, were people whom Papa liked and admired. I said: 'Let him see, dear, how clever *you* are, and how many things you know – and you can't imagine what a high place you will have in his opinion. I hope you don't think I am taking too much on myself in telling you how to behave.'

He relieved that doubt in a manner which I despair of describing. His eyes rested on me with such a look of exquisite sweetness and love, that I was obliged to hold by his arm, I trembled so with the pleasure of feeling it.

'I do sincerely believe,' he said, 'that you are the most innocent girl, the sweetest, truest girl that ever lived. I wish I was a better man, Eunice; I wish I was good enough to be worthy of you!'

To hear him speak of himself in that way jarred on me. If such words had fallen from any other man's lips, I should have been afraid that he had done something or thought something, of which he had reason to feel ashamed. With Philip this was impossible.

He was eager to walk on rapidly, and to turn a corner in the path, before we could be seen. 'I want to be alone with you,' he said.

I looked back. We were too late; Helena and Miss Jillgall had nearly overtaken us. My sister was on the point of speaking to Philip, when she seemed to change her mind, and only looked at him. Instead of looking at her in return, he kept his eyes cast down, and drew figures on the pathway with his stick. I think Helena was out of temper; she suddenly turned my way. 'Why didn't you wait for me?' she asked.

Philip took her up sharply. 'If Eunice likes seeing the river better than waiting in the street,' he said, 'isn't she free to do as she pleases?'

Helena said nothing more; Philip walked on slowly by himself. Not knowing what to make of it, I turned to Miss Jillgall.

'Surely Philip can't have quarrelled with Helena?' I said.

Miss Jillgall answered in an odd off-hand manner: 'Not he! He is a great deal more likely to have quarrelled with himself.'

'Why?'

'Suppose you ask him why?'

It was not to be thought of; it would have looked like prying into his thoughts. 'Selina!' I said, 'there is something odd about you to-day. What is the matter? I don't understand you.'

'My poor dear, you will find yourself understanding me before long.' I thought I saw something like pity in her face when she said that.

'My poor dear?' I repeated. 'What makes you speak to me in that way?'

'I don't know - I'm tired; I'm an old fool – I'll go back to the house.'

Without another word, she left me. I turned to look for Philip, and saw that my sister had joined him while I had been speaking to Miss Jillgall. It pleased me to find that they were talking in a friendly way when I joined them. A quarrel between Helena and my husband that is to be – no, my husband that *shall* be – would have been too distressing, too unnatural I might almost call it.

Philip looked along the backward path, and asked what had become of Miss Jillgall. 'Have you any objection to follow her example?' he said to me, when I told him that Selina had returned to the town. 'I don't care for the banks of this river.'

Helena, who used to like the river at other times, was as ready as Philip to leave it now. I fancy they had both been kindly waiting to change our walk, till I came to them, and they could study my wishes too. Of course I was ready to go where they pleased. I asked Philip if there was anything he would like to see, when we got into the streets again.

Clever Helena suggested what seemed to be a strange amusement to offer to Philip. 'Let's take him to the Girls' School,' she said.

It appeared to be a matter of perfect indifference to him; he was, what they call, ironical. 'Oh, yes, of course. Deeply interesting! deeply interesting!' He suddenly broke into the wildest good spirits, and tucked my hand under his arm with a gaiety which it was impossible to resist. 'What a boy you are!' Helena said, enjoying his delightful hilarity as I did.

## CHAPTER XXIV

### EUNICE'S DIARY

On entering the schoolroom we lost our gaiety, all in a moment. Something unpleasant had evidently happened.

Two of the eldest girls were sitting together in a corner, separated from the rest, and looking most wickedly sulky. The teachers were at the other end of the room, appearing to be ill at ease. And there, standing in the midst of them, with his face flushed and his eyes angry – there was Papa, sadly unlike his gentle self in the days of his health and happiness. On former occasions, when the exercise of his authority was required in the school, his forbearing temper always set things right. When I saw him now, I thought of what the doctor had said of his health, on my way home from the station

Papa advanced to us the moment we showed ourselves at the door.

He shook hands – cordially shook hands – with Philip. It was delightful to see him, delightful to hear him say: 'Pray don't suppose, Mr Dunboyne, that you are intruding; remain with us by all means if you like.' Then he spoke to Helena and to me, still excited, still not like himself: 'You couldn't have come here, my dears, at a time when your presence was more urgently needed.' He turned to the teachers. 'Tell my daughters what has happened; tell them, why they see me here – shocked and distressed, I don't deny it.'

We now heard that the two girls in disgrace had broken the rules, and in such a manner as to deserve severe punishment.

One of them had been discovered hiding a novel in her desk. The other had misbehaved herself more seriously still – she had gone to the theatre. Instead of expressing any regret, they had actually dared to complain of having to learn Papa's improved catechism. They had even accused him of treating them with severity, because they were poor girls brought up on charity. 'If we had been young ladies,' they were audacious enough to say, 'more indulgence would have been shown to us; we should have been allowed to read stories and to see plays.'

All this time I had been asking myself what Papa meant, when he told us we could not have come to the schoolroom at a better time. His meaning now appeared. When he spoke to the offending girls, he pointed to Helena and to me.

'Here are my daughters,' he said. 'You will not deny that they are young ladies. Now listen. They shall tell you themselves whether my rules make any difference between them and you. Helena! Eunice! do I allow you to read novels? do I allow you to go to the play?'

We said, 'No' – and hoped it was over. But he had not done yet. He turned to Helena.

'Answer some of the questions,' he went on, 'from my Manual of Christian Obligation, which the girls call my catechism.' He asked one of the questions: 'If you are told to do unto others as you would they should do unto you, and if you find a difficulty in obeying that Divine Precept, what does your duty require?'

It is my belief that Helena has the material in her for making another Joan of Arc. She rose, and answered without the slightest sign of timidity: 'My duty requires me to go to the minister, and to seek for advice and encouragement.'

'And if these fail?'

'Then I am to remember that my pastor is my friend. He claims no priestly authority or priestly infallibility. He is my fellow-christian who loves me. He will tell me how he has himself failed; how he has struggled against himself; and what a blessed reward has followed his victory – a purified heart, a peaceful mind.'

Then Papa released my sister, after she had only repeated two out of all the answers in the Christian Obligation, which we first began to learn when we were children. He then addressed himself again to the girls.

'Is what you have just heard a part of my catechism? Has my daughter been excused from repeating it because she is a young lady? Where is the difference between the religious education which is given to my own child, and that given to you?'

The wretched girls still sat silent and obstinate, with their heads down. I tremble again as I write of what happened next. Papa fixed his eyes on me. He said, out loud: 'Eunice!' – and waited for me to rise and answer, as my sister had done.

It was entirely beyond my power to get on my feet.

Philip had (innocently, I am sure) discouraged me; I saw displeasure, I saw contempt in his face. There was a dead silence in the room. Everybody looked at me. My heart beat furiously, my hands turned cold, the questions and answers in Christian Obligation all left my memory together. I looked imploringly at Papa.

For the first time in his life, he was hard on me. His eyes were as angry as ever; they showed me no mercy. Oh, what had come to me? what evil spirit possessed me? I felt resentment; horrid, undutiful resentment, at being treated in this cruel way. My fists clenched themselves in my lap, my face felt as hot as fire. Instead of asking my father to excuse me, I said: 'I can't do it.' He was astounded, as well he might be. I went on from bad to worse. I said: 'I won't do it.'

He stooped over me; he whispered: 'I am going to ask you something; I insist on your answering. Yes or No.' He raised his voice, and drew himself back so that they could all see me.

'Have you been taught like your sister?' he asked. 'Has the catechism that has been her religious lesson, for all her life, been your religious lesson, for all your life, too?'

I said: 'Yes' – and I was in such a rage that I said it out loud. If Philip had handed me his cane, and had advised me to give the young hussies who were answerable for this dreadful state of things a good beating, I believe I should have done it. Papa turned his back on me, and offered the girls a last chance: 'Do you feel sorry for what you have done? Do you ask to be forgiven?'

Neither the one nor the other answered him. He called across the room to the teachers: 'Those two pupils are expelled the school.'

Both the women looked horrified. The elder of the two approached him, and tried to plead for a milder sentence. He answered in one stern word: 'Silence!' – and left the schoolroom, without even a passing bow to Philip. And this, after he had cordially shaken hands with my poor dear, not half an hour before.

I ought to have made affectionate allowance for his nervous miseries; I ought to have run after him, and begged his pardon. There must be something wrong, I am afraid, in girls loving anybody but their fathers. When Helena led the way out by another door, I ran after Philip; and I asked *him* to forgive me.

I don't know what I said; it was all confusion. The fear of having forfeited his fondness must, I suppose, have shaken my mind. I remember entreating Helena to say a kind word for me. She was so clever, she had behaved so well, she had deserved that Philip should listen to her. 'Oh,' I cried out to him desperately, 'what must you think of me?'

'I will tell you what I think of you,' he said. 'It is your father who is in fault, Eunice – not you. Nothing could have been in worst taste than his management of that trumpery affair in the schoolroom; it was a complete mistake from beginning to end. Make your mind easy; I don't blame You.'

'Are you, really and truly, as fond of me as ever?'

'Yes, to be sure!'

Helena seemed to be hardly as much interested in this happy ending of my anxieties as I might have anticipated. She walked on by herself. Perhaps she was thinking of poor Papa's strange outbreak of excitement, and grieving over it.

We had only a little way to walk, before we passed the door of Philip's hotel. He had not yet received the expected letter from his father – the cruel letter which might recall him to Ireland. It was then the hour of delivery by our second post; he went to look at the letter-rack in the hall. Helena saw that I was anxious. She was as kind again as ever; she consented to wait with me for Philip, at the door.

He came out to us with an open letter in his hand.

'From my father, at last,' he said – and gave me the letter to read. It only contained these few lines:

'Do not be alarmed, my dear boy, at the change for the worse in my handwriting. I am suffering for my devotion to the studious habits of a lifetime: my right hand is attacked by the malady called Writer's Cramp. The doctor here can do nothing. He tells me of some foreign woman, mentioned in his newspaper, who cures nervous derangements of all kinds by hand-rubbing, and who is coming to London. When you next hear from me, I may be in London too.' – There the letter ended.

Of course I knew who the foreign woman, mentioned in the newspaper, was.

But what does Miss Jillgall's friend matter to me? The one important thing is, that Philip has not been called back to Ireland. Here is a fortunate circumstance, which perhaps means more good luck. I may be Mrs Philip Dunboyne before the year is out.

## CHAPTER XXV

### HELENA'S DIARY

They all notice at home that I am looking worn and haggard. That hideous old maid, Miss Jillgall, had her malicious welcome ready for me when we met at breakfast this morning: 'Dear Helena, what has become of your beauty? One would think you had left it in your room!' Poor deluded Eunice showed her sisterly sympathy: 'Don't joke about it, Selina: can't you see that Helena is ill?'

I *have* been ill; ill of my own wickedness.

But the recovery of my tranquillity will bring with it the recovery of my good looks. My fatal passion for Philip promises to be the utter destruction of everything that is good in me. Well! what is good in me may not be worth keeping. There is a fate in these things. If I am destined to rob Eunice of the one dear object of her love and hope – how can I resist? The one kind thing I can do is to keep her in ignorance of what is coming, by acts of affectionate deceit.

Besides, if she suffers, I suffer too. In the length and breadth of England, I doubt if there is a much more wicked young woman to be found than myself. Is it nothing to feel that, and to endure it as I do?

Upon my word, there is no excuse for me!

Is this sheer impudence? No; it is the bent of my nature. I have a tendency to self-examination, accompanied by one merit – I don't spare myself.

There are excuses for Eunice. She lives in a fools' paradise; and she sees in her lover a radiant creature, shining in the halo thrown over him by her own self-delusion. Nothing of this sort is to be said for me. I see Philip as he is. My penetration looks into the lowest depths of his character – when I am not in his company. There seems to be a foundation of good, somewhere in his nature. He despises and hates himself (he has confessed it to me), when Eunice is with him – still believing in her false sweetheart. But how long do these better influences last? I have only to show myself, in my sister's absence, and Philip is mine body and soul. His vanity and his weakness take possession of him the moment he sees my face. He is one of those men – even in my little experience I have met with them – who are born to be led by women. If Eunice had possessed my strength of character, he would have been true to her for life.

Ought I not, in justice to myself, to have lifted my heart high above the reach of such a creature as this? Certainly I ought! I know it, I feel it. And yet, there is some fascination in loving him which I am absolutely unable to resist.

What, I ask myself, has fed the new flame which is burning in me? Did it begin with gratified pride? I might well feel proud when I found myself admired by a man of his beauty, set off by such manners and such accomplishments as his. Or, has the growth of this masterful feeling been encouraged by the envy and jealousy stirred in me, when I found Eunice (my inferior in every respect) distinguished by the devotion of a handsome lover, and having a brilliant marriage in view – while I was left neglected, with no prospect of changing my title from Miss to Mrs? Vain inquiries! My wicked heart seems to have secrets of its own, and to keep them a mystery to me.

What has become of my excellent education?

I don't care to inquire; I have got beyond the reach of good books and religious examples. Among my other blameable actions there may now be reckoned disobedience to my father. I have been reading novels in secret.

At first I tried some of the famous English works, published at a price within the reach of small purses. Very well written, no doubt – but with one unpardonable drawback, so far as I am concerned. Our celebrated native authors address themselves to good people, or to penitent people who want to be made good; not to wicked readers like me.

Arriving at this conclusion, I tried another experiment. In a small bookseller's shop I discovered some cheap translations of French novels. Here, I found what I wanted – sympathy with sin. Here, there was opened to me a new world inhabited entirely by unrepentant people; the magnificent women diabolically beautiful; the satanic men dead to every sense of virtue, and alive – perhaps rather dirtily alive – the splendid fascinations of crime. I know now that Love is above everything but itself. Love is the one law that we are bound to obey. How deep! how consoling! how admirably true! The novelists of England have reason indeed to hide their heads before the novelists of France. All that I have felt, and have written here, is inspired by these wonderful authors.

I have relieved my mind, and may now return to the business of my diary – the record of domestic events.

An overwhelming disappointment has fallen on Eunice. Our dinner-party has been put off.

The state of father's health is answerable for this change in our arrangements. That wretched scene at the school, complicated by my sister's undutiful behaviour at the time, so seriously excited him that he passed a sleepless night, and kept to his bedroom throughout the day. Eunice's total want of discretion added, no doubt, to his sufferings: she rudely intruded on him to express her regret and to ask his pardon. Having carried her point, she was at leisure to come to me, and to ask (how amazingly simple of her!) what she and Philip were to do next.

'We had arranged it all so nicely,' the poor wretch began.

'Philip was to have been so clever and agreeable at dinner, and was to have chosen his time so very discreetly, that Papa would have been ready to listen to anything he said. Oh, we should have succeeded; I haven't a doubt of it! Our only hope, Helena, is in you. What are we to do now?'

'Wait,' I answered.

'Wait?' she repeated hotly. 'Is my heart to be broken? and, what is more cruel still, is Philip to be disappointed? I expected something more sensible, my dear, from you. What possible reason can there be for waiting?'

The reason – if I could only have mentioned it – was beyond dispute. I wanted time to quiet Philip's uneasy conscience, and to harden his weak mind against outbursts of violence, on Eunice's part, which would certainly exhibit themselves when she found that she had lost her lover, and lost him to me. In the meanwhile, I had to produce my reason for advising her to wait. It was easily done. I reminded her of the irritable condition of our father's nerves, and gave it as my opinion that he would certainly say No, if she was unwise enough to excite him on the subject of Philip, in his present frame of mind.

These unanswerable considerations seemed to produce the right effect on her. 'I suppose you know best,' was all she said. And then she left me.

I let her go without feeling any distrust of this act of submission on her part; it was such a common experience, in my life, to find my sister guiding herself by my advice. But experience is not always to be trusted. Events soon showed that I had failed to estimate Eunice's resources of obstinacy and cunning at their true value.

Half an hour later I heard the street door close, and looked out of the window. Miss Jillgall was leaving the house; no one was with her. My dislike of this person led me astray once more. I ought to have suspected her of being bent on some mischievous errand, and to have devised some means of putting my suspicions to the test. I did nothing of the kind. In the moment when I turned my head away from the window, Miss Jillgall was a person forgotten – and I was a person who had made a serious mistake.

## CHAPTER XXVI

### HELENA'S DIARY

The event of to-day began with the delivery of a message summoning me to my father's study. He had decided – too hastily, as I feared – that he was sufficiently recovered to resume his usual employments. I was writing to his dictation, when we were interrupted. Maria announced a visit from Mr Dunboyne.

Hitherto, Philip had been content to send one of the servants of the hotel to make inquiry after Mr Gracedieu's health. Why had he now called personally? Noticing that father seemed to be annoyed, I tried to make an opportunity of receiving Philip myself. 'Let me see him,' I suggested; 'I can easily say you are engaged.'

Very unwillingly, as it was easy to see, my father declined to allow this. 'Mr Dunboyne's visit pays me a compliment,' he said; 'and I must receive him.' I made a show of leaving the room, and was called back to my chair. 'This is not a private interview, Helena; stay where you are.'

Philip came in – handsomer than ever, beautifully dressed – and paid his respects to my father with his customary grace. He was too well bred to allow any visible signs of embarrassment to escape him. But when he shook hands with me, I felt a little trembling in his fingers, through the delicate gloves which fitted him like a second skin. Was it the true object of his visit to try the experiment designed by Eunice and himself, and deferred by the postponement of our dinner-party? Impossible surely that my sister could have practised on his weakness, and persuaded him to return to his first love! I waited, in breathless interest, for his next words. They were not worth listening to. Oh, the poor common-place creature!

'I am glad, Mr Gracedieu, to see that you are well enough to be in your study again,' he said. The writing materials on the table attracted his attention. 'Am I one of the idle people,' he asked, with his charming smile, 'who are always interrupting useful employment?'

He spoke to my father, and he was answered by my father.

Not once had he addressed a word to me – no, not even when we shook hands. I was angry enough to force him into taking some notice of me, and to make an attempt to confuse him at the same time.

'Have you seen my sister?' I asked.

'No.'

It was the shortest reply that he could choose. Having flung it at me, he still persisted in looking at my father and speaking to my father: 'Do you think of trying a change of air, Mr Gracedieu, when you feel strong enough to travel?'

'My duties keep me here,' father answered; 'and I cannot honestly say that I enjoy travelling. I dislike manners and customs that are strange to me; I don't find that hotels reward me for giving up the comforts of my own house. How do you find the hotel here?'

'I submit to the hotel, sir. They are sad savages in the kitchen; they put mushroom ketchup into their soup, and mustard and cayenne pepper into their salads. I am half starved at dinner-time, but I don't complain.'

Every word he said was an offence to me. With or without reason, I attacked him again.

'I have heard you acknowledge that the landlord and landlady are very obliging people,' I said. 'Why don't you ask them to let you make your own soup and mix your own salad?'

I wondered whether I should succeed in attracting his notice, after this. Even in these private pages, my self-esteem finds it hard to confess what happened. I succeeded in reminding Philip that he had his reasons for requesting me to leave the room.

'Will you excuse me, Miss Helena,' he said, 'if I ask leave to speak to Mr Gracedieu in private?'

The right thing for me to do was, let me hope, the thing that I did. I rose, and waited to see if my father would interfere. He looked at Philip with suspicion in his face, as well as surprise. 'May I ask,' he said coldly, 'what is the object of the interview?'

'Certainly,' Philip answered, 'when we are alone.' This cool reply placed my father between two alternatives; he must either give way, or be guilty of an act of rudeness to a guest in his own house. The choice reserved for me was narrower still – I had to decide between being told to go, or going of my own accord. Of course, I left them together.

The door which communicated with the next room was pulled to, but not closed. On the other side of it, I found Eunice.

'Listening!' I said, in a whisper.

'Yes,' she whispered back. 'You listen, too!'

I was so indignant with Philip, and so seriously interested in what was going on in the study, that I yielded to temptation. We both degraded ourselves. We both listened.

Eunice's base lover spoke first. Judging by the change in his voice, he must have seen something in my father's face that daunted him. Eunice heard it too. 'He's getting nervous,' she whispered; 'he'll forget to say the right thing at the right time.'

'Mr Gracedieu,' Philip began, 'I wish to speak to you——'

Father interrupted him: 'We are alone now, Mr Dunboyne. I want to know why you consult me in private.'

'I am anxious to consult you, sir, on a subject——'

'On what subject? Any religious difficulty?'

'No.'

'Anything I can do for you in the town?'

'Not at all. If you will only allow me——'

'I am still waiting, sir, to know what it is about.'

Philip's voice suddenly became an angry voice. 'Once and for all, Mr Gracedieu,' he said, 'will you let me speak? It's about your daughter——'

'No more of it, Mr Dunboyne!' (My father was now as loud as Philip.) 'I don't desire to hold a private conversation with you on the subject of my daughter.'

'If you have any personal objection to me, sir, be so good as to state it plainly.'

'You have no right to ask me to do that.'

'You refuse to do it?'

'Positively.'

'You are not very civil, Mr Gracedieu.'

'If I speak without ceremony, Mr Dunboyne, you have yourself to thank for it.'

Philip replied to this in a tone of savage irony. 'You are a

minister of religion, and you are an old man. Two privileges –
and you presume on them both. Good-morning.'

I drew back into a corner, just in time to escape discovery in
the character of a listener. Eunice never moved. When Philip
dashed into the room, banging the door after him, she threw
herself impulsively on his breast: 'Oh Philip! Philip! what have
you done? Why didn't you keep your temper?'

'Did you hear what your father said to me?' he asked.

'Yes, dear; but you ought to have controlled yourself – you
ought, indeed, for my sake.'

Her arms were still round him. It struck me that he felt her
influence. 'If you wish me to recover myself,' he said gently,
'you had better let me go.'

'Oh, how cruel, Philip, to leave me when I am so wretched!
Why do you want to go?'

'You told me just now what I ought to do,' he answered, still
restraining himself. 'If I am to get the better of my temper, I
must be left alone.'

'I never said anything about your temper, darling.'

'Didn't you tell me to control myself?'

'Oh, yes! Go back to Papa, and beg him to forgive you.'

'I'll see him damned first!'

If ever a stupid girl deserved such an answer as this, the girl
was my sister. I had hitherto (with some difficulty) refrained
from interfering. But when Eunice tried to follow Philip out of
the house, I could hesitate no longer; I held her back. 'You
fool,' I said; 'haven't you made mischief enough already?'

'What am I to do?' she burst out helplessly.

'Do what I told you to do yesterday – wait.'

Before she could reply, or I could say anything more, the
door that led to the landing was opened softly and slyly, and
Miss Jillgall peeped in. Eunice instantly left me, and ran to the
meddling old maid. They whispered to each other. Miss
Jillgall's skinny arm encircled my sister's waist; they disappeared
together.

I was only too glad to get rid of them both, and to take the
opportunity of writing to Philip. I insisted on an explanation of
his conduct while I was in the study – to be given within an

hour's time, at a place which I appointed. 'You are not to attempt to justify yourself in writing,' I added in conclusion. 'Let your reply merely inform me if you can keep the appointment. The rest, when we meet.'

Maria took the letter to the hotel, with instructions to wait.

Philip's reply reached me without delay. It pledged him to justify himself as I had desired, and to keep the appointment. My own belief is that the event of to-day will decide his future and mine.


# CHAPTER XXVII

### EUNICE'S DIARY

Indeed, I am a most unfortunate creature; everything turns out badly with me. My good true friend, my dear Selina, has become the object of a hateful doubt in my secret mind. I am afraid she is keeping something from me.

Talking with her about my troubles, I heard for the first time that she had written again to Mrs Tenbruggen. The object of her letter was to tell her friend of my engagement to young Mr Dunboyne. I asked her why she had done this. The answer informed me that there was no knowing, in the present state of my affairs, how soon I might not want the help of a clever woman. I ought, I suppose, to have been satisfied with this. But there seemed to be something not fully explained yet.

Then again, after telling Selina what I heard in the study, and how roughly Philip had spoken to me afterwards, I asked her what she thought of it. She made an incomprehensible reply: 'My sweet child, I mustn't think of it – I am too fond of you.'

It was impossible to make her explain what this meant. She began to talk of Philip; assuring me (which was quite needless) that she had done her best to fortify and encourage him, before he called on Papa. When I asked her to help me in another way – that is to say, when I wanted to find out where Philip was at that moment – she had no advice to give me. I told her that I should not enjoy a moment's ease of mind until I and my dear one were reconciled. She only shook her head, and declared that she was sorry for me. When I hit on the idea of ringing for Maria, this little woman, so bright, and quick and eager to help me at other times, she said: 'I leave it to you, dear,' and turned to the piano (close to which I was sitting), and played softly and badly stupid little tunes.

'Maria, did you open the door for Mr Dunboyne when he went away just now?'

'No, Miss.'

Nothing but ill-luck for me! If I had been left to my own devices, I should now have let the housemaid go. But Selina contrived to give me a hint, on a strange plan of her own. Still at the piano, she began to confuse talking to herself with playing to herself. The notes went *tinkle, tinkle* – and the tongue mixed up words with the notes in this way: 'Perhaps they have been talking in the kitchen about Philip?'

The suggestion was not lost on me. I said to Maria – who was standing at the other end of the room, near the door – 'Did you happen to hear which way Mr Dunboyne went when he left us?'

'I know where he was, Miss, half an hour ago.'

'Where was he?'

'At the hotel.'

Selina went on with her hints in the same way as before. 'How does she know – ah, how does she know?' was the vocal part of the performance this time. My clever inquiries followed the vocal part as before:

'How do you know that Mr Dunboyne was at the hotel?'

'I was sent there with a letter for him, and waited for the answer.'

There was no suggestion required this time. The one possible question was: 'Who sent you?'

Maria replied, after first reserving a condition: 'You won't tell upon me, Miss?'

I promised not to tell. Selina suddenly left off playing.

'Well,' I repeated, 'who sent you?'

'Miss Helena.'

Selina looked round at me. Her little eyes seemed to have suddenly become big, they stared me so strangely in the face. I don't know whether she was in a state of fright or of wonder. As for myself, I simply lost the use of my tongue. Maria, having no more questions to answer, discreetly left us together.

Why should Helena write to Philip at all – and especially without mentioning it to me? Here was a riddle which was more than I could guess. I asked Selina to help me. She might at least have tried, I thought; but she looked uneasy, and made excuses

I said: 'Suppose I go to Helena, and ask her why she wrote to Philip?' And Selina said: 'Suppose you do, dear.'

I rang for Maria once more: 'Do you know where my sister is?'

'Just gone out, Miss.'

There was no help for it but to wait till she came back, and to get through the time in the interval as I best might. But for one circumstance, I might not have known what to do. The truth is, there was a feeling of shame in me when I remembered having listened at the study door. Curious notions come into one's head – one doesn't know how or why. It struck me that I might make a kind of atonement for having been mean enough to listen, if I went to Papa, and offered to keep him company in his solitude. If we fell into pleasant talk, I had a sly idea of my own – I meant to put in a good word for poor Philip.

When I confided my design to Selina, she shut up the piano and ran across the room to me. But somehow she was not like her old self again, yet.

'You good little soul, you are always right. Look at me again, Euneece. Are you beginning to doubt me? Oh, my darling, don't do that! It isn't using me fairly. I can't bear it!'

I took her hand; I was on the point of speaking to her with the kindness she deserved from me. On a sudden she snatched her hand away, and ran back to the piano. When she was seated on the music-stool, her face was hidden from me. At that moment she broke into a strange cry – it began like a laugh, and it ended like a sob.

'Go away to Papa! Don't mind me – I'm a creature of

impulse – ha! ha! ha! a little hysterical – the state of the weather
– I get rid of these weaknesses, my dear, by singing to myself. I
have a favourite song: "My heart is light, my will is free." – Go
away! oh, for God's sake, go away!'

I had heard of hysterics, of course; knowing nothing about
them, however, by my own experience. What could have
happened to agitate her in this extraordinary manner?

Had Helena's letter anything to do with it? Was my sister
indignant with Philip for swearing in my presence; and had she
written him an angry letter, in her zeal on my behalf? But
Selina could not possibly have seen the letter – and Helena
(who is often hard on me when I do stupid things) showed little
indulgence for me, when I was so unfortunate as to irritate
Philip. I gave up the hopeless attempt to get at the truth by
guessing, and went away to forget my troubles, if I could, in my
father's society.

After knocking twice at the door of the study, and receiving
no reply, I ventured to look in.

The sofa in this room stood opposite the door. Papa was
resting on it, but not in comfort. There were twitching
movements in his feet, and he shifted his arms this way and that
as if no restful posture could be found for them. But what
frightened me was this. His eyes, staring straight at the door by
which I had gone in, had an inquiring expression, as if he
actually did not know me! I stood midway between the door
and the sofa, doubtful about going nearer to him.

He said: 'Who is it?' This to me – to his own daughter. He
said: 'What do you want?'

I really could *not* bear it. I went up to him. I said: 'Papa, have
you forgotten Eunice?'

My name seemed (if one may say such a thing) to bring him
to himself again. He sat upon the sofa – and laughed as he
answered me.

'My dear child, what delusion has got into that pretty little
head of yours? Fancy her thinking that I had forgotten my own
daughter! I was lost in thought, Eunice. For the moment, I was
what they call an absent man. Did I ever tell you the story of
the absent man? He went to call upon some acquaintance of his;

and when the servant said, "What name, sir?" he couldn't answer. He was obliged to confess he had forgotten his own name. The servant said, "That's very strange." The absent man at once recovered himself. "That's it!" he said: "my name is Strange." Droll, isn't it? If I had been calling on a friend to-day, I dare say *I* might have forgotten my name, too. Much to think of, Eunice — too much to think of.'

Leaving the sofa with a sigh, as if he was tired of it, he began walking up and down. He seemed to be still in good spirits. 'Well, my dear,' he said, 'what can I do for you?'

'I came here, Papa, to see if there was anything I could do for you.'

He looked at some sheets of paper, strung together, and laid on the table. They were covered with writing (from his dictation) in my sister's hand. 'I ought to get on with my work,' he said. 'Where is Helena?'

I told him that she had gone out, and begged leave to try what I could do to supply her place.

The request seemed to please him; but he wanted time to think. I waited, noticing that his face grew gradually worried and anxious. There came a vacant look into his eyes which it grieved me to see; he appeared to have quite lost himself again. 'Read the last page,' he said, pointing to the manuscript on the table; 'I don't remember where I left off.'

I turned to the last page. As well as I could tell, it related to some publication, which he was recommending to religious persons of our way of thinking.

Before I had read half-way through it, he began to dictate, speaking so rapidly that my pen was not always able to follow him. My handwriting is as bad as bad can be when I am hurried. To make matters worse still, I was confused. What he was now saying seemed to have nothing to do with what I had been reading.

Let me try if I can call to mind the substance of it.

He began in the most strangely sudden way by asking:

'Why should there be any fear of discovery, when every possible care had been taken to prevent it? The danger from unexpected events was far more disquieting. A man might find himself bound in honour to disclose what it had been the chief anxiety of his life to conceal. For example, could he let an innocent person be the victim of deliberate suppression of the truth – no matter how justifiable that suppression might appear to be? On the other hand, dreadful consequences might follow an honourable confession. There might be a cruel sacrifice of tender affection; there might be a shocking betrayal of innocent hope and trust.'

I remember those last words, just as he dictated them, because he suddenly stopped there; looking, poor dear, distressed and confused. He put his hand to his head, and went back to the sofa.

'I'm tired,' he said. 'Wait for me while I rest.'

In a few minutes he fell asleep. It was a deep repose that came to him now; and, though I don't think it lasted much longer than half an hour, it produced a wonderful change in him for the better when he woke. He spoke quietly and kindly; and when he returned to me at the table, and looked at the page on which I had been writing, he smiled.

'Oh, my dear, what bad writing! I declare I can't read what I myself told you to write. No! no! don't be downhearted about it. You are not used to writing from dictation; and I dare say I have been too quick for you.' He kissed me and encouraged me. 'You know how fond I am of my little girl,' he said; 'I am afraid I like my Eunice just the least in the world more than I like my Helena. Ah, you are beginning to look a little happier now!'

He had filled me with such confidence and such pleasure that I could not help thinking of my sweetheart. Oh dear, when shall I learn to be distrustful of my own feelings? The temptation to say a good word for Philip quite mastered any little discretion that I possessed.

I said to Papa: 'If you knew how to make me happier than I have ever been in all my life before, would you do it?'

'Of course I would.'

'Then send for Philip, dear, and be a little kinder to him, this time.'

His pale face turned red with anger; he pushed me away from him.

'That man again!' he burst out. 'Am I never to hear the last of him? Go away, Eunice. You are of no use here.' He took up my unfortunate page of writing, and ridiculed it with a bitter laugh. 'What is this fit for?' He crumpled it up in his hand, and tossed it into the fire.

I ran out of the room in such a state of mortification that I hardly knew what I was about. If some hardhearted person had come to me with a cup of poison, and had said: 'Eunice, you are not fit to live any longer; take this,' I do believe I should have taken it. If I thought of anything, I thought of going back to Selina. My ill luck still pursued me; she had disappeared. I looked about in a helpless way, completely at a loss what to do next – so stupefied, I may even say, that it was some time before I noticed a little three-cornered note on the table by which I was standing. The note was addressed to me:

'EVER-DEAREST EUNEECE,

'I have tried to make myself useful to you, and have failed. But how can I see the sad sight of your wretchedness, and not feel the impulse to try again? I have gone to the hotel to find Philip, and to bring him back to you a penitent and faithful man. Wait for me, and hope for great things. A hundred thousand kisses to my sweet Euneece.

'S.J.'

Wait for her, after reading that note! How could she expect it? I had only to follow her, and to find Philip. In another minute, I was on my way to the hotel.

## CHAPTER XXVIII

### HELENA'S DIARY

Looking at the last entry in my Journal, I see myself anticipating that the event of to-day will decide Philip's future and mine. This has proved prophetic. All further concealment is now at an end.

Forced to it by fate, or helped to it by chance, Eunice has made the discovery of her lover's infidelity. 'In all human probability' (as my father says in his sermons), we two sisters are enemies for life.

I am not suspected, as Eunice is, of making appointments with a sweetheart. So I am free to go out alone, and to go where I please. Philip and I were punctual to our appointment this afternoon.

Our place of meeting was in a secluded corner of the town park. We found a rustic seat in our retirement, set up (one would suppose) as a concession to the taste of visitors who are fond of solitude. The view in front of us was bounded by the park wall and railings, and our seat was prettily approached on one side by a plantation of young trees. No entrance-gate was near; no carriage road crossed the grass. A more safe and more solitary nook for conversation, between two persons desiring to be alone, it would be hard to find in most public parks. Lovers are said to know it well, and to be especially fond of it towards evening. We were there in broad daylight, and we had the seat to ourselves.

My memory of what passed between us is, in some degree, disturbed by the formidable interruption which brought our talk to an end.

But among other things, I remember that I showed him no mercy at the outset. At one time I was indignant; at another I was scornful. I declared, in regard to my object in meeting him, that I had changed my mind, and had decided to shorten a disagreeable interview by waiving my right to an explanation, and bidding him farewell. Eunice, as I pointed out, had the first claim to him; Eunice was much more likely to suit him, as a companion for life, than I was. 'In short,' I said, in conclusion, 'my inclination for once takes sides with my duty, and leaves my sister in undisturbed possession of young Mr Dunboyne.' With this satirical explanation, I rose to say good-bye.

I had merely intended to irritate him. He showed a surperiority to anger for which I was not prepared.

'Be so kind as to sit down again,' he said quietly.

He took my letter from his pocket, and pointed to that part of it which alluded to his conduct, when we had met in my father's study.

'You have offered me the opportunity of saying a word in my own defence,' he went on. 'I prize that privilege far too highly to consent to your withdrawing it, merely because you have changed your mind. Let me at least tell you what my errand was, when I called on your father. Loving you, and you only, I had forced myself to make a last effort to be true to your sister. Remember that, Helena, and then say – is it wonderful if I was beside myself, when I found you in the study?'

'When you tell me you were beside yourself,' I said, 'do you mean, ashamed of yourself?'

That touched him. 'I mean nothing of the kind,' he burst out. 'After the hell on earth in which I have been living between you two sisters, a man hasn't virtue enough left in him to be ashamed. He's half mad – that's what he is. Look at my position! I had made up my mind never to see you again; I had made up my mind (if I married Eunice) to rid myself of my own miserable life when I could endure it no longer. In that state of feeling, when my sense of duty depended on my speaking with Mr Gracedieu alone, whose was the first face I saw when I entered the room? If I had dared to look at you, or to speak to you, what do you think would have become of my resolution to sacrifice myself?'

'What has become of it now?' I asked.

'Tell me first if I am forgiven,' he said – 'and you shall know.'

'Do you deserve to be forgiven?'

It has been discovered by wiser heads than mine that weak people are always in extremes. So far, I had seen Philip in the vain and violent extreme. He now shifted suddenly to the sad and submissive extreme. When I asked him if he deserved to be forgiven, he made the humblest of all replies – he sighed and said nothing.

'If I did my duty to my sister,' I reminded him, 'I should refuse to forgive you, and send you back to Eunice.'

'Your father's language and your father's conduct,' he

answered, 'have released me from that entanglement. I can never go back to Eunice. If you refuse to forgive me, neither you nor she will see anything more of Philip Dunboyne; I promise you that. Are you satisfied now?'

After holding out against him resolutely, I felt myself beginning to yield. When a man has once taken their fancy, what helplessly weak creatures women are! I saw through his vacillating weakness – and yet I trusted him, with both eyes open. My looking-glass is opposite to me while I write. It shows me a contemptible Helena. I lied, and said I was satisfied – to please *him*.

'Am I forgiven?' he asked.

It is absurd to put it on record. Of course I forgave him. What a good Christian I am, after all!

He took my willing hand. 'My lovely darling, ' he said, 'our marriage rests with you. Whether your father approves of it or not, say the word; claim me, and I am yours for life.'

I must have been infatuated by his voice and his look; my heart must have been burning under the pressure of his hand on mine. Was it my modesty or my self-control that deserted me? I let him take me in his arms. Again, and again, and again I kissed him. We were deaf to what we ought to have heard; we were blind to what we ought to have seen. Before we were conscious of a movement among the trees, we were discovered. My sister flew at me like a wild animal. Her furious hands fastened themselves on my throat. Philip started to his feet. When he touched her, in the act of forcing her back from me, Eunice's raging strength became utter weakness in an instant. Her arms fell helpless at her sides – her head drooped – she looked at him in silence which was dreadful, at such a moment as that. He shrank from the unendurable reproach in those tearless eyes. Meanly, he turned away from her. Meanly, I followed him. Looking back for an instant, I saw her step forward; perhaps to stop him, perhaps to speak to him. The effort was too much for her strength; she staggered back against the trunk of a tree. Like strangers, walking separate one from the other, we left her to her companion – the hideous traitress who was my enemy and her friend.

## CHAPTER XXIX

### HELENA'S DIARY

On reaching the street which led to Philip's hotel, we spoke to each other for the first time.

'What are we to do?' I said.

'Leave this place,' he answered.

'Together?' I asked.

'Yes.'

To leave us (for a while), after what had happened, might be the wisest thing which a man, in Philip's critical position, could do. But if I went with him − unprovided as I was with any friend of my own sex, whose character and presence might sanction the step I had taken − I should be lost beyond redemption. Is any man that ever lived worth that sacrifice? I thought of my father's house closed to me, and of our friends ashamed of me. I have owned, in some earlier part of my Journal, that I am not very patient under domestic cares. But the possibility of Eunice being appointed housekeeper, with my power, in my place, was more than I could calmly contemplate. 'No,' I said to Philip. 'Your absence, at such a time as this, may help us both; but, come what may of it, I must remain at home.'

He yielded, without an attempt to make me alter my mind. There was a sullen submission in his manner which it was not pleasant to see. Was he despairing already of himself and of me? Had Eunice aroused the watchful demons of shame and remorse?

'Perhaps you are right,' he said gloomily. 'Good-bye.'

My anxiety put the all-important question to him without hesitation:

'Is it good-bye for ever, Philip?'

His reply instantly relieved me: 'God forbid!'

But I wanted more: 'You still love me?' I persisted.

'More dearly than ever!'

'And yet you leave me?'

He turned pale. 'I leave you because I am afraid.'

'Afraid of what?'

'Afraid to face Eunice again.'

The only possible way out of our difficulty that I could see, now occurred to me. 'Suppose my sister can be prevailed on to give you up?' I suggested. 'Would you come back in that case?'

'Certainly!'

'And you would ask my father to consent to our marriage?'

'On the day of my return, if you like.'

'Suppose obstacles get in our way,' I said – 'suppose time passes and tries your patience – will you still consider yourself engaged to me?'

'Engaged to you,' he answered, 'in spite of obstacles and in spite of time.'

'And, while you are away from me,' I ventured to add, 'we shall write to each other?'

'Go where I may,' he said, 'you shall always hear from me.'

I could ask no more; and he could concede no more. The impression evidently left on him by Eunice's terrible outbreak, was far more serious than I had anticipated. I was myself depressed and ill at ease. No expressions of tenderness were exchanged between us. There was something horrible in our barren farewell. We merely clasped hands, at parting. He went his way – and I went mine.

There are some occasions when women set an example of courage to men. I was ready to endure whatever might happen to me, when I got home. What a desperate wretch! some people might say, if they could look into this diary.

Maria opened the door; she told me that my sister had already returned, accompanied by Miss Jillgall. There had been apparently some difference of opinion between them, before they entered the house. Eunice had attempted to go on to some other place; and Miss Jillgall had remonstrated. Maria had heard her say: 'No, you would degrade yourself' – and, with that, she had led Eunice indoors. I understood, of course, that my sister had been prevented from following Philip to the hotel. There was probably a serious quarrel in store for me. I went straight to the bedroom, expecting to find Eunice there, and prepared to brave the storm that might burst on me. There was a woman at

Eunice's end of the room, removing dresses from the wardrobe. I could only see her back, but it was impossible to mistake *that* figure – Miss Jillgall.

She laid the dresses on Eunice's bed, without taking the slightest notice of me. In significant silence I pointed to the door. She went on as coolly with her occupation as if the room had been, not mine but hers; I stepped up to her, and spoke plainly.

'You oblige me to remind you,' I said, 'that you are not in your own room.' There, I waited a little, and found that I had produced no effect. 'With every disposition,' I resumed, 'to make allowance for the disagreeable peculiarities of your character, I cannot consent to overlook an act of intrusion, committed by a Spy. Now, do you understand me?'

She looked round her. 'I see no third person here,' she said. 'May I ask if you mean me?'

'I mean you.'

'Will you be so good, Miss Helena, as to explain yourself?'

Moderation of language would have been thrown away on this woman. 'You followed me to the park,' I said. 'It was you who found me with Mr Dunboyne, and betrayed me to my sister. You are a Spy, and you know it. At this very moment you daren't look me in the face.'

Her insolence forced its way out of her at last. Let me record it – and repay it, when the time comes.

'Quite true,' she replied. 'If I ventured to look you in the face, I am afraid I might forget myself. I have always been brought up like a lady, and I wish to show it even in the company of such a wretch as you are. There is not one word of truth in what you have said of me. I went to the hotel to find Mr Dunboyne. Ah, you may sneer! I haven't got your good looks – and a vile use you have made of them. My object was to recall that base young man to his duty to my dear charming injured Euneece. The hotel servant told me that Mr Dunboyne had gone out. Oh, I had the means of persuasion in my pocket! The man directed me to the park, as he had already directed Mr Dunboyne. It was only when I had found the place, that I heard some one behind me. Poor innocent

Euneece had followed me to the hotel, and had got her directions, as I had got mine. God knows how hard I tried to persuade her to go back, and how horribly frightened I was – No! I won't distress myself by saying a word more. It would be too humiliating to let *you* see an honest woman in tears. Your sister has a spirit of her own, thank God! She won't inhabit the same room with you; she never desires to see your false face again. I take the poor soul's dresses and things away – and as a religious person I wait, confidently wait, for the judgment that will fall on you!'

She caught up the dresses all together; some of them were in her arms, some of them fell on her shoulders, and one of them towered over her head. Smothered in gowns, she bounced out of the room like a walking milliner's shop. I have to thank the wretched old creature for a moment of genuine amusement, at a time of devouring anxiety. The meanest insect, they say, has its use in this world – and why not Miss Jillgall?

In half an hour more, an unexpected event raised my spirits. I heard from Philip.

On his return to the hotel he had found a telegram waiting for him. Mr Dunboyne the elder had arrived in London; and Philip had arranged to join his father by the next train. He sent me the address, and begged that I would write and tell him my news from home by the next day's post.

Welcome, thrice welcome to Mr Dunboyne the elder! If Philip can manage, under my advice, to place me favourably in the estimation of this rich old man, his presence and authority may do for us what we cannot do for ourselves. Here is surely an influence to which my father must submit, no matter how unreasonable or how angry he may be when he hears what has happened. I begin already to feel hopeful of the future.

# CHAPTER XXX

### EUNICE'S DIARY

Through the day, and through the night, I feel a misery that never leaves me – I mean the misery of fear.

I am trying to find out some harmless means of employing myself, which will keep evil remembrances from me. If I don't succeed, my fear tells me what will happen. I shall be in danger of going mad

I dare not confide in any living creature. I don't know what other persons might think of me, or how soon I might find myself perhaps in an asylum. In this helpless condition, doubt and fright seem to be driving me back to my Journal. I wonder whether I shall find harmless employment here.

I have heard of old people losing their memories. What would I not give to be old! I remember! oh, how I remember! One day after another I see Philip, I see Helena, as I first saw them when I was among the trees in the park. My sweetheart's arms, that once held me, hold my sister now. She kisses him, kisses him, kisses him.

Is there no way of making myself see something else? I want to get back to remembrances that don't burn in my head, and tear at my heart. How is it to be done?

I have tried books – no! I have tried going out to look at the shops – no! I have tried saying my prayers – no! And now I am making my last effort; trying my pen. My black letters fall from it, and take their places on the white paper. Will my black letters help me? Where can I find something consoling to write down? Where? Where?

Selina – poor Selina, so fond of me, so sorry for me. When I was happy, she was happy too. It was always amusing to hear her talk. Oh, my memory, be good to me! Save me from Philip and Helena. I want to remember the pleasant days when my kind little friend and I used to gossip in the garden.

No, the days in the garden won't come back. What else can I think of?

      \*     \*     \*     \*     \*

The recollections that I try to encourage keep away from me. The other recollections that I dread, come crowding back. Still Philip! Still Helena!

But Selina mixes herself up with them. Let me try again if I can think of Selina.

How delightfully good to me and patient with me she was, on our dismal way home from the park! And how affectionately she excused herself for not having warned me of it, when she first suspected that my own sister and my worst enemy were one and the same!

'I know I was wrong, my dear, to let my love and pity close my lips. But remember how happy you were at the time. The thought of making you miserable was more than I could endure – I am so fond of you! Yes; I began to suspect them, on the day when they first met at the station. And, I am afraid, I thought it just likely that you might be as cunning as I was, and have noticed them too.'

Oh, how ignorant she must have been of my true thoughts and feelings! How strangely people seem to misunderstand their dearest friends! Knowing, as I did, that I could never love any man but Philip, could I be wicked enough to suppose that Philip would love any woman but me?

I explained to Selina how he had spoken to me, when we were walking together on the bank of the river. Shall I ever forget those exquisite words? 'I wish I was a better man, Eunice; I wish I was good enough to be worthy of you.' I asked Selina if she thought he was deceiving me when he said that. She comforted me by owning that he must have been in earnest, at the time – and then she distressed me by giving the reason why.

'My love, you must have innocently said something to him, when you and he were alone, which touched his conscience (when he *had* a conscience), and made him ashamed of himself. Ah, you were too fond of him to see how he changed for the worse, when your vile sister joined you, and took possession of him again! It made my heart ache to see you so unsuspicious of them. You asked me, my poor dear, if they had quarrelled – you believed they were tired of walking by the river, when it was you they were tired of – and you wondered why Helena took him to see the school. My child! she was the leading spirit at the school, and you were nobody. Her vanity saw the chance of making him compare you at a disadvantage with your clever sister. I declare, Euneece, I lose my head if I only think of it! All the strong points in my character seem to slip away from me. Would you believe it? – I have neglected that sweet infant at the cottage; I have even let Mrs Molly have her baby back again. If I had the making of the laws, Philip Dunboyne and Helena Gracedieu should be hanged together on the same gallows. I see I shock you. Don't let us talk of it! Oh, don't let us talk of it!'

And here I am writing of it! What I had determined not to do, is what I have done. Am I losing my senses already? The very names that I was most anxious to keep out of my memory, stare me in the face in the lines that I have just written. Philip again! Helena again!

*     *     *     *     *

Another day; and something new that must and will be remembered, shrink from it as I may. This afternoon, I met Helena on the stairs.

She stopped, and eyed me with a wicked smile; she held out her hand. 'We are likely to meet often, while we are in the same house,' she said; 'hadn't we better consult appearances, and pretend to be as fond of each other as ever?'

I took no notice of her hand; I took no notice of her shameless proposal. She tried again: 'After all, it isn't my fault if Philip likes me better than he likes you. Don't you see that?' I still refused to speak to her. She still persisted. 'How black you look, Eunice! Are you sorry you didn't kill me, when you had your hands on my throat?'

I said: 'Yes.'

She laughed, and left me. I was obliged to sit down on the stair – I trembled so. My own reply frightened me. I tried to find out why I had said Yes. I don't remember being conscious of meaning anything. It was as if somebody else had said Yes –

not I. Perhaps I was provoked and the word escaped me before I could stop it. Could I have stopped it? I don't know.

*     *     *     *     *

Another sleepness night. Did I pass the miserable hours in writing letters to Philip, and then tearing them up? Or did I only fancy that I wrote to him? I have just looked at the fireplace, the torn paper in it tells me that I did write. Why did I destroy my letters? I might have sent one of them to Philip. After what has happened? Oh, no! no!

Having been many days away from the Girls' Scripture Class, it seemed to be possible that going back to the school and the teaching might help me to escape from myself.

Nothing succeeds with me. I found it impossible to instruct the girls as usual; their stupidity soon reached the limit of my patience — suffocated me with rage. One of them, a poor, fat, feeble creature, began to cry when I scolded her. I looked with envy at the tears rolling over her big round cheeks. If I could only cry, I might perhaps bear my hard fate with submission

I walked towards home by a roundabout way; feeling as if want of sleep was killing me by inches.

In the High Street, I saw Helena; she was posting a letter, and was not aware that I was near her. Leaving the post-office, she crossed the street, and narrowly escaped being run over. Suppose the threatened accident had really taken place — how should I have felt, if it had ended fatally? What a fool I am to be putting questions to myself about things that have not happened!

The walking tired me; I went straight home.

Before I could ring the bell, the house door opened, and the doctor came out. He stopped to speak to me. While I had been away (he said), something had happened at home (he neither knew nor wished to know what) which had thrown my father into a state of violent agitation. The doctor had administered composing medicine. 'My patient is asleep now,' he told me; 'but remember what I said to you the last time we met; a longer rest than any doctor's prescription can give him is what he wants. You are not looking well yourself my dear. What is the matter?'

I told him of my wretched restless nights; and asked if I might take some of the composing medicine which he had given to my father. He forbade me to touch a drop of it. 'What is physic for your father, you foolish child, is not physic for a young creature like you,' he said. 'Count a thousand, if you can't sleep to-night, or turn your pillow. I wish you pleasant dreams.' He went away, amused at his own humour.

I found Selina waiting to speak with me, on the subject of poor Papa.

She had been startled on hearing his voice, loud in anger. In the fear that something serious had happened, she left her room to make inquiries, and saw Helena on the landing of the flight of stairs beneath, leaving the study. After waiting till my sister was out of the way, Selina ventured to present herself at the study door, and to ask if she could be of any use. My father, walking excitedly up and down the room, declared that both his daughters had behaved infamously, and that he would not suffer them to speak to him again until they had come to their senses, on the subject of Mr Dunboyne. He would enter into no further explanation; and he had ordered, rather than requested, Selina to leave him. Having obeyed, she tried next to find me, and had just looked into the dining-room to see if I was there, when she was frightened by the sound of a fall in the room above – that is to say, in the study. Running upstairs again, she had found him insensible on the floor, and had sent for the doctor.

'And mind this,' Selina continued, 'the person who has done the mischief, is the person whom I saw leaving the study. What your unnatural sister said to provoke her father——'

'That your unnatural sister will tell you herself,' Helena's voice added. She had opened the door, while we were too much absorbed in our talk to hear her.

Selina attempted to leave the room. I caught her by the hand, and held her back. I was afraid of what I might do if she left me by myself. Never have I felt anything like the rage that tortured me, when I saw Helena looking at us with the same wicked smile on her lips that had insulted me when we met on the stairs.

'Have *we* anything to be ashamed of?' I said to Selina. 'Stay where you are.'

'You may be of some use, Miss Jillgall, if you stay,' my sister suggested. 'Eunice seems to be trembling. Is she angry, or is she ill?'

The sting of this was in the tone of her voice. It was the hardest thing I ever had to do in my life – but I did succeed in controlling myself.

'Go on with what you have to say,' I answered, 'and don't notice me.'

'You are not very polite, my dear, but I can make allowances. Oh, come! come! putting up your hands to stop your ears is too childish. You would do better to express regret for having misled your father. Yes! you did mislead him. Only a few days since, you left him to suppose that you were engaged to Philip. It became my duty, after that, to open his eyes to the truth; and if I unhappily provoked him, it was your fault. I was strictly careful in the language I used. I said: "Dear father, you have been misinformed on a very serious subject. The only marriage engagement for which your kind sanction is requested, is *my* engagement. *I* have consented to become Mrs Philip Dunboyne."'

'Stop!' I said.

'Why am I to stop?'

'Because I have something to say. You and I are looking at each other. Does my face tell you what is passing in my mind?'

'Your face seems to be paler than usual,' she answered – 'that's all.'

'No.' I said; 'that is not all. The devil that possessed me, when I discovered you with Philip, is not cast out of me yet. Silence the sneering devil that is in you, or we may both live to regret it.'

Whether I did or did not frighten her, I cannot say. This only I know – she turned away silently to the door, and went out.

I dropped on the sofa. That horrid hungering for revenge, which I felt for the first time when I knew how Helena had

wronged me, began to degrade and tempt me again. In the
effort to get away from this new evil self of mine, I tried to find
sympathy in Selina, and called to her to come and sit by me.
She seemed to be startled when I looked at her, but she
recovered herself, and came to me, and took my hand.

'I wish I could comfort you!' she said, in her kind simple
way.

'Keep my hand in your hand,' I told her; 'I am drowning in
dark water – and I have nothing to hold by but you.'

'Oh, my darling, don't talk in that way!'

'Good Selina! dear Selina! You shall talk to me. Say
something harmless – tell me a melancholy story – try to make
me cry.'

My poor little friend looked sadly bewildered.

'I'm more likely to cry myself,' she said. 'This is so heartbreaking – I almost wish I was back in the time, before you
came home, the time when your detestable sister first showed
how she hated me. I was happy, meanly happy, in the spiteful
enjoyment of provoking her. Oh, Euneece, I shall never
recover my spirits again! All the pity in the world would not be
pity enough for *you*. So hardly treated! so young! so forlorn!
Your good father too ill to help you; your poor mother——'

I interrupted her; she had interested me in something better
than my own wretched self. I asked directly if she had known
my mother.

'My dear child, I never even saw her!'

'Has my father never spoken to you about her?'

'Only once, when I asked him how long she had been dead.
He told me you lost her while you were an infant, and he told
me no more. I was looking at her portrait in the study, only
yesterday. I think it must be a bad portrait; your mother's face
disappoints me.'

I had arrived at the same conclusion years since. But I shrank
from confessing it.

'At any rate,' Selina continued, 'you are not like her. Nobody
would ever guess that you were the child of that lady, with the
long slanting forehead and the restless look in her eyes.

What Selina had said of me and my mother's portrait, other

friends had said. There was nothing that I know of to interest me in hearing it repeated – and yet it set me pondering on the want of resemblance between my mother's face and mine, and wondering (not for the first time) what sort of woman my mother was. When my father speaks of her, no words of praise that he can utter seem to be good enough for her. Oh, me, I wish I was a little more like my mother!

It began to get dark; Maria brought in the lamp. The sudden brightness of the flame struck my aching eyes, as if it had been a blow from a knife. I was obliged to hide my face in my handkerchief. Compassionate Selina entreated me to go to bed. 'Rest your poor eyes, my child, and your weary head – and try at least to get some sleep.' She found me very docile; I kissed her, and said good-night. I had my own idea.

When all was quiet in the house, I stole out into the passage, and listened at the door of my father's room.

I heard his regular breathing, and opened the door and went in. The composing medicine, of which I was in search, was not on the table by his bedside. I found it in the cupboard – perhaps placed purposely out of his reach. They say that some physic is poison, if you take too much of it. The label on the bottle told me what the dose was. I dropped it into the medicine glass, and swallowed it, and went back to my father.

Very gently, so as not to wake him, I touched poor Papa's forehead with my lips. 'I must have some of your medicine,' I whispered to him; 'I want it, dear, as badly as you do.'

Then I returned to my own room – and lay down in bed, waiting to be composed.

## CHAPTER XXXI

### EUNICE'S DIARY

My restless nights are passed in Selina's room.

Her bed remains near the window. My bed has been placed opposite, near the door. Our night-light is hidden in a corner, so that the faint glow of it is all that we see. What trifles these are to write about! But they mix themselves up with what I am determined to set down in my Journal, and then to close the book for good and all.

I had not disturbed my little friend's enviable repose, either when I left our bedchamber, or when I returned to it. The night was quiet, and the stars were out. Nothing moved but the throbbing at my temples. The lights and shadows in our half-darkened room, which at other times suggest strange resemblances to my fancy, failed to disturb me now. I was in a darkness of my own making, having bound a handkerchief, cooled with water, over my hot eyes. There was nothing to interfere with the soothing influence of the dose that I had taken, if my father's medicine would only help me.

I began badly. The clock in the hall struck the quarter past the hour, the half-past, the three-quarters past, the new hour. Time was awake – and I was awake with Time.

It was such a trial to my patience that I thought of going back to my father's room, and taking a second dose of the medicine, no matter what the risk might be. On attempting to get up, I became aware of a change in me. There was a dull sensation in my limbs which seemed to bind them down on the bed. It was the strangest feeling. My will said, Get up – and my heavy limbs said, No.

I lay quite still, thinking desperate thoughts, and getting nearer and nearer to the end that I have been dreading for so many days past. Having been as well educated as most girls, my lessons in history had made me acquainted with assassination and murder. Horrors which I had recoiled from reading in past happy days, now returned to my memory; and, this time, they interested instead of revolting me. I counted the three first ways of killing as I happened to remember them, in my books of instruction: – a way by stabbing; a way by poison; a way in a bed, by suffocation with a pillow. On that dreadful night, I never once called to mind what I find myself remembering now – the harmless past time, when our friends used to say: 'Eunice is a good girl; we are all fond of Eunice.' Shall I ever be the same lovable creature again?

While I lay thinking, a strange thing happened. Philip, who had haunted me for days and nights together, vanished out of my thoughts. My memory of the love which had begun so brightly, and had ended to miserably, became a blank. Nothing was left but my own horrid visions of vengeance and death.

For a while, the strokes of the clock still reached my ears. But it was an effort to count them; I ended in letting them pass unheeded. Soon afterwards, the round of my thoughts began to circle slowly and more slowly. The strokes of the clock died out. The round of my thoughts stopped.

All this time, my eyes were still covered by the handkerchief which I had laid over them.

The darkness began to weigh on my spirits, and to fill me with distrust. I found myself suspecting that there was some change – perhaps an unearthly change – passing over the room. To remain blindfolded any longer was more than I could endure. I lifted my hand – without being conscious of the heavy sensation which, some time before, had laid my limbs helpless on the bed – I lifted my hand, and drew the handkerchief away from my eyes.

The faint glow of the night-light was extinguished.

But the room was not quite dark. There was a ghastly light trembling over it; like nothing that I have ever seen by day; like nothing that I have ever seen by night. I dimly discerned Selina's bed, and the frame of the window, and the curtains on either side of it – but not the starlight, and not the shadowy tops of the trees in the garden.

The light grew fainter and fainter; the objects in the room faded slowly away. Darkness came.

It may be a saying hard to believe – but, when I declare that I was not frightened, I am telling the truth. Whether the room was lit by awful light, or sunk in awful dark, I was equally interested in the expectation of what might happen next. I listened calmly for what I might hear: I waited calmly for what I might feel.

A touch came first. I felt it creeping on my face – like a little fluttering breeze. The sensation pleased me for awhile. Soon it grew colder, and colder, and colder, till it froze me.

'Oh, no more!' I cried out. 'You are killing me with an icy death!'

The dead-cold touches lingered a moment longer – and left me.

The first sound came.

It was the sound of a whisper on my pillow, close to my ear. My strange insensibility to fear remained undisturbed. The whisper was welcome, it kept me company in the dark room.

It said to me: 'Do you know who I am?'

I answered: 'No.'

It said: 'Who have you been thinking of this evening?'

I answered: 'My mother.'

The whisper said: 'I am your mother.'

'Oh, mother, command the light to come back! Show yourself to me!'

'No.'

'Why not?'

'My face was hidden when I passed from life to death. My face no mortal creature may see.'

'Oh, mother, touch me! Kiss me!'

'No.'

'Why not?'

'My touch is poison. My kiss is death.'

The sense of fear began to come to me now. I moved my head away on the pillow. The whisper followed my movement.

'Leave me,' I said. 'You are an Evil Spirit.'

The whisper answered: 'I am your mother.'

'You come to tempt me.'

'I come to harden your heart. Daughter of mine, whose blood is cool; daughter of mine, who tamely submits – you have loved. Is it true?'

'It is true.'

'A woman has lured him away to herself. A woman has had no mercy on you, or on him. Is it true?'

'It is true.'

'If she lives, what crime towards you will she commit next?'

'If she lives, she will marry him.'

'Will you let her live?'

'Never.'

'Have I hardened your heart against her?'

'Yes.'

'Will you kill her?'

'Show me how.'

There was a sudden silence. I was still left in the darkness; feeling nothing, hearing nothing. Even the consciousness that I was lying on my bed deserted me. I had no idea that I was in the bedroom; I had no knowledge of where I was.

The ghastly light that I had seen already dawned on me once more. I was no longer in my bed, no longer in my room, no longer in the house. Without wonder, without even a feeling of surprise, I looked round. The place was familiar to me. I was alone in the Museum of our town.

The light flowed along in front of me. I followed, from room to room in the Museum, where the light led.

First, through the picture gallery, hung with the works of modern masters. Then, through the room filled with specimens of stuffed animals. The lion and the tiger, the vulture of the Alps and the great albatross, looked like living creatures threatening me, in the supernatural light. I entered the third room, devoted to the exhibition of ancient armour, and the weapons of all nations. Here the light rose higher, and, leaving me in darkness where I stood, showed a collection of swords, daggers, and knives arranged on the wall in imitation of the form of a star.

The whisper sounded again, close at my ear. It echoed my own throught, when I called to mind the ways of killing which history had taught me. It said: 'Kill her with the knife.'

No. My heart failed me when I thought of the blood. I hid the dreadful weapons from my view. I cried out: 'Let me go! Let me go!'

Again, I was lost in darkness. Again, I had no knowledge in me of where I was. Again, after an interval, the light showed me the new place in which I stood.

I was alone in the burial ground of our parish church. The light led me on, among the graves, to the lonely corner in which the great yew tree stands; and, rising higher, revealed the solemn foliage, brightened by the fatal red fruit which hides in itself the seeds of death.

The whisper tempted me again. It followed again the train of my own thought. It said: 'Kill her by poison.'

No. Revenge by poison steals its way to its end. The base deceitfulness of Helena's crime against me seemed to call for a day of reckoning that hid itself under no disguise. I raised my cry to be delivered from the sight of the deadly tree. The changes which I have tried to describe, followed once more the confession of what I felt; the darkness was dispelled for the third time.

I was standing in Helena's room, looking at her as she lay asleep in her bed.

She was quite still now; but she must have been restless at some earlier time. The bed-clothes were disordered, her head had sunk so low, that the pillow rose high and vacant above her. There, coloured by a tender flush of sleep, was the face whose beauty put my poor face to shame. There, was the sister who had committed the worst of murders – the wretch who had killed in me all that made life worth having. While that thought was in my mind, I heard the whisper again. 'Kill her openly,' the tempting mother said. 'Kill her daringly. Faint heart, do you still want courage? Rouse your spirit; look! see yourself in the act!'

The temptation took a form which now tried me for the first time.

As if a mirror had reflected the scene, I saw myself standing by the bedside, with the pillow that was to smother the sleeper in my hands. I heard the whipering voice telling me how to speak the words that warned and condemned her: 'Wake! you who have taken him from me! Wake! and meet your doom.'

I saw her start up in bed. The sudden movement disordered the nightdress over her bosom, and showed the miniature portrait of a man, hung round her neck.

The man was Philip. The likeness was looking at me.

So dear, so lovely – those eyes that had once been the light of my heart, mourned for me and judged me now. They saw the guilty thought that polluted me; they brought me to my knees, imploring him to help me back to my better self: 'One last mercy, dear, to comfort me under the loss of you. Let the love that was once my life, be my good angel still. Save me, Philip, even though you forsake me – save me from myself!'

*    *    *    *    *

There was a sudden cry.

The agony of it pierced my brain – drove away the ghastly light – silenced the tempting whispers. I came to myself. I saw – and not in a dream.

Helena *had* started up in her bed. That cry of terror, at the sight of me in her room at night, *had* burst from her lips. The miniature of Philip hung round her neck, a visible reality. Though my head was dizzy, though my heart was sinking, I had not lost my senses yet. All that the night lamp could show me, I still saw; and I heard the sound, faintly, when the door of the bedchamber was opened. Alarmed by that piercing cry, my father came hurrying into the room.

Not a word passed between us three. The whispers that I had heard were wicked; the thoughts that had been in my mind were vile. Had they left some poison in the air of the room which killed the words on our lips?

My father looked at Helena. With a trembling hand, she pointed to me. He put his arm round me, and held me up. I remember his leading me away – and I remember nothing more.

My last words are written. I lock up this journal of misery – never, I hope and pray, to open it again.

# SECOND PERIOD (continued)

## EVENTS IN THE FAMILY, RELATED BY THE GOVERNOR

### CHAPTER XXXII

#### THE MIDDLE-AGED LADY

In the year 1870, I found myself compelled to submit to the demands of two hard task-masters. Advancing age and failing health reminded the Governor of the Prison of his duty to his successor, in one unanswerable word – Resign.

When they have employed us and interested us, for the greater part of our lives, we bid farewell to our duties – even to the gloomy duties of a prison – with a sense of regret. My view of the future presented a vacant prospect indeed, when I looked at my idle life to come, and wondered what I should do with it. Loose on the world – at my age! – I drifted into domestic refuge, under the care of my two dear and good sons. After a while (never mind how long a while) I began to grow restless under the heavy burden of idleness. Having nothing else to complain of, I complained of my health, and consulted a doctor. That sagacious man hit on the right way of getting rid of me – he recommended travelling.

This was unexpected advice. After some hesitation, I accepted it reluctantly.

The instincts of age recoil from making new acquaintances, contemplating new places, and adopting new habits. Besides, I hate railway travelling. However, I contrived to get as far as Italy, and stopped to rest at Florence. Here, I found pictures by the old masters that I could really enjoy, a public park that I could honestly admire, and an excellent friend and colleague of former days; once chaplain to the prison, now clergyman in charge of the English Church. We met in the gallery of the Pitti Palace; and he recognized me immediately. I was pleased to find that the lapse of years had made so little difference in my personal appearance.

The traveller who advances as far as Florence, and does not go on to Rome, must be regardless indeed of the opinions of his friends. Let me not attempt to conceal it – I am that insensible traveller. Over and over again, I said to myself: 'Rome must be done;' and over and over again, I put off doing it. To own the truth, the fascinations of Florence, aided by the society of my friend, laid so strong a hold on me that I believe I should have ended my days in the delightful Italian city, but for the dangerous illness of one of my sons. This misfortune hurried me back to England, in dread, every step of the way, of finding that I had arrived too late. The journey (thank God) proved to have been taken without need. My son was no longer in danger, when I reached London in the year 1875.

At that date, I was near enough to the customary limit of human life to feel the necessity of rest and quiet. In other words, my days of travel had come to their end.

Having established myself in my own country, I did not forget to let old friends know where they might find me. Among those to whom I wrote was another colleague of past years, who still held his medical appointment in the prison. When I received the doctor's reply, it enclosed a letter directed to me at my old quarters in the Governor's rooms. Who could possibly have sent a letter to an address which I had left five years since? My correspondent proved to be no less a person than the Congregational Minister – the friend whom I had estranged from me by the tone in which I had written to him, on the long-past occasion of his wife's death.

It was a distressing letter to read. I beg permission to give only the substance of it in this place.

Entreating me, with touching expressions of humility and sorrow, to forgive his long silence, the writer appealed to my friendly remembrance of him. He was in sore need of counsel, under serious difficulties; and I was the only person to whom he could apply for help. In the disordered state of his health at that time, he ventured to hope that I would visit him at his present place of abode, and would let him have the happiness of seeing me as speedily as possible. He concluded with this extraordinary postscript:

'When you see my daughters, say nothing to either of them which relates, in any way, to the subject of their ages. You shall hear why when we meet.'

The reading of this letter naturally reminded me of the claims which my friend's noble conduct had established on my admiration and respect, at the past time when we met in the prison. I could not hesitate to grant his request – strangely as it was expressed, and doubtful as the prospect appeared to be of my answering the expectations which he had founded on the renewal of our intercourse. Answering his letter by telegraph, I promised to be with him on the next day.

On arriving at the station, I found that I was the only traveller, by a first-class carriage, who left the train. A young lady, remarkable by her good looks and good dressing, seemed to have noticed this trifling circumstance. She approached me with a ready smile. 'I believe I am speaking to my father's friend,' she said; 'my name is Helena Gracedieu.'

Here was one of the Minister's two 'daughters'; and that one of the two – as I discovered the moment I shook hands with her – who was my friend's own child. Miss Helena recalled to me her mother's face, infinitely improved by youth and health, and by a natural beauty which that cruel and deceitful woman could never have possessed. The slanting forehead and the shifting flashing eyes, that I recollected in the parent, were reproduced (slightly reproduced, I ought to say) in the child. As for the other features, I had never seen a more beautiful nose and mouth, or a more delicately-shaped outline, than was presented by the lower part of the face. But Miss Helena somehow failed to charm me. I doubt if I should have fallen in love with her, even in the days when I was a foolish young man.

The first question that I put, as we drove from the station to the house, related naturally to her father.

'He is very ill,' she began; 'I am afraid you must prepare yourself to see a sad change. Nerves. The mischief first showed itself, the doctor tells us, in derangement of his nervous system.

He has been, I regret to tell you, obstinate in refusing to give up his preaching and pastoral work. He ought to have tried rest at the seaside. Things have gone on from bad to worse. Last Sunday, at the beginning of his sermon, he broke down. Very, very sad, is it not? The doctor says that precious time has been lost, and he must make up his mind to resign his charge. He won't hear of it. You are his old friend. Please try to persuade him.'

Fluently spoken; the words well chosen; the melodious voice reminding me of the late Mrs Gracedieu's advantages in that respect; little sighs judiciously thrown in here and there, just at the right places; everything, let me own, that could present a dutiful daughter as a pattern of propriety – and nothing, let me add, that could produce an impression on my insensible temperament. If I had not been too discreet to rush at a hasty conclusion, I might have been inclined to say: her mother's child, every inch of her!

The interest which I was still able to feel in my friend's domestic affairs centred in the daughter whom he had adopted.

In her infancy I had seen the child, and liked her; I was the one person living (since the death of Mrs Gracedieu) who knew how the Minister had concealed the sad secret of her parentage; and I wanted to discover if the hereditary taint had begun to show itself in the innocent offspring of the murderess. Just as I was considering how I might harmlessly speak of Miss Helena's 'sister', Miss Helena herself introduced the subject.

'May I ask,' she resumed, 'if you were disappointed when you found nobody but me to meet you at our station?'

Here was an opportunity of paying her a compliment, if I had been a younger man, or if she had produced a favourable impression on me. As it was, I hit – if I may praise myself – on an ingenious compromise.

'What excuse could I have,' I asked, 'for feeling disappointed?'

'Well, I hear you are an official personage – I ought to say, perhaps, retired official personage. We might have received you more respectfully, if *both* my father's daughters had been present at the station. It's not my fault that my sister was not with me.'

The tone in which she said this strengthened my prejudice against her. It told me that the two girls were living together on not very friendly terms; and it suggested – justly or unjustly I could not then decide – that Miss Helena was to blame.

'Perhaps your sister is ill?' I said.

'My sister is away from home.'

'Surely, Miss Helena, that is a good reason for her not coming to meet me?'

'I beg your pardon – it is a bad reason. She has been sent away for the recovery of her health – and the loss of her health is entirely her own fault.'

What did this matter to me? I decided on dropping the subject. My memory reverted, however, to past occasions on which the loss of *my* health had been entirely my own fault. There was something in these personal recollections, which encouraged my perverse tendency to sympathize with a young lady to whom I had not yet been introduced. The young lady's sister appeared to be discouraged by my silence. She said: 'I hope you don't think the worse of me for what I have just mentioned?'

'Certainly not.'

'Perhaps, you will fail to see any need of my speaking of my sister at all? Will you kindly listen, if I try to explain myself?'

'With pleasure.'

She slyly set the best construction on my perfectly commonplace reply.

'Thank you,' she said. 'The fact is, my father (I can't imagine why) wishes you to see my sister as well as me. He has written to the farmhouse at which she is now staying, to tell her to come home to-morrow. It is possible – if your kindness offers me an opportunity – that I may ask to be guided by your experience, in a little matter which interests me. My sister is rash, and reckless, and has a terrible temper. I should be very sorry indeed if you were induced to form an unfavourable opinion of me, from anything you might notice if you see us together. You understand me, I hope?'

'I quite understand you.'

To set me against her sister, in her own private interests –

there, as I felt sure, was the motive under which she was acting. As hard as her mother, as selfish as her mother, and, judging from those two bad qualities, probaby as cruel as her mother. That was how I understood Miss Helena Gracedieu, when our carriage drew up at her father's house.

A middle-aged lady was on the door step, when we arrived, just ringing the bell. She looked round at us both; being evidently as complete a stranger to my fair companion as she was to me. When the servant opened the door, she said:

'Is Miss Jillgall at home?'

At the sound of that odd name, Miss Helena tossed her head disdainfully. She took no sort of notice of the stranger-lady who was at the door of her father's house. This young person's contempt for Miss Jillgall appeared to extend to Miss Jillgall's friends.

In the meantime, the servant's answer was: 'Not at home.'

The middle-aged lady said: 'Do you expect her back soon?'

'Yes, ma'am.'

'I will call again, later in the day.'

'What name, if you please?'

The lady stole another look at me, before she replied.

'Never mind the name,' she said – and walked away.


## CHAPTER XXXIII

### THE MINISTER'S MISFORTUNE

'Do you know that lady?' Miss Helena asked, as we entered the house.

'She is a perfect stranger to me,' I answered.

'Are you sure you have not forgotten her?'

'Why do you think I have forgotten her?'

'Because she evidently remembered you.'

The lady had no doubt looked at me twice. If this meant that my face was familiar to her, I could only repeat what I had already said. Never, to my knowledge, had I seen her before.

Leading the way upstairs, Miss Helena apologised for taking me into her father's bedroom. 'He is able to sit up in an arm-chair,' she said; 'and he might do more, I think, if he would exert himself. He won't exert himself. Very sad. Would you like to look at your room, before you see my father? It is quite ready for you. We hope' — she favoured me with a fascinating smile, devoted to winning my heart when her interests required it — 'we hope you will pay us a long visit; we look on you as one of ourselves.'

I thanked her, and said I would shake hands with my old friend before I went to my room. We parted at the bedroom door.

It is out of my power to describe the shock that overpowered me when I first saw the Minister again, after the long interval of time that had separated us. Nothing that his daughter said, nothing that I myself anticipated, had prepared me for that lamentable change. For the moment, I was not sufficiently master of myself to be able to speak to him. He added to my embarrassment by the humility of his manner, and the formal elaboration of his apologies.

'I feel painfully that I have taken a liberty with you,' he said, 'after the long estrangement between us — for which my want of Christian forbearance is to blame. Forgive it, sir, and forget it. I hope to show that necessity justifies my presumption, in subjecting you to a wearisome journey for my sake.'

Beginning to recover myself, I begged that he would make no more excuses. My interruption seemed to confuse him.

'I wished to say,' he went on, 'that you are the one man who can understand me. There is my only reason for asking to see you, and looking forward as I do to your advice. You remember the night — or was it the day? — before that miserable woman was hanged? You were the only person present when I agreed to adopt the poor little creature, stained already (one may say) by its mother's infamy. I think your wisdom foresaw what a terrible responsibility I was undertaking; you tried to prevent it. Well! well! you have been in my confidence — you only. Mind! nobody in this house knows that one of the two girls is not really my daughter. Pray stop me, if you find me wandering from the point. My wish is to show that you are the only man I can open my heart to. She——' He paused, as if in search of a lost idea, and left the sentence uncompleted. 'Yes,' he went on, 'I was thinking of my adopted child. Did I ever tell you that I baptized her myself? and by a good Scripture name too – Eunice. Ah, sir, that little helpless baby is a grown-up girl now; of an age to inspire love, and to feel love. I blush to acknowledge it; I have behaved with a want of self-control, with a cowardly weakness——. No! I am, indeed, wandering this time. I ought to have told you first that I have been brought face to face with the possibility of Eunice's marriage. And, to make it worse still, I can't help liking the young man. He comes of a good family – excellent manners, highly educated, plenty of money, a gentleman in every sense of the word. And poor little Eunice is so fond of him! Isn't it dreadful to be obliged to check her dearly-loved Philip? The young gentleman's name is Philip. Do you like the name? I say I am obliged to check her sweetheart in the rudest manner, when all he wants to do is to ask me modestly for my sweet Eunice's hand. Oh, what have I not suffered, without a word of sympathy to comfort me, before I had courage enough to write to you! Shall I make a dreadful confession? If my religious convictions had not stood in my way, I believe I should have committed suicide. Put yourself in my place. Try to see yourself shrinking from a necessary explanation, when the happiness of a harmless girl – so dutiful, so affectionate – depended on a word of kindness from your lips. And that word you are afraid to speak! Don't take offence, sir; I mean myself, not you. Why don't you say something?' he burst out fiercely, incapable of perceiving that he had allowed me no opportunity of speaking to him. 'Good God! don't you understand me, after all?'

The signs of mental confusion in his talk had so distressed me, that I had not been composed enough to feel sure of what he really meant, until he described himself as 'shrinking from a necessary explanation'. Hearing those words, my knowledge of the circumstances helped me; I realised what his situation really was.

'Compose yourself,' I said, 'I understand you at last.'

He had suddenly become distrustful.

'Prove it;' he muttered, with a furtive look at me. 'I want to be satisfied that you understand my position.'

'This is your position,' I told him. 'You are placed between two deplorable alternatives. If you tell this young gentleman that Miss Eunice's mother was a criminal hanged for murder, his family – even if he himself doesn't recoil from it – will unquestionably forbid the marriage; and your adopted daughter's happiness will be the sacrifice.'

'True!' he said. 'Frightfully true! Go on.'

'If, on the other hand, you sanction the marriage, and conceal the truth, you commit a deliberate act of deceit; and you leave the lives of the young couple at the mercy of a possible discovery, which might part husband and wife – cast a slur on their children – and break up the household.'

He shuddered while he listened to me. 'Come to the end of it,' he cried.

I had no more to say, and I was obliged to answer him to that effect.

'No more to say?' he replied. 'You have not told me yet what I most want to know.'

I did a rash thing; I asked what it was that he most wanted to know.

'Can't you see it for yourself?' he demanded indignantly. 'Suppose you were put between those two alternatives which you mentioned just now.'

'Well?'

'What would you do, sir, in my place? Would you own the disgraceful truth – before the marriage – or run the risk, and keep the horrid story to yourself?'

Either way, my reply might lead to serious consequences. I hesitated.

He threatened me with his poor feeble hand. It was only the anger of a moment; his humour changed to supplication. He reminded me piteously of bygone days: 'You used to be a kind-hearted man. Has age hardened you? Have you no pity left for your old friend? My poor heart is sadly in want of a word of wisdom, spoken kindly.'

Who could have resisted this? I took his hand: 'Be at ease, dear Minister. In your place I should run the risk, and keep that horrid story to myself.'

He sank back gently in his chair. 'Oh, the relief of it!' he said. 'How can I thank you as I ought for quieting my mind?'

I seized the opportunity of quieting his mind to good purpose by suggesting a change of subject. 'Let us have done with serious talk for the present,' I proposed. 'I have been an idle man for the last five years, and I want to tell you about my travels.'

His attention began to wander, he evidently felt no interest in my travels. 'Are you sure,' he asked anxiously, 'that we have said all we ought to say? No!' he cried, answering his own question. 'I believe I have forgotten something – I am certain I have forgotten something. Perhaps I mentioned it in the letter I wrote to you. Have you got my letter?'

I showed it to him. He read the letter, and gave it back to me with a heavy sigh. 'Not there!' he said despairingly. 'Not there!'

'Is the lost remembrance connected with anybody in the house?' I asked, trying to help him. 'Does it relate, by any chance, to one of the young ladies?'

'You wonderful man! Nothing escapes you. Yes; the thing I have forgotten concerns one of the girls. Stop! Let me get at it by myself. Surely it relates to Helena?' He hesitated; his face clouded over with an expression of anxious thought. 'Yes; it relates to Helena,' he repeated – 'but how?' His eyes filled with tears. 'I am ashamed of my weakness,' he said faintly. 'You don't know how dreadful it is to forget things in this way.'

The injury that his mind had sustained now assumed an aspect that was serious indeed. The subtle machinery which stimulates the memory, by means of the association of ideas, appeared to have lost its working power in the intellect of this unhappy man. I made the first suggestion that occurred to me, rather than add to his distress by remaining silent.

'If we talk of your daughter,' I said, 'the merest accident – a word spoken at random by you or me – may be all your memory wants to rouse it.'

He agreed eagerly to this: 'Yes! Yes! Let me begin. Helena

met you, I think, at the station. Of course, I remember that; it
only happened a few hours since. Well?' he went on, with a
change in his manner to parental pride, which it was pleasant to
see, 'did you think my daughter a fine girl? I hope Helena
didn't disappoint you?'

'Quite the contrary.' Having made that necessary reply, I saw
my way to keeping his mind occupied by a harmless subject. 'It
must, however, be owned,' I went on, 'that your daughter
surprised me.'

'In what way?'

'When she mentioned her name. Who could have supposed
that you – an inveterate enemy to the Roman Catholic Church
– would have christened your daughter by the name of a
Roman Catholic Saint?'

He listened to this with a smile. Had I happily blundered on
some association which his mind was still able to pursue?

'You happen to be wrong this time,' he said pleasantly, 'I
never gave my girl the name of Helena; and, what is more, I
never baptized her. You ought to know that. Years and years
ago, I wrote to tell you that my poor wife had made me a
proud and happy father. And surely I said that the child was
born while she was on a visit to her brother's rectory. Do you
remember the name of the place? I told you it was a remote
little village called—— Suppose we put *your* memory to a test?
Can you remember the name?' he asked, with a momentary
appearance of triumph showing itself, poor fellow, in his face.

After the time that had elapsed, the name had slipped my
memory. When I confessed this, he exulted over me, with an
unalloyed pleasure which it was cheering to see.

'*Your* memory is failing you now,' he said. 'The name is Long
Lanes. And what do you think my wife did – this is so
characteristic of her! – when I presented myself at her bedside.
Instead of speaking of our own baby, she reminded me of the
name that I had given to our adopted daughter when I baptized
the child. "You chose the ugliest name that a girl can have,"
she said. I begged her to remember that "Eunice" was a name
in Scripture. She persisted in spite of me. (What firmness of
character!) "I detest the name of Eunice!" she said; "and now

that I have a girl of my own, it's my turn to choose the name; I claim it as my right." She was beginning to get excited; I allowed her to have her own way, of course. "Only let me know," I said, "what the name is to be when you have thought of it." My dear sir, she had the name already, without thinking about it: "My baby shall be called by the name that is sweetest in my ears, the name of my dear lost mother." We had – what shall I call it? – a slight difference of opinion when I heard that the name was to be Helena. I really could *not* reconcile it to my conscience to baptize a child of mine by the name of a Popish saint. My wife's brother set things right between us. A worthy good man; he died not very long ago – I forget the date. Not to detain you any longer, the rector of Long Lanes baptized our daughter. That is how she comes by her un-English name; and so it happens that her birth is registered in a village which her father has never inhabited. I hope, sir, you think a little better of my memory now?'

I was afraid to tell him what I really did think.

He was not fifty years old yet; and he had just exhibited one of the sad symptoms which mark the broken memory of old age. Lead him back to the events of many years ago, and (as he had just proved to me) he could remember well and relate coherently. But let him attempt to recall circumstances which had only taken place a short time since, and forgetfulness and confusion presented the lamentable result, just as I have related it.

The effort that he had made, the agitation that he had undergone in talking to me, had confirmed my fears that he would overtask his wasted strength. He lay back in his chair. 'Let us go on with our conversation,' he murmured. 'We haven't recovered what I had forgotten, yet.' His eyes closed, and opened again languidly. 'There was something I wanted to recall,' he resumed, 'and you were helping me.' His weak voice died away; his weary eyes closed again. After waiting until there could be no doubt that he was resting peacefully in sleep, I left the room.

# CHAPTER XXXIV

### THE LIVELY OLD MAID

A perfect stranger to the interior of the house (seeing that my experience began and ended with the Minister's bedchamber), I descended the stairs, in the character of a guest in search of domestic information.

On my way down, I heard the door of a room on the ground floor open, and a woman's voice below, speaking in a hurry: 'My dear, I have not a moment to spare; my patients are waiting for me.' This was followed by a confidential communication, judging by the tone. 'Mind! not a word about me to that old gentleman!' Her patients were waiting for her – had I discovered a female doctor? And there was some old gentleman whom she was not willing to trust – surely I was not that much-injured man?

Reaching the hall just as the lady said her last words, I caught a glimpse of her face, and discovered the middle-aged stranger who had called on 'Miss Jillgall', and had promised to repeat her visit. A second lady was at the door, with her back to me, taking leave of her friend. Having said good-bye, she turned round – and we confronted each other.

I found her to be a little person, wiry and active; past the prime of life, and ugly enough to encourage prejudice, in persons who take a superficial view of their fellow-creatures. Looking impartially at the little sunken eyes which rested on me with a comical expression of embarrassment, I saw signs that said: There is some good here, under a disagreeable surface, if you can only find it.

She saluted me with a carefully-performed curtsey, and threw open the door of a room on the ground floor.

'Pray walk in, sir, and permit me to introduce myself. I am Mr Gracedieu's cousin – Miss Jillgall. Proud indeed to make the acquaintance of a gentleman distinguished in the service of his country – or perhaps I ought to say, in the service of the Law. The Governor offers hospitality to prisoners. And who introduces prisoners to board and lodging with the Governor? –

the Law. Beautiful weather for the time of year, is it not? May I ask – have you seen your room?'

The embarrassment which I had already noticed had extended by this time to her voice and her manner. She was evidently trying to talk herself into a state of confidence. It seemed but too probable that I was indeed the person mentioned by her prudent friend at the door.

Having acknowledged that I had not seen my room yet, my politeness attempted to add that there was no hurry. The wiry little lady was of the contrary opinion; she jumped out of her chair as if she had been shot out of it. 'Pray let me make myself useful. The dream of my life is to make myself useful to others; and to such a man as you – I consider myself honoured. Besides, I do enjoy running up and downstairs. This way, dear sir; this way to your room.'

She skipped up the stairs, and stopped on the first landing. 'Do you know, I am a timid person, though I may not look like it. Sometimes, curiosity gets the better of me – and then I grow bold. Did you notice a lady who was taking leave of me just now at the house door?'

I replied that I had seen the lady for a moment, but not for the first time. 'Just as I arrived here from the station,' I said, 'I found her paying a visit when you were not at home.'

'Yes – and do tell me one thing more.' My readiness in answering seemed to have inspired Miss Jillgall with confidence. I heard no more confessions of overpowering curiosity. 'Am I right,' she proceeded, 'in supposing that Miss Helena accompanied you, on your way here from the station?'

'Quite right.'

'Did she say anything particular, when she saw the lady asking for me at the door?'

'Miss Helena thought,' I said, 'that the lady recognized me as a person whom she had seen before.'

'And what did you think yourself?'

'I thought Miss Helena was wrong.'

'Very extraordinary!' With that remark Miss Jillgall dropped the subject. The meaning of her reiterated inquiries was now, as it seemed to me, clear enough. She was eager to discover how I could have inspired the distrust of me, expressed in the caution addressed to her by her friend.

When we reached the upper floor, she paused before the Minister's room.

'I believe many years have passed,' she said, 'since you last saw Mr Gracedieu. I am afraid you have found him a sadly changed man? You won't be angry with me, I hope, for asking more questions? I owe Mr Gracedieu a debt of gratitude which no devotion, on my part, can ever repay. You don't know what a favour I shall consider it, if you will tell me what you think of him. Did it seem to you that he was not quite himself? I don't mean in his looks, poor dear – I mean in his mind.'

There was true sorrow and sympathy in her face. I believe I should hardly have thought her ugly, if we had first met at that moment. Thus far, she had only amused me. I began really to like Miss Jillgall now.

'I must not conceal from you,' I replied, 'that the state of Mr Gracedieu's mind surprised and distressed me. But I ought also to tell you that I saw him perhaps at his worst. The subject on which he wished to speak with me would have agitated any man, in his state of health. He consulted me about his daughter's marriage.'

Miss Jillgall suddenly turned pale.

'His daughter's marriage?' she repeated. 'Oh, you frighten me!'

'Why should I frighten you?'

She seemed to find some difficulty in expressing herself. 'I hardly know how to put it, sir. You will excuse me (won't you?) if I say what I feel. You have influence – not the sort of influence that finds places for people who don't deserve them, and gets mentioned in the newspapers – I only mean influence over Mr Gracedieu. That's what frightens me. How do I know ——? Oh, dear, I'm asking another question! Allow me, for once, to be plain and positive. I'm afraid, sir, you have encouraged the Minister to consent to Helena's marriage.'

'Pardon me,' I answered, 'you mean Eunice's marriage.'

'No, sir! Helena.'

'No, Madam! Eunice.'

'What does he mean?' said Miss Jillgall to herself.

I heard her. 'This is what I mean,' I asserted, in my most positive manner. 'The only subject on which the Minister has consulted me is Miss Eunice's marriage.'

My tone left her no alternative but to believe me. She looked not only bewildered but alarmed. 'Oh, poor man, has he lost himself in such a dreadful way as that?' She said to herself. 'I daren't believe it.' She turned to me. 'You have been talking with him for some time. Please try to remember. While Mr Gracedieu was speaking of Euneece, did he say nothing of Helena's infamous conduct to her sister?'

Not the slightest hint of any such thing, I assured her, had reached my ears.

'Then,' she cried, 'I can tell you what he has forgotten! We kept as much of that miserable story to ourselves as we could, in mercy to him. Besides, he was always fondest of Euneece; she would live in his memory when he had forgotten the other – the wretch, the traitress, the plotter, the fiend!' Miss Jillgall's good manners slipped, as it were, from under her; she clenched her fists as a final means of expressing her sentiments. 'The wretched English language isn't half strong enough for me,' she declared with a look of fury.

I took a liberty. 'May I ask what Miss Helena has done?' I said.

'*May* you ask? Oh, Heavens! you must ask, you shall ask. Mr Governor, if your eyes are not opened to Helena's true character, I can tell you what she will do; she will deceive you into taking her part. Do you think she went to the station out of regard for the great man? Pooh! she went with an eye to her own interests; and she means to make the great man useful. Thank God, I can stop that!'

She checked herself there, and looked suspiciously at the door of Mr Gracedieu's room.

'In the interest of our conversation,' she whispered, 'we have not given a thought to the place we have been talking in. Do you think the Minister has heard us?'

'Not if he is asleep – as I left him.'

Miss Jillgall shook her head ominously. 'The safe way is this way,' she said. 'Come with me.'

## CHAPTER XXXV

### THE FUTURE LOOKS GLOOMY

My ever-helpful guide led me to my room – well out of Mr Gracedieu's hearing, if he happened to be awake – at the other end of the passage. Having opened the door, she paused on the threshold. The decrees of that merciless English despot, Propriety, claimed her for their own. 'Oh, dear!' she said to herself, 'ought I to go in?'

My interest as a man (and, what is more, an old man) in the coming disclosure, was too serious to be trifled with in this way. I took her arm, and led her into my room as if I was at a dinner-party, leading her to the table. Is it the good or the evil fortune of mortals that the comic side of life, and the serious side of life, are perpetually in collision with each other? We burst out laughing, at a moment of grave importance to us both. Perfectly inappropriate, and perfectly natural. But we were neither of us philosophers, and we were ashamed of our own merriment the moment it had ceased.

'When you hear what I have to tell you,' Miss Jillgall began, 'I hope you will think as I do. What has slipped Mr Gracedieu's memory, it may be safer to say – for he is sometimes irritable, poor dear – where he won't know anything about it.'

With that she told the lamentable story of the desertion of Eunice.

In silence I listened, from first to last. How could I trust myself to speak, as I must have spoken, in the presence of a woman? The cruel injury inflicted on the poor girl, who had interested and touched me in the first innocent year of her life – who had grown to womanhood to be the victim of two wretches, both trusted by her, both bound to her by the sacred debt of love – so fired my temper that I longed to be within reach of the man, with a horsewhip in my hand. Seeing in my face, as I suppose, what was passing in my mind, Miss Jillgall expressed sympathy and admiration in her own quaint way: 'Ah, I like to see you so angry! It's grand to know that a man who has governed prisoners has got such a pitying heart. Let me tell you one thing, sir. You will be more angry than ever, when you see my sweet girl to-morrow. And mind this – it is Helena's devouring vanity, Helena's wicked jealousy of her sister's good fortune, that has done the mischief. Don't be too hard on Philip? I do believe, if the truth was told, he is ashamed of himself.'

I felt inclined to be harder on Philip than ever. 'Where is he?' I asked.

Miss Jillgall started. 'Oh, Mr Governor, don't show the severe side of yourself, after the pretty compliment I have just paid to you! What a masterful voice! and what eyes, dear sir; what terrifying eyes! I feel as if I was one of your prisoners, and had misbehaved myself,'

I repeated my question with improvement, I hope, in my looks and tones: 'Don't think me obstinate, my dear lady. I only want to know if he is in this town.'

Miss Jillgall seemed to take a curious pleasure in disappointing me; she had not forgotten my unfortunate abruptness of look and manner. 'You won't find him here,' she said.

'Perhaps he has left England?'

'If you must know, sir, he is in London – with Mr Dunboyne.'

The name startled me.

In a moment more it recalled to my memory a remarkable letter, addressed to me many years ago, which will be found in my introductory narrative. The writer – an Irish gentleman, named Dunboyne – confided to me that his marriage had associated him with the murderess, who had then been recently executed, as brother-in-law to that infamous woman. This circumstance he had naturally kept a secret from everyone, including his son, then a boy. I alone was made an exception to the general rule, because I alone could tell him what had become of the poor little girl, who in spite of the disgraceful end of her mother was still his niece. If the child had not been provided for, he felt it his duty to take charge of her education, and to watch over her prospects in the future. Such had been his object in writing to me; and such was the substance of his letter. I had merely informed him, in reply, that his kind intentions had been anticipated, and that the child's prosperous future was assured.

Miss Jillgall's keen observation noticed the impression that had been produced upon me. 'Mr Dunboyne's name seems to surprise you,' she said.

'This is the first time I have heard you mention it,' I answered.

She looked as if she could hardly believe me. 'Surely you must have heard the name,' she said, 'when I told you about poor Euneece?'

'No.'

'Well, then, Mr Gracedieu must have mentioned it?'

'No.'

This second reply in the negative irritated her.

'At any rate,' she said sharply, 'you appeared to know Mr Dunboyne's name, just now.'

'Certainly!'

'And yet,' she persisted, 'the name seemed to come upon you as a surprise. I don't understand it. If I have mentioned Philip's name once, I have mentioned it a dozen times.'

We were completely at cross-purposes. She had taken something for granted which was an unfathomable mystery to me.

'Well,' I objected, 'if you did mention his name a dozen times – excuse me for asking the question – what then?'

'Good Heavens!' cried Miss Jillgall, 'do you mean to say you never guessed that Philip was Mr Dunboyne's son?'

I was petrified.

His son! Dunboyne's son! How could I have guessed it?

At a later time only, the good little creature who had so innocently deceived me, remembered that the mischief might have been wrought by the force of habit. While he had still a claim on their regard, the family had always spoken of Eunice's worthy lover by his Christian name; and what had been familiar in their mouths felt the influence of custom, before time enough had elapsed to make them think as readily of the enemy as they had hitherto thought of the friend.

But I was ignorant of this: and the disclosure by which I

found myself suddenly confronted was more than I could support. For the moment, speech was beyond me.

His son! Dunboyne's son!

What a position that young man had occupied, unsuspected by his father, unknown to himself! Kept in ignorance of the family disgrace, he had been a guest in the house of the man who had consoled his infamous aunt on the eve of her execution – who had saved his unhappy cousin from poverty, from sorrow, from shame. And but one human being knew this. And that human being was myself!

Observing my agitation, Miss Jillgall placed her own construction on it.

'Do you know anything bad of Philip?' she asked eagerly. 'If it's something that will prevent Helena from marrying him, tell me what it is, I beg and pray.'

I knew no more of 'Philip' (whom she still called by his Christian name!) than she had told me herself: there was no help for it but to disappoint her. At the same time I was unable to conceal that I was ill at ease, and that it might be well to leave me by myself. After a look round the bed-chamber to see that nothing was wanting to my comfort, she made her quaint curtsey, and left me with her own inimitable form of farewell.

'Oh, indeed, I have been here too long! And I'm afraid I have been guilty, once or twice, of vulgar familiarity. You will excuse me, I hope. This has been an exciting interview – I think I am going to cry.'

She ran out of the room; and carried away with her some of my kindliest feelings, short as the time of our acquaintance had been. What a wife and what a mother was lost there – and all for want of a pretty face!

Left alone, my thoughts inevitably reverted to Dunboyne the elder, and to all that had happened in Mr Gracedieu's family since the Irish gentleman had written to me in bygone years.

The terrible choice of responsibilities which had preyed on the Minister's mind had been foreseen by Mr Dunboyne, when he first thought of adopting his infant niece, and had warned him to dread what might happen in the future, if he brought her up as a member of the family with his own boy, and if the two young people became at a later period attached to each other. How had the wise foresight, which offered such a contrast to the poor Minister's impulsive act of mercy, met with its reward? Fate or Providence (call it which we may) had brought Dunboyne's son and the daughter of the murderess together; had inspired those two strangers with love; and had emboldened them to plight their troth by a marriage engagement. Was the man's betrayal of the trust placed in him by the faithful girl, to be esteemed a fortunate circumstance by the two persons who knew the true story of her parentage, the Minister and myself? Could we rejoice in an act of infidelity which had embittered and darkened the gentle harmless life of the victim? Or could we, on the other hand, encourage the ruthless deceit, the hateful treachery, which had put the wicked Helena – with no exposure to dread if *she* married – into her wronged sister's place? Impossible! In the one case as in the other, impossible!

Equally hopeless did the prospect appear, when I tried to determine what my own individual course of action ought to be.

In my calmer moments, the idea had occurred to my mind of going to Dunboyne the younger, and, if he had any sense of shame left, exerting my influence to lead him back to his betrothed wife. How could I now do this, consistently with my duty to the young man's father; knowing what I knew, and not forgetting that I had myself advised Mr Gracedieu to keep the truth concealed, when I was equally ignorant of Philip Dunboyne's parentage and of Helena Gracedieu's treachery?

Even if events so ordered it that the marriage of Eunice might yet take place – without any interference exerted to produce that result, one way or the other, on my part – it would be just as impossible for me to speak out now, as it had been in the long-past years when I had so cautiously answered Mr Dunboyne's letter. But what would he think of me if accident led, sooner or later, to the disclosure which I had felt bound to conceal? The more I tried to forecast the chances of the future, the darker and the darker was the view that faced me.

To my sinking heart and wearied mind, good Dame Nature presented a more acceptable prospect, when I happened to look out of the window of my room. There I saw the trees and flower-beds of a garden, tempting me irresistibly under the cloudless sunshine of a fine day. I was on my way out, to recover heart and hope, when a knock at the door stopped me.

Had Miss Jillgall returned? When I said 'Come in,' Mr Gracedieu opened the door, and entered the room.

He was so weak that he staggered as he approached me. Leading him to a chair, I noticed a wild look in his eyes, and a flush on his haggard cheeks. Something had happened.

'When you were with me in my room,' he began, 'did I not tell you that I had forgotten something?'

'Certainly you did.'

'Well, I have found the lost remembrance. My misfortune – I ought to call it the punishment for my sins, is recalled to me now. The worst curse that can fall on a father is the curse that has come to me. I have a wicked daughter. My own child, sir! my own child!'

Had he been awake, while Miss Jillgall and I had been talking outside his door? Had he heard her ask me if Mr Gracedieu had said nothing of Helena's infamous conduct to her sister, while he was speaking of Eunice? The way to the lost remembrance had perhaps been found there. In any case, after that bitter allusion to his 'wicked daughter' some result must follow. Helena Gracedieu and a day of reckoning might be nearer to each other already than I had ventured to hope.

I waited anxiously for what he might say to me next.

## CHAPTER XXXVI

### THE WANDERING MIND

For the moment, the Minister disappointed me.

Without speaking, without even looking up, he took out his pocket-book, and began to write in it. Constantly interrupted – either by a trembling in the hand that held the pencil, or by a difficulty (as I imagined) in expressing thoughts imperfectly realized – his patience gave way; he dashed the book on the floor.

'My mind is gone!' he burst out. 'Oh, Father in Heaven, let death deliver me from a body without a mind!'

Who could hear him, and be guilty of the cruelty of preaching self-control? I picked up the pocket-book, and offered to help him.

'Do you think you can?' he asked.

'I can at least try.'

'Good fellow! What should I do without you? See now; here is my difficulty. I have got so many things to say, I want to separate them – or else they will all run into each other. Look at the book,' my poor friend said mournfully; 'they have run into each other in spite of me.'

The entries proved to be nearly incomprehensible. Here and there I discovered some scattered words, which showed themselves more or less distinctly in the midst of the surrounding confusion. The first word that I could make out was 'Education'. Helped by that hint, I trusted to guess-work to guide me in speaking to him. It was necessary to be positive, or he would have lost all faith in me.

'Well?' he said impatiently

'Well,' I answered, 'you have something to say to me about the education which you have given to your daughters.'

'Don't put them together!' he cried. 'Dear, patient, sweet Eunice must not be confounded with that she-devil——'

'Hush, hush, Mr Gracedieu! Badly as Miss Helena has behaved, she is your own child.'

'I repudiate her, sir! Think for a moment of what she has done – and then think of the religious education that I have given her. Heartless! Deceitful! The most ignorant creature in the lowest dens of this town could have done nothing more basely cruel. And this, after years on years of patient Christian instruction on my part! What is religion? What is education? I read a horrible book once (I forget who was the author); it called religion superstition, and education empty form. I don't know; upon my word I don't know that the book may not – Oh, my tongue! Why don't I keep a guard over my tongue!

Are you a father, too? Don't interrupt me. Put yourself in my place, and think of it. Heartless, deceitful, and *my* daughter. Give me the pocket-book; I want to see which memorandum comes first.'

He had now wrought himself into a state of excitement, which relieved his spirits of the depression that had weighed on them up to this time. His harmless vanity always, as I suspect, a latent quality in his kindly nature, had already restored his confidence. With a self-sufficient smile, he consulted his own unintelligible entries, and made his own wild discoveries.

'Ah, yes; "M" stands for Minister; I come first. Am I to blame? Am I – God forgive me my many sins – am I heartless? Am I deceitful?'

'My good friend, not even your enemies could say that!'

'Thank you. Who comes next?' He consulted the book again. 'Her mother, her sainted mother, comes next. People say she is like her mother. Was my wife heartless? Was the angel of my life deceitful?'

('That,' I thought to myself, 'is exactly what your wife was – and exactly what reappears in your wife's child.')

'Where does her wickedness come from?' he went on. 'Not from her mother; not from me; not from a neglected education.' He suddenly stepped up to me, and laid his hands on my shoulders; his voice dropped to hoarse, moaning, awe-struck tones. 'Shall I tell you what it is? A possession of the devil.'

It was so evidently desirable to prevent any continuation of such a train of thought as this, that I could feel no hesitation in interrupting him.

'Will you hear what I have to say?' I asked bluntly.

His humour changed again; he made me a low bow, and went back to his chair. 'I will hear you with pleasure,' he answered politely. 'You are the most eloquent man I know, with one exception – myself. Of course – myself.'

'It is mere waste of time,' I continued, 'to regret the excellent education which your daughter has misused.' Making that reply, I was tempted to add another word of truth. All education is at the mercy of two powerful counter-influences:

the influence of temperament, and the influence of circumstances. But this was philosophy. How could I expect him to submit to philosophy? 'What we know of Miss Helena,' I went on, 'must be enough for us. She has plotted, and she means to succeed. Stop her.'

'Just my idea!' he declared firmly. 'I refuse my consent to that abominable marriage.'

In the popular phrase, I struck while the iron was hot. 'You must do more than that, sir,' I told him.

His vanity suddenly took the alarm — I was leading him rather too undisguisedly. He handed his book back to me. 'You will find,' he said loftily, 'that I have put it all down there.'

I pretended to find it, and read an imaginary entry to this effect: 'After what she has already done, Helena is capable of marrying in defiance of my wishes and commands. This must be considered and provided against.' So far, I had succeeded in flattering him. But when (thinking of his paternal authority) I alluded next to his daughter's age, his eyes rested on me with a look of downright terror.

'No more of that!' he said. 'I won't talk of the girls' ages even with you.'

What did he mean? It was useless to ask. I went on with the matter in hand — still deliberately speaking to him, as I might have spoken to a man with an intellect as clear as my own. In my experience, this practice generally stimulates a weak intelligence to do its best. We all know how children receive talk that is lowered, or books that are lowered, to their presumed level.

'I shall take it for granted,' I continued, 'that Miss Helena is still under your lawful authority. She can only arrive at her ends by means of a runaway marriage. In that case, much depends on the man. You told me you couldn't help liking him. This was, of course, before you knew of the infamous manner in which he has behaved. You must have changed your opinion now.'

He seemed to be at a loss how to reply. 'I am afraid,' he said, 'the young man was drawn into it by Helena.'

Here was Miss Jillgall's apology for Philip Dunboyne repeated in other words. Despising and detesting the fellow as I did, I was forced to admit to myself that he must be recommended by personal attractions which it would be necessary to reckon with. I tried to get some more information from Mr Gracedieu.

'The excuse you have just made for him,' I resumed, 'implies that he is a weak man; easily persuaded, easily led.'

The Minister answered by nodding his head.

'Such weakness as that,' I persisted, 'is a vice in itself. It has led already, sir, to the saddest results.'

He admitted this by another nod.

'I don't wish to shock you Mr Gracedieu; but I must recommend employing the means that present themselves. You must practise on this man's weakness, for the sake of the good that may come of it. I hear he is in London with his father. Try the strong influence, and write to his father. There is another reason besides for doing this. It is quite possible that the truth has been concealed from Mr Dunboyne the elder. Take care that he is informed of what has really happened. Are you looking for pen, ink, and paper? Let me offer you the writing materials which I use in travelling.'

I placed them before him. He took up the pen; he arranged the paper; he was eager to begin.

After writing a few words, he stopped – reflected – tried again – stopped again – tore up the little that he had done – and began a new letter, ending in the same miserable result. It was impossible to witness his helplessness, to see how pitiably patient he was over his own incapacity, and to let the melancholy spectacle go on. I proposed to write the letter; authenticating it, of course, by his signature. When he allowed me to take the pen, he turned away his face, ashamed to let me see what he suffered. Was this the same man, whose great nature had so nobly asserted itself in the condemned cell? Poor mortality!

The letter was easily written.

I had only to inform Mr Dunboyne of his son's conduct; repeating, in the plainest language that I could use, what Miss Jillgall had related to me. Arrived at the conclusion, I contrived to make Mr Gracedieu express himself in these strong terms: 'I protest against the marriage in justice to you, sir, as well as to myself. We can neither of us consent to be accomplices in an act of domestic treason of the basest kind.'

In silence, the Minister read the letter, and attached his signature to it. In silence, he rose and took my arm. I asked if he wished to go to his room. He only replied by a sign. I offered to sit with him, and try to cheer him. Gratefully, he pressed my hand: gently, he put me back from the door. Crushed by the miserable discovery of the decay of his own faculties! What could I do? what could I say? Nothing!

Miss Jillgall was in the drawing-room. With the necessary explanations, I showed her the letter. She read it with breathless interest. 'It terrifies one to think how much depends on old Mr Dunboyne,' she said. 'You know him. What sort of man is he?'

I could only assure her (after what I remembered of his letter to me) that he was a man whom we could depend upon.

Miss Jillgall possessed treasures of information to which I could lay no claim. Mr Dunboyne, she told me, was a scholar, and a writer, and a rich man. His views on marriage were liberal in the extreme. Let his son find good principles, good temper, and good looks, in a wife, and he would promise to find the money.

'I get these particulars,' said Miss Jillgall, 'from dear Euneece. They are surely encouraging? That Helena may carry out Mr Dunboyne's views in her personal appearance is, I regret to say, what I can't deny. But as to the other qualifications, how hopeful is the prospect! Good principles, and good temper? Ha! ha! Helena has the principles of Jezebel, and the temper of Lady Macbeth.'

After dashing off this striking sketch of character, the fair artist asked to look at my letter again, and observed that the address was wanting. 'I can set this right for you,' she resumed, 'thanks, as before, to my sweet Euneece. And (don't be in a hurry) I can make myself useful in another way. Oh, how I do enjoy making myself useful! If you trust your letter to the basket in the hall, Helena's lovely eyes – capable of the meanest conceivable actions – are sure to take a peep at the address. In that case, do you think your letter would get to London? I am afraid you detect a faint infusion of spitefulness in that question. Oh, for shame! I'll post the letter myself.'

## CHAPTER XXXVII

### THE SHAMELESS SISTER

For some reason, which my unassisted penetration was unable to discover, Miss Helena Gracedieu kept out of my way.

At dinner, on the day of my arrival, and at breakfast on the next morning, she was present of course; ready to make herself agreeable in a modest way, and provided me with the necessary supply of cheerful small-talk. But the meal having come to an end, she had her domestic excuse ready, and unostentatiously disappeared like a well-bred young lady. I never met her on the stairs, never found myself intruding on her in the drawing-room, never caught her getting out of my way in the garden. As much at a loss for an explanation of these mysteries as I was, Miss Jillgall's interest in my welfare led her to caution me in a vague and general way.

'Take my word for it, dear Mr Governor, she has some design on you. Will you allow an insignificant old maid to offer a suggestion? Oh, thank you; I will venture to advise. Please look back at your experience of the very worst female prisoner you ever had to deal with – and be guided accordingly if Helena catches you at a private interview.'

In less than half an hour afterwards, Helena caught me. I was writing in my room, when the maidservant came in with a message: 'Miss Helena's compliments, sir, and would you please spare her half an hour, downstairs?'

My first excuse was of course that I was engaged. This was disposed of by a second message, provided beforehand, no doubt, for an anticipated refusal: 'Miss Helena wished me to say, sir, that her time is your time.' I was still obstinate; I pledged next that my day was filled up. A third message had evidently been prepared, even for this emergency: 'Miss Helena will regret, sir, having the pleasure deferred, but she will leave you to make your own appointment for to-morrow.' Persistency so inveterate as this led to a result which Mr Gracedieu's cautious daughter had not perhaps contemplated: it put me on my guard. There seemed to be a chance, to say the least of it, that I might serve Eunice's interests if I discovered what the enemy had to say. I locked up my writing – declared myself incapable of putting Miss Helena to needless inconvenience – and followed the maid to the lower floor of the house.

The room to which I was conducted proved to be empty. I looked round me.

If I had been told that a man lived there who was absolutely indifferent to appearances, I should have concluded that his views were faithfully represented by his place of abode. The chairs and tables reminded me of a railway waiting-room. The shabby little bookcase was the mute record of a life indifferent to literature. The carpet was of that dreadful drab colour, still the cherished favourite of the average English mind, in spite of every protest that can be entered against it, on behalf of Art. The ceiling, recently whitewashed, made my eyes ache when they looked at it. On either side of the window, flaccid green curtains hung helplessly with nothing to loop them up. The writing-desk and the paper-case, viewed as specimens of woodwork, recalled the ready-made bedrooms on show in cheap shops. The books, mostly in slate-coloured bindings, were devoted to the literature which is called religious; I only discovered three worldly publications among them – *Domestic Cookery, Etiquette for Ladies*, and *Hints on the Breeding of Poultry*. An ugly little clock, ticking noisily in a black case, and two candlesticks of base metal placed on either side of it, completed the ornaments on the chimney-piece. Neither pictures nor prints hid the barrenness of the walls. I saw no needlework and no flowers. The one object in the place which showed any pretensions to beauty was a looking-glass in an elegant gilt frame – sacred to vanity, and worthy of the office that it filled. Such was Helena Gracedieu's sitting-room. I really could not help thinking: How like her!

She came in with a face perfectly adapted to the circumstances – pleased and smiling; amiably deferential, in consideration of the claims of her father's guest – and, to my surprise, in some degree suggestive of one of those incorrigible female prisoners, to whom Miss Jillgall had referred me when she offered a word of advice.

'How kind of you to come so soon! Excuse my receiving you in my housekeeping-room; we shall not be interrupted here. Very plainly furnished, is it not? I dislike ostentation and display. Ornaments are out of place in a room devoted to domestic necessities. I hate domestic necessities. You notice the looking-glass? It's a present. I should never have put such a thing up. Perhaps my vanity excuses it.'

She pointed the last remark by a look at herself in the glass; using it, while she despised it. Yes: there was a handsome face, paying her its reflected compliment – but not so well matched as it might have been by a handsome figure. Her feet were too large; her shoulders were too high; the graceful undulations of a well-made girl were absent when she walked; and her bosom was, to my mind, unduly developed for her time of life.

She sat down by me with her back to the light. Happening to be opposite to the window, I offered her the advantage of a clear view of my face. She waited for me, and I waited for her – and there was an awkward pause before we spoke. She set the example.

'Isn't it curious?' she remarked. 'When two people have something particular to say to each other, and nothing to hinder them, they never seem to know how to say it. You are the oldest, sir. Why don't you begin?'

'Because I have nothing particular to say.'

'In plain words, you mean that I must begin?'

'If you please.'

'Very well. I want to know whether I have given you (and Miss Jillgall, of course) as much time as you want, and as many opportunities as you could desire?'

'Pray go on, Miss Helena.'

'Have I not said enough already?'

'Not enough, I regret to say, to convey your meaning to me.'

She drew her chair a little farther away from me. 'I am sadly disappointed,' she said. 'I had such a high opinion of your perfect candour. I thought to myself, there is such a striking expression of frankness in his face. Another illusion gone! I hope you won't think I am offended, if I say a bold word. I am only a young girl, to be sure; but I am not quite such a fool as

you take me for. Do you really think I don't know that Miss
Jillgall has been telling you everything that is bad about me;
putting every mistake that I have made, every fault that I have
committed, in the worst possible point of view? And you have
listened to her – quite naturally! And you are prejudiced,
strongly prejudiced, against me – what else could you be, under
the circumstances? I don't complain; I have purposely kept out
of your way, and out of Miss Jillgall's way; in short, I have
afforded you every facility, as the prospectuses say. I only want
to know if my turn has come at last. Once more, have I given
you time enough, and opportunities enough?'

'A great deal more than enough.'

'Do you mean that you have made up your mind about me
without stopping to think?'

'That is exactly what I mean. An act of treachery, Miss
Helena, *is* an act of treachery; no honest person need hesitate to
condemn it. I am sorry you sent for me.'

I got up to go. With an ironical gesture of remonstrance, she
signed to me to sit down again.

'Must I remind you, dear sir, of our famous native virtue?
Fair play is surely due to a young person who has nobody to
take her part. You talked of treachery, just now. I deny the
treachery. Please give me a hearing.'

I returned to my chair.

'Or would you prefer waiting,' she went on, 'till my sister
comes here later in the day, and continues what Miss Jillgall has
begun, with the great advantage of being young and nice-
looking?'

When the female mind gets into this state, no wise man
answers the female questions.

'Am I to take silence as meaning Go on?' Miss Helena
inquired.

I begged her to interpret my silence in the sense most
agreeable to herself.

This naturally encouraged her. She made a proposal: 'Do you
mind changing places, sir?'

'Just as you like, Miss Helena.'

We changed chairs; the light now fell full on her face. Had she deliberately challenged me to look into her secret mind if I could? Anything like the stark insensibility of that young girl to every refinement of feeling, to every becoming doubt of herself, to every customary timidity of her age and sex in the presence of a man who had not disguised his unfavourable opinion of her, I never met with in all my experience of the world and of women.

'I wish to be quite mistress of myself,' she explained; 'your face, for some reason which I really don't know, irritates me. The fact is, I have great pride in keeping my temper. Please make allowances. Now about Miss Jillgall. I suppose she told you how my sister first met with Philip Dunboyne?'

'Yes.'

'She also mentioned, perhaps, that he was a highly-cultivated man?'

'She did.'

'Now we shall get on. When Philip came to our town here, and saw me for the first time – do you object to my speaking familiarly of him, by his Christian name?'

'In the case of anyone else in your position, Miss Helena, I should venture to call it bad taste.'

I was provoked into saying that. It failed entirely as a well-meant effort in the way of implied reproof. Miss Helena smiled.

'You grant me a liberty which you would not concede to another girl.' That was how she viewed it. 'We are getting on better already. To return to what I was saying. When Philip first saw me – I have it from himself, mind – he felt that I should have been his choice, if he had met with me before he met with my sister. Do you blame him?'

'If you will take my advice,' I said, 'you will not inquire too closely into my opinion of Mr Philip Dunboyne.'

'Perhaps you don't wish me to say any more?' she suggested.

'On the contrary; pray go on, if you like.'

After that concession, she was amiability itself. 'Oh, yes,' she assured me, 'that's easily done.' And she went on accordingly: 'Philip having informed me of the state of his affections, I naturally followed his example. In fact, we exchanged confessions. Our marriage engagement followed as a matter of course. Do you blame me?'

'I will wait till you have done.'

'I have no more to say.'

She made that amazing reply with such perfect composure, that I began to fear there must have been some misunderstanding between us. 'Is that really all you have to say for yourself?' I persisted.

Her patience with me was most exemplary. She lowered herself to my level. Not trusting to words only on this occasion, she (so to say) beat her meaning into my head by gesticulating on her fingers, as if she was educating a child.

'Philip and I,' she began, 'are the victims of an accident, which kept us apart when we ought to have met together – we are not responsible for an accident.' She impressed this on me by touching her forefinger. 'Philip and I fell in love with each other at first sight – we are not responsible for the feelings implanted in our natures by an all-wise Providence.' She assisted me in understanding this by touching her middle finger. 'Philip and I owe a duty to each other, and accept a responsibility under those circumstances – the responsibility of getting married.' A touch on her third finger, and an indulgent bow, announced that the lesson was ended. 'I am not a clever man like you,' she modestly acknowledged, 'but I ask you to help us, when you next see my father, with some confidence. You know exactly what to say to him, by this time. Nothing has been forgotten.'

'Pardon me,' I said, 'a person has been forgotten.'

'Indeed? What person?'

'Your sister.'

A little perplexed at first, Miss Helena reflected, and recovered herself.

'Ah, yes,' she said; 'I was afraid I might be obliged to trouble you for an explanation – I see it now. You are shocked (very properly) when feelings of enmity exist between near relations; and you wish to be assured that I bear no malice towards Eunice. She is violent, she is sulky, she is stupid, she is selfish; and she cruelly refuses to live in the same house with me. Make your mind easy, sir, I forgive my sister.'

Let me not attempt to disguise it – Miss Helena Gracedieu confounded me.

Ordinary audacity is one of those forms of insolence which mature experience dismisses with contempt. This girl's audacity struck down all resistance, for one shocking reason: it was unquestionably sincere. Strong conviction of her own virtue stared at me in her proud and daring eyes. At that time, I was not aware of what I have learned since. The horrid hardening of her moral sense had been accomplished by herself. In her diary, there has been found the confession of a secret course of reading – with supplementary reflections flowing from it, which need only to be described as worthy of their source.

A person capable of repentance and reform would, in her place, have seen that she had disgusted me. Not a suspicion of this occurred to Miss Helena. 'I see you are embarrassed,' she remarked, 'and I am at no loss to account for it. You are too polite to acknowledge that I have not made a friend of you yet. Oh, I mean to do it!'

'No.' I said, 'I think not.'

'We shall see,' she replied. 'Sooner or later, you will find yourself saying a kind word to my father for Philip and me.' She rose, and took a turn in the room – and stopped, eyeing me attentively. 'Are you thinking of Eunice?' she asked.

'Yes.'

'She had your sympathy, I suppose?'

'My heart-felt sympathy.'

'I needn't ask how I stand in your estimation, after that. Pray express yourself freely. Your looks confess it – you view me with a feeling of aversion.'

'I view you with a feeling of horror.'

The exasperating influences of her language, her looks, and her tones would, as I venture to think, have got to the end of another man's self-control before this. Anyway, she had at last irritated me into speaking as strongly as I felt. What I said had been so plainly (perhaps so rudely) expressed, that misinterpretation of it seemed to be impossible. She mistook me, nevertheless. The most merciless disclosure of the dreary side of human destiny is surely to be found in the failure of words, spoken or written, so to answer their purpose that we can trust them, in our attempts to communicate with each other. Even when he seems to be connected, by the nearest and dearest relations, with his fellow-mortals, what a solitary creature, tried by the test of sympathy, the human being really is in the teeming world that he inhabits! Affording one more example, of the impotence of human language to speak for itself, my misinterpreted words had found their way to the one sensitive place in Helena Gracedieu's impenetrable nature. She betrayed it in the quivering and flushing of her hard face, and in the appeal to the looking-glass which escaped her eyes the next moment. My hasty reply had roused the idea of a covert insult addressed to her handsome face. In other words, I had wounded her vanity. Driven by resentment, out came the secret distrust of me which had been lurking in that cold heart, from the moment when we first met.

'I inspire you with horror, and Eunice inspires you with compassion,' she said. 'That, Mr Governor, is not natural.'

'May I ask why?'

'You know why.'

'No.'

'You will have it?'

'I want an explanation, Miss Helena, if that is what you mean.'

'Take your explanation, then! You are not the stranger you are said to be to my sister and to me. Your interest in Eunice is a personal interest of some kind. I don't pretend to guess what it is. As for myself, it is plain that somebody else has been setting you against me, before Miss Jillgall got possession of your private ear.'

In alluding to Eunice, she had blundered, strangely enough, on something like the truth. But when she spoke of herself, the headlong malignity of her suspicions – making every allowance for the anger that had hurried her into them – seemed to call for some little protest against a false assertion. I told her that she was completely mistaken.

'I am completely right,' she answered; 'I saw it.'

'Saw what?'

'Saw you pretending to be a stranger to me.'

'When did I do that?'

'You did it when we met at the station.'

The reply was too ridiculous for the preservation of any control over my own sense of humour. It was wrong; but it was inevitable – I laughed. She looked at me with a fury, revealing a concentration of evil passion in her which I had not seen yet. I asked her pardon; I begged her to think a little before she persisted in taking a view of my conduct unworthy of her, and unjust to myself.

'Unjust to You!' she burst out. 'Who are You? A man who has driven your trade has spies always at his command – yes! and knows how to use them. You were primed with private information – you had, for all I know, a stolen photograph of me in your pocket – before ever you came to our town. Do you still deny it? Oh, sir, why degrade yourself by telling a lie?'

No such outrage as this had ever been inflicted on me, at any time in my life. My forbearance must, I suppose, have been more severely tried than I was aware of myself. With or without excuse for me, I was weak enough to let a girl's spiteful tongue sting me, and, worse still, to let her see that I felt it.

'You shall have no second opportunity, Miss Gracedieu, of insulting me.' With that foolish reply, I opened the door violently, and went out.

She ran after me, triumphing in having roused the temper of a man old enough to have been her grandfather, and caught me by the arm. 'Your own conduct has exposed you.' (That was literally how she expressed herself.) 'I saw it in your eyes when we met at the station. You, the stranger – you who allowed poor ignorant me to introduce myself – you knew me all the time, knew me by sight!'

I shook her hand off with an inconsiderable roughness, humiliating to remember. 'It's false!' I cried. 'I knew you by your likeness to your mother.'

The moment the words had passed my lips. I came to my senses again; I remembered what fatal words they might prove to be, if they reached the Minister's ears.

Heard only by his daughter, my reply seemed to cool the heat of her anger in an instant.

'So you knew my mother?' she said. 'My father never told us that, when he spoke of your being such a very old friend of his. Strange, to say the least of it.'

I was wise enough – now when wisdom had come too late – not to attempt to explain myself, and not to give her an opportunity of saying more. 'We are neither of us in a state of mind,' I answered, 'to allow this interview to continue. I must try to recover my composure; and I leave you to do the same.'

In the solitude of my room, I was able to look my position fairly in the face.

Mr Gracedieu's wife had come to me, in the long-past time, without her husband's knowledge. Tempted to a cruel resolve by the maternal triumph of having an infant of her own, she had resolved to rid herself of the poor little rival in her husband's fatherly affection, by consigning the adopted child to the keeping of a charitable asylum. She had dared to ask me to help her. I had kept the secret of her shameful visit – I can honestly say, for the Minister's sake. And now, long after time had doomed those events to oblivion, they were revived – and revived by me. Thanks to my folly, Mr Gracedieu's daughter knew what I had concealed from Mr Gracedieu himself.

What course did respect for my friend, and respect for myself, counsel me to take?

I could only see before me a choice of two evils. To wait for events – with the too certain prospect of a vindictive betrayal of my indiscretion by Helena Gracedieu. Or to take the initiative into my own hands, and risk consequences which I might regret to the end of my life, by making my confession to the Minister.

Before I had decided, somebody knocked at the door. It was the maid-servant again. Was it possible she had been sent by Helena?

'Another message?'

'Yes, sir. My master wishes to see you.'

# CHAPTER XXXVIII

### THE GIRLS' AGES

Had the Minister's desire to see me been inspired by his daughter's betrayal of what I had unfortunately said to her? Although he would certainly not consent to receive her personally, she would be at liberty to adopt a written method of communication with him, and the letter might be addressed in such a manner as to pique his curiosity. If Helena's vindictive purpose had been already accomplished – and if Mr Gracedieu left me no alternative but to present his unworthy wife in her true character – I can honestly say that I dreaded the consequences, not as they might affect myself, but as they might affect my unhappy friend in his enfeebled state of body and mind.

When I entered his room, he was still in bed.

The bed-curtains were so drawn, on the side nearest to the window, as to keep the light from falling too brightly on his weak eyes. In the shadow thus thrown on him, it was not possible to see his face plainly enough, from the open side of the bed, to arrive at any definite conclusion as to what might be passing in his mind. After having been awake for some hours during the earlier part of the night, he had enjoyed a long and undisturbed sleep. 'I feel stronger this morning,' he said, 'and I wish to speak to you while my mind is clear.'

If the quiet tone of his voice was not an assumed tone, he was surely ignorant of all that had passed between his daughter and myself.

'Eunice will be here soon,' he proceeded, 'and I ought to explain why I have sent for her to come and meet you. I have reasons, serious reasons, mind, for wishing you to compare her personal appearance with Helena's personal appearance, and then to tell me which of the two, on a fair comparison, looks the eldest. Pray bear in mind that I attach the greatest importance to the conclusion at which you may arrive.'

He spoke more clearly and collectedly than I had heard him speak yet.

Here and there I detected hesitations and repetitions, which I have purposely passed over. The substance of what he said to me is all that I shall present in this place. Careful as I have been to keep my record of events within strict limits, I have written at a length which I was far indeed from contemplating when I accepted Mr Gracedieu's invitation.

Having promised to comply with the strange request which he had addressed to me, I ventured to remind him of past occasions on which he had pointedly abstained, when the subject presented itself, from speaking of the girls' ages. 'You have left it to my discretion,' I added, 'to decide a question in which you are seriously interested, relating to your daughters. Have I no excuse for regretting that I have not been admitted to your confidence a little more freely?'

'You have every excuse,' he answered. 'But you trouble me all the same. There was something else that I had to say to you – and your curiosity gets in the way.'

He said this with a sullen emphasis. In my position, the worst of evils was suspense. I told him that my curiosity could wait; and I begged that he would relieve his mind of what was pressing on it at the moment.

'Let me think a little,' he said.

I waited anxiously for the decision at which he might arrive. Nothing came of it to justify my misgivings. 'Leave what I have in my mind to ripen in my mind,' he said. 'The mystery about the girls' ages seems to irritate you. If I put my good friend's temper to any further trial, he will be of no use to me. Never mind if my head swims; I'm used to that. Now listen!'

Strange as the preface was, the explanation that followed was stranger yet. I offer a shortened and simplified version, giving accurately the substance of what I heard.

The Minister entered without reserve on the mysterious subject of the ages. Eunice, he informed me, was nearly two years older than Helena. If she outwardly showed her superiority of age, any person acquainted with the circumstances under which the adopted infant had been received into Mr Gracedieu's childless household, need only compare the so-called sisters in after-life, and would thereupon identify the eldest-looking young lady of the two as the offspring of the woman who had been hanged for murder. With such a misfortune as this presenting itself as a possible prospect, the Minister was bound to prevent the girls from ignorantly betraying each other by allusions to their ages and their birthdays. After much thought, he had devised a desperate means of meeting the difficulty – already made known, as I am told, for the information of strangers who may read the pages that have gone before mine. My friend's plan of proceeding had, by the nature of it, exposed him to injurious comment, to embarrassing questions, and to doubts and misconceptions, all patiently endured in consideration of the security that had been attained. Proud of his explanation, Mr Gracedieu's vanity called upon me to acknowledge that my curiosity had been satisfied, and my doubts completely set at rest.

No: my obstinate common sense was not reduced to submission, even yet. Looking back over a lapse of seventeen years, I asked what had happened, in that long interval, to justify the anxieties which still appeared to trouble my friend.

This time, my harmless curiosity could be gratified by a reply expressed in three words – nothing had happened.

Then what, in Heaven's name, was the Minister afraid of?

His voice dropped to a whisper. He said: 'I am afraid of the women.'

Who were the women?

Two of them actually proved to be the servants employed in Mr Gracedieu's house, at the bygone time when he had brought the child home with him from the prison! To point out the absurdity of the reasons that he gave for fearing what female curiosity might yet attempt, if circumstances happened to encourage it, would have been a mere waste of words. Dismissing the subject, I next ascertained that the Minister's doubts extended even to the two female warders, who had been appointed to watch the murderess in turn, during her last days in prison. I easily relieved his mind in this case. One of the warders was dead. The other had married a farmer in Australia. Had we exhausted the list of suspected persons yet? No: there was one more left; and the Minister declared that he had first met with her in my official residence, at the time when I was Governor of the prison.

'She presented herself to me by name,' he said; 'and she spoke rudely. A Miss——' He paused to consult his memory, and this time (thanks perhaps to his night's rest) his memory answered the appeal. 'I have got it!' he cried – 'Miss Chance.'

My friend had interested me in his imaginary perils at last. It was just possible that he might have a formidable person to deal with now.

During my residence at Florence, the Chaplain and I had taken many a retrospective look (as old men will) at past events in our lives. My former colleague spoke of the time when he had performed clerical duty for his friend, the rector of a parish church in London. Neither he nor I had heard again of the 'Miss Chance' of our disagreeable prison experience, whom he had married to the dashing Dutch gentleman, Mr Tenbruggen. We could only wonder what had become of that mysterious married pair.

Mr Gracedieu being undoubtedly ignorant of the woman's marriage, it was not easy to say what the consequence might be, in his excitable state, if I informed him of it. He would, in all probability, conclude that I knew more of the woman than he did. I decided on keeping my own counsel, for the present at least.

Passing at once, therefore, to the one consideration of any importance, I endeavoured to find out whether Mr Gracedieu and Mrs Tenbruggen had met, or had communicated with each other in any way, during the long period of separation that had taken place between the Minister and myself. If he had been so unlucky as to offend her, she was beyond all doubt an enemy to be dreaded. Apart, however, from a misfortune of this kind, she would rank, in my opinion, with the other harmless objects of Mr Gracedieu's morbid distrust.

In making my inquiries, I found that I had an obstacle to contend with.

While he felt the renovating influence of the repose that he enjoyed, the Minister had been able to think and to express himself with less difficulty than usual. But the reserves of strength, on which the useful exercise of his memory depended, began to fail him as the interview proceeded. He distinctly recollected that 'something unpleasant had passed between that audacious woman and himself.' But at what date – and whether by word of mouth or by correspondence – was more than his memory could now recall. He believed he was not mistaken in telling me that he 'had been in two minds about her'. At one time, he was satisfied that he had taken wise measures for his own security, if she attempted to annoy him. But there was another and a later time, when doubts and fears had laid hold of him again. If I wanted to know how this had happened, he fancied it was through a dream; and if I asked what the dream was, he could only beg and pray that I would spare his poor head.

Unwilling even yet to submit unconditionally to defeat, it occurred to me to try a last experiment on my friend, without calling for any mental effort on his own part. The 'Miss Chance' of former days might, by a bare possibility, have written to him. I asked accordingly if he was in the habit of keeping his letters, and if he would allow me (when he had rested a little) to lay them open before him, so that he could look at the signatures. 'You might find the lost recollection in that way,' I suggested, 'at the bottom of one of your letters.'

He was in that state of weariness, poor fellow, in which a man will do anything for the sake of peace. Pointing to a cabinet in his room, he gave me a key taken from a little basket on his bed. 'Look for yourself,' he said. After some hesitation – for I naturally recoiled from examining another man's correspondence – I decided on opening the cabinet, at any rate.

The letters – a large collection – were, to my relief, all neatly folded, and endorsed with the names of the writers. I could run harmlessly through bundle after bundle in search of the one name that I wanted, and still respect the privacy of the letters. My perseverance deserved a reward – and failed to get it. The name I wanted steadily eluded my search. Arriving at the upper shelf of the cabinet, I found it so high that I could barely reach it with my hand. Instead of getting more letters to look over, I pulled down two newspapers.

One of them was an old copy of *The Times*, dating back as far as the 13th December, 1858. It was carefully folded, longwise, with the title-page uppermost. On the first column, at the left-hand side of the sheet, appeared the customary announcements of Births. A mark with a blue pencil, against one of the advertisements, attracted my attention. I read these lines:

> On the 10th inst., the wife of the Revd Abel Gracedieu, of a daughter.

The second newspaper bore a later date, and contained nothing that interested me. I naturally assumed that the advertisement in *The Times* had been inserted at the desire of Mrs Gracedieu; and, after all that I had heard, there was little difficulty in attributing the curious omission of the place in which the child had been born to the caution of her husband. If Mrs Tenbruggen (then Miss Chance) had happened to see the advertisement in the great London newspaper, Mr Gracedieu might yet have good reason to congratulate himself on his prudent method of providing against mischievous curiosity.

I turned towards the bed and looked at him. His eyes were closed. Was he sleeping? Or was he trying to remember what he had desired to say to me, when the demands which I made on his memory had obliged him to wait for a later opportunity?

Either way, there was something that quickened my sympathies, in the spectacle of his helpless repose. It suggested to me personal reasons for his anxieties, which he had not mentioned, and which I had not thought of, up to this time. If the discovery that he dreaded took place, his household would be broken up, and his position as pastor would suffer in the estimation of the flock. His own daughter would refuse to live under the same roof with the daugher of an infamous woman. Popular opinion, among his congregation, judging a man who had passed off the child of other parents as his own, would find that man guilty of an act of deliberate deceit.

Still oppressed by reflections which pointed to the future in this discouraging way, I was startled by a voice outside the door – a sweet sad voice – saying, 'May I come in?'

The Minister's eyes opened instantly: he raised himself in his bed.

'Eunice at last!' he cried. 'Let her in.'


## CHAPTER XXXIX

### THE ADOPTED CHILD

I opened the door.

Eunice passed me with the suddenness almost of a flash of light. When I turned towards the bed, her arms were round her father's neck. 'Oh, poor Papa, how ill you look!' Commonplace expressions of fondness, and no more; but the tone gave them a charm that subdued me. Never had I felt so indulgent towards Mr Gracedieu's unreasonable fears as when I saw him in the embrace of his adopted daughter. She had already reminded me of the bygone day when a bright little child had sat on my knee and listened to the ticking of my watch.

The Minister gently lifted her head from his breast. 'My darling,' he said, 'you don't see my old friend. Love him, and look up to him, Eunice. He will be your friend too, when I am gone.'

She came to me and offered her cheek to be kissed. It was sadly pale, poor soul – and I could guess why. But her heart was now full of her father. 'Do you think he is seriously ill?' she whispered. What I ought to have said I don't know. Her eyes, the sweetest, truest, loveliest eyes I ever saw in a human face, were pleading with me. Let my enemies make the worst of it, if they like – I did certainly lie. And if I deserved my punishment, I got it; the poor child believed me! 'Now I am happier,' she said gratefully. 'Only to hear your voice seems to encourage me. On our way here, Selina did nothing but talk of you. She told me I shouldn't have time to feel afraid of the great man; he would make me fond of him directly. I said. "Are *you* fond of him?" She said, "Madly in love with him, my dear." My little friend really thinks you like her, and is very proud of it. There are some people who call her ugly. I hope you don't agree with them?'

I believe I should have lied again, if Mr Gracedieu had not called me to the bedside.

'How does she strike you?' he whispered eagerly. 'Is it too soon to ask if she shows her age in her face?'

'Neither in her face nor her figure,' I answered: 'it astonishes me that you can ever have doubted it. No stranger, judging by personal appearance, could fail to make the mistake of thinking Helena the oldest of the two.

He looked fondly at Eunice. 'Her figure seems to bear out what you say,' he went on. 'Almost childish, isn't it?'

I could not agree to that. Slim, supple, simply graceful in every movement, Eunice's figure, in the charm of first youth, only waited its perfect development. Most men, looking at her as she stood at the other end of the room with her back towards us, would have guessed her age to be sixteen.

Finding that I failed to agree with him, Mr Gracedieu's misgivings returned. 'You speak very confidently,' he said, 'considering that you have not seen the girls together. Think what a dreadful blow it would be to me if you made a mistake.'

I declared, with perfect sincerity, that there was no fear of a mistake. The bare idea of making the proposed comparison was hateful to me. If Helena and I had happened to meet at that moment, I should have turned away from her by instinct – she would have disturbed my impressions of Eunice.

The Minister signed to me to move a little nearer to him. 'I must say it,' he whispered, 'and I am afraid of her hearing me. Is there anything in her face that reminds you of her miserable mother?'

I had hardly patience to answer the question: it was simply preposterous. Her hair was by many shades darker than her mother's hair; her eyes were of a different colour. There was an exquisite tenderness and sincerity in their expression – made additionally beautiful, to my mind, by a gentle uncomplaining sadness. It was impossible even to think of the eyes of the murderess when I looked at her child. Eunice's lower features, again, had none of her mother's regularity of proportion. Her smile, simple and sweet, and soon passing away, was certainly not an inherited smile on the maternal side. Whether she resembled her father, I was unable to conjecture – having never seen him. The one thing certain was, that not the faintest trace, in feature or expression, of Eunice's mother was to be seen in Eunice herself. Of the two girls, Helena – judging by something in the colour of her hair, and by something in the shade of her complexion – might possibly have suggested, in those particulars only, a purely accidental resemblance to my terrible prisoner of past times.

The revival of Mr Gracedieu's spirits indicated a temporary change only, and was already beginning to pass away. The eyes which had looked lovingly at Eunice began to look languidly now: his head sank on the pillow with a sigh of weak content. 'My pleasure has been almost too much for me,' he said. 'Leave me for a while to rest, and get used to it.'

Eunice kissed his forehead – and we left the room.

## CHAPTER XL

### THE BRUISED HEART

When we stepped out on the landing, I observed that my companion paused. She looked at the two flights of stairs below us before she descended them. It occurred to me that there must be somebody in the house whom she was anxious to avoid.

Arrived at the lower hall, she paused again, and proposed in a whisper that we should go into the garden. As we advanced along the backward division of the hall, I saw her eyes turn distressfully towards the door of the room in which Helena had received me. At last, my slow perceptions felt with her and understood her. Eunice's sensitive nature recoiled from a chance meeting with the wretch, who had laid waste all that had once been happy and hopeful in that harmless young life.

'Will you come with me to the part of the garden that I am fondest of?' she asked.

I offered her my arm. She led me in silence to a rustic seat, placed under the shade of a mulberry tree. I saw a change in her face as we sat down – a tender and beautiful change. At that moment the girl's heart was far away from me. There was some association with this corner of the garden, on which I felt that I must not intrude.

'I was once very happy here,' she said. 'When the time of the heartache came soon after, I was afraid to look at the old tree and the bench under it. But that is all over now. I like to remember the hours that were once dear to me, and to see the place that recalls them. Do you know who I am thinking of? Don't be afraid of distressing me. I never cry now.'

'My dear child, I have heard your sad story – but I can't trust myself to speak of it.'

'Because you are so sorry for me?'

'No words can say how sorry I am!'

'But you are not angry with Philip?'

'Not angry! My poor dear, I am afraid to tell you how angry I am with him.'

'Oh, no! You mustn't say that. If you wish to be kind to me – and I am sure you do wish it – don't think bitterly of Philip.'

When I remember that the first feeling she roused in me was nothing worthier of a professing Christian than astonishment, I drop in my own estimation to the level of a savage. 'Do you really mean,' I was base enough to ask, 'that you have forgiven him?'

She said gently: 'How could I help forgiving him?'

The man who could have been blessed with such love as this, and who could have cast it away from him, can have been nothing but an idiot. On that ground – though I dared not confess it to Eunice – I forgave him too.

'Do I surprise you?' she asked simply. 'Perhaps love will bear any humiliation. Or perhaps I am only a poor weak creature. You don't know what a comfort it was to me to keep the few letters that I received from Philip. When I heard that he had gone away, I gave his letters the kiss that bade him good-bye.

That was the time, I think, when my poor bruised heart got used to the pain; I began to feel that there was one consolation still left for me – I might end in forgiving him. Why do I tell you this? I think you must have bewitched me. Is this really the first time I have seen you?'

She put her little trembling hand into mine; I lifted it to my lips, and kissed it. Sorely I was tempted to own that I had pitied and loved her in her infancy. It was almost on my lips to say: 'I remember you an easily-pleased little creature, amusing yourself with the broken toys which were once the playthings of my own children.' I believe I should have said it, if I could have trusted myself to speak composedly to her. This was not to be done. Old as I was, versed as I was in the hard knowledge of how to keep the mask on in the hour of need, this was not to be done.

Still trying to understand that I was little better than a stranger to her, and still bent on finding the secret of the sympathy that united us, Eunice put a strange question to me.

'When you were young yourself,' she said, 'did you know what it was to love, and to be loved – and then to lose it all?'

It is not given to many men to marry the woman who has been the object of their first love. My early life had been darkened by a sad story; never confided to any living creature; banished resolutely from my own thoughts. For forty years past, that part of my buried self had lain quiet in its grave – and the chance touch of an innocent hand had raised the dead, and set us face to face again! Did I know what it was to love, and to be loved, and then to lose it all? 'Too well, my child; too well!'

That was all I could say to her. In the last days of my life, I shrank from speaking of it. When I had first felt that calamity, and had felt it most keenly, I might have given an answer worthier of me, and worthier of her.

She dropped my hand, and sat by me in silence, thinking. Had I – without meaning it, God knows! – had I disappointed her?

'Did you expect me to tell my own story,' I said, 'as frankly and as trustfully as you have told yours?'

'Oh, don't think that! I know what an effort it was to you to

answer me at all. Yes, indeed! I wonder whether I may ask
something. The sorrow you have just told me of is not the only
one − is it? You have had other troubles?'

'Many of them.'

'There are times,' she went on, 'when one can't help
thinking of one's own miserable self. I try to be cheerful, but
those times come now and then.'

She stopped, and looked at me with a pale fear confessing
itself in her face.

'You know who Selina is?' she resumed. 'My friend! The
only friend I had, till you came here.'

I guessed that she was speaking of the quaint kindly little
woman, whose ugly surname had been hitherto the only name
known to me.

'Selina has, I dare say, told you that I have been ill,' she
continued, 'and that I am staying in the country for the benefit
of my health.'

It was plain that she had something to say to me, far more
important than this, and that she was dwelling on trifles to gain
time and courage. Hoping to help her, I dwelt on trifles too;
asking commonplace questions about the part of the country in
which she was staying. She answered absently − then, little by
little, impatiently. The one poor proof of kindness that I could
offer, now, was to say no more.

'Do you know what a strange creature I am?' she broke out.
'Shall I make you angry with me? or shall I make you laugh at
me? What I have shrunk from confessing to Selina − what I
dare not confess to my father − I must, and will confess to You!'

There was a look of horror in her face that alarmed me. I
drew her to me so that she could rest her head on my shoulder.
My own agitation threatened to get the better of me. For the
first time since I had seen this sweet girl, I found myself
thinking of the blood that ran in her veins, and of the nature of
the mother who had borne her.

'Did you notice how I behaved upstairs?' she said. 'I mean
when we left my father, and came out on the landing.'

It was easily recollected; I begged her to go on.

'Before I went downstairs,' she proceeded, 'you saw me look

and listen. Did you think I was afraid of meeting some person? and did you guess who it was I wanted to avoid?'

'I guessed that – and I understood you.'

'No! You are not wicked enough to understand me. Will you do me a favour? I want you to look at me.'

It was said seriously. She lifted her head for a moment, so that I could examine her face.

'Do you see anything,' she asked, 'which makes you fear that I am not in my right mind?'

'Good God! how can you ask such a horrible question?'

She laid her head back on my shoulder with a sad little sigh of resignation. 'I ought to have known better,' she said; 'there is no such easy way out of it as that. Tell me – is there one kind of wickedness more deceitful than another? Can it lie hidden in a person for years together, and show itself when a time of suffering – no; I mean when a sense of injury comes? Did you ever see that, when you were master in the prison?'

I had seen it – and, after a moment's doubt, I said I had seen it.

'Did you pity those poor wretches?'

'Certainly! They deserved pity.'

'I am one of them!' she said. 'Pity *me*. If Helena looks at me – if Helena speaks to me – if I only see Helena by accident – do you know what she does? She tempts me! Tempts me to do dreadful things! Tempts me——' The poor child threw her arms round my neck, and whispered the next fatal words in my ear.

The mother! Prepared as I was for the accursed discovery, the horror of it shook me.

She left me, and started to her feet. The inherited energy showed itself in furious protest against the inherited evil. 'What does it mean?' she cried. 'I'll submit to anything. I'll bear my hard lot patiently, if you will only tell me what it means. Where does this horrid transformation of me out of myself come from? Look at my good father. In all this world there is no man so perfect as he is. And oh, how he has taught me! there isn't a single good thing that I have not learnt from him since I was a little girl. Did you ever hear him speak of my mother? You must have heard him. My mother was an angel. I could never be worthy of her at my best – but I have tried! I have tried! The wickedest girl in the world doesn't have worse thoughts than the thoughts that have come to me. Since when? Since Helena – oh, how can I tell her by her name as if I still loved her? Since my sister – can she be my sister, I ask myself sometimes! Since my enemy – there's the word for her – since my enemy took Philip away from me. What does it mean? I have asked in my prayers – and have got no answer. I ask you. What does it mean? You must tell me! You shall tell me! What does it mean?'

Why did I not try to calm her? I had vainly tried to calm her – I who knew who her mother was, and what her mother had been.

At last, she had forced the sense of my duty on me. The simplest way of calming her was to put her back in the place by my side that she had left. It was useless to reason with her, it was impossible to answer her. I had my own idea of the one way in which I might charm Eunice back to her sweeter self.

'Let us talk of Philip,' I said.

The fierce flush on her face softened, the swelling trouble of her bosom began to subside, as that dearly-loved name passed my lips! But there was some influence left in her which resisted me.

'No,' she said: 'we had better not talk of him.'

'Why not?'

'I have lost all my courage. If you speak of Philip, you will make me cry.'

I drew her nearer to me. If she had been my own child, I don't think I could have felt for her more truly than I felt at that moment. I only looked at her; I only said:

'Cry!'

The love that was in her heart rose, and poured its tenderness into her eyes. I had longed to see the tears that would comfort her. The tears came.

There was silence between us for a while. It was possible for me to think.

In the absence of physical resemblance between parent and child, is an unfavourable influence exercised on the tendency to moral resemblance? Assuming the possibility of such a result as this, Eunice (entirely unlike her mother) must, as I concluded, have been possessed of qualities formed to resist, as well as of qualities doomed to undergo, the infection of evil. While, therefore, I resigned myself to recognize the existence of the hereditary maternal taint, I firmly believed in the counterbalancing influences for good which had been part of the girl's birthright. They had been derived, perhaps, from the better qualities in her father's nature; they had been certainly developed by the tender care, the religious vigilance, which had guarded the adopted child so lovingly in the Minister's household; and they had served their purpose until time brought with it the change, for which the tranquil domestic influences were not prepared. With the great, the vital transformation, which marks the ripening of the girl into the woman's maturity of thought and passion, a new power for Good, strong enough to resist the latent power for Evil, sprang into being, and sheltered Eunice under the supremacy of Love. Love ill-fated and ill-bestowed – but love that no profanation could stain, that no hereditary evil could conquer – the True Love that had been, and was, and would be, the guardian angel of Eunice's life.

If I am asked whether I have ventured to found this opinion on what I have observed in one instance only, I reply that I have had other opportunities of investigation, and that my conclusions are derived from experience which refers to more instances than one.

No man in his senses can doubt that physical qualities are transmitted from parents to children. But inheritance of moral qualities is less easy to trace. Here, the exploring mind finds its progress beset by obstacles. That those obstacles have been sometimes overcome I do not deny. Moral resemblances have been traced between parents and children. While, however, I admit this, I doubt the conclusion which sees, in inheritance of moral qualities, a positive influence exercised on moral destiny. There are inherent emotional forces in humanity to which the inherited influences must submit; they are essentially influences under control – influences which can be encountered and forced back. That we, who inhabit this little planet, may be the doomed creatures of fatality, from the cradle to the grave, I am not prepared to dispute. But I absolutely refuse to believe that it is a fatality with no higher origin than can be found in our accidental obligation to our fathers and mothers.

Still absorbed in these speculations, I was disturbed by a touch on my arm.

I looked up. Eunice's eyes were fixed on a shrubbery, at some little distance from us, which closed the view of the garden on that side. I noticed that she was trembling. Nothing to alarm her was visible that I could discover. I asked what she had seen to startle her. She pointed to the shrubbery.

'Look again,' she said.

This time I saw a woman's dress among the shrubs. The woman herself appeared in a moment more.

It was Helena. She carried a small portfolio, and she approached us with a smile.

## CHAPTER XLI

### THE WHISPERING VOICE

I looked at Eunice. She had risen, startled by her first suspicion of the person who was approaching us through the shrubbery; but she kept her place near me, only changing her position so as to avoid confronting Helena. Her quickened breathing was all that told me of the effort she was making to preserve her self-control.

Entirely free from unbecoming signs of hurry and agitation, Helena opened her business with me by means of an apology.

'Pray excuse me for disturbing you. I am obliged to leave the house on one of my tiresome domestic errands. If you will kindly permit it, I wish to express, before I go, my very sincere regret for what I was rude enough to say, when I last had the honour of seeing you. May I hope to be forgiven? How-do-you-do, Eunice? Have you enjoyed your holiday in the country?'

Eunice neither moved nor answered. Having some doubt of what might happen if the two girls remained together, I proposed to Helena to leave the garden and to let me hear what she had to say, in the house.

'Quite needless,' she replied; 'I shall not detain you for more than a minute. Please look at this.'

She offered to me the portfolio that she had been carrying, and pointed to a morsel of paper attached to it, which contained this inscription:

Philip's Letters To Me. Private. Helena Gracedieu.

'I have a favour to ask,' she said, 'and a proof of confidence in you to offer. Will you be so good as to look over what you find in my portfolio? I am unwilling to give up the hopes that I had founded on our interview, when I asked for it. The letters will, I venture to think, plead my cause more convincingly than I was able to plead it for myself. I wish to forget what passed between us, to the last word. To the last word,' she repeated emphatically – with a look which sufficiently informed me that I had not been betrayed to her father yet. 'Will you indulge me?' she asked, and offered her portfolio for the second time.

A more impudent bargain could not well have been proposed to me.

I was to read, and to be favourably impressed by, Mr Philip Dunboyne's letters; and Miss Helena was to say nothing of that unlucky slip of the tongue, relating to her mother, which she had discovered to be a serious act of self-betrayal – thanks to my confusion at the time. If I had not thought of Eunice, and of the desolate and loveless life to which the poor girl was so patiently resigned, I should have refused to read Miss Gracedieu's love-letters.

But, as things were, I was influenced by the hope (innocently encouraged by Eunice herself) that Philip Dunboyne might not be so wholly unworthy of the sweet girl whom he had injured, as I had hitherto been too hastily disposed to believe. To act on this view with the purpose of promoting a reconciliation was impossible, unless I had the means of forming a secret estimate of the man's character. It seemed to me that I had found the means. A fair chance of putting his sincerity to a trustworthy test, was surely offered by the letters (the confidential letters) which I had been requested to read. To feel this as strongly as I felt it, brought me at once to a decision. I consented to take the portfolio – on my own conditions.

'Understand, Miss Helena,' I said, 'that I make no promises. I reserve my own opinion, and my own right of action.'

'I am not afraid of your opinions or your actions,' she answered confidently, 'if you will only read the letters. In the meantime, let me relieve my sister, there, of my presence. I hope you will soon recover, Eunice, in the country air.'

If the object of the wretch was to exasperate her victim, she had completely failed. Eunice remained as still as a statue. To all appearances, she had not even heard what had been said to her. Helena looked at me, and touched her forehead with a significant smile. 'Sad, isn't it?' she said – and bowed, and went briskly away on her household errand.

We were alone again.

Still, Eunice never moved. I spoke to her, and produced no impression. Beginning to feel alarmed, I tried the effect of touching her. With a wild cry, she started into a state of animation. Almost at the same moment, she weakly swayed to and fro as if the pleasant breeze in the garden moved her at its will, like the flowers. I held her up, and led her to the seat.

'There is nothing to be afraid of,' I said. 'She had gone.'

Eunice's eyes rested on me in vacant surprise.

'How do you know?' she asked. 'I hear her; but I never see her. Do you see her?'

'My dear child! of what person are you speaking?'

She answered: 'Of no person. I am speaking of a Voice that whispers and tempts me, when Helena is near.'

'What voice, Eunice?'

'The whispering Voice. It said to me, "I am your mother;" it called me Daughter when I first heard it. My father speaks of my mother, the angel. That good spirit has never come to me from the better world. It is a mock-mother who comes to me – some spirit of evil. Listen to this. I was awake in my bed. In the dark I heard the mock-mother whispering, close at my ear. Shall I tell you how she answered me, when I longed for light to see her by, when I prayed to her to show herself to me? She said: 'My face was hidden when I passed from life to death; my face no mortal creature may see." I have never seen her – how can *you* have seen her? But I heard her again, just now. She whispered to me when Helena was standing there – where you are standing. She freezes the life in me. Did she freeze the life in *you*? Did you hear her tempting me? Don't speak of it, if you did. Oh, not a word! not a word!'

A man who has governed a prison may say with Macbeth, 'I have supped full with horrors'. Hardened as I was – or ought to have been – the effect of what I had just heard turned me cold. If I had not known it to be absolutely impossible, I might have believed that the crime and the death of the murderess were known to Eunice, as being the crime and the death of her mother, and that the horrid discovery had turned her brain. This was simply impossible. What did it mean? Good God! what did it mean?

My sense of my own helplessness was the first sense in me that recovered. I thought of Eunice's devoted little friend. A woman's sympathy seemed to be needed now. I rose to lead the way out of the garden.

'Selina will think we are lost,' I said. 'Let us go and find Selina.'

'Not for the world,' she cried.

'Why not?'

'Because I don't feel sure of myself. I might tell Selina something which she must never know; I should be so sorry to frighten her. Let me stop here with you.'

I resumed my place at her side.

'Let me take your hand.'

I gave her my hand. What composing influence this simple act may, or may not, have exercized, it is impossible to say. She was quiet, she was silent. After an interval, I heard her breathe a long-drawn sigh of relief.

'I am afraid I have surprised you,' she said. 'Helena brings the dreadful time back to me——' She stopped and shuddered.

'Don't speak of Helena, my dear.'

'But I am afraid you will think – because I have said strange things – that I have been talking at random,' she insisted. 'The doctor will say that, if you meet with him. He believes I am deluded by a dream. I tried to think so myself. It was of no use; I am quite sure he is wrong.'

I privately determined to watch for the doctor's arrival, and to consult with him. Eunice went on:

'I have the story of a terrible night to tell you; but I haven't the courage to tell it now. Why shoudn't you come back with me to the place that I am staying at? A pleasant farmhouse, and such kind people. You might read the account of that night in my journal. I shall not regret the misery of having written it, if it helps you to find out how this hateful second self of mine has come to me. Hush! I want to ask you something. Do you think Helena is in the house?'

'No – she has gone out.'

'Did she say that herself? Are you sure?'

'Quite sure.'

She decided on going back to the farm, while Helena was out of the way. We left the garden together. For the first time, my companion noticed the portfolio. I happened to be carrying it in the hand that was nearest to her, as she walked by my side.

'Where did you get that?' she asked.

It was needless to reply in words. My hesitation spoke for me.

'Carry it in your other hand,' she said – 'the hand that's farthest away from me. I don't want to see it! Do you mind waiting a moment while I find Selina? You will go to the farm with us, won't you?'

I had to look over the letters, in Eunice's own interests; and I begged her to let me defer my visit to the farm until the next day. She consented, after making me promise to keep my appointment. It was of some importance to her, she told me, that I should make acquaintance with the farmer and his wife and children, and tell her how I liked them. Her plans for the future depended on what those good people might be willing to do. When she had recovered her health, it was impossible for her to go home again while Helena remained in the house. She had resolved to earn her own living, if she could get employment as a governess. The farmer's children liked her; she had already helped their mother in teaching them; and there was reason to hope that their father would see his way to employing her permanently. His house offered the great advantage of being near enough to the town, to enable her to hear news of the Minister's progress towards recovery, and to see him herself when safe opportunities offered, from time to time. As for her salary, what did she care about money? Anything would be acceptable, if the good man would only realize her hopes for the future.

It was disheartening to hear that hope, at her age, began and ended within such narrow limits as these. No prudent man would have tried to persuade her, as I now did, that the idea of reconciliation offered the better hope of the two.

'Suppose I see Mr Philip Dunboyne when I go back to London,' I began, 'what shall I say to him?'

'Say I have forgiven him.'

'And suppose,' I went on, 'that the blame really rests, where you all believe it to rest, with Helena. If that young man returns to you, truly ashamed of himself, truly penitent, will you——?'

She resolutely interrupted me: 'No!'

'Oh, Eunice, you surely mean Yes?'

'I mean No!'

'Why?'

'Don't ask me! Good-bye till to-morrow.'

# CHAPTER XLII

### THE QUAINT PHILOSOPHER

No person came to my room, and nothing happened to interrupt me while I was reading Mr Philip Dunboyne's letters.

One of them, let me say at once, produced a very disagreeable impression on me. I have unexpectedly discovered Mrs Tenbruggen – in a postscript. She is making a living as a Medical Rubber (or Masseuse), and is in professional attendance on Mr Dunboyne the elder. More of this, a little farther on.

Having gone through the whole collection of young Dunboyne's letters, I set myself to review the differing conclusions which the correspondence had produced on my mind.

I call the papers submitted to me a correspondence, because the greater part of Philip's letters exhibit notes in pencil, evidently added by Helena. These express, for the most part, the interpretation, which she had placed on passages that perplexed or displeased her; and they have, as Philip's rejoinders show, been employed as materials when she wrote her replies.

On reflection, I find myself troubled by complexities and contradictions in the view presented of this young man's character. To decide positively whether I can justify to myself and to my regard for Eunice, an attempt to reunite the lovers, requires more time for consideration than I can reasonably expect that Helena's patience will allow. Having a quiet hour or two still before me, I have determined to make extracts from the letters for my own use, with the intention of referring to them, while I am still in doubt which way my decision ought to incline. I shall present them here, to speak for themselves. Is there any objection to this? None that I can see.

In the first place, these extracts have a value of their own. They add necessary information to the present history of events.

In the second place, I am under no obligation to Mr Gracedieu's daughter which forbids me to make use of her portfolio. I told her that I only consented to receive it, under reserve of my own right of action – and her assent to that stipulation was expressed in the clearest terms.

## EXTRACTS FROM MR PHILIP DUNBOYNE'S LETTERS

### First Extract

You blame me, dear Helena, for not having paid proper attention to the questions put to me in your last letter. I have only been waiting to make up my mind, before I replied.

First question: Do I think it advisable that you should write to my father? No, my dear; I beg you will defer writing, until you hear from me again.

Second question: Considering that he is still a stranger to you, is there any harm in your asking me what sort of man my father is? No harm, my sweet one; but, as you will presently see, I am afraid you have addressed yourself to the wrong person.

My father is kind, in his own odd way – and learned, and rich – a more high-minded and honourable man (as I have every reason to believe) doesn't live. But if you ask me which he prefers, his books or his son, I hope I do him no injustice when I answer, his books. His reading and his writing are obstacles between us which I have never been able to overcome. This is the more to be regretted because he is charming, on the few occasions when I find him disengaged. If you wish I knew more about my father, we are in complete agreement as usual – I wish, too.

But there is a dear friend of yours and mine, who is just the person we want to help us. Need I say that I allude to Mrs Staveley?

I called on her yesterday, not long after she had paid a visit to my father. Luck had favoured her. She arrived just at the time when hunger had obliged him to shut up his books, and ring for something to eat. Mrs Staveley secured a favourable reception with her customary tact and delicacy. He had a fowl for his dinner. She knows his weakness of old; she volunteered to carve it for him.

If I can only repeat what this clever woman told me of their talk, you will have a portrait of Mr Dunboyne the elder – not perhaps a highly-finished picture, but, as I hope and believe, a good likeness.

Mrs Staveley began by complaining to him of the conduct of his son. I had promised to write to her, and I had never kept my word. She had reasons for being especially interested in my plans and prospects, just then; knowing me to be attached (please take notice that I am quoting her own language) to a charming friend of hers, whom I had first met at her house. To aggravate the disappointment that I had inflicted, the young lady had neglected her too. No letters, no information. Perhaps my father would kindly enlighten her? Was the affair going on? or was it broken off?

My father held out his plate and asked for the other wing of the fowl. 'It isn't a bad one for London,' he said; 'won't you have some yourself?'

'I don't seem to have interested you,' Mrs Staveley remarked.

'What did you expect me to be interested in?' my father inquired: 'I was absorbed in the fowl. Favour me by returning to the subject.'

Mrs Staveley admits that she answered this rather sharply: 'The subject, sir, was your son's admiration for a charming girl: one of the daughters of Mr Gracedieu, the famous preacher.'

My father is too well-bred to speak to a lady while his attention is absorbed by a fowl. He finished the second wing, and then he asked if 'Philip was engaged to be married'.

'I am not quite sure,' Mrs Staveley confessed.

'Then, my dear friend, we will wait till we *are* sure.'

'But, Mr Dunboyne, there is really no need to wait, I suppose your son comes here, now and then, to see you?'

'My son is most attentive. In course of time he will contrive to hit on the right hour for his visit. At present, poor fellow, he interrupts me every day.'

'Suppose he hits upon the right time to-morrow?'

'Yes?'

'You might ask him if he is engaged?'

'Pardon me. I think I might wait till Philip mentions it without asking.'

'What an extraordinary man you are!'

'Oh, no, no – only a philosopher.'

This tried Mrs Staveley's temper. You know what a perfectly candid person our friend is. She owned to me that she felt inclined to make herself disagreeable. 'That's thrown away upon me,' she said: 'I don't know what a philosopher is.'

Let me pause for a moment, dear Helena. I have inexcusably forgotten to speak of my father's personal appearance. It won't take long. I need only notice one interesting feature which, so to speak, lifts his face out of the common. He has an eloquent nose. Persons possessing this rare advantage are blessed with powers of expression not granted to their ordinary fellow-creatures. My father's nose is a mine of information to friends familiarly acquainted with it. It changes colour like a modest young lady's cheek. It works flexibly from side to side like the rudder of a ship. On the present occasion, Mrs Staveley saw it shift towards the left-hand side of his face. A sigh escaped the poor lady. Experience told her that my father was going to hold forth.

'You don't know what a philosopher is!' he repeated. 'Be so kind as to look at me. I am a philosopher.'

Mrs Staveley bowed.

'And a philosopher, my charming friend, is a man who has discovered a system of life. Some systems assert themselves in volumes – *my* system asserts itself in two words: Never think of anything until you have first asked yourself if there is an absolute necessity for doing it, at that particular moment. Thinking of things, when things needn't be thought of, is offering an opportunity to Worry; and Worry is the favourite agent of Death when the destroyer handles his work in a lingering way, and achieves premature results. Never look back, and never look forward, as long as you can possibly help it. Looking back leads the way to sorrow. And looking forward ends in the cruellest of all delusions: it encourages hope. The present time is the precious time. Live for the passing day: the passing day is all that we can be sure of. You suggested, just now, that I should ask my son if he was engaged to be married. How do we know what wear and tear of your nervous texture I

succeeded in saving when I said: "Wait till Philip mentions it
without asking"? There is the personal application of my
system. I have explained it in my time to every woman on the
list of my acquaintance, including the female servants. Not one
of them has rewarded me by adopting my system. How do you
feel about it?'

Mrs Staveley declined to tell me whether she had offered a
bright example of gratitude to the rest of the sex. When I asked
why, she declared that it was my turn now to tell her what I
had been doing.

You will anticipate what followed. She objected to the
mystery in which my prospects seemed to be involved. In plain
English, was I, or was I not, engaged to marry her dear Eunice?
I said, No. What else could I say? If I had told Mrs Staveley the
truth, when she insisted on my explaining myself, she would
have gone back to my father, and would have appealed to his
sense of justice to forbid our marriage. Finding me obstinately
silent, she has decided on writing to Eunice. So we parted. But
don't be disheartened. On my way out of the house, I met Mr
Staveley coming in, and had a little talk with him. He and his
wife and his family are going to the seaside, next week. Mrs
Staveley once out of our way, I can tell my father of our
engagement without any fear of consequences. If she writes to
him, the moment he sees my name mentioned, and finds
violent language associated with it, he will hand the letter to
me. 'Your business, Philip: don't interrupt me.' He will say
that, and go back to his books. There is my father, painted to
the life! Farewell, for the present.

*      *      *      *      *

*Remarks by H.G.* – Philip's grace and gaiety of style might be
envied by any professional Author. He amuses me, but he
rouses my suspicion at the same time. This slippery lover of
mine tells me to defer writing to his father, and gives no
reason for offering that strange advice to the young lady who
is soon to be a member of the family. Is this merely one more
instance of the weakness of his character? Or, now that he is

away from my influence, is he beginning to regret Eunice already?

*Added by the Governor.* – I too have my doubts. Is the flippant nonsense which Philip has written, inspired by the effervescent good spirits of a happy young man? Or is it assumed for a purpose? In this latter case, I should gladly conclude, that he was regarding his conduct to Eunice with becoming emotions of sorrow and shame.

## CHAPTER XLIII

### THE MASTERFUL MASSEUSE

My next quotations will suffer a process of abridgement. I intend them to present the substance of three letters, reduced as follows:

### *Second Extract*

Weak as he may be, Mr Philip Dunboyne shows (in his second letter) that he can feel resentment, and that he can express his feelings, in replying to Miss Helena. He protests against suspicions which he has not deserved. That he does sometimes think of Eunice he sees no reason to deny. He is conscious of errors and misdeeds, which – traceable as they are to Helena's irresistible fascinations – may perhaps be considered rather his misfortune than his fault. Be that as it may, he does indeed feel anxious to hear good accounts of Eunice's health. If this honest avowal excites her sister's jealousy, he will be disappointed in Helena for the first time.

His third letter shows that this exhibition of spirit has had its effect.

The imperious young lady regrets that she has hurt his feelings, and is rewarded for the apology by receiving news of the most gratifying kind. Faithful Philip has told his father that he is engaged to be married to Miss Helena Gracedieu, daughter of the celebrated Congregational preacher – and so on, and so on. Has Mr Dunboyne the elder expressed any objection to the young lady? Certainly not! He knows nothing of the other engagement to Eunice; and he merely objects, on principle, to looking forward. 'How do we know,' says the philosopher, 'what accidents may happen, or what doubts and hesitations may yet turn up? I am not to burden my mind in this matter, till I know that I must do it. Let me hear when she is ready to go to church, and I will be ready with the settlements. My compliments to Miss and her Papa, and let us wait a little.'

Dearest Helena – isn't he funny?

The next letter has been already mentioned.

In this there occurs the first startling reference to Mrs Tenbruggen, by name. She is in London, finding her way to lucrative celebrity by twisting, turning, and pinching the flesh of credulous persons, afflicted with nervous disorders; and she has already paid a few medical visits to Mr Dunboyne. He persists in poring over his books while Mrs Tenbruggen operates, sometimes on his cramped right hand, sometimes (in the fear that his brain may have something to do with it) on the back of his neck. One of them frowns over her rubbing, and the other frowns over his reading. It would be delightfully ridiculous, but for a drawback; Mr Philip Dunboyne's first impressions of Mrs Tenbruggen do not incline him to look at that lady from a humorous point of view.

Helena's remarks follow as usual. She has seen Mrs Tenbruggen's name on the address of a letter written by Miss Jillgall – which is quite enough to condemn Mrs Tenbruggen. As for Philip himself, she feels not quite sure of him, even yet. No more do I.

### Third Extract

The letter that follows must be permitted to speak for itself:

I have flown into a passion, dearest Helena; and I am afraid I shall make you fly into a passion too. Blame Mrs Tenbruggen; don't blame me.

On the first occasion when I found my father under the hands of the Medical Rubber, she took no notice of me. On the second occasion – when she had been in daily attendance on him for a week, at an exorbitant fee – she said in the coolest manner: 'Who is this young gentleman?' My father laid down his book, for a moment only: 'Don't interrupt me again, Ma'am. The young gentleman is my son Philip.' Mrs Tenbruggen eyed me with an appearance of interest which I was at a loss to account for. I hate an impudent woman. My visit came suddenly to an end.

The next time I saw my father, he was alone.

I asked him how he got on with Mrs Tenbruggen. As badly as possible, it appeared. 'She takes liberties with my neck; she interrupts me in my reading; and she does me no good. I shall end, Philip, in applying a medical rubbing to Mrs Tenbruggen.'

A few days later, I found the masterful 'Masseuse' torturing the poor old gentleman's muscles again. She had the audacity to say to me: 'Well, Mr Philip, when are you going to marry Miss Eunice Gracedieu?' My father looked up. 'Eunice?' he repeated. 'When my son told me he was engaged to Miss Gracedieu, he said "Helena!" Philip, what does this mean?' Mrs Tenbruggen was so obliging as to answer for me. 'Some mistake, sir; it's Eunice he is engaged to.' I confess I forgot myself. 'How the devil do you know that?' I burst out. Mrs Tenbruggen ignored me and my language. 'I am sorry to see, sir, that your son's education has been neglected; he seems to be grossly ignorant of the laws of politeness.' 'Never mind the laws of politeness,' says my father. 'You appear to be better acquainted with my son's matrimonial prospects than he is himself. How is that?' Mrs Tenbruggen favoured him with another ready reply: 'My authority is a letter, addressed to me by a relative of Mr Gracedieu – my dear and intimate friend, Miss Jillgall.' My father's keen eyes travelled backwards and forwards between his female surgeon and his son. 'Which am I to believe?' he inquired. 'I am surprised at your asking the question,' I said. Mrs Tenbruggen pointed to me. 'Look at Mr Philip, sir – and you will allow him one merit. He is capable of showing it, when he knows he has disgraced himself.' Without intending it,

I am sure, my father infuriated me; he looked as if he believed her. Out came one of the smallest and strongest words in the English language before I could stop it: 'Mrs Tenbruggen, you lie!' The illustrious Rubber dropped my father's hand – she had been operating on him all the time – and showed us that she could assert her dignity when circumstances called for the exertion: 'Either your son or I, sir, must leave the room. Which is it to be?' She met her match in my father. Walking quietly to the door, he opened it for Mrs Tenbruggen with a low bow. She stopped on her way out, and delivered her parting words: 'Messieurs Dunboyne, father and son, I keep my temper, and merely regard you as a couple of blackguards.' With that pretty assertion of her opinion, she left us.

When we were alone, there was but one course to take; I made my confession. It is impossible to tell you how my father received it – for he sat down at his library table with his back to me. The first thing he did was to ask me to help his memory.

'Did you say that the father of these girls was a parson?'

'Yes – a Congregational Minister.'

'What does the Minister think of you?'

'I don't know, sir.'

'Find out.'

That was all; not another word could I extract from him. I don't pretend to have discovered what he really has in his mind. I only venture on a suggestion. If there is any old friend in your town, who has some influence over your father, leave no means untried of getting that friend to say a kind word for us. And then ask your father to write to mine. This is, as I see it, our only chance.

*    *    *    *    *

There the letter ends. Helena's notes on it show that her pride is fiercely interested in securing Philip as a husband. Her victory over poor Eunice will, as she plainly intimates, be only complete when she is married to young Dunboyne. For the rest, her desperate resolution to win her way to my good graces is sufficiently intelligible, now.

My own impressions vary. Philip rather gains upon me; he

appears to have some capacity for feeling ashamed of himself. On the other hand, I regard the discovery of an intimate friendship existing between Mrs Tenbruggen and Miss Jillgall with the gloomiest views. Is this formidable Masseuse likely to ply her trade in the country towns? And is it possible that she may come to this town? God forbid!

Of the other letters in the collection, I need take no special notice. I returned the whole correspondence to Helena, and waited to hear from her.

The one recent event in Mr Gracedieu's family, worthy of record, is of a melancholy nature. After paying his visit to-day, the doctor has left word that nobody but the nurse is to go near the Minister. This seems to indicate, but too surely, a change for the worse.

Helena has been away all the evening at the Girls' School. She left a little note, informing me of her wishes: 'I shall expect to be favoured with your decision to-morrow morning, in my housekeeping room.'

At breakfast time, the report of the poor Minister was still discouraging. I noticed that Helena was absent from the table. Miss Jillgall suspected that the cause was bad news from Mr Philip Dunboyne, arriving by that morning's post. 'If you will excuse the use of strong language by a lady,' she said, 'Helena looked perfectly devilish when she opened the letter. She rushed away, and locked herself up in her own shabby room. A serious obstacle, as I suspect, in the way of her marriage. Cheering, isn't it?' As usual, good Selina expressed her sentiments without reserve.

I had to keep my appointment; and the sooner Helena Gracedieu and I understood each other the better.

I knocked at the door. It was loudly unlocked, and violently thrown open. Helena's temper had risen to boiling heat; she stammered with rage when she spoke to me.

'I mean to come to the point at once,' she said.

'I am glad to hear it, Miss Helena.'

'May I count on your influence to help me? I want a positive answer.'

I gave her what she wanted. I said: 'Certainly not.'

She took a crumpled letter from her pocket, opened it, and smoothed it out on the table with a blow of her open hand.

'Look at that,' she said.

I looked. It was the letter addressed to Mr Dunboyne the elder, which I had written for Mr Gracedieu — with the one object of preventing Helena's marriage.

'Of course, I can depend on you to tell me the truth?' she continued.

'Without fear or favour,' I answered, 'you may depend on *that.*'

'The signature to the letter, Mr Governor, is written by my father. But the letter itself is in a different hand. Do you, by any chance, recognize the writing?'

'I do.'

'Whose writing is it?'

'Mine.'


# CHAPTER XLIV

### THE RESURRECTION OF THE PAST

After having identified my handwriting, I waited with some curiosity to see whether Helena would let her anger honestly show itself, or whether she would keep it down. She kept it down.

'Allow me to return good for evil.' (The devil was uppermost, nevertheless, when Miss Gracedieu expressed herself in these self-denying terms.) 'You are no doubt anxious to know if Philip's father has been won over to serve your purpose. Here is Philip's own account of it; the last of his letters that I shall trouble you to read.'

I looked it over. The memorandum follows which I made for my own use:

An eccentric philosopher is as capable as the most commonplace human being in existence of behaving like an

honourable man. Mr Dunboyne read the letter which bore the
Minister's signature, and handed it to his son. 'Can you answer
that?' was all he said. Philip's silence confessed that he was
unable to answer it – and Philip himself, I made add, rose
accordingly in my estimation. His father pointed to the writing-
desk. 'I must spare my cramped hand,' the philosopher
resumed, 'and I must answer Mr Gracedieu's letter. Write, and
leave a place for my signature.' He began to dictate his reply.
'Sir, – My son Philip has seen your letter, and has no defence to
make. In this respect he has set an example of candour which I
propose to follow. There is no excuse for him. What I can do
to show that I feel for you, and agree with you, shall be done.
At the age which this young man has reached, the laws of
England abolish the authority of his father. If he is sufficiently
infatuated to place his honour and his happiness at the mercy of
a lady, who has behaved to her sister as your daughter has
behaved to Miss Eunice, I warn the married couple not to
expect a farthing of my money, either during my lifetime or
after my death. Your faithful servant, DUNBOYNE, SENIOR.'
Having performed his duty as secretary, Philip received his
dismissal: 'You may send my reply to the post,' his father said;
'and you may keep Mr Gracedieu's letter. Morally speaking, I
regard that last document as a species of mirror, in which a
young gentleman like yourself may see how ugly he looks.'
This, Philip declared, was his father's form of farewell.

I handed back the letter to Helena. Not a word passed
between us. In sinister silence she opened the door and left me
alone in the room.

That Mrs Gracedieu and I had met in the bygone time, and –
this was the only serious part of it – had met in secret, would
now be made known to the Minister. Was I to blame for
having shrunk from distressing my good friend, by telling him
that his wife had privately consulted me on the means of
removing his adopted child from his house? And, even if I had
been cruel enough to do this, would he have believed my
statement against the positive denial with which the woman
whom he loved and trusted would have certainly met it? No!
let the consequences of the coming disclosure be what they

might, I failed to see any valid reason for regretting my conduct in the past time.

I found Miss Jillgall waiting in the passage to see me come out.

Before I could tell her what had happened, there was a ring at the house-bell. The visitor proved to be Mr Wellwood, the doctor. I was anxious to speak to him on the subject of Mr Gracedieu's health. Miss Jillgall introduced me, as an old and dear friend of the Minister, and left us together in the dining-room.

'What do I think of Mr Gracedieu?' he said, repeating the first question that I put. 'Well, sir, I think badly of him.'

Entering into details, after that ominous reply, Mr Wellwood did not hesitate to say that his patient's nerves were completely shattered. Disease of the brain had, as he feared, been already set up. 'As to the causes which have produced this lamentable break-down,' the doctor continued, 'Mr Gracedieu has been in the habit of preaching extempore twice a day on Sundays, and sometimes in the week as well – and has uniformly refused to spare himself when he was in most urgent need of rest. If you have ever attended his chapel, you have seen a man in a state of fiery enthusiasm, feeling intensely every word that he utters. Think of such exhaustion as that implies going on for years together, and accumulating its wasting influences on a sensitively-organized constitution. Add that he is tormented by personal anxieties, which he confesses to no one, not even to his own children – and the sum of it all is that a worse case of its kind, I am grieved to say, has never occurred in my experience.'

Before the doctor left me to go to his patient, I asked leave to occupy a minute more of his time. My object was, of course, to speak about Eunice.

The change of subject seemed to be agreeable to Mr Wellwood. He smiled good-humouredly.

'You need feel no alarm about the health of that interesting girl,' he said. 'When she complained to me – at her age! – of not being able to sleep, I should have taken it more seriously if I had been told that she too had her troubles, poor little soul.

Love-troubles, most likely – but don't forget that my professional limits keep me in the dark! Have you heard that she took some composing medicine, which I had prescribed for her father? The effect (certain, in any case, to be injurious to a young girl) was considerably aggravated by the state of her mind at the time. A dream that frightened her, and something resembling delirium, seems to have followed. And she made matters worse, poor child, by writing in her diary about the visions and supernatural appearances that had terrified her. I was afraid of fever, on the day when they first sent for me. We escaped that complication, and I was at liberty to try the best of all remedies – quiet and change of air. I have no fears for Miss Eunice.'

With that cheering reply he went up to the Minister's room.

All that I had found perplexing in Eunice was now made clear. I understood how her agony at the loss of her lover, and her keen sense of the wrong that she had suffered, had been strengthened in their disastrous influence by her experiment on the sleeping draught intended for her father. In mind and body, both, the poor girl was in the condition which offered its opportunity to the lurking hereditary taint. It was terrible to think of what might have happened, if the all-powerful counter-influence had not been present to save her.

Before I had been long alone the servant-maid came in, and said the doctor wanted to see me.

Mr Wellwood was waiting in the passage, outside the Minister's bedchamber. He asked if he could speak to me without interruption, and without the fear of being overheard. I led him at once to the room which I occupied as a guest.

'At the very time when it is most important to keep Mr Gracedieu quiet,' he said, 'something has happened to excite – I might almost say to infuriate him. He has left his bed, and is walking up and down the room; and, I don't scruple to say, he is on the verge of madness. He insists on seeing you. Being wholly unable to control him in any other way, I have consented to this. But I must not allow you to place yourself in what may be a disagreeable position, without a word of warning. Judging by his tones and his looks, he seems to have no very friendly motive for wishing to see you.'

Knowing perfectly well what had happened, and being one of those impatient people who can never endure suspense, I offered to go at once to Mr Gracedieu's room. The doctor asked leave to say one word more.

'Pray be careful that you neither say nor do anything to thwart him,' Mr Wellwood resumed. 'If he expresses an opinion, agree with him. In the state of his brain, the one hopeful course to take is to let him have his own way. Pray remember that. I will be within call, in case of your wanting me.'


## CHAPTER XLV

### THE FATAL PORTRAIT

I knocked at the bedroom door.

'Who's there?'

Only two words – but the voice that uttered them, hoarse and peremptory, was altered almost beyond recognition. If I had not known whose room it was, I might have doubted whether the Minister had really spoken to me.

At the instant when I answered him, I was allowed to pass in. Having admitted me, he closed the door, and placed himself with his back against it. The customary pallor of his face had darkened to a deep red; there was an expression of ferocious mockery in his eyes. Helena's vengeance had hurt her unhappy father far more severely than it seemed likely to hurt me. The doctor had said he was on the verge of madness. To my thinking, he had already passed the boundary line.

He received me with a boisterous affectation of cordiality.

'My excellent friend! My admirable, honourable, welcome guest, you don't know how glad I am to see you. Stand a little nearer to the light; I want to admire you.'

Remembering the doctor's advice, I obeyed him in silence.

'Ah, you were a handsome fellow when I first knew you,' he said, 'and you have some remains of it still left. Do you remember the time when you were a favourite with the ladies? Oh, don't pretend to be modest; don't turn your back, now you are old, on what you were in the prime of your life. Do you own that I am right?'

What his object might be in saying this – if, indeed, he had an object – it was impossible to guess. The doctor's advice left me no alternative; I hastened to own that he was right. As I made that answer, I observed that he held something in his hand which was half hidden up the sleeve of his dressing-gown. What the nature of the object was I failed to discover.

'And when I happened to speak of you somewhere,' he went on, 'I forget where – a member of my congregation – I don't recollect who it was – told me you were connected with the aristocracy. How were you connected?'

He surprised me; but, however he had got his information, he had not been deceived. I told him that I was connected, through my mother, with the family to which he had alluded.

'The aristocracy!' he repeated. 'A race of people who are rich, without earning their money, and noble because their great-grandfathers were noble before them. They live in idleness and luxury – profligates who gratify their passions without shame and without remorse. Deny, if you dare, that this is a true description of them.'

It was really pitiable. Heartily sorry for him, I pacified him again.

'And don't suppose I forget that you are one of them. Do you hear me, my noble friend?'

There was no help for it – I made another conciliatory reply.

'So far,' he resumed, 'I don't complain of you. You have not attempted to deceive me – yet. Absolute silence is what I require next. Though you may not suspect it, my mind is a ferment; I must try to think.'

To some extent at least, his thoughts betrayed themselves in his actions. He put the object that I had half seen in his hand into the pocket of his dressing-gown, and moved to the toilet-table. Opening one of the drawers, he took from it a folded sheet of paper, and came back to me.

'A minister of the Gospel,' he said, 'is a sacred man, and has a horror of crime. You are safe, so far – provided you obey me. I have a solemn and terrible duty to perform. This is not the right place for it. Follow me downstairs.'

He led the way out. The doctor, waiting in the passage, was not near the stairs, and so escaped notice. 'What is it?' Mr Wellwood whispered. In the same guarded way, I said: 'He has not told me yet; I have been careful not to irritate him.' When we descended the stairs, the doctor followed us at a safe distance. He mended his pace when the Minister opened the door of the study, and when he saw us both pass in. Before he could follow, the door was closed and locked in his face. Mr Gracedieu took out the key and threw it, through the open window, into the garden below.

Turning back into the room, he laid the folded sheet of paper on the table. That done, he spoke to me.

'I distrust my own weakness,' he said. 'A dreadful necessity confronts me – I might shrink from the horrid idea, and, if I could open the door, might try to get away. Escape is impossible now. We are prisoners together. But don't suppose that we are alone. There is a third person present, who will judge between you and me. Look there!'

He pointed solemnly to the portrait of his wife. It was a small picture, very simply framed; representing the face in a 'three-quarter' view, and part of the figure only. As a work of art it was contemptible; but, as a likeness, it answered its purpose. My unhappy friend stood before it, in an attitude of dejection, covering his face with his hands.

In the interval of silence that followed, I was reminded that an unseen friend was keeping watch outside.

Alarmed by having heard the key turned in the lock, and realizing the embarrassment of the position in which I was placed, the doctor had discovered a discreet way of communicating with me. He slipped one of his visiting cards under the door, with these words written on it: 'How can I help you?'

I took the pencil from my pocket-book, and wrote on the blank side of the card: 'He has thrown the key into the garden; look for it under the window.' A glance at the Minister, before

I returned my reply, showed that his attitude was unchanged. Without being seen or suspected, I, in my turn, slipped the card under the door.

The slow minutes followed each other – and still nothing happened.

My anxiety to see how the doctor's search for the key was succeeding, tempted me to approach the window. On my way to it, the tail of my coat, threw down a little tray containing pens and pencils, which had been left close to the edge of the table. Slight as the noise of the fall was, it disturbed Mr Gracedieu. He looked round vacantly.

'I have been comforted by prayer,' he told me. 'The weakness of poor humanity has found strength in the Lord.' He pointed to the portrait once more: 'My hands must not presume to touch it, while I am still in doubt. Take it down.'

I removed the picture and placed it, by his directions, on a chair that stood midway between us. To my surprise his tones faltered; I saw tears rising in his eyes.

'You may think you see a picture there,' he said. 'You are wrong. You see my wife herself. Stand here, and look at my wife with me.'

We stood together, with our eyes fixed on the portrait.

Without anything said or done on my part to irritate him, he suddenly turned to me in a state of furious rage. 'Not a sign of sorrow!' he burst out. 'Not a blush of shame! Wretch, you stand condemned by the atrocious composure that I see in your face!'

A first discovery of the odious suspicion of which I was the object, dawned on my mind at that moment. My capacity for restraining myself completely failed me. I spoke to him as if he had been an accountable being. 'Once for all,' I said, 'tell me what I have a right to know. You suspect me of something. What is it?'

Instead of directly replying, he seized my arm, and led me to the table. 'Take up that paper,' he said. 'There is writing on it. Read – and let Her judge between us. Your life depends on how you answer me.'

Was there a weapon concealed in the room? or had he got it in the pocket of his dressing-gown? I listened for the sound of the doctor's returning footsteps in the passage outside, and heard nothing. My life had once depended, years since, on my success in heading the arrest of an escaped prisoner. I was not conscious, then, of feeling my energies weakened by fear. But *that* man was not mad; and I was younger, in those days, by a good twenty years or more. At my later time of life, I could show my old friend that I was not afraid of him – but I was conscious of an effort in doing it.

I opened the paper. 'Am I to read this to myself?' I asked. 'Or am I to read it aloud?'

'Read it aloud!'

In these terms, his daughter addressed him:

'I have been so unfortunate, dearest father, as to displease you, and I dare not hope that you will consent to receive me. What it is my painful duty to tell you, must be told in writing.

'Grieved as I am to distress you, in your present state of health, I must not hesitate to reveal what it has been my misfortune – I may even say my misery, when I think of my mother – to discover.

'But let me make sure, in such a serious matter as this is, that I am not mistaken.

'In those happy past days, when I was still dear to my father, you said you thought of writing to invite a dearly-valued friend to pay a visit to this house. You had first known him, as I understood, when my mother was still living. Many interesting things you told me about this old friend, but you never mentioned that he knew, or that he had even seen, my mother. I was left to suppose that those two had remained strangers to each other to the day of her death.

'If there is any misinterpretation here of what you said, or perhaps of what you meant to say, pray destroy what I have written without turning to the next page; and forgive me for having innocently startled you by a false alarm.'

Mr Gracedieu interrupted me.

'Put it down!' he cried; 'I won't wait till you have got to the end – I shall question you now. Give me the paper; it will help me to keep this mystery of iniquity clear in my own mind.'

I gave him the paper.

He hesitated – and looked at the portrait once more. 'Turn her away from me,' he said; 'I can't face my wife.'

I placed the picture with its back to him.

He consulted the paper, reading it with but little of the confusion and hesitation which my experience of him had induced me to anticipate. Had the mad excitement that possessed him exercised an influence in clearing his mind, resembling in some degree the influence exercised by a storm in clearing the air? Whatever the right explanation may be, I can only report what I saw. I could hardly have mastered what his daughter had written more readily, if I had been reading it myself.

'Helena tells me,' he began, 'that you said you knew her by her likeness to her mother. Is that true?'

'Quite true.'

'And you made an excuse for leaving her – see! here it is, written down. You made an excuse, and left her when she asked for an explanation.'

'I did.'

He consulted the paper again.

'My daughter says – No! I won't be hurried and I won't be interrupted – she says you were confused. Is that so?'

'It is so. Let your questions wait for a moment. I wish to tell you why I was confused.'

'Haven't I said I won't be interrupted? Do you think you can shake *my* resolution?' He referred to the paper again. 'I have lost the place. It's your fault – find it for me.'

The evidence which was intended to convict me was the evidence which I was expected to find! I pointed it out to him.

His natural courtesy asserted itself in spite of his anger. He said 'Thank you,' and questioned me the moment after as fiercely as ever. 'Go back to the time, sir, when we met in your rooms at the prison. Did you know my wife then?'

'Certainly not.'

'Did you and she see each other – ha! I've got it now – did you see each other after I had left the town? No prevarication! You own to telling Helena that you knew her by her likeness to her mother. You must have seen her mother. Where?'

I made another effort to defend myself. He again refused furiously to hear me. It was useless to persist. Whatever the danger that threatened me might be, the sooner it showed itself the easier I should feel. I told him that Mrs Gracedieu had called on me, after he and his wife had left the town.

'Do you mean to tell me,' he cried, 'that she came to you?'

'I do.'

After that answer, he no longer required the paper to help him. He threw it from him on the floor.

'And you received her,' he said, 'without inquiring whether I knew of her visit or not? Guilty deception on your part – guilty deception on her part. Oh, the hideous wickedness of it!'

When his mad suspicion that I had been his wife's lover betrayed itself in this way, I made a last attempt, in the face of my own conviction that it was hopeless, to place my conduct and his wife's conduct before him in the true light.

'Mrs Gracedieu's object was to consult me——' Before I could say the next words, I saw him put his hand into the pocket of his dressing-gown.

'An innocent man,' he sternly declared, 'would have told me that my wife had been to see him – you kept it a secret. An innocent woman would have given me a reason for wishing to go to you – she kept it a secret, when she left my house; she kept it a secret when she came back.'

'Mr Gracedieu, I insist on being heard! Your wife's motive——'

He drew from his pocket the thing that he had hidden from me. This time, there was no concealment; he let me see that he was opening a razor. It was no time for asserting my innocence; I had to think of preserving my life. When a man is without firearms, what defence can avail against a razor in the hands of a madman? A chair was at my side; it offered the one poor means of guarding myself that I could see. I laid my hand on it, and kept my eye on him.

He paused, looking backwards and forwards between the picture and me.

'Which of them shall I kill first?' he said to himself. 'The man who was my trusted friend? Or the woman whom I believed to be an angel on earth?' He stopped once more, in a state of fierce self-concentration, debating what he should do. 'The woman,' he decided. 'Wretch! Fiend! Harlot! How I loved her!!!'

With a yell of fury, he pounced on the picture – ripped the canvas out of the frame – and cut it malignantly into fragments. As they dropped from the razor on the floor, he stamped on them, and ground them under his foot. 'Go, wife of my bosom,' he cried, with a dreadful mockery of voice and look – 'go, and burn everlastingly in the place of torment!' His eyes glared at me. 'Your turn now,' he said – and rushed at me with his weapon ready in his hand. I hurled the chair at his right arm. The razor dropped on the floor. I caught him by the wrist. Like a wild animal he tried to bite me. With my free hand – if I had known how to defend myself in any other way, I would have taken that way – with my free hand I seized him by the throat; forced him back; and held him against the wall. My grasp on his throat kept him quiet. But the dread of seriously injuring him so completely overcame me, that I forgot I was a prisoner in the room, and was on the point of alarming the household by a cry for help.

I was still struggling to preserve my self-control, when the sound of footsteps broke the silence outside. I heard the key turn in the lock, and saw the doctor at the open door.

## CHAPTER XLVI

### THE CUMBERSOME LADIES

I cannot prevail upon myself to dwell at any length on the events that followed.

We secured my unhappy friend, and carried him to his bed. It was necessary to have men in attendance who could perform the duty of watching him. The doctor sent for them, while I went downstairs to make the best I could of the miserable news which it was impossible entirely to conceal.

All that I could do to spare Miss Jillgall, I did. I was obliged to acknowledge that there had been an outbreak of violence, and that the portrait of the Minister's wife had been destroyed by the Minister himself. Of Helena's revenge on me I said nothing. It had led to consequences which even her merciless malice could not have contemplated. There were no obstacles in the way of keeping secret the attempt on my life. But I was compelled to own that Mr Gracedieu had taken a dislike to me, which rendered it necessary that my visit should be brought to an end. I hastened to add that I should go to the hotel, and should wait there until the next day, in the hope of hearing better news.

Of the multitude of questions with which poor Miss Jillgall overwhelmed me – of the wild words of sorrow and alarm that escaped her – of the desperate manner in which she held me by my arm, and implored me not to go away, when I must see for myself that 'she was a person entirely destitute of presence of mind' – I shall say nothing. The undeserved suffering that is inflicted on innocent persons by the sins of others demands silent sympathy; and, to that extent at least, I can say that I honestly felt for my quaint and pleasant little friend.

In the evening the doctor called on me at the hotel. The medical treatment of his patient had succeeded in calming the maddened brain under the influence of sleep. If the night passed quietly, better news might be hoped for in the morning.

On the next day I had arranged to drive to the farm, being resolved not to disappoint Eunice. But I shrank from the prospect of having to distress her as I had already distressed Miss Jillgall. The only alternative left was to repeat the sad story in writing, subject to the concealments which I had already observed. This I did, and sent the letter by messenger, overnight, so that Eunice might know when to expect me.

The medical report, in the morning, justified some hope. Mr Gracedieu had slept well, and there had been no reappearance of insane violence on his waking. But the doctor's opinion was far from encouraging when we spoke of the future. He did not anticipate the cruel necessity of placing the Minister under restraint – unless some new provocation led to a new outbreak.

The misfortune to be feared was imbecility.

I was just leaving the hotel to keep my appointment with Eunice, when the waiter announced the arrival of a young lady who wished to speak with me. Before I could ask if she had mentioned her name, the young lady herself walked in – Helena Gracedieu.

She explained her object in calling on me, with the exasperating composure which was peculiarly her own. No parallel to it occurs to me in my official experience of shameless women.

'I don't wish to speak of what happened yesterday, so far as I know anything about it,' she began. 'It is quite enough for me that you have been obliged to leave the house and to take refuge in this hotel. I have come to say a word about the future. Are you honouring me with your attention?'

I signed to her to go on. If I had answered in words, I should have told her to leave the room.

'At first,' she resumed, 'I thought of writing; but it occurred to me that you might keep my letter, and show it to Philip, by way of lowering me in his good opinion, as you have lowered me in the good opinion of his father. My object in coming here is to give you a word of warning. If you attempt to make mischief next between Philip and myself, I shall hear of it – and you know what to expect, when you have me for an enemy. It is not worth while to say any more. We understand each other, I hope?'

She was determined to have a reply – and she got it.

'Not quite yet,' I said. 'I have been hitherto, as becomes a gentleman, always mindful of a woman's claims to forbearance. You will do well not to tempt me into forgetting that *you* are a woman, by prolonging your visit. Now, Miss Helena Gracedieu, we understand each other.'

She made me a low curtsey, and answered in her finest tone of irony: 'I only desire to wish you a pleasant journey home.'

I rang for the waiter. 'Show this lady out,' I said.

Even this failed to have the slightest effect on her. She sauntered to the door, as perfectly at her ease as if the room had been hers – not mine.

I had thought of driving to the farm. Shall I confess it? My temper was so completely upset that active movement of some kind offered the one means of relief in which I could find refuge. The farm was not more than five miles distant, and I had been a good walker all my life. After making the needful inquiries, I set forth to visit Eunice on foot.

My way through the town led me past the Minister's house. I had left the door some fifty yards behind me, when I saw two ladies approaching. They were walking, in the friendliest manner, arm in arm. As they came nearer, I discovered Miss Jillgall. Her companion was the middle-aged lady who had declined to give her name, when we met accidentally at Mr Gracedieu's door.

Hysterically impulsive, Miss Jillgall seized both my hands, and overwhelmed me with entreaties that I would go back with her to the house. I listened rather absently. The middle-aged lady happened to be nearer to me now than on either of the former occasions on which I had seen her. There was something in the expression of her eyes which seemed to be familiar to me. But the effort of my memory was not helped by what I observed in the other parts of her face. The iron-grey hair, the baggy lower eyelids, the fat cheeks, the coarse complexion, and the double chin, were features, and very disagreeable features too, which I had never seen at any former time.

'Do pray come back with us,' Miss Jillgall pleaded. 'We were just talking of you. I and my friend——' There she stopped, evidently on the point of blurting out the name which she had been forbidden to utter in my hearing.

The lady smiled; her provokingly familiar eyes rested on me with a humorous enjoyment of the scene.

'My dear,' she said to Miss Jillgall, 'caution ceases to be a virtue when it ceases to be of any use. The Governor is beginning to remember me, and the inevitable recognition – with *his* quickness of perception – is likely to be a matter of minutes now.' She turned to me. 'In more ways than one, sir, women are hardly used by Nature. As they advance in years they lose more in personal appearance than the men do. You are white-haired, and (pray excuse me) you stoop at the shoulders – but you have not entirely lost your good looks. *I am no longer recognizable.* Allow me to prompt you, as they say on the stage. I am Mrs Tenbruggen.'

As a man of the world, I ought to have been capable of concealing my astonishment and dismay. She struck me dumb.

Mrs Tenbruggen in the town! The one woman whose appearance Mr Gracedieu had dreaded, and justly dreaded, stood before me – free, as a friend of his kinswoman, to enter his house, at the very time when he was a helpless man, guarded by watchers at his bedside. My first clear idea was to get away from both the women, and consider what was to be done next. I bowed – and begged to be excused – and said I was in a hurry, all in a breath.

Hearing this, the best of genial old maids was unable to restrain her curiosity. 'Where are you going?' she asked.

Too confused to think of an excuse, I said I was going to the farm.

'To see my dear Euneece?' Miss Jillgall burst out. 'Oh, we will go with you!' Mrs Tenbruggen's politeness added immediately, 'With the greatest pleasure.'

## CHAPTER XLVII

### THE JOURNEY TO THE FARM

My first ungrateful impulse was to get rid of the two cumbersome ladies who had offered to be my companions. It was needless to call upon my invention for an excuse; the truth, as I gladly perceived, would serve my purpose. I had only to tell them that I had arranged to walk to the farm.

Lean, wiry, and impetuous, Miss Jillgall received my excuse with the sincerest approval of it, as a new idea. 'Nothing could be more agreeable to me,' she declared; 'I have been a wonderful walker all my life.' She turned to her friend. 'We will go with him, my dear, won't we?'

Mrs Tenbruggen's reception of this proposal inspired me with

hope; she asked how far it was to the farm. 'Five miles!' she
repeated. 'And five miles back again, unless the farmer lends us
a cart. My dear Selina, you might as well ask me to walk to the
North Pole. You have got rid of one of us, Mr Governor,' she
added pleasantly; 'and the other, if you only walk fast enough,
you will leave behind you on the road. If I believed in luck –
which I don't – I should call you a fortunate man.'

But companionable Selina would not hear of a separation.
She asked, in her most irresistible manner, if I objected to
driving instead of walking. Her heart's dearest wish, she said,
was to make her bosom friend and myself better acquainted
with each other. To conclude, she reminded me that there was
a cab-stand in the next street.

Perhaps I might have been influenced by my distrust of Mrs
Tenbruggen, or perhaps by my anxiety to protect Eunice. It
struck me that I might warn the defenceless girl to be on her
guard with Mrs Tenbruggen to better purpose, if Eunice was in
a position to recognize her in any future emergency that might
occur. To my mind, this dangerous woman was doubly
formidable – and for a good reason: she was the bosom friend of
that innocent and unwary person, Miss Jillgall.

So I amiably consented to forego my walk, yielding to the
superior attraction of Mrs Tenbruggen's company. On that day
the sunshine was tempered by a delightful breeze. If we had
been in the biggest and worst-governed city on the civilized
earth, we should have found no public vehicle, open to the air,
which could offer accommodation to three people. Being only
in a country town, we had a light four-wheeled chaise at our
disposal as a matter of course.

No wise man expects to be mercifully treated, when he is
shut into a carriage with a mature single lady, inflamed by
curiosity. I was not unprepared for Miss Jillgall when she
alluded, for the second time, to the sad events which had
happened in the house on the previous day – and especially to
the destruction by Mr Gracedieu of the portrait of his wife.

'Why didn't he destroy something else?' she pleaded
piteously. 'It is such a disappointment to me. I never liked that
picture myself. Of course I ought to have admired the portrait

of the wife of my benefactor. But no – that disagreeable painted face was too much for me. I should have felt inexpressibly relieved, if I could have shown it to Elizabeth, and heard her say that she agreed with me.'

'Perhaps I saw it when I called on you,' Mrs Tenbruggen suggested. 'Where did the picture hang?'

'My dear! I received you in the dining-room, and the portrait hung in Mr Gracedieu's study.'

What they said to each other next, escaped my attention. Quite unconsciously, Miss Jillgall had revealed to me a danger which neither the Minister nor I had discovered, though it had conspicuously threatened us both on the wall of the study. The act of mad destruction which, if I had possessed the means of safely interfering, I should certainly have endeavoured to prevent, now assumed a new and startling aspect. If Mrs Tenbruggen really had some motive of her own for endeavouring to identify the adopted child, the preservation of the picture must have led her straight to the end in view. The most casual opportunity of comparing Helena with the portrait of Mrs Gracedieu would have revealed the likeness between mother and daughter – and, that result attained, the identification of Eunice with the infant whom the 'Miss Chance' of those days had brought to the prison must inevitably have followed. It was perhaps natural that Mr Gracedieu's infatuated devotion to the memory of his wife, should have blinded him to the betrayal of Helena's parentage, which met his eyes every time he entered his study. But that I should have been too stupid to discover what he had failed to see, was a wound dealt to my self-esteem which I was vain enough to feel acutely.

Mrs Tenbruggen's voice, cheery and humorous, broke in on my reflections, with an odd question:

'Mr Governor, do you ever condescend to read novels?'

'It's not easy to say, Mrs Tenbruggen, how grateful I am to the writers of novels.'

'Ah! I read novels, too. But I blush to confess – do I blush? – that I never thought of feeling grateful till you mentioned it. Selina and I don't complain of your preferring your own reflections to our company. On the contrary, you have reminded us agreeably of the heroes of fiction, when the author describes them as being "absorbed in thought". For some minutes, Mr Governor, you have been a hero; absorbed, as I venture to guess, in unpleasant remembrances of the time when I was a single lady. You have not forgotten how badly I behaved, and what shocking things I said, in those bygone days. Am I right?'

'You are entirely wrong.'

It is possible that I may have spoken a little too sharply. Anyway, faithful Selina interceded for her friend. 'Oh, dear Sir, don't be hard on Elizabeth! She always means well.' Mrs Tenbruggen, as facetious as ever, made a grateful return for a small compliment. She chucked Miss Jillgall under the chin, with the air of an amorous old gentleman expressing his approval of a pretty servant-girl. It was impossible to look at the two, in their relative situations, without laughing. But Mrs Tenbruggen failed to cheat me into altering my opinion of her. Innocent Miss Jillgall clapped her ugly hands, and said: 'Isn't she good company?'

Mrs Tenbruggen's social resources were not exhausted yet. She suddenly shifted to the serious side of her character.

'Perhaps I have improved a little,' she said, 'as I have advanced in years. The sorrows of an unhappy married life may have had a purifying influence on my nature. My husband and I began badly. Mr Tenbruggen thought I had money; and I thought Mr Tenbruggen had money. He was taken in by me; and I was taken in by him. When he repeated the words of the marriage service (most impressively read by your friend the Chaplain): "With all my worldy goods I thee endow" – his eloquent voice suggested one of the largest incomes in Europe. When I promised and vowed, in my turn, the delightful prospect of squandering my rich husband's money made quite a new woman of me. I declare solemnly, when I said I would love, honour, and obey Mr T., I looked as if I really meant it. Wherever he is now, poor dear, he is cheating somebody. Such a handsome gentlemanlike man, Selina! And, oh, Mr Governor, such a blackguard!'

Having described her husband in those terms, she got tired of the subject. We were now favoured with another view of this many-sided woman. She appeared in her professional character.

'Ah, what a delicious breeze is blowing, out here in the country!' she said. 'Will you excuse me if I take off my gloves? I want to air my hands.' She held up her hands to the breeze; firm, muscular, deadly white hands. 'In my professional occupation,' she explained, 'I am always rubbing, tickling, squeezing, tapping, kneading, rolling, striking the muscles of patients. Selina, do you know the movements of your own joints? Flexion, extension, abduction, adduction, rotation, circumduction, pronation, supination, and the lateral movements. Be proud of those accomplishments, my dear, but beware of attempting to become a Masseuse. There are drawbacks to that vocation – and I am conscious of one of them at this moment.' She lifted her hands to her nose. 'Pah! my hands smell of other people's flesh. The delicious country air will blow it away – the luxury of purification!' Her fingers twisted and quivered, and got crooked at one moment and straight again at another, and showed themselves in succession singly, and flew into each other fiercely interlaced, and then spread out again like the sticks of a fan, until it really made me giddy to look at them. As for Miss Jillgall, she lifted her poor little sunken eyes rapturously to the sky, as if she called the honest sunlight to witness that this was the most lovable woman on the face of the earth.

But elderly female fascination offers its allurements in vain to the rough animal, man. Suspicion of Mrs Tenbruggen's motives had established itself firmly in my mind. Why had the popular Masseuse abandoned her brilliant career in London, and plunged into the obscurity of a country town? An opportunity of clearing up the doubt thus suggested seemed to have presented itself now. 'Is it indiscreet to ask,' I said, 'if you are here in your professional capacity?'

Her cunning seized its advantage and put a sly question to me. 'Do you wish to be one of my patients yourself?'

'That is unfortunately impossible,' I replied; 'I have arranged to return to London.'

'Immediately?'

'To-morrow at the latest.'

Artful as she was, Mrs Tenbruggen failed to conceal a momentary expression of relief which betrayed itself, partly in her manner, partly in her face. She had ascertained, to her own complete satisfaction, that my speedy departure was an event which might be relied on.

'But I have not yet answered you,' she resumed. 'To tell the truth, I am eager to try my hands on you. Massage, as I practise it, would lighten your weight, and restore your figure; I may even say would lengthen your life. You will think of me, one of these days, won't you? In the meanwhile – yes! I am here in my professional capacity. Several interesting cases; and one very remarkable person, brought to death's door by the doctors; a rich man who is liberal in paying his fees. There is my quarrel with London, and Londoners. Some of their papers, medical newspapers of course, declare that my fees are exorbitant; and there is a tendency among the patients – I mean the patients who are rolling in riches – to follow the lead of the newspapers. I am no worm to be trodden on, in that way. The London people shall wait for me, until they miss me – and, when I do go back, they will find the fees increased. *My* fingers and thumbs, Mr Governor, are not to be insulted with impunity.'

Miss Jillgall nodded her head at me. It was an eloquent nod. 'Admire my spirited friend,' was the interpretation I put on it.

At the same time, my private sentiments suggested that Mrs Tenbruggen's reply was too perfectly satisfactory, viewed as an explanation. My suspicions were by no means set at rest; and I was resolved not to let the subject drop yet. 'Speaking of Mr Gracedieu, and of the chances of his partial recovery,' I said, 'do you think the Minister would benefit by Massage?'

'I haven't a doubt of it, if you can get rid of the doctor.'

'You think he would be an obstacle in the way?'

'There are some medical men who are honourable exceptions to the general rule; and he may be one of them,' Mrs Tenbruggen admitted. 'Don't be too hopeful. As a doctor, he belongs to the most tyrannical trades-union in existence. May I make a personal remark?'

'Certainly.'

'I find something in your manner – pray don't suppose that I am angry – which looks like distrust; I mean, distrust of me.'

Miss Jillgall's ever ready kindness interfered in my defence: 'Oh, no, Elizabeth! You are not often mistaken; but indeed you are wrong now. Look at my distinguished friend. I remember my copy-book, when I was a small creature learning to write, in England. There were first lines that we copied, in big letters, and one of them said, "Distrust Is Mean". I know a young person, whose name begins with H, who is one mass of meanness. But' – excellent Selina paused, and pointed to me with a gesture of triumph – 'no meanness there!'

Mrs Tenbruggen waited to hear what I had to say, scornfully insensible to Miss Jillgall's well-meant interruption.

'You are not altogether mistaken,' I told her. 'I can't say that my mind is in a state of distrust, but I own that you puzzle me.'

'How, if you please?'

'May I presume that you remember the occasion when we met at Mr Gracedieu's house-door? You saw that I failed to recognize you, and you refused to give your name when the servant asked it. A few days afterwards, I heard you (quite accidentally) forbid Miss Jillgall to mention your name in my hearing. I am at a loss to understand it.'

Before she could answer me, the chaise drew up at the gate of the farm-house. Mrs Tenbruggen carefully promised to explain what had puzzled me, at the first opportunity. 'If it escapes my memory,' she said, 'pray remind me of it.'

I determined to remind her of it. Whether I could depend on her to tell the truth, might be quite another thing.

## CHAPTER XLVIII

### THE DECISION OF EUNICE

Eunice ran out to meet us, and opened the gate. She was instantly folded in Miss Jillgall's arms. On her release, she came to me, eager for news of her father's health. When I had communicated all that I thought it right to tell her of the doctor's last report, she noticed Mrs Tenbruggen. The appearance of a stranger seemed to embarrass her. I left Miss Jillgall to introduce them to each other.

'Darling Euneece, you remember Mrs Tenbruggen's name, I am sure? Elizabeth, this is my sweet girl; I mentioned her in my letters to you.'

'I hope she will be *my* sweet girl, when we know each other a little better. May I kiss you, dear? You have lovely eyes; but I am sorry to see that they don't look like happy eyes. You want Mamma Tenbruggen to cheer you. What a charming old house!'

She put her arm round Eunice's waist, and led her to the house-door. Her enjoyment of the creepers that twined their way up the pillars of the porch was simply perfection, as a piece of acting. When the farmer's wife presented herself, Mrs Tenbruggen was so irresistibly amiable, and took such flattering notice of the children, that the harmless British matron actually blushed with pleasure. 'I'm sure, ma'am, you must have children of your own,' she said. Mrs Tenbruggen cast her eyes on the floor, and sighed with pathetic resignation. A sweet little family, and all cruelly swept away by death. If the performance meant anything, it did most assuredly mean that.

'What wonderful self-possession!' somebody whispered in my ear. The children in the room were healthy, well-behaved little creatures – but the name of the innocent one among them was Selina.

Before dinner we were shown over the farm.

The good woman of the house led the way, and Miss Jillgall and I accompanied her. The children ran on in front of us. Still keeping possession of Eunice, Mrs Tenbruggen followed at some distance behind. I looked back, after no very long interval, and saw that a separation had taken place. Mrs Tenbruggen passed me, not looking so pleasantly as usual, joined the children, and walked with two of them, hand in hand, a pattern of maternal amiability. I dropped back a little, and gave Eunice an opportunity of joining me; having purposely left her to form her own opinion, without any adverse influence exercised on my part.

'Is that lady a friend of yours?' she asked.

'No; only an acquaintance. What do you think of her?'

'I thought I should like her at first; she was so kind, and seemed to take such an interest in me. But she said such strange things – asked if I was reckoned like my mother, and which of us was the eldest, my sister or myself, and whether we were my father's only two children, and if one of us was more his favourite than the other. What I could tell her, I did tell. But when I said I didn't know which of us was the oldest, she gave me an impudent tap on the cheek, and said, "I don't believe you, child," and left me. How can Selina be so fond of her? Don't mention it to anyone else; I hope I shall never see her again.'

'I will keep your secret, Eunice; and you must keep mine. I entirely agree with you.'

'You agree with me in disliking her?'

'Heartily.'

We could say no more at that time. Our friends in advance were waiting for us. We joined them at once.

If I had felt any doubt of the purpose which had really induced Mrs Tenbruggen to leave London, all further uncertainty on my part was at an end. She had some vile interest of her own to serve by identifying Mr Gracedieu's adopted child – but what the nature of that interest might be, it was impossible to guess. The future, when I thought of it now, filled me with dismay. A more utterly helpless position than mine it was not easy to conceive. To warn the Minister, in his present critical state of health, was simply impossible. My relations with Helena forbade me even to approach her. And, as for Selina, she was little less than a mere tool in the hands of her well-beloved friend. What, in God's name, was I to do?

At dinner-time, we found the master of the house waiting to bid us welcome

Personally speaking, he presented a remarkable contrast to the typical British farmer. He was neither big nor burly; he spoke English as well as I did; and there was nothing in his dress which would have made him a fit subject for a picture of rustic life. When he spoke, he was able to talk on subjects unconnected with agricultural pursuits; nor did I hear him grumble about the weather and the crops. It was pleasant to see that his wife was proud of him, and that he was, what all fathers ought to be, his children's best and dearest friend. Why do I dwell on these details, relating to a man whom I was not destined to see again? Only because I had reason to feel grateful to him. When my spirits were depressed by anxiety, he made my mind easy about Eunice, as long as she remained in his house.

The social arrangements, when our meal was over, fell of themselves into the right train.

Miss Jillgall went upstairs, with the mother and the children, to see the nursery and the bedrooms. Mrs Tenbruggen discovered a bond of union between the farmer and herself; they were both skilled players at backgammon, and they sat down to try conclusions at their favourite game. Without any wearisome necessity for excuses or stratagems, Eunice took my arm and led me to the welcome retirement of her own sitting-room.

I could honestly congratulate her, when I heard that she was established at the farm as a member of the family. While she was governess to the children, she was safe from dangers that might have threatened her, if she had been compelled by circumstances to return to the Minister's house.

The entry in her Journal, which she was anxious that I should read, was placed before me next.

I followed the poor child's account of the fearful night that she had passed, with an interest that held me breathless to the end. A terrible dream, which had impressed a sense of its reality on the sleeper by reaching its climax in somnambulism – this was the obvious explanation, no doubt; and a rational mind would not hesitate to accept it. But a rational mind is not a universal gift, even in a country which prides itself on the idol-worship of Fact. Those good friends who are always better acquainted with our faults, failings, and weaknesses that we can pretend to be ourselves, had long since discovered that my nature was superstitious, and my imagination likely to mislead me in the presence of events which encouraged it. Well! I was weak enough to recoil from the purely rational view of all that Eunice had suffered, and heard, and seen, on the fateful night recorded in her journal. Good and Evil walk the ways of this unintelligible world, on the same free conditions. If we cling, as many of us do, to the comforting belief that departed spirits can minister to earthly creatures for good – can be felt moving in us, in a train of thought, and seen as visible manifestations, in a dream – with what pretence of reason can we deny that the same freedom of supernatural influence which is conceded to the departed spirit, working for good, is also permitted to the departed spirit, working for evil? If the grave cannot wholly part mother and child, when the mother's life has been good, does eternal annihilation separate them when the mother's life has been wicked? No! If the departed spirit can bring with it a blessing, the departed spirit can bring with it a curse. I dared not confess to Eunice that the influence of her murderess-mother might, as I thought possible, have been supernaturally present when she heard temptation whispering in her ear; but I dared not deny it to myself. All that I could say to satisfy and sustain her, I did say. And when I declared – with my whole heart declared – that the noble passion which had elevated her whole being, and had triumphed over the sorest trials that desertion could inflict, would still triumph to the end, I saw hope, in that brave and true heart, showing its bright promise for the future in Eunice's eyes.

She closed and locked her Journal. By common consent we sought the relief of changing the subject. Eunice asked me if it was really necessary that I should return to London.

I shrank from telling her that I could be of no further use to her father, while he regarded me with an enmity which I had not deserved. But I saw no reason for concealing that it was my purpose to see Philip Dunboyne.

'You told me yesterday,' I reminded her, 'that I was to say you had forgiven him. Do you still wish me to do that?'

'Indeed I do!'

'Have you thought of it seriously? Are you sure of not having been hurried by a generous impulse into saying more than you mean?'

'I have been thinking of it,' she said, 'through the wakeful hours of last night – and many things are plain to me, which I was not sure of in the time when I was so happy. He has caused me the bitterest sorrow of my life, but he can't undo the good that I owe to him. He has made a better girl of me, in the time when his love was mine. I don't forget that. Miserably as it has ended, I don't forget that.'

Her voice trembled; the tears rose in her eyes. It was impossible for me to conceal the distress that I felt. The noble creature saw it. 'No,' she said faintly; 'I am not going to cry. Don't look so sorry for me.' Her hand pressed my hand gently – *she* pitied *me*. When I saw how she struggled to control herself, and did control herself, I declare to God I could have gone down on my knees before her.

She asked to be allowed to speak of Philip again, and for the last time.

'When you meet with him in London, he may perhaps ask if you have seen Eunice.'

'My child! he is sure to ask.'

'Break it to him gently – but don't let him deceive himself. In this world, he must never hope to see me again.'

I tried – very gently – to remonstrate. 'At your age, and at his age,' I said, 'surely there is hope?'

'There is no hope.' She pressed her hand on her heart. 'I know it, I feel it, here.'

'Oh, Eunice, it's hard for me to say that!'

'I will try to make it easier for you. Say that I have forgiven him – and say no more.'

## CHAPTER XLIX

### THE GOVERNOR ON HIS GUARD

After leaving Eunice, my one desire was to be alone. I had much to think of, and I wanted an opportunity of recovering myself. On my way out of the house, in search of the first solitary place that I could discover, I passed the room in which we had dined. The door was ajar. Before I could get by it, Mrs Tenbruggen stepped out and stopped me.

'Will you come in here for a moment?' she said. 'The farmer has been called away, and I want to speak to you.'

Very unwillingly – but how could I have refused without giving offence? – I entered the room.

'When you noticed my keeping my name from you,' Mrs Tenbruggen began, 'while Selina was with us, you placed me in an awkward position. Our little friend is an excellent creature, but her tongue runs away with her sometimes; I am obliged to be careful of taking her too readily into my confidence. For instance, I have never told her what my name was before I married. Won't you sit down?'

I had purposely remained standing as a hint to her not to prolong the interview. The hint was thrown away; I took a chair.

'Selina's letters had informed me,' she resumed, 'that Mr Gracedieu was a nervous invalid. When I came to England, I had hoped to try what massage might do to relieve him. The cure of their popular preacher might have advertized me through the whole of the Congregational sect. It was essential to my success that I should present myself as a stranger. I could trust time and change, and my married name (certainly not known to Mr Gracedieu) to keep up my incognito. He would have refused to see me if he had known that I was once Miss Chance.'

I began to be interested.

Here was an opportunity, perhaps, of discovering what the Minister had failed to remember when he had been speaking of this woman, and when I had asked if he had ever offended her. I was especially careful in making my inquiries.

'I remember how you spoke to Mr Gracedieu,' I said, 'when you and he met, long ago, in my rooms. But surely you don't think him capable of vindictively remembering some thoughtless words, which escaped you sixteen or seventeen years since?'

'I am not quite such a fool as that, Mr Governor. What I was

thinking of was an unpleasant correspondence between the
Minister and myself. Before I was so unfortunate as to meet
with Mr Tenbruggen, I obtained a chance of employment in a
public Institution, on condition that I included a clergyman
among my references. Knowing nobody else whom I could
apply to, I rashly wrote to Mr Gracedieu, and received one of
those cold and cruel refusals which only the strictest religious
principle can produce. I was mortally offended at the time; and
if your friend the Minister had been within my reach——' She
paused, and finished the sentence by a significant gesture.

'Well,' I said, 'he is within your reach now.'

'And out of his mind,' she added. 'Besides, one's sense of
injury doesn't last (except in novels and plays) through a series
of years. I don't pity him – and if an opportunity of shaking his
high position among his admiring congregation presented itself,
I dare say I might make a mischievous return for his letter to
me. In the meanwhile, we may drop the subject. I suppose you
understand, now, why I concealed my name from you, and
why I kept out of the house while you were in it.'

It was plain enough, of course. If I had known her again, or
had heard her name, I might have told the Minister that Mrs
Tenbruggen and Miss Chance were one and the same. And if I
had seen her and talked with her in the house, my memory
might have shown itself capable of improvement. Having
politely presented the expression of my thanks, I rose to go.

She stopped me at the door.

'One word more,' she said, 'while Selina is out of the way. I
need hardly tell you that I have not trusted her with the
Minister's secret. You and I are, as I take it, the only people
now living who know the truth about these two girls. And we
keep our advantage.'

'What advantage?' I asked.

'Don't you know?'

'I don't indeed.'

'No more do I. Female folly, and a slip of the tongue; I am
old and ugly, but I am still a woman. About Miss Eunice.
Somebody has told the pretty little fool never to trust strangers.
You would have been amused if you had heard that sly young

person prevaricating with me. In one respect, her appearance strikes me. She is not like either the wretch who was hanged, or the poor victim who was murdered. Can she be the adopted child? Or is it the other sister, whom I have not seen yet? Oh come! come! Don't try to look as if you didn't know. That is really too ridiculous.'

'You alluded just now,' I answered, 'to our "advantage" in being the only persons who know the truth about the two girls. Well, Mrs Tenbruggen, I keep *my* advantage.'

'In other words,' she rejoined, 'you leave me to make the discovery myself. Well, my friend, I mean to do it!'

★   ★   ★   ★   ★

In the evening, my hotel offered to me the refuge of which I stood in need. I could think, for the first time that day, without interruption.

Being resolved to see Philip, I prepared myself for the interview by consulting my extracts once more. The letter, in which Mrs Tenbruggen figures, inspired me with the hope of protection for Mr Gracedieu, attainable through no less a person than Helena herself.

To begin with, she would certainly share Philip's aversion to the Masseuse, and her dislike of Miss Jillgall would, just as possibly, extend to Miss Jillgall's friend. The hostile feeling thus set up might be trusted to keep watch on Mrs Tenbruggen's proceedings, with a vigilance not attainable by the coarser observation of a man. In the event of an improvement in the Minister's health, I should hear of it both from the doctor and from Miss Jillgall, and in that case I should instantly return to my unhappy friend and put him on his guard.

I started for London by the early train in the morning.

My way home from the terminus took me past the hotel at which the elder Mr Dunboyne was staying. I called on him. He was reported to be engaged; that is to say, immersed in his books. The address on one of Philip's letters had informed me that he was staying at another hotel. Pursuing my inquiries in this direction, I met with a severe disappointment. Mr Philip

Dunboyne had left the hotel that morning; for what destination neither the landlord nor the waiter could tell me.

The next day's post brought with it the information which I had failed to obtain. Miss Jillgall wrote, informing me in her strongest language that Philip Dunboyne had returned to Helena. Indignant Selina added: 'Helena means to make him marry her; and I promise you she shall fail, if I can stop it.'

In taking leave of Eunice, I had given her my address; had warned her to be careful, if she and Mrs Tenbruggen happened to meet again; and had begged her to write to me, or to come to me, if anything happened to alarm her in my absence.

In two days more, I received a line from Eunice, written evidently in the greatest agitation.

'Philip has discovered me. He has been here, and has insisted on seeing me. I have refused. The good farmer has so kindly taken my part. I can write no more.'

## CHAPTER L

### THE NEWS FROM THE FARM

When I next heard from Miss Jillgall, the introductory part of her letter merely reminded me that Philip Dunboyne was established in the town, and that Helena was in daily communication with him. I shall do Selina no injustice if my extract begins with her second page.

'You will sympathize, I am sure' (she writes), 'with the indignation which urged me to call on Philip, and tell him the way to the farmhouse. Think of Helena being determined to marry him, whether he wants to or not! I am afraid this is bad grammar. But there are occasions when even a cultivated lady fails in her grammar, and almost envies the men their privilege of swearing when they are in a rage. My state of mind is truly indescribable. Grief mingles with anger, when I tell you that my sweet Euneece has disappointed me, for the first time since I had the happiness of knowing and admiring her. What can have been the motive of her refusal to receive her penitent lover? Is it pride? We are told that Satan fell through pride. Euneece satanic? Impossible! I feel inclined to go and ask her what has hardened her heart against a poor young man, who bitterly regrets his own folly. Do you think it was bad advice from the farmer or his wife? In that case, I shall exert my influence, and take her away. You would do the same, wouldn't you?

'I am ashamed to mention the poor dear Minister in a postscript. The truth is, I don't very well know what I am about. Mr Gracedieu is quiet, sleeps better than he did, eats with a keener appetite, gives no trouble. But, alas, that glorious intellect is in a state of eclipse! Do not suppose, because I write figuratively, that I am not sorry for him. He understands nothing; he remembers nothing; he has my prayers.

'You might come to us again, if you would only be so kind. It would make no difference now; the poor man is so sadly altered. I must add, most reluctantly, that the doctor recommends your staying at home. Between ourselves, he is little better than a coward. Fancy his saying; "No; we must not run that risk yet." I am barely civil to him, and no more.

'In any other affair (excuse me for troubling you with a second postscript), my sympathy with Euneece would have penetrated her motives; I should have felt with her feelings. But I have never been in love; no gentleman gave me the opportunity when I was young. Now I am middle-aged, neglect has done its dreary work – my heart is an extinct crater. Figurative again! I had better put my pen away, and say farewell for the present.'

Miss Jillgall may now give place to Eunice. The same day's post brought me both letters.

I should be unworthy indeed of the trust which this affectionate girl has placed in me, if I failed to receive her explanation of her conduct towards Philip Dunboyne as a sacred secret confided to my fatherly regard. In those later portions of her letter, which are not addressed to me confidentially, Eunice writes as follows:

'I get news – and what heartbreaking news! – of my father, by sending a messenger to Selina. It is more than ever impossible that I can put myself in the way of seeing Helena again. She has written to me about Philip, in a tone so shockingly insolent and cruel, that I have destroyed her letter. Philip's visit to the farm, discovered I don't know how, seems to have infuriated her. She accuses me of doing all that she might herself have done in my place, and threatens me – No! I am afraid of the wicked whisperings of that second self of mine if I think of it. They were near to tempting me when I read Helena's letter. But I thought of what you said, after I had shown you my journal; and your words took my memory back to the days when I was happy with Philip. The trial and the terror passed away.

'Consolation has come to me from the best of good women. Mrs Staveley writes as lovingly as my mother might have written, if death had spared her. I have replied with all the gratitude that I really feel, but without taking advantage of the services which she offers. Mrs Staveley has it in her mind, as you had it in your mind, to bring Philip back to me. Does she forget, do you forget, that Helena claims him? But you both mean kindly, and I love you both for the interest that you feel in me.

'The farmer's wife – dear good soul! – hardly understands me so well as her husband does. She confesses to pitying Philip. "He is so wretched," she says. "And, dear heart, how handsome, and what nice winning manners! I don't think I should have had your courage, in your place. To tell the truth, I should have jumped for joy when I saw him at the door; and I should have run down to let him in – and perhaps been sorry for it afterwards. If you really wish to forget him, my dear, I will do all I can to help you.

'These are trifling things to mention, but I am afraid you may think I am unhappy – and I want to prevent that.

'I have so much to be thankful for, and the children are so fond of me. Whether I teach them as well as I might have done, if I had been a more learned girl, may perhaps be doubtful. They do more for their governess, I am afraid, than their governess does for them. When they come into my room in the morning, and rouse me with their kisses, the hour of waking, which used to be so hard to endure after Philip left me, is now the happiest hour of my day.'

With that reassuring view of her life as a governess, the poor child's letter comes to an end.

# CHAPTER LI

## THE TRIUMPH OF MRS TENBRUGGEN

Miss Jillgall appears again, after an interval, on the field of my extracts. My pleasant friend deserves this time a serious reception. She informs me that Mrs Tenbruggen has begun the inquiries which I have the best reason to dread – for I alone know the end which they are designed to reach.

The arrival of this news affected me in two different ways.

It was discouraging to find that circumstances had not justified my reliance on Helena's enmity as a counter-influence to Mrs Tenbruggen. On the other hand, it was a relief to be assured that my return to London would serve, rather than compromise, the interests which it was my chief anxiety to defend. I had foreseen that Mrs Tenbruggen would wait to set her enterprise on foot, until I was out of her way; and I had calculated on my absence as an event which would at least put an end to suspense by encouraging her to begin.

The first sentences in Miss Jillgall's letter explain the nature of her interest in the proceedings of her friend, and are, on that account, worth reading.

'Things are sadly changed for the worse' (Selina writes); 'but I don't forget that Philip was once engaged to Euneece, and that Mr Gracedieu's extraordinary conduct towards him puzzled us all. The mode of discovery which dear Elizabeth suggested by letter, at that time, appears to be the mode which she is following now. When I asked why, she said: "Philip may return to Euneece; the Minister may recover – and will be all the more likely to do so if he tries Massage. In that case, he will probably repeat the conduct which surprised you; and your natural curiosity will ask me again to find out what it means. Am I your friend, Selina, or am I not?" This was so delightfully kind, and so irresistibly conclusive, that I kissed her in a transport of gratitude. With what breathless interest I have watched her progress towards penetrating the mystery of the girls' ages, it is quite needless to tell you.'

\*     \*     \*     \*     \*

Mrs Tenbruggen's method of keeping Miss Jillgall in ignorance of what she was really about, and Miss Jillgall's admirable confidence in the integrity of Mrs Tenbruggen, being now set forth on the best authority, an exact presentation of the state of affairs will be completed if I add a word more, relating to the positions actually occupied towards Mrs Tenbruggen's enterprise, by my correspondent and myself.

On her side, Miss Jillgall was entirely ignorant that one of the two girls was not Mr Gracedieu's daugher, but his adopted child. On my side, I was entirely ignorant of Mrs Tenbruggen's purpose in endeavouring to identify the daughter of the murderess. Speaking of myself, individually, let me add that I only waited the event to protect the helpless ones – my poor demented friend, and the orphan whom his mercy received into his heart and his home.

Miss Jillgall goes on with her curious story, as follows:

'Always desirous of making myself useful, I thought I would give my dear Elizabeth a hint which might save time and trouble. "Why not begin," I suggested, "by asking the Governor to help you?" That wonderful woman never forgets anything. She had already applied to you, without success.

'In my next attempt to be useful I did violence to my most cherished convictions, by presenting the wretch Helena to the admirable Elizabeth. That the former would be cold as ice, in her reception of any friend of mine, was nothing wonderful. Mrs Tenbruggen passed it over with the graceful composure of a woman of the world. In the course of conversation with Helena, she slipped in a question: "Might I ask if you are older than your sister?" The answer was, of course: "I don't know."

And here, for once, the most deceitful girl in existence spoke the truth.

'When we were alone again, Elizabeth made a remark: "If personal appearance could decide the question," she said, "the disagreeable young woman is the oldest of the two. The next thing to be done is to discover if looks are to be trusted in this case."

'My friend's lawyer received confidential instructions (not shown to me, which seems rather hard) to trace the two Miss Gracedieus' registers of birth. Elizabeth described this proceeding (not very intelligibly to my mind) as a means of finding out which of the girls could be identified by name as the elder of the two.

'The report arrived this morning. I was only informed that the result, in one case, had entirely defeated the inquiries. In the other case, Elizabeth had helped her agent by referring him to a birth, advertized in the customary columns of *The Times* newspaper. Even here, there was a fatal obstacle. The name of the place in which Mr Gracedieu's daughter had been born was not added as usual.

'I still tried to be useful. Had my friend known the Minister's wife? My friend had never even seen the Minister's wife. And, as if by a fatality, her portrait was no longer in existence. I could only mention that Helena was like her mother. But Elizabeth seemed to attach very little importance to my evidence, if I may call it by so grand a name. "People have such strange ideas about likenesses," she said, "and arrive at such contradictory conclusions. One can only trust one's own eyes in a matter of that kind."

'My friend next asked me about our domestic establishment. We had only a cook and a housemaid. If they were old servants who had known the girls as children, they might be made of some use. Our luck was as steadily against us as ever. They had both been engaged when Mr Gracedieu assumed his new pastoral duties, after having resided with his wife at her native place.

'I asked Elizabeth what she proposed to do next.

'She deferred her answer, until I had first told her whether the visit of the doctor might be expected on that day. I could reply to this in the negative. Elizabeth, thereupon, made a sterling request; she begged me to introduce her to Mr Gracedieu.

'I said: "Surely, you have forgotten the sad state of his mind?" No; she knew perfectly well that he was imbecile. "I want to try," she explained, "if I can rouse him for a few minutes."

'"By Massage?" I inquired.

'She burst out laughing. "Massage, my dear, doesn't act in that way. It is an elaborate process, pursued patiently for weeks together. But my hands have more than one accomplishment at their finger-ends. Oh, make your mind easy! I shall do no harm, if I do no good. Take me, Selina, to the Minister."

'We went to his room. Don't blame me for giving way; I am too fond of Elizabeth to be able to disappoint her.

'It was a sad sight when we went in. He was quite happy, playing like a child, at cup-and-ball. The attendant retired at my request. I introduced Mrs Tenbruggen. He smiled and shook hands with her. He said: "Are you a Christian or a Pagan? You are very pretty. How many times can you catch the ball in the cup?" The effort to talk to her ended there. He went on with his game, and seemed to forget that there was anybody in the room. It made my heart ache to remember what he was – and to see him now.

'Elizabeth whispered: "Leave me alone with him."

'I don't know why I did such a rude thing – I hesitated.

'Elizabeth asked me if I had no confidence in her. I was ashamed of myself; I left them together.

'A long half-hour passed. Feeling a little uneasy, I went upstairs again, and looked into the room. He was leaning back in his chair; his plaything was on the floor, and he was looking vacantly at the light that came in through the window. I found Mrs Tenbruggen at the other end of the room, in the act of ringing the bell. Nothing in the least out of the ordinary way seemed to have happened. When the attendant had answered the bell, we left the room together. Mr Gracedieu took no notice of us.

'"Well," I said, "how has it ended?"

'Quite calmly, my noble Elizabeth answered: "In total failure."

"'What did you say to him after you sent me away?"

"'I tried, in every possible way, to get him to tell me which of his two daughters was the oldest."

"'Did he refuse to answer?"

"'He was only too ready to answer. First, he said Helena was the oldest – then he corrected himself, and declared that Eunice was the oldest – then he said they were twins – then he went back to Helena and Eunice. Now one was the oldest, and now the other. He rang the changes on those two names, I can't tell you how often, and seemed to think it a better game then cup-and-ball."

"'What is to be done?"

"'Nothing is to be done, Selina."

"'What!" I cried, "you give it up?"

'My heroic friend answered: "I know when I am beaten, my dear – I give it up." She looked at her watch; it was time to operate on the muscles of one of her patients. Away she went, on her glorious mission of massage, without a murmur of regret. What strength of mind! But, oh, dear, what a disappointment for poor little me! On one thing I am determined. If I find myself getting puzzled or frightened, I shall instantly write to you.'

With that expression of confidence in me, Selina's narrative came to an end. I wish I could have believed, as she did, that the object of her admiration had been telling her the truth.

A few days later, Mrs Tenbruggen honoured me with a visit at my house in the neighbourhood of London. Thanks to this circumstance, I am able to add a postscript, which will complete the revelations in Miss Jillgall's letter.

The illustrious Masseuse, having much to conceal from her faithful Selina, was well aware that she had only one thing to keep hidden from me – namely: the advantage which she would have gained, if her inquiries had met with success.

'I thought I might have got at what I wanted,' she told me, 'by mesmerising our reverend friend. He is as weak as a

woman; I threw him into hysterics, and had to give it up, and
quiet him, or he would have alarmed the house. You look as if
you don't believe in mesmerism.'

'My looks, Mrs Tenbruggen, exactly express my opinion.
Mesmerism is humbug.'

'You amusing old Tory! Shall I throw you into a state of
trance? No! I'll give you a shock of another kind – a shock of
surprise. I know as much as you do about Mr Gracedieu's
daughters. What do you think of that?'

'I think I should like to hear you tell me, which is the
adopted child.'

'Helena, to be sure!'

Her manner was defiant, her tone was positive; I doubted
both. Under the surface of her assumed confidence, I saw
something which told me that she was trying to read my
thoughts in my face. Many other women had tried to do that.
They succeeded when I was young. When I had reached the
wrong side of fifty, my face had learned discretion, and they
failed.

'How did you arrive at your discovery?' I asked. 'I know of
nobody who could have helped you.'

'I helped myself, sir! I reasoned it out. A wonderful thing for
a woman to do, isn't it? I wonder whether you could follow the
process?'

My reply to this was made by a bow. I was sure of my
command over my face; but perfect control of the voice is a
rare power. Here and there, a great actor or a great criminal
possesses it.

Mrs Tenbruggen's vanity took me into her confidence. 'In
the first place,' she said, 'Helena is plainly the wicked one of the
two. I was not prejudiced by what Selina had told me of her: I
saw it, and felt it, before I had been five minutes in her
company. If lying tongues ever provoke her as lying tongues
provoked her mother, she will follow her mother's example.
Very well. Now – in the second place – though it is very slight,
there is a certain something in her hair and her complexion
which reminds me of the murderess: there is no other
resemblance, I admit. In the third place, the girls' names point

to the same conclusion. Mr Gracedieu is a Protestant and a Dissenter. Would he call a child of his own by the name of a Roman Catholic saint? No! he would prefer a name in the Bible; Eunice is *his* child. And Helena was once the baby whom I carried into the prison. Do you deny that?'

'I don't deny it.'

Only four words! But they were deceitfully spoken, and the deceit — practised in Eunice's interest, it is needless to say — succeeded. Mrs Tenbruggen's object in visiting me was attained; I had confirmed her belief in the delusion that Helena was the adopted child.

She got up to take her leave. I asked if she proposed remaining in London. No; she was returning to her country patients that night.

As I attended her to the house door, she turned to me with her mischievous smile. 'I have taken some trouble in finding the clue to the Minister's mystery,' she said. 'Don't you wonder why?'

'If I did wonder,' I answered, 'would you tell me why?'

She laughed at the bare idea of it. 'Another lesson,' she said, 'to assist a helpless man in studying the weaker sex. I have already shown you that a woman can reason. Learn next that a woman can keep a secret. Good-bye. God bless you!'

Of the events which followed Mrs Tenbruggen's visit it is not possible for me, I am thankful to say, to speak from personal experience. Ought I to conclude with an expression of repentence for the act of deception to which I have already pleaded guilty? I don't know. Yes! the force of circumstances does really compel me to say it, and say it seriously — I declare, on my word of honour, I don't know.

# THIRD PERIOD: 1876

*HELENA'S DIARY RESUMED*

## CHAPTER LII

HELENA'S DIARY RESUMED

While my father remains in his present helpless condition, somebody must assume a position of command in this house. There cannot be a moment's doubt that I am the person to do it.

In my agitated state of mind, sometimes doubtful of Philip, sometimes hopeful of him, I find Mrs Tenbruggen simply unendurable. A female doctor is, under any circumstances, a creature whom I detest. She is, at her very best, a bad imitation of a man. The Medical Rubber is worse than this; she is a bad imitation of a mountebank. Her grinning good-humour, adopted no doubt to please the fools who are her patients, and her impudent enjoyment of hearing herself talk, make me regret for the first time in my life that I am a young lady. If I belonged to the lowest order of the population, I might take the first stick I could find, and enjoy the luxury of giving Mrs Tenbruggen a good beating.

She literally haunts the house, encouraged, of course, by her wretched little dupe, Miss Jillgall. Only this morning, I tried what a broad hint would do towards suggesting that her visits had better come to an end.

'Really, Mrs Tenbruggen,' I said, 'I must request Miss Jillgall to moderate her selfish enjoyment of your company, for your own sake. Your time is too valuable in a professional sense, to be wasted on an idle woman who has no sympathy with your patients, waiting for relief perhaps, and waiting in vain.'

She listened to this, all smiles and good-humour: 'My dear, do you know how I might answer you, if I was an ill-natured woman?'

'I have no curiosity to hear it, Mrs Tenbruggen.'

'I might ask you,' she persisted, 'to allow me to mind my own business. But I am incapable of making an ungrateful return for the interest which you take in my medical welfare. Let me venture to ask if you understand the value of time.'

' Are you going to say much more, Mrs Tenbruggen?'

'I am going to make a sensible remark, my child. If you feel tired, permit me – here is a chair. Father Time, dear Miss Gracedieu, has always been a good friend of mine, because I know how to make the best use of him. The author of the famous saying *Tempus fugit* (you understand Latin, of course) was, I take leave to think, an idle man. The more I have to do, the readier Time is to wait for me. Let me impress this on your mind by some interesting examples. The greatest conqueror of the century – Napoleon – had time enough for everything. The greatest novelist of the century – Sir Walter Scott – had time enough for everything. At my humble distance, I imitate those illustrious men, and my patients never complain of me.'

'Have you done?' I asked.

'Yes, dear – for the present.'

'You are a clever woman, Mrs Tenbruggen – and you know it. You have an eloquent tongue, and you know it. But you are something else, which you don't seem to be aware of. You are a bore.'

She burst out laughing, with the air of a woman who thoroughly enjoyed a good joke. I looked back when I left the room, and saw the friend of Father Time in the easy-chair opening our newspaper.

This is a specimen of the customary encounter of our wits. I place it on record in my Journal, to excuse myself *to* myself. When she left us at last, later in the day, I sent a letter after her to the hotel. Not having kept a copy of it, let me present the substance, like a sermon, under three heads: I begged to be excused for speaking plainly; I declared that there was a total want of sympathy between us, on my side; and I proposed that she should deprive me of future opportunities of receiving her in this house. The reply arrived immediately in these terms: 'Your letter received, dear girl. I am not in the least angry; partly because I am very fond of you, partly because I know that you will ask me to come back again. P.S.: Philip sends his love.'

This last piece of insolence was unquestionably a lie. Philip detests her. They are both staying at the same hotel. But I happen to know that he won't even look at her, if they meet by accident on the stairs.

People who can enjoy the melancholy spectacle of human nature in a state of degradation would be at a loss which exhibition to prefer – an ugly old maid in a rage, or an ugly old maid in tears. Miss Jillgall presented herself in both characters when she heard what had happened. To my mind, Mrs Tenbruggen's bosom-friend is a creature not fit to be seen or heard when she loses her temper. I only told her to leave the room. To my great amusement, she shook her bony fist at me, and expressed a frantic wish: 'Oh, if I was rich enough to leave this wicked house!' I wonder whether there is insanity (as well as poverty) in Miss Jillgall's family?

Last night my mind was in a harassed state. Philip was, as usual, the cause of it.

Perhaps I acted indiscreetly when I insisted on his leaving London, and returning to this place. But what else could I have done? It was not merely my interest, it was an act of downright necessity, to withdraw him from the influence of his hateful father – whom I now regard as the one serious obstacle to my marriage. There is no prospect of being rid of Mr Dunboyne the elder by his returning to Ireland. He is trying a new remedy for his crippled hand – electricity. I wish it was lightning, to kill him! If I had given that wicked old man the chance, I am firmly convinced he would not have let a day pass without doing his best to depreciate me in his son's estimation. Besides, there was the risk, if I had allowed Philip to remain long away from me, of losing – no, while I keep my beauty I cannot be in such danger as that – let me say, of permitting time and absence to weaken my hold on him. However sullen and silent he may be, when we meet – and I find him in that condition far too often – I can, sooner or later, recall him to his brighter self. My eyes preserve their charm, my talk can still amuse him, and, better even than that, I feel the answering thrill in him, which tells me how precious my kisses are – not too lavishly bestowed! But the time when I am obliged to leave him to himself, is the time that I dread. How do I know that his thoughts are not wandering away to Eunice! He denies it; he declares that he only went to the farmhouse to express his regret for his own thoughtless conduct, and to offer her the brotherly regard due to the sister of his promised wife. Can I believe it? Oh, what would I not give to be able to believe it! How can I feel sure that her refusal to see him was not a cunning device to make him long for another interview, and plan perhaps in private to go back and try again. Marriage! Nothing will quiet these frightful doubts of mine, nothing will reward me for all that I have suffered, nothing will warm my heart with the delightful sense of triumph over Eunice, but my marriage to Philip. And what does he say, when I urge it on him? – yes, I have fallen as low as that, in the despair which sometimes possesses me. He has his answer, always the same, and always ready: 'How are we to live? where is the money?' The maddening part of it is that I cannot accuse him of raising objections that don't exist. We are poorer then ever here, since my father's illness – and Philip's allowance is barely enough to suffice him as a single man. Oh, how I hate the rich!

It was useless to think of going to bed. How could I hope to sleep, with my head throbbing, and my thoughts in this disturbed state? I put on my comfortable dressing-gown, and sat down to try what reading would do to quiet my mind.

I had borrowed the book from the Library, to which I have been a subscriber in secret for some time past. It was an old volume, full of what we should now call gossip; relating strange adventures, and scandalous incidents in family history which had been concealed from public notice.

One of these last romances in real life caught a strong hold on my interest

It was a strange case of intended poisoning, which had never been carried out. A young married lady of rank, whose name was concealed under an initial letter, had suffered some unendurable wrong (which was not mentioned) at the hands of her husband's mother. The wife was described as a woman of strong passions, who had determined on a terrible revenge by taking the life of her mother-in-law. There were difficulties in the way of her committing the crime without an accomplice to help her; and she decided on taking her maid, an elderly woman, into her confidence. The poison was secretly obtained by this person; and the safest manner of administering it was under discussion between the mistress and the maid, when the door of the room was suddenly opened. The husband, accompanied by his brother, rushed in, and charged his wife with plotting the murder of his mother. The young lady (she was only twenty-three) must have been a person of extraordinary courage and resolution. She saw at once that her maid had betrayed her, and, with astonishing presence of mind, she turned on the traitress, and said to her husband: 'There is the wretch who has been trying to persuade me to poison your mother!' As it happened, the old lady's temper was violent and overbearing; and the maid had complained of being ill-treated by her, in the hearing of the other servants. The circumstances made it impossible to decide which of the two was really the guilty woman. The servant was sent away, and the husband and wife separated soon afterwards, under the excuse of incompatibility of temper. Years passed; and the truth was only discovered by the death-bed confession of the wife. A remarkable story, which has made such an impression on me that I have written it in my Journal. I am not rich enough to buy the book.

For the last two days, I have been confined to my room with a bad feverish cold – caught, as I suppose, by sitting at an open window reading my book till nearly three o'clock in the morning. I sent a note to Philip, telling him of my illness. On the first day, he called to inquire after me. On the second day, no visit, and no letter. Here is the third day – and no news of him as yet. I am better, but not fit to go out. Let me wait another hour, and, if that exercise of patience meets with no reward, I shall send a note to the hotel.

No news of Philip. I have sent to the hotel.

The servant has just returned, bringing me back my note. The waiter informed her that Mr Dunboyne had gone away to London by the morning train. No apology or explanation left for me.

*Can* he have deserted me? I am in such a frenzy of doubt and rage that I can hardly write that horrible question. Is it possible – oh, I feel it *is* possible that he has gone away with Eunice. Do I know where to find them? If I did know, what could I do? I feel as if I could kill them both!

## CHAPTER LIII

### HELENA'S DIARY RESUMED

After the heat of my anger had cooled, I made two discoveries. One cost me a fee to a messenger, and the other exposed me to the insolence of a servant. I pay willingly in my purse and my pride, when the gain is peace of mind. Through my messenger I ascertained that Eunice had never left the farm. Through my own inquiries, answered by the waiter with an impudent grin, I heard that Philip had left orders to have his room kept for him. What misery our stupid housemaid might have spared me, if she had thought of putting that question when I sent her to the hotel!

The rest of the day passed in vain speculations on Philip's motive for this sudden departure. What poor weak creatures we are! I persuaded myself to hope that anxiety for our marriage had urged him to make an effort to touch the heart of his mean father. Shall I see him to-morrow? And shall I have reason to be fonder of him then ever?

We met again to-day as usual. He has behaved infamously.

When I asked what had been his object in going to London, I was told that it was 'a matter of business'. He made that idiotic excuse as coolly as if he really thought I should believe it. I submitted in silence, rather than mar his return to me by the

disaster of a quarrel. But this was an unlucky day. A harder trial
of my self-control was still to come. Without the slightest
appearance of shame, Philip informed me that he was charged
with a message from Mrs Tenbruggen! She wanted some Irish
lace, and would I be so good as to tell her which was the best
shop at which she could buy it?

Was he really in earnest? 'You,' I said, 'who distrusted and
detested her – you are on friendly terms with that woman?'

He remonstrated with me. 'My dear Helena, don't speak in
that way of Mrs Tenbruggen. We have both been mistaken
about her. That good creature has forgiven the brutal manner in
which I spoke to her, when she was in attendance on my father.
She was the first to propose that we should shake hands and
forget it. My darling, don't let all the good feeling be on one
side. You have no idea how kindly she speaks of you, and how
anxious she is to help us to be married. Come! come! meet her
half-way. Write down the name of the shop on my card, and I
will take it back to her.'

Sheer amazement kept me silent: I let him go on. He was a
mere child in the hands of Mrs Tenbruggen: she had only to
determine to make a fool of him, and she could do it.

But why did she do it? What advantage had she to gain by
insinuating herself in this way into his good opinion, evidently
with the intention of urging him to reconcile us to each other?
How could we two poor young people be of the smallest use to
the fashionable Masseuse?

My silence began to irritate Philip. 'I never knew before how
obstinate you could be,' he said; 'you seem to be doing your
best – I can't imagine why – to lower yourself in my
estimation.'

I held my tongue; I assumed my smile. It is all very well for men
to talk about the deceitfulness of women. What chance (I should
like to ask somebody who knows about it) do the men give us of
making our lives with them endurable, except by deceit! I gave
way, of course, and wrote down the address of the shop.

He was so pleased that he kissed me. Yes! the most fondly
affectionate kiss that he had given me, for weeks past, was my
reward for submitting to Mrs Tenbruggen. She is old enough to

be his mother, and almost as ugly as Miss Jillgall – and she has made her interests his interests already!

On the next day, I fully expected to receive a visit from Mrs Tenbruggen. She knew better than that. I only got a polite little note, thanking me for the address, and adding an artless confession: 'I earn more money than I know what to do with; and I adore Irish lace.'

The next day came, and still she was careful not to show herself too eager for a personal reconciliation. A splendid nosegay was sent to me, with another little note: 'A tribute, dear Helena, offered by one of my grateful patients. Too beautiful a present for an old woman like me. I agree with the poet: "Sweets to the sweet". A charming thought of Shakspere's is it not? I should like to verify the quotation. Would you mind leaving the volume for me in the hall, if I call to-morrow?'

Well done, Mrs Tenbruggen! She doesn't venture to intrude on Miss Gracedieu in the drawing-room; she only wants to verify a quotation in the hall. Oh, goddess of Humility (if there is such a person), how becomingly you are dressed when your milliner is an artful old woman!

While this reflection was passing through my mind, Miss Jillgall came in – saw the nosegay on the table – and instantly pounced on it. 'Oh, for me! for me!' she cried. 'I noticed it this morning on Elizabeth's table. How very kind of her!' She plunged her inquisitive nose into the poor flowers, and looked up sentimentally at the ceiling. 'The perfume of goodness,' she remarked, 'mingled with the perfume of flowers!' 'When you have quite done with it,' I said, 'perhaps you will be so good as to return my nosegay?' '*Your* nosegay!' she exclaimed. 'There is Mrs Tenbruggen's letter,' I replied, 'if you would like to look at it.' She did look at it. All the bile in her body flew up into her eyes, and turned them green; she looked as if she longed to scratch my face. I gave the flowers afterwards to Maria; Miss Jillgall's nose had completely spoilt them.

It would have been too ridiculous to have allowed Mrs Tenbruggen to consult Shakspere in the hall. I had the honour of receiving her in my own room. We accomplished a touching reconciliation, and we quite forgot Shakspere.

She troubles me; she does indeed trouble me.

Having set herself entirely right with Philip, she is determined on performing the same miracle with me. Her reform of herself is already complete. Her vulgar humour was kept under strict restraint; she was quiet and well-bred, and readier to listen than to talk. This change was not presented abruptly. She contrived to express her friendly interests in Philip and in me by hints dropped here and there, assisted in their effect by answers on my part, into which I was tempted so skilfully that I only discovered the snare set for me, on reflection. What is it, I ask again, that she has in view in taking all this trouble? Where is her motive for encouraging a love affair, which Miss Jillgall must have denounced to her as an abominable wrong inflicted on Eunice? Money (even if there was a prospect of such a thing, in our case) cannot be her object; it is quite true that her success sets her above pecuniary anxiety. Spiteful feeling against Eunice is out of the question. They have only met once; and her opinion was expressed to me with evident sincerity: 'Your sister is a nice girl, but she is like other nice girls – she doesn't interest me.' There is Eunice's character, drawn from the life in few words. In what an irritating position do I find myself placed! Never before have I felt so interested in trying to look into a person's secret mind; and never before have I been so completely baffled.

I had written as far as this, and was on the point of closing my Journal, when a third note arrived from Mrs Tenbruggen.

She had been thinking about me at intervals (she wrote) all through the rest of the day; and, kindly as I had received her, she was conscious of being the object of doubts on my part which her visit had failed to remove. Might she ask leave to call on me, in the hope of improving her position in my estimation? An appointment followed for the next day.

What can she have to say to me which she has not already said? Is it anything about Philip, I wonder?

## CHAPTER LIV

### HELENA'S DIARY RESUMED

At our interview of the next day, Mrs Tenbruggen's capacity for self-reform appeared under a new aspect. She dropped all familiarity with me, and she stated the object of her visit without a superfluous word of explanation or apology.

I thought this a remarkable effort for a woman; and I recognized the merit of it by leaving the lion's share of the talk to my visitor. In these terms she opened her business with me:

'Has Mr Philip Dunboyne told you why he went to London?'

'He made a commonplace excuse,' I answered. 'Business, he said, took him to London. I know no more.'

'You have a fair prospect of happiness, Miss Helena, when you are married — your future husband is evidently afraid of you. I am not afraid of you; and I shall confide to your private ear something which you have an interest in knowing. The business which took young Mr Dunboyne to London was to consult a competent person, on a matter concerning himself. The competent person is the sagacious (not to say sly) old gentleman, whom we used to call the Governor. You know him, I believe?'

'Yes. But I am at a loss to imagine why Philip should have consulted him.'

'Have you ever heard or read, Miss Helena, of such a thing as "an old man's fancy"?'

'I think I have.'

'Well, the Governor has taken an old man's fancy to your sister. They appeared to understand each other perfectly when I was at the farmhouse.'

'Excuse me, Mrs Tenbruggen, that is what I know already. Why did Philip go to the Governor?'

She smiled. 'If anybody is acquainted with the true state of your sister's feelings, the Governor is the man. I sent Mr Dunboyne to consult him — and there is the reason for it.'

This open avowal of her motives perplexed and offended me.

After declaring herself to be interested in my marriage-engagement, had she changed her mind, and resolved on favouring Philip's return to Eunice? What right had he to consult anybody about the state of that girl's feelings? *My* feelings form the only subject of inquiry that was properly open to him. I should have said something which I might have afterwards regretted, if Mrs Tenbruggen had allowed me the opportunity. Fortunately for both of us, she went on with her narrative of her own proceedings.

'Philip Dunboyne is an excellent fellow,' she continued: 'I really like him – but he has his faults. He sadly wants strength of purpose; and, like weak men in general, he only knows his own mind when a resolute friend takes him in hand and guides him. I am his resolute friend. I saw him veering about between you and Eunice; and I decided for his sake – may I say for your sake also? – on putting an end to that mischievous state of indecision. You have the claim on him; you are the right wife for him – and the Governor was (as I thought likely from what I had myself observed) the man to make him see it. I am not in anybody's secrets; it was pure guess-work on my part, and it has succeeded. There is no more doubt now about Miss Eunice's sentiments. The question is settled.'

'In my favour?'

'Certainly in your favour – or I should not have said a word about it.'

'Was Philip's visit kindly received? Or did the old wretch laugh at him?'

'My dear Miss Gracedieu, the old wretch is a man of the world, and never makes mistakes of that sort. Before he could open his lips, he had to satisfy himself that your lover deserved to be taken into his confidence, on the delicate subject of Eunice's sentiments. He arrived at a favourable conclusion. I can repeat Philip's questions and the Governor's answers – after putting the young man through a stiff examination – just as they passed: "May I inquire, sir, if she has spoken to you about me?" "She has often spoken about you." "Did she seem to be angry with me?" "She is too good and too sweet to be angry with you." "Do you think she will forgive me?" "She has forgiven

you." "Did she say so herself?" "Yes, of her own free will."
"Why did she refuse to see me when I called at the farm?" "She
had her own reasons – good reasons." "Has she regretted it
since?" "Certainly not." "Is it likely that she would consent, if I
proposed a reconciliation?" "I put that question to her myself."
"How did she take it, sir?" "She declined to take it." "You
mean that she declined a reconciliation?" "Yes." "Are you sure
she was in earnest?" "I am positively sure." That last answer
seems, by young Dunboyne's own confession, to have been
enough, and more than enough for him. He got up to go – and
then an odd thing happened. After giving him the most
unfavourable answers, the Governor patted him paternally on
the shoulder, and encouraged him to hope. "Before we say
good-bye, Mr Philip, one word more. If I was as young as you
are, I should not despair." There is a sudden change of front!
Who can explain it?'

The Governor's mischievous resolution to reconcile Philip
and Eunice explained it, of course. With the best intentions
(perhaps) Mrs Tenbruggen had helped that design by bringing
the two men together. 'Go on,' I said; 'I am prepared to hear
next that Philip has paid another visit to my sister, and has been
received this time.'

I must say this for Mrs Tenbruggen; she kept her temper
perfectly.

'He has not been to the farm,' she said, 'but he has done
something nearly as foolish. He has written to your sister.'

'And he has received a favourable reply, of course?'

She put her hand into the pocket of her dress.

'There is your sister's reply,' she said.

Any persons who have had a crushing burden lifted,
unexpectedly and instantly, from off their minds, will know
what I felt when I read the reply. In the most positive language,
Eunice refused to correspond with Philip, or to speak with him.
The concluding words proved that she was in earnest: 'You are
engaged to Helena. Consider me as a stranger until you are
married. After that time you will be my brother-in-law, and
then I may pardon you for writing to me.'

Nobody who knows Eunice would have supposed that she

possessed those two valuable qualities – common-sense and proper pride. It is pleasant to feel that I can now send cards to my sister, when I am Mrs Philip Dunboyne.

I returned the letter to Mrs Tenbruggen, with the sincerest expressions of regret for having doubted her. 'I have been unworthy of your generous interest in me,' I said; 'I am almost ashamed to offer you my hand.'

She took my hand, and gave it a good, hearty shake.

'Are we friends?' she asked in the simplest and prettiest manner. 'Then let us be easy and pleasant again,' she went on. 'Will you call me Elizabeth; and shall I call you Helena? Very well. Now I have got something else to say; another secret which must be kept from Philip (I call *him* by his name now, you see) for a few days more. Your happiness, my dear, must not depend on his miserly old father. He must have a little income of his own to marry on. Among the hundreds of unfortunate wretches whom I have relieved from torture of mind and body, there is a grateful minority. Small! small! but there they are. I have influence among powerful people; and I am trying to make Philip private secretary to a member of Parliament. When I have succeeded, you shall tell him the good news.'

What a vile humour I must have been in, at the time, not to have appreciated the delightful gaiety of this good creature; I went to the other extreme now, and behaved like a gushing young Miss fresh from school. I kissed her.

She burst out laughing. 'What a sacrifice!' she cried. 'A kiss for me, which ought to have been kept for Philip! By-the-bye, do you know what I should do, Helena, in your place? I should take your handsome young man away from that hotel!'

'I will do anything that you advise,' I said.

'And you will do well, my child. In the first place, the hotel is too expensive for Philip's small means. In the second place, two of the chambermaids have audaciously presumed to be charming girls; and the men, my dear – well! well! I will leave you to find that out for yourself. In the third place, you want to have Philip under your own wing; domestic familiarity will make him fonder of you than ever. Keep him out of the sort of company that he meets with in the billiard-room and the smoking-room. You have got a spare bed here, I know, and your poor father is in no condition to use his authority. Make Philip one of the family.

This last piece of advice staggered me. I mentioned the proprieties. Mrs Tenbruggen laughed at the proprieties.

'Make Selina of some use,' she suggested. 'While you have got *her* in the house, propriety is rampant. Why condemn poor helpless Philip to cheap lodgings? Time enough to cast him out to the feather-bed and the fleas, on the night before your marriage. Besides, I shall be in and out constantly – for I mean to cure your father. The tongue of scandal is silent in my awful presence; an atmosphere of virtue surrounds Mamma Tenbruggen. Think of it.'

## CHAPTER LV

### HELENA'S DIARY RESUMED

I did think of it. Philip came to us, and lived in our house.

Let me hasten to add that the protest of propriety was duly entered, on the day before my promised husband arrived. Standing in the doorway – nothing would induce her to take a chair, or even to enter the room – Miss Jillgall delivered her opinion on Philip's approaching visit. Mrs Tenbruggen reported it in her pocket-book, as if she was representing a newspaper at a public meeting. Here it is, copied from her notes:

'Miss Helena Gracedieu, my first impulse under the present disgusting circumstances, was to leave the house, and earn a bare crust in the cheapest garret I could find in the town. But my grateful heart remembers Mr Gracedieu. My poor afflicted cousin was good to me when I was helpless. I cannot forsake him when *he* is helpless. At whatever sacrifice of my own self-respect, I remain under this roof, so dear to me for the Minister's sake. I notice, Miss, that you smile. I see my once dear Elizabeth, the friend who has so bitterly disappointed me——' she stopped, and put her handkerchief to her eyes, and went on again – 'the friend who has so bitterly disappointed me, taking satirical notes of what I say. I am not ashamed of what I say. The virtue which will not stretch a little, where the motive is good, is feeble virtue indeed. I shall stay in the house, and witness horrors, and rise superior to them. Good-morning, Miss Gracedieu. Good-morning, Elizabeth.' She performed a magnificent curtsey, and (as Mrs Tenbruggen's experience of the stage informed me) made a very creditable exit.

A week has passed, and I have not opened my Diary.

My days have glided away in one delicious flow of happiness. Philip has been delightfully devoted to me. His fervent courtship, far exceeding any similar attentions which he may once have paid to Eunice, has shown such variety and such steadfastness of worship, that I despair of describing it. My enjoyment of my new life is to be felt – not to be coldly considered, and reduced to an imperfect statement in words.

For the first time I feel capable, if the circumstances encouraged me, of acts of exalted virtue. For instance, I could save my country if my country was worth it. I could die a martyr to religion if I had a religion. In one word, I am exceedingly well satisfied with myself.

The little disappointments of life pass over me harmless. I do not even regret the failure of good Mrs Tenbruggen's efforts to find an employment for Philip, worthy of his abilities and accomplishments. The member of Parliament to whom she had applied has chosen a secretary possessed of political influence. That is the excuse put forward in his letter to Mrs Tenbruggen. Wretched corrupt creature! If he was worth a thought I should pity him. He has lost Philip's services.

Three days more have slipped by. The aspect of my heaven on earth is beginning to alter.

Perhaps the author of that wonderful French novel 'L'Ame Damnée' is right when he tells us that human happiness is misery in masquerade. It would be wrong to say that I am miserable. But I may be on the way to it; I am anxious.

To-day, when he did not know that I was observing him, I discovered a preoccupied look in Philip's eyes. He laughed when I asked if anything had happened to vex him. Was it a natural laugh? He put his arm round me and kissed me. Was it done mechanically? I dare say I am out of humour myself. I think I had a little headache. Morbid, probably. I won't think of it any more.

It has occurred to me this morning that he may dislike being left by himself, while I am engaged in my household affairs. If this is the case, intensely as I hate her, utterly as I loathe the idea of putting her in command over my domestic dominions, I shall ask Miss Jillgall to take my place as housekeeper.

I was away to-day in the kitchen regions rather longer than usual. When I had done with my worries, Philip was not to be found. Maria, looking out of one of the bedroom windows instead of doing her work, had seen Mr Dunboyne leave the house. It was possible that he had charged Miss Jillgall with a message for me. I asked if she was in her room. No; she, too, had gone out. It was a fine day, and Philip had no doubt taken a stroll – but he might have waited till I could join him. There were some orders to be given to the butcher and the greengrocer. I, too, left the house, hoping to get rid of some little discontent, caused by thinking of what had happened.

Returning by the way of High Street – I declare I can hardly believe it even now – I did positively see Miss Jillgall coming out of a pawnbroker's shop!

The direction in which she turned prevented her from seeing me. She was quite unaware that I had discovered her; and I have said nothing about it since. But I noticed something unusual in the manner in which her watch-chain was hanging, and I asked her what o'clock it was. She said, 'You have got your own watch.' I told her my watch had stopped. 'So has mine,' she said. There is no doubt about it now; she has pawned her watch. What for? She lives here for nothing, and she has not had a new dress since I have known her. Why does she want money?

Philip had not returned when I got home. Another

mysterious journey to London? No. After an absence of more than two hours, he came back.

Naturally enough, I asked what he had been about. He had been taking a long walk. For his health's sake? No: to think. To think of what? Well, I might be surprised to hear it, but his idle life was beginning to weigh on his spirits; he wanted employment. Had he thought of an employment? Not yet. Which way had he walked? Anyway: he had not noticed where he went. These replies were all made in a tone that offended me. Besides, I observed there was no dust on his boots (after a week of dry weather), and his walk of two hours did not appear to have heated or tired him. I took an opportunity of consulting Mrs Tenbruggen.

She had anticipated that I should appeal to her opinion, as a woman of the world.

I shall not set down in detail what she said. Some of it humiliated me; and from some of it I recoiled. The expression of her opinion came to this. In the absence of experience, a certain fervour of temperament was essential to success in the art of fascinating men. Either my temperament was deficient, or my intellect overpowered it. It was natural that I should suppose myself to be as susceptible to the tender passion as the most excitable woman living. Delusion, my Helena, amiable delusion! Had I ever observed or had any friend told me, that my pretty hands were cold hands? I had beautiful eyes, expressive of vivacity, of intelligence, of every feminine charm, except the one inviting charm that finds favour in the eyes of a man. She then entered into particulars, which I don't deny showed a true interest in helping me. I was ungrateful, sulky, self-opinionated. Dating from that day's talk with Mrs Tenbruggen, my new friendship began to show signs of having caught a chill.

But I did my best to follow her instructions – and failed.

It is perhaps true that my temperament is overpowered by my intellect. Or it is possibly truer still that the fire in my heart, when it warms to love, is a fire that burns low. My belief is that I surprised Philip instead of charming him. He responded to my advances, but I felt that it was not done in earnest, not spontaneously. Had I any right to complain? Was I in earnest? Was I spontaneous? We were making love to each other under false pretences. Oh, what a fool I was to ask Mrs Tenbruggen's advice!

A humiliating doubt has come to me suddenly. Has his heart been inclining to Eunice again? After such a letter as she has written to him? Impossible!

Three events since yesterday, which I consider, trifling as they may be, intimations of something wrong.

First, Miss Jillgall, who at one time was eager to take my place, has refused to relieve me of my housekeeping duties. Secondly, Philip has been absent again, on another long walk. Thirdly, when Philip returned, depressed and sulky, I caught Miss Jillgall looking at him with interest and pity visible in her skinny face. What do these things mean?

I am beginning to doubt everybody. Not one of them, Philip included, cares for me – but I can frighten them, at any rate. Yesterday evening, I dropped on the floor as suddenly as if I had been shot: a fit of some sort. The doctor honestly declared that he was at a loss to account for it. He would have laid me under an eternal obligation if he had failed to bring me back to life again.

As it is, I am more clever than the doctor. What brought the fit on is well known to me. Rage – furious, overpowering, deadly rage – was the cause. I am now in the cold-blooded state, which can look back at the event as composedly as if it had happened to some other girl. Suppose that girl had let her sweetheart know how she loved him, as she had never let him know it before. Suppose she opened the door again the instant after she had left the room, eager, poor wretch, to say, once more, for the fiftieth time, 'My angel, I love you!' Suppose she found her angel standing with his back towards her, so that his face was reflected in the glass. And suppose she discovered in that face, so smiling and so sweet when his head had rested on her bosom only the moment before, the most hideous expression of disgust that features can betray. There could be no doubt of it; I had made my poor offering of love to a man who secretly loathed me. I wonder that I survived my sense of my own degradation. Well! I am alive; and I know him in his true character at last. Am I a woman who submits when an outrage is offered to her? What will happen next? Who knows?

I am in a fine humour. What I have just written has set me laughing at myself. Helena Gracedieu has one merit at least – she is a very amusing person.

I slept last night.

This morning, I am strong again, calm, wickedly capable of deceiving Mr Philip Dunboyne, as he has deceived me. He has not the faintest suspicion that I have discovered him. I wish he had courage enough to kill somebody. How I should enjoy hiring the nearest window to the scaffold, and seeing him hanged!

Miss Jillgall is in better spirits than ever. She is going to take a little holiday; and the cunning creature makes a mystery of it. 'Good-bye, Miss Helena. I am going to stay for a day or two with a friend.' What friend? Who cares?

Last night, I was wakeful. In the darkness a daring idea came to me. To-day, I have carried out the idea. Something has followed which is well worth entering in my Diary.

I left the room at the usual hour for attending to my domestic affairs. The obstinate cook did me a service; she was insolent; she wanted to have her own way. I gave her her own way. In less than five minutes I was on the watch in the pantry, which has a view of the house door. My hat and my parasol were waiting for me on the table, in case of my going out, too.

In a few minutes more, I heard the door opened. Mr Philip Dunboyne stepped out. He was going to take another of his long walks.

I followed him to the street in which the cabs stand. He hired the first one on the rank, an open chaise; while I kept myself hidden in a shop door.

The moment he started on his drive, I hired a closed cab. 'Double your fare,' I said to the driver, 'whatever it may be, if you follow that chaise cleverly, and do what I tell you.'

He nodded and winked at me. A wicked-looking old fellow; just the man I wanted.

We followed the chaise.

## CHAPTER LVI

### HELENA'S DIARY RESUMED

When we had left the town behind us, the coachman began to drive more slowly. In my ignorance, I asked what this change in the pace meant. He pointed with his whip to the open road and to the chaise in the distance.

'If we keep too near the gentleman, Miss, he has only got to look back, and he'll see we are following him. The safe thing to do is to let the chaise get on a bit. We can't lose sight of it, out here.'

I had felt inclined to trust in the driver's experience, and he had already justified my confidence in him. This encouraged me to consult his opinion on a matter of some importance to my present interests. I could see the necessity of avoiding discovery when we had followed the chaise to its destination; but I was totally at a loss to know how it could be done. My wily old man was ready with his advice the moment I asked for it.

'Wherever the chaise stops, Miss, we must drive past it as if we were going somewhere else. I shall notice the place while we go by; and you will please sit back in the corner of the cab so that the gentleman can't see you.'

'Well,' I said, 'and what next?'

'Next, Miss, I shall pull up, wherever it may be, out of sight of the driver of the chaise. He bears an excellent character, I don't deny it; but I've known him for years – and we had better not trust him. I shall tell you where the gentleman stopped; and you will go back to the place (on foot, of course), and see for yourself what's to be done, especially if there happens to be a lady in the case. No offence, Miss; it's in my experience that there's generally a lady in the case. Anyhow, you can judge for yourself, and you'll know where to find me waiting when you want me again.'

'Suppose something happens,' I suggested, 'that we don't expect?'

'I shan't lose my head, Miss, whatever happens.'

'All very well, coachman; but I have only your word for it.' In the irritable state of my mind, the man's confident way of thinking annoyed me.

'Begging your pardon, my young lady, you've got (if I may say so) what they call a guarantee. When I was a young man, I drove a cab in London for ten years. Will that do?'

'I suppose you mean,' I answered, 'that you have learned deceit in the wicked ways of the great city.'

He took this as a compliment. 'Thank you, Miss. That's it exactly.'

After a long drive, or so it seemed to my impatience, we passed the chaise drawn up at a lonely house, separated by a front garden from the road. In two or three minutes more, we stopped where the road took a turn, and descended to lower ground. The farmhouse which we had left behind us was known to the driver. He led the way to a gate at the side of the road, and opened it for me.

'In your place, Miss,' he said slily, 'the private way back is the way I should wish to take. Try it by the fields. Turn to the right when you have passed the barn, and you'll find yourself at the back of the house.' He stopped, and looked at his big silver watch. 'Half-past twelve,' he said, 'the Chawbacons − I mean the farmhouse servants, Miss − will be at their dinner. All in your favour, so far. If the dog happens to be loose, don't forget that his name's Grinder; call him by his name, and pat him before he has time enough to think, and he'll let you be. When you want me, here you'll find me waiting for orders.

I looked back as I crossed the field. The driver was sitting on the gate, smoking his pipe, and the horse was nibbling the grass at the roadside. Two happy animals, without a burden on their minds!

After passing the barn, I saw nothing of the dog. Far or near, no living creature appeared; the servants must have been at dinner, as the coachman had foreseen. Arriving at a wooden fence, I opened a gate in it, and found myself on a bit of waste ground. On my left, there was a large duck-pond. On my right, I saw the fowl-house and the pigsties. Before me was a high impenetrable hedge; and at some distance behind it – an orchard or a garden, as I supposed, filling the intermediate space – rose at the back of the house. I made for the shelter of the hedge, in the fear that someone might approach a window and see me. Once sheltered from observation, I might consider what I should do next. It was impossible to doubt that this was the house in which Eunice was living. Neither could I fail to conclude that Philip had tried to persuade her to see him, on those former occasions when he told me he had taken a long walk.

As I crouched behind the hedge, I heard voices approaching on the other side of it. At last fortune had befriended me. The person speaking at the moment was Miss Jillgall; and the person who answered her was Philip.

'I am afraid, dear Mr Philip, you don't quite understand my sweet Euneece. Honourable, high-minded, delicate in her feelings, and, oh, so unselfish! I don't want to alarm you, but when she hears you have been deceiving Helena——'

'Upon my word, Miss Jillgall, you are too provoking! I have *not* been deceiving Helena. Haven't I told you what discouraging answers I got, when I went to see the Governor? Haven't I shown you Eunice's reply to my letter? You can't have forgotten it already?'

'Oh, yes, I have. Why should I remember it? Don't I know poor Euneece was in your mind, all the time?'

'You're wrong again! Eunice was *not* in my mind all the time. I was hurt – I was offended by the cruel manner in which she had treated me. And what was the consequence? So far was I from deceiving Helena—— she rose in my estimation by comparison with her sister.'

'Oh, come, come, Mr Philip! that won't do. Helena rising in anybody's estimation? Ha! ha! ha!'

'Laugh as much as you like, Miss Jillgall, you won't laugh

away the facts. Helena loved me; Helena was true to me. Don't be hard on a poor fellow who is half distracted. What a man finds he can do on one day, he finds he can't do on another. Try to understand that a change does sometimes come over one's feelings.'

'Bless my soul, Mr Philip, that's just what I have been understanding all the time! I know your mind as well as you know it yourself. You can't forget my sweet Euneece.'

'I tell you I tried to forget her! On my word of honour as a gentleman, I tried to forget her, in justice to Helena. Is it my fault that I failed? Eunice was in my mind, as you said just now. Oh, my friend — for you are my friend, I am sure — persuade her to see me, if it's only for a minute!'

(Was there ever a man's mind in such a state of confusion as this! First, I rise in his precious estimation, and Eunice drops. Then Eunice rises, and I drop. Idiot! Mischievous idiot! Even Selina seemed to be disgusted with him, when she spoke next.)

'Mr Philip, you are hard and unreasonable. I have tried to persuade her, and I have made my darling cry. Nothing you can say will induce me to distress her again. Go back, you very undetermined man — go back to your Helena.'

'Too late.'

'Nonsense!'

'I say too late. If I could have married Helena when I first went to stay in the house, I might have faced the sacrifice. As it is, I can't endure her; and (I tell you this in confidence) she has herself to thank for what has happened.'

'Is that really true?'

'Quite true.'

'Tell me what she did.

'Oh, don't talk of her! Persuade Eunice to see me. I shall come back again, and again, and again till you bring her to me.'

'Please don't talk nonsense. If she changes her mind, I will bring her with pleasure. If she still shrinks from it, I regard Eunice's feelings as sacred. Take my advice; don't press her. Leave her time to think of you, and to pity you — and that true heart may be yours again, if you are worthy of it.'

'Worthy of it? What do you mean?'

'Are you quite sure, my young friend, that you won't go back to Helena?'

'Go back to *her*? I would cut my throat if I thought myself capable of doing it!'

'How did she set you against her? Did the wretch quarrel with you?'

'It might have been better for both of us if she had done that. Oh her fulsome endearments! What a contrast to the charming modesty of Eunice! If I was rich, I would make it worth the while of the first poor fellow I could find to rid me of Helena by marrying her. I don't like saying such a thing of a woman, but if you will have the truth——'

'Well, Mr Philip – and what is the truth?'

'Helena disgusts me.'

## CHAPTER LVII

### HELENA'S DIARY RESUMED

So it was all settled between them. Philip is to throw me away, like one of his bad cigars, for this unanswerable reason: 'Helena disgusts me'. And he is to persuade Eunice to take my place, and be his wife. Yes! if I let him do it.

I heard no more of their talk. With that last, worst outrage burning in my memory, I left the place.

On my way back to the carriage, the dog met me. Truly, a grand creature. I called him by his name, and patted him. He licked my hand. Something made me speak to him. I said: 'If I was to tell you to tear Mr Philip Dunboyne to pieces, would you do it?' The great good-natured brute held out his paw to shake hands. Well! well! I was not an object of disgust to the dog.

But the coachman was startled, when he saw me again. He said something, I did not know what it was; and he produced a pocket-flask, containing some spirits, I suppose. Perhaps he thought I was going to faint. He little knew me. I told him to

drive back to the place at which I had hired the cab, and earn
his money. He earned it.

On getting home, I found Mrs Tenbruggen walking up and
down the dining-room, deep in thought. She was startled when
we first confronted each other. 'You look dreadfully ill,' she
said.

I answered that I had been out for a little exercise, and had
over-fatigued myself; and then changed the subject. 'Does my
father seem to improve under your treatment?' I asked.

'Very far from it, my dear. I promised that I would try what
massage would do for him, and I find myself compelled to give
it up.'

'Why?'

'It excites him dreadfully.'

'In what way?'

'He has been talking wildly of events in his past life. His brain
is in some condition which is beyond my powers of
investigation. He pointed to a cabinet in his room, and said his
past life was locked up there. I asked if I should unlock it. He
shook with fear; he said I should let out the ghost of his dead
brother-in-law. Have you any idea of what he meant?'

The cabinet was full of old letters. I could tell her that – and
could tell her no more. I had never heard of his brother-in-law.
Another of his delusions, no doubt. 'Did you ever hear him
speak,' Mrs Tenbruggen went on, 'of a place called Low Lanes?'

She waited for my reply to this last inquiry, with an
appearance of anxiety that surprised me. I had never heard him
speak of Low Lanes.

'Have you any particular interest in the place?' I asked.

'None whatever.'

She went away to attend on a patient. I retired to my
bedroom, and opened my Diary. Again and again, I read that
remarkable story of the intended poisoning, and of the manner
in which it had ended. I sat thinking over this romance in real
life, till I was interrupted by the annoucement of dinner.

Mr Philip Dunboyne had returned. In Miss Jillgall's absence
we were alone at the table. My appetite was gone. I made a
pretence of eating, and another pretence of being glad to see

my devoted lover. I talked to him in the prettiest manner. As a hypocrite, he thoroughly matched me; he was gallant, he was amusing. If baseness like ours had been punishable by the law, a prison was the right place for both of us.

Mrs Tenbruggen came in again, after dinner, still not quite easy about my health. 'How flushed you are!' she said. 'Let me feel your pulse.' I laughed, and left her with Mr Philip Dunboyne.

Passing my father's door, I looked in, anxious to see if he was in the excitable state which Mrs Tenbruggen had described. Yes; the effect which she had produced on him – how, she knows best – had not passed away yet: he was still talking. The attendant told me it had gone on for hours together. On my approaching his chair, he called out: 'Which are you? Eunice or Helena!' When I had answered him, he beckoned me to come nearer. 'I'm getting stronger every minute,' he said. 'We will go travelling to-morrow, and see the place where you were born.'

Where had I been born? He had never told me where. Had he mentioned the place in Mrs Tenbruggen's hearing? I asked the attendant if he had been present while she was in the room. Yes; he had remained at his post; he had also heard the allusion to the place with the odd name. Had Mr Gracedieu said anything more about that place? Nothing more; the poor Minister's mind had wandered off to other things. He was wandering now. Sometimes, he was addressing his congregation; sometimes, he wondered what they would give him for supper; sometimes, he talked of the flowers in the garden. And then he looked at me, and frowned, and said I prevented him from thinking.

I went back to my bedroom, and opened my Diary, and read the story again.

Was the poison of which that resolute young wife proposed to make use, something that acted slowly, and told the doctors nothing if they looked for it after death?

Would it be running too great a risk to show the story to the doctor, and try to get a little valuable information in that way? It would be useless. He would make some feeble joke; he would say, girls and poisons are not fit company for each other.

But I might discover what I want to know in another way. I might call on the doctor, after he has gone out on his afternoon round of visits, and might tell the servant I would wait for his master's return. Nobody would be in my way; I might get at the medical literature in the consulting-room, and find the information for myself.

A knock at my door interrupted me in the midst of my plans. Mrs Tenbruggen again! – still in a fidgety state of feeling on the subject of my health. 'Which is it?' she said. 'Pain of body, my dear, or pain of mind? I am anxious about you.'

'My dear Elizabeth, your sympathy is thrown away on me. As I have told you already, I am over-tired – nothing more.'

She was relieved to hear that I had no mental troubles to complain of. 'Fatigue,' she remarked, 'sets itself right with rest. Did you take a very long walk?'

'Yes.'

'Beyond the limits of the town, of course? Philip has been taking a walk in the country, too. He doesn't say that he met you.'

These clever people sometimes overreach themselves. How she suggested it to me, I cannot pretend to have discovered. But I did certainly suspect that she had led Philip, while they were together downstairs, into saying to her what he had already said to Miss Jillgall. I was so angry that I tried to pump my excellent friend, as she had been trying to pump me – a vulgar expression, but vulgar writing is such a convenient way of writing sometimes. My first attempt to entrap the Masseuse failed completely. She coolly changed the subject.

'Have I interrupted you in writing?' she asked, pointing to my Diary.

'No; I was idling over what I have written already – an extraordinary story which I copied from a book.'

'May I look at it?'

I pushed the open Diary across the table. If I was the object of any suspicions which she wanted to confirm, it would be curious to see if the poisoning story helped her. 'It's a piece of family history,' I said; 'I think you will agree with me that it is really interesting.'

She began to read. As she went on, not all her power of controlling herself could prevent her from turning pale. This change of colour (in such a woman) a little alarmed me. When a girl is devoured by deadly hatred of a man, does the feeling show itself to other persons in her face? I must practise before the glass, and train my face into a trustworthy state of discipline.

'Coarse melodrama!' Mrs Tenbruggen declared. 'Mere sensation. No analysis of character. A made-up story!'

'Well made up, surely?' I answered.

'I don't agree with you.' Her voice was not quite so steady as usual. She asked suddenly if my clock was right – and declared that she should be late for an appointment. On taking leave she pressed my hand strongly – eyed me with distrustful attention – and said very emphatically: 'Take care of yourself, Helena; pray take care of yourself.'

I am afraid I did a very foolish thing when I showed her the poisoning story. Has it helped the wily old creature to look into my inmost thoughts?

Impossible!

To-day, Miss Jillgall returned, looking hideously healthy and spitefully cheerful. Although she tried to conceal it, while I was present, I could see that Philip had recovered his place in her favour. After what he had said to her behind the hedge at the farm, she would be relieved from all fear of my becoming his wife, and would joyfully anticipate his marriage to Eunice. There are thoughts in me which I don't set down in my book. I only say: We shall see.

This afternoon, I decided on visiting the doctor.

The servant was quite sorry for me when he answered the door. His master had just left the house for a round of visits. I said I would wait. The servant was afraid I should find waiting very tedious. I reminded him that I could go away if I found it tedious. At last, the polite old man left me.

I went into the consulting-room, and read the backs of the medical books ranged round the walls, and found a volume that interested me. There was such curious information in it that I amused myself by making extracts using the first sheets of paper that I could find. They had printed directions at the top, which showed that the doctor was accustomed to write his prescriptions on them. We had many, too many, of his prescriptions in our house.

The servant's doubts of my patience proved to have been well founded. I got tired of waiting, and went home before the doctor returned.

From morning to night, nothing has been seen of Mrs Tenbruggen to-day. Nor has any apology for her neglect of us, been received, fond as she is of writing little notes.

Has that story in my Diary driven her away? Let me see what to-morrow may bring forth.

To-day has brought forth - nothing. Mrs Tenbruggen still keeps away from us. It looks as if my Diary had something to do with the mystery of her absence.

I am not in good spirits to-day. My nerves – if I have such things, which is more than I know by my own experience – have been a little shaken by a horrid dream. The medical information, which my thirst for knowledge absorbed in the doctor's consulting-room, turned traitor – armed itself with the grotesque horrors of nightmare – and so thoroughly frightened me that I was on the point of being foolish enough to destroy my notes. I thought better of it, and my notes are safe under lock and key.

Mr Philip Dunboyne is trying to pave the way for his flight from this house. He speaks of friends in London, whose interests will help him to find the employment which is the object of his ambition. 'In a few days more,' he said, 'I shall ask for leave of absence.'

Instead of looking at me, his eyes wandered to the window; his fingers played restlessly with his watch-chain while he spoke. I thought I would give him a chance, a last chance, of making the atonement that he owes to me. This shows shameful weakness, on my part. Does my own resolution startle me? Or does the wretch appeal – to what? To my pity? It cannot be my love; I am positively sure that I hate him. Well, I am not the first girl who has been an unanswerable riddle to herself.

'Is there any other motive for your departure?' I asked.

'What other motive can there be?' he replied.

I put what I had to say to him in plainer words still.

'Tell me, Philip, are you beginning to wish that you were a free man again?'

He still prevaricated. Was this because he is afraid of me, or because he is not quite brute enough to insult me to my face? I tried again for the third and last time. I almost put the words into his mouth.

'I fancy you have been out of temper lately,' I said. 'You have not been your own kinder and better self. Is this the right interpretation of the change that I think I see in you?'

He answered: 'I have not been very well lately.'

'And that is all?'

'Yes – that is all.'

There was no more to be said; I turned away to leave the room. He followed me to the door. After a momentary hesitation, he made the attempt to kiss me. I only looked at him – he drew back from me in silence. I left the new Judas, standing alone, while the shades of evening began to gather over the room.

# THIRD PERIOD (continued)

*EVENTS IN THE FAMILY, RELATED BY MISS JILLGALL*

## CHAPTER LVIII

### DANGER

'If anything of importance happens, I trust to you to write an account of it, and to send the writing to me. I will come to you at once, if I see reason to believe that my presence is required.' Those lines, in your last kind reply to me, rouse my courage, dear Mr Governor, and sharpen the vigilance which has always been one of the strong points in my character. Every suspicious circumstance which occurs in this house will be (so to speak) seized on by my pen, and will find itself (so to speak again) placed on its trial, before your unerring judgment. Let the wicked tremble! I mention no names.

Taking up my narrative where it came to an end, when I last wrote, I have to say a word first on the subject of my discoveries, in regard to Philip's movements.

The advertisement of a private inquiry office, which I read in a newspaper, put the thing into my head. I provided myself with money to pay the expenses by – I blush while I write it – pawning my watch. This humiliation of my poor self has been rewarded by success. Skilled investigation has proved that our young man has come to his senses again, exactly as I supposed. On each occasion when he was suspiciously absent from the house, he has been followed to the farm. I have been staying there myself for a day or two, in the hope of persuading Eunice to relent. The hope has not yet been realized. But Philip's devotion, assisted by my influence, will yet prevail. Let me not despair.

Whether Helena knows positively that she has lost her wicked hold on Philip I cannot say. It seems hardly possible that she could have made the discovery just yet. The one thing of which I am certain is, that she looks like a fiend.

Philip has wisely taken my advice, and employed pious fraud. He will get away from the wretch, who had tempted him once and may tempt him again, under pretence of using the interest of his friends in London to find a place under Government. He has not been very well for the last day or two, and the execution of our project is in consequence delayed.

I have news of Mrs Tenbruggen which will, I think, surprise you.

She has kept away from us in a most unaccountable manner. I called on her at the hotel, and heard she was engaged with her lawyer. On the next day, she suddenly returned to her old habits, and paid the customary visit. I observed a similar alteration in her state of feeling. She is now coldly civil to Helena; and she asks after Eunice with a maternal interest touching to see. I said to her: 'Elizabeth, you appear to have changed your opinion of the two girls, since I saw you.' She answered, with a delightful candour which reminded me of old times: 'Completely!' I said: 'A woman of your intellectual calibre, dear, doesn't change her mind without a good reason for it.' Elizabeth cordially agreed with me. I ventured to be a little more explicit: 'You have no doubt made some interesting discovery.' Elizabeth agreed again; and I ventured again: 'I suppose I may not ask what the discovery is?' 'No. Selina, you may not ask.'

This is curious; but it is nothing to what I have got to tell you next. Just as I was longing to take her to my bosom again as my friend and confidant, Elizabeth has disappeared. And, alas! alas! there is a reason for it which no sympathetic person can dispute.

I have just received some overwhelming news, in the form of a neat parcel, addressed to myself.

There has been a scandal at the hotel. That monster in human form, Elizabeth's husband, is aware of his wife's professional fame, has heard of the large sums of money which she earns as the greatest living professor of Massage, has been long on the look-out for her, and has discovered her at last. He has not only forced his way into her sitting-room at the hotel: he insists on her living with him again; her money being the attraction, it is needless to say. If she refuses, he threatens her with the law, the barbarous law, which, to use his own coarse expression, will 'restore his conjugal rights'.

All this I gather from the narrative of my unhappy friend, which forms one of the two enclosures in her parcel. She has already made her escape. Ha! the man doesn't live who can circumvent Elizabeth. The English Court of Law isn't built which can catch her when she roams the free and glorious Continent.

The vastness of this amazing woman's mind is what I must pause to admire. In the frightful catastrophe that has befallen her, she can still think of Philip and Euneece. She is eager to hear of their marriage, and renounces Helena with her whole heart. 'I too was deceived by that cunning young woman,' she writes. 'Beware of her, Selina. Unless I am much mistaken, she is going to end badly. Take care of Philip, take care of Euneece. If you want help, apply at once to my favourite hero in real life, The Governor.' I don't presume to correct Elizabeth's language. I should have called you The Idol of the Women.

The second enclosure contains, as I suppose, a wedding present. It is carefully sealed – it feels no bigger than an ordinary letter – and it contains an inscription which your highly-cultivated intelligence may be able to explain. I copy it as follows:

'To be enclosed in another envelope, addressed to Mr Dunboyne the elder, at Percy's Private Hotel, London, and delivered by a trustworthy messenger, on the day when Mr Philip Dunboyne is married to Miss Eunice Gracedieu. Placed meanwhile under the care of Miss Selina Jillgall.'

Why is this mysterious letter to be sent to Philip's father? I wonder whether that circumstance will puzzle you as it has puzzled me.

I have kept my report back, so as send you the last news relating to Philip's state of health. To my great regret, his illness seems to have made a serious advance since yesterday. When I ask if he is in pain, he says: 'It isn't exactly pain; I feel as if I was sinking. Sometimes I am giddy; and sometimes I find myself feeling thirsty and sick.' I have no opportunity of looking after him as I could wish; for Helena insists on nursing him, assisted by the housemaid. Maria is a very good girl in her way, but too stupid to be of much use. If he is not better to-morrow, I shall insist on sending for the doctor.

He is no better; and he wishes to have medical help. Helena doesn't seem to understand his illness. It was not until Philip had insisted on seeing him that she consented to send for the doctor.

You had some talk with this experienced physician when you were here, and you know what a clever man he is. When I tell you that he hesitates to say what is the matter with Philip, you will feel as much alarmed as I do. I will wait to send this to the post until I can write in a more definite way.

Two days more have passed. The doctor has put two very strange questions to me.

He asked, first, if there was anybody staying with us besides the regular members of the household. I said we had no visitor. He wanted to know, next, if Mr Philip Dunboyne had made any enemies since he has been living in our town. I said none that I knew of – and I took the liberty of asking what he meant. He answered to this, that he has a few more inquiries to make, and that he will tell me what he means to-morrow.

For God's sake come here as soon as you possibly can. The whole burden is thrown on me – and I am quite unequal to it.

I received the doctor to-day in the drawing-room. To my amazement, he begged leave to speak with me in the garden. When I asked why, he answered: 'I don't want to have a listener at the door. Come out on the lawn, where we can be sure that we are alone.'

When we were in the garden, he noticed that I was trembling.

'Rouse your courage, Miss Jillgall,' he said. 'In the Minister's helpless state there is nobody whom I can speak to but yourself.'

I ventured to remind him that he might speak to Helena as well as to myself.

He looked as black as thunder when I mentioned her name. All he said was, 'No!' But, oh, if you had heard his voice – and he so gentle and sweet-tempered at other times – you would have felt, as I did, that he had Helena in his mind!

'Now, listen to this,' he went on. 'Everything that my art can do for Mr Philip Dunboyne, while I am at his bedside, is undone while I am away by some other person. He is worse to-day than I have seen him yet.'

'Oh, sir, do you think he will die?'

'He will certainly die unless the right means are taken to save him, and taken at once. It is my duty not to flinch from telling you the truth. I have made a discovery since yesterday which satisfies me that I am right. Somebody is trying to poison Mr Dunboyne; and somebody will succeed unless he is removed from this house.'

I am a poor feeble creature. The doctor caught me, or I should have dropped on the grass. It was not a fainting-fit. I only shook and shivered so that I was too weak to stand up. Encouraged by the doctor, I recovered sufficiently to be able to ask him where Philip was to be taken to. He said: 'To the hospital. No poisoner can follow my patient there. Persuade him to let me take him away, when I call again in an hour's time.'

As soon as I could hold a pen, I sent a telegram to you. Pray, pray come by the earliest train. I also telegraphed to old Mr Dunboyne, at the hotel in London.

It was impossible for me to face Helena; I own I was afraid. The cook kindly went upstairs to see who was in Philip's room. It was the housemaid's turn to look after him for a while. I went instantly to his bedside.

There was no persuading him to allow himself to be taken to the hospital. 'I am dying,' he said. 'If you have any pity for me, send for Euneece. Let me see her once more, let me hear her say that she forgives me, before I die.'

I hesitated. It was too terrible to think of Euneece in the

same house with her sister. Her life might be in danger! Philip gave me a look, a dreadful ghastly look. 'If you refuse,' he said wildly, 'the grave won't hold me. I'll haunt you for the rest of your life.'

'She shall hear that you are ill,' I answered – and ran out of the room before he could speak again.

What I had promised to write, I did write. But, placed between Euneece's danger and Philip's danger, my heart was all for Euneece. Would Helena spare her, if she came to Philip's bedside? In such terror as I never felt before in my life, I added a word more, entreating her not to leave the farm. I promised to keep her regularly informed on the subject of Philip's illness; and I mentioned that I expected the Governor to return to us immediately. 'Do nothing,' I wrote, 'without his advice.' My letter having been completed, I sent the cook away with it, in a chaise. She belonged to the neighbourhood, and she knew the farmhouse well.

Nearly two hours afterwards, I heard the chaise stop at the door, and ran out, impatient to hear how my sweet girl had received my letter. God help us all! When I opened the door, the first person whom I saw was Euneece herself.

## CHAPTER LIX

### DEFENCE

One surprise followed another, after I had encountered Euneece at the door.

When my fondness had excused her for setting the well-meant advice in my letter at defiance, I was conscious of expecting to see her in tears; eager, distressingly eager, to hear what hope there might be of Philip's recovery. I saw no tears, I heard no inquiries. She was pale, and quiet, and silent. Not a word fell from her when we met, not a word when she kissed me, not a word when she led the way into the nearest room – the dining-room. It was only when we were shut in together that she spoke.

'Which is Philip's room?' she asked.

Instead of wanting to know how he was, she desired to know where he was! I pointed towards the back dining-room, which had been made into a bedroom for Philip. He had chosen it himself, when he first came to stay with us, because the window opened into the garden, and he could slip out and smoke at any hour of the day or night, when he pleased.

'Who is with him now?' was the next strange thing this sadly-changed girl said to me.

'Maria is taking her turn,' I answered; 'she assists in nursing Philip.'

'Where is——?' Euneece got no farther than that. Her breath quickened, her colour faded away. I had seen people look as she was looking now, when they suffered under some sudden pain. Before I could offer to help her, she rallied, and went on: 'Where,' she began again, 'is the other nurse?'

'You mean Helena?' I said.

'I mean the Poisoner.'

When I remind you, dear Mr Governor, that my letter had carefully concealed from her the horrible discovery made by the doctor, your imagination will picture my state of mind. She saw that I was overpowered. Her sweet nature, so strangely frozen up thus far, melted at last. 'You don't know what I have heard,' she said, 'you don't know what thoughts have been roused in me.' She left her chair, and sat on my knee with the familiarity of the dear old times, and took the letter that I had written to her from her pocket.

'Look at it yourself,' she said, 'and tell me if anybody could read it, and not see that you were concealing something. My dear, I have driven round by the doctor's house – I have seen him – I have persuaded him, or perhaps I ought to say surprised him, into telling me the truth. But the kind old man is obstinate. He wouldn't believe me when I told him I was on my way here to save Philip's life. He said: "My child, you will only put your own life in jeopardy. If I had not seen that danger, I should never have told you of the dreadful state of things at home. Go back to the good people at the farm, and leave the saving of Philip to me."'

'He was right, Euneece, entirely right.'

'No, dear, he was wrong. I begged him to come here and judge for himself; and I ask you to do the same.'

I was obstinate. 'Go back!' I persisted. 'Go back to the farm!'

'Can I see Philip?' she asked.

I have heard some insolent men say that women are like cats. If they mean that we do, figuratively speaking, scratch at times, I am afraid they are not altogether wrong. An irresistible impulse made me say to poor Euneece: 'This is a change indeed, since you refused to receive Philip.'

'Is there no change in the circumstances?' she asked sadly. 'Isn't he ill and in danger?'

I begged her to forgive me; I said I meant no harm.

'I gave him up to my sister,' she continued, 'when I believed that his happiness depended, not on me, but on her. I take him back to myself, when he is at the mercy of a demon who threatens his life. Come, Selina, let us go to Philip.'

She put her arm round me, and made me get up from my chair. I was so easily persuaded by her, that the fear of what Helena's jealousy and Helena's anger might do was scarcely present in my thoughts. The door of communication was locked on the side of the bedchamber. I went into the hall, to enter Philip's room by the other door. She followed, waiting behind me. I heard what passed between them when Maria went out to her.

'Where is Miss Gracedieu?'

'Resting upstairs, Miss, in her room.'

'Look at the clock, and tell me when you expect her to come down here.'

'I am to call her, Miss, in ten minutes more.'

'Wait in the dining-room, Maria, till I come back to you.'

She joined me. I held the door open for her to go into Philip's room. It was not out of curiosity; the feeling that urged me was sympathy, when I waited a moment to see their first meeting. She bent over the poor, pallid, trembling, suffering man, and raised him in her arms, and laid his head on her bosom. 'My Philip!' She murmured those words in a kiss. I closed the door; I had a good cry; and, oh, how it comforted me!

There was only a minute to spare when she came out of the room. Maria was waiting for her. Euneece said, as quietly as ever: 'Go and call Miss Gracedieu.'

The girl looked at her, and saw — I don't know what. Maria became alarmed. But she went up the stairs, and returned in haste to tell us that her young mistress was coming down.

The faint rustling of Helena's dress as she left her room reached us in the silence. I remained at the open door of the dining-room, and Maria approached and stood near me. We were both frightened. Euneece stepped forward, and stood on the mat at the foot of the stairs, waiting. Her back was towards me; I could only see that she was as still as a statue. The rustling of the dress came nearer. Oh, Heavens! what was going to happen? My teeth chattered in my head; I held by Maria's shoulder. Drops of perspiration showed themselves on the girl's forehead; she stared in vacant terror at the slim little figure, posted firm and still on the mat.

Helena turned the corner of the stairs, and waited a moment on the last landing, and saw her sister.

'You here?' she said. 'What do you want?'

There was no reply. Helena descended, until she reached the last stair but one. There, she stopped. Her staring eyes grew large and wild: her hand shook as she stretched it out, feeling for the bannister; she staggered as she caught at it, and held herself up. The silence was still unbroken. Something in me, stronger than myself, drew my steps along the hall, nearer and nearer to the stair, till I could see the face which had struck that murderous wretch with terror.

I looked

No! it was not my sweet girl; it was a horrid transformation of her. I saw a fearful creature, with glittering eyes that threatened some unimaginable vengeance. Her lips were drawn back; they showed her clenched teeth. A burning red flush dyed her face. The hair of her head rose, little by little, slowly. And, most dreadful sight of all, she seemed, in the stillness of the house, to be *listening to something*. If I could have moved, I should have fled to the first place of refuge I could find. If I could have raised my voice, I should have cried for help. I could do neither the one nor the other. I could only look, look, look; held by the horror of it with a hand of iron.

Helena must have roused her courage, and resisted her terror. I heard her speak:

'Let me by!'

'No.'

Slowly, steadily, in a whisper, Euneece made that reply. Helena tried once more – still fighting against her own terror: I knew it by the trembling of her voice:

'Let me by,' she repeated; 'I am on my way to Philip's room.'

'You will never enter Philip's room again.'

'Who will stop me?'

'I will.'

She had spoken in the same steady whisper throughout – but now she moved. I saw her set her foot on the first stair. I saw the horrid glitter in her eyes flash close into Helena's face. I heard her say:

'Poisoner, go back to your room.'

Silent and shuddering, Helena shrank away from her – daunted by her glittering eyes; mastered by her lifted hand pointing up the stairs.

Helena slowly ascended till she reached the landing. She turned and looked down; she tried to speak. The pointing hand struck her dumb, and drove her up the next flight of stairs. She was lost to view. Only the small rustling sound of the dress was to be heard, growing fainter and fainter; then an interval of stillness; then the noise of a door opened and closed again; then no sound more – but a change to be seen: the transformed creature was crouching on her knees, still and silent, her face covered by her hands. I was afraid to approach her; I was afraid to speak to her. After a time, she rose. Suddenly, swiftly, with her head turned away from me, she opened the door of Philip's room – and was gone.

I looked round. There was only Maria in the lonely hall. Shall I try to tell you what my sensations were? It may sound strangely, but it is true – I felt like a sleeper, who has half awakened from a dream.

# CHAPTER LX

### DISCOVERY

A little later, on that eventful day, when I was most in need of all that your wisdom and kindness could do to guide me, came the telegram which announced that you were helpless under an attack of gout. As soon as I had in some degree got over my disappointment, I remembered having told Euneece in my letter that I expected her kind old friend to come to us. With the telegram in my hand I knocked softly at Philip's door.

The voice that bade me come in was the gentle voice that I knew so well. Philip was sleeping. There, by his bedside, with his hand resting in her hand, was Euneece, so completely restored to her own sweet self that I could hardly believe what I had seen, not an hour since. She talked of you, when I showed her your message, with affectionate interest and regret. Look back, my admirable friend, at what I have written on the two or three pages which precede this, and explain the astounding contrast if you can.

I was left alone to watch by Philip, while Euneece went away to see her father. Soon afterwards, Maria took my place; I had been sent for to the next room to receive the doctor.

He looked care-worn and grieved. I said I was afraid he had brought bad news with him.

'The worst possible news,' he answered. 'A terrible exposure threatens this family, and I am powerless to prevent it.'

He then asked me to remember the day when I had been surprised by the singular questions which he had put to me, and when he had engaged to explain himself after he had made some inquiries. Why, and how, he had set those inquiries on foot, was what he had now to tell. I will repeat what he said, in his own words, as nearly as I can remember them. While he was in attendance on Philip, he had observed symptoms which made him suspect that Digitalis had been given to the young man, in doses often repeated. Cases of attempted poisoning by this medicine were so rare, that he felt bound to put his suspicions to the test by going round among the chemists' shops

– excepting of course the shop at which his own prescriptions were made up – and asking if they had lately dispensed any preparation of Digitalis, ordered perhaps in a larger quantity than usual. At the second shop he visited, the chemist laughed. 'Why, doctor,' he said, 'have you forgotten your own prescription?' After this, the prescription was asked for, and produced. It was on the paper used by the doctor – paper which had his address printed at the top, and a notice added, telling patients who came to consult him for the second time to bring their prescriptions with them. Then, there followed in writing: 'Tincture of Digitalis, one ounce' – with his signature at the end, not badly imitated, but a forgery nevertheless. The chemist noticed the effect which this discovery had produced on the doctor, and asked if that was his signature. He could hardly, as an honest man, have asserted that a forgery was a signature of his own writing. So he made the true reply, and asked who had presented the prescription. The chemist called to his assistant to come forward. 'Did you tell me that you knew, by sight, the young lady who brought this prescription?' The assistant admitted it. 'Did you tell me she was Miss Helena Gracedieu?' 'I did.' 'Are you sure of not having made any mistake?' 'Quite sure.' The chemist then said: 'I myself supplied the Tincture of Digitalis, and the young lady paid for it, and took it away with her. You have had all the information that I can give you, sir; and I may now ask if you can throw any light on the matter.' Our good friend thought of the poor Minister, so sorely afflicted, and of the famous name so sincerely respected in the town and in the country around, and said he could not undertake to give an immediate answer. The chemist was excessively angry. 'You know as well as I do,' he said, 'that Digitalis, given in certain doses, is a poison, and you cannot deny that I honestly believed myself to be dispensing your prescription. While you are hesitating to give me an answer, my character may suffer; I may be suspected myself.' He ended in declaring he should consult his lawyer. The doctor went home, and questioned his servant. The man remembered the day of Miss Helena's visit in the afternoon, and the intention that she expressed of waiting for his master's return. He had shown her into the parlour which opened into the consulting-room. No other visitor was in the house at that time, or had arrived during the rest of the day. The doctor's own experience, when he got home, led him to conclude that Helena had gone into the consulting-room. He had entered that room, for the purpose of writing some prescriptions, and had found the leaves of paper that he used diminished in number. After what he had heard, and what he had discovered (to say nothing of what he suspected), it occurred to him to look along the shelves of his medical library. He found a volume (treating of Poisons) with a slip of paper left between the leaves; the poison described at the place so marked being Digitalis, and the paper used being one of his own prescription-papers. 'If, as I fear, a legal investigation into Helena's conduct is a possible event,' the doctor concluded, 'there is the evidence that I shall be obliged to give, when I am called as witness.'

It is my belief that I could have felt no greater dismay, if the long arm of the Law had laid its hold on me while he was speaking. I asked what was to be done.

'If she leaves the house at once,' the doctor replied, 'she may escape the infamy of being charged with an attempt at murder by poison; and, in her absence, I can answer for Philip's life. I don't urge you to warn her, because that might be a dangerous thing to do. It is for you to decide, as a member of the family, whether you will run the risk.'

I tried to speak to him of Euneece, and to tell him what I had already related to yourself. He was in no humour to listen to me. 'Keep it for a fitter time,' he answered; 'and think of what I have just told you.' With that, he left me, on his way to Philip's room.

Mental exertion was completely beyond me. Can you understand a poor middle-aged spinster being frightened into doing a dangerous thing? That may seem to be nonsense. But if you ask why I took a morsel of paper, and wrote the warning which I was afraid to communicate by word of mouth – why I went upstairs with my knees knocking together, and opened the door of Helena's room just wide enough to let my hand pass through – why I threw the paper in, and banged the door to again, and ran downstairs as I have never run since I was a little girl – I can only say, in the way of explanation, what I have said already: I was frightened into doing it.

What I have written, thus far, I shall send to you by to-night's post.

The doctor came back to me, after he had seen Philip, and spoken with Euneece. He was very angry; and, I must own, not without reason. Philip had flatly refused to let himself be removed to the hospital; and Euneece – 'a mere girl' – had declared that she would be answerable for consequences! The doctor warned me that he meant to withdraw from the case, and to make his declaration before the magistrates. At my entreaties he consented to return in the evening, and to judge by results before taking the terrible step that he had threatened.

While I remained at home on the watch, keeping the doors of both rooms locked, Euneece went out to get Philip's medicine. She came back, followed by a boy carrying a portable apparatus for cooking. 'All that Philip wants, and all that we want,' she explained, 'we can provide for ourselves. Give me a morsel of paper to write on.'

Unhooking the little pencil attached to her watch-chain, she paused, and looked towards the door. 'Somebody is listening,' she whispered. 'Let them listen.' She wrote a list of necessities, in the way of things to eat and things to drink, and asked me to go out and get them myself. 'I don't doubt the servants,' she said, speaking distinctly enough to be heard outside; 'but I am afraid of what a Poisoner's cunning and a Poisoner's desperation may do, in a kitchen which is open to her.' I went away on my errand – discovering no listener outside, I need hardly say. On my return, I found the door of communication with Philip's room closed, but no longer locked. 'We can now attend on him in turn,' she said, 'without opening either of the doors which lead into the hall. At night we can relieve each other, and each of us can get sleep as we want it in the large arm-chair in the dining-room. Philip must be safe under our charge, or the doctor will insist on taking him to the hospital. When we want Maria's help, from time to time, we can employ her under our own superintendence. Have you anything else, Selina, to suggest?'

There was nothing left to suggest. Young and inexperienced as she was, how (I asked) had she contrived to think of all this? She answered simply: 'I'm sure I don't know; my thoughts came to me while I was looking at Philip.'

Soon afterwards I found an opportunity of inquiring if Helena had left the house. She had just rung her bell; and Maria had found her, quietly reading, in her room. Hours afterwards, when I was on the watch at night, I heard Philip's door softly tried from the outside. Her dreadful purpose had not been given up, even yet.

The doctor came in the evening, as he had promised, and found an improvement in Philip's health. I mentioned what precautions we had taken, and that they had been devised by Euneece. 'Are you going to withdraw from the case?' I asked. 'I am coming back to the case,' he answered, 'to-morrow morning.'

It had been a disappointment to me to receive no answer to the telegram which I had sent to Mr Dunboyne the elder. The next day's post brought the explanation in a letter to Philip from his father, directed to him at the hotel here. This showed that my telegram, giving my address at this house, had not been received. Mr Dunboyne announced that he had returned to Ireland, finding the air of London unendurable, after the sea-breezes at home. If Philip had already married, his father would leave him to a life of genteel poverty with Helena Gracedieu. If he had thought better of it, his welcome was waiting for him.

Little did Mr Dunboyne know what changes had taken place since he and his son had last met, and what hope might yet present itself of brighter days for poor Euneece! I thought of writing to him. But how would that crabbed old man receive a confidential letter from a lady who was a stranger?

My doubts were set at rest by Philip himself. He asked me to write a few lines of reply to his father; declaring that his marriage with Helena was broken off – that he had not given up all hope of being permitted to offer the sincere expression of his penitence to Euneece – and that he would gladly claim his welcome, as soon as he was well enough to undertake the journey to Ireland. When he had signed the letter, I was so pleased that I made a smart remark. I said, 'This is a treaty of peace between father and son.'

When the doctor arrived in the morning, and found the change for the better in his patient confirmed, he did justice to us at last. He spoke kindly, and even gratefully, to Euneece. No more allusions to the hospital as a place of safety escaped him. He asked me cautiously for news of Helena. I could only tell him that she had gone out at her customary time, and had returned at her customary time. He did not attempt to conceal that my reply had made him uneasy.

'Are you still afraid that she may succeed in poisoning Philip?' I asked.

'I am afraid of her cunning,' he said. 'If she is charged with attempting to poison young Dunboyne, she has some system of defence, you may rely on it, for which we are not prepared. There, in my opinion, is the true reason for her extraordinary insensibility to her own danger.'

Two more days passed, and we were still safe under the protection of lock and key.

On the evening of the second day (which was a Monday) Maria came to me, in great tribulation. On inquiring what was the matter, I received a disquieting reply: 'Miss Helena is tempting me. She is so miserable at being prevented from seeing Mr Philip, and helping to nurse him, that it is quite distressing to see her. At the same time, Miss, it's hard on a poor servant. She asks me to take the key secretly out of the door, and lend it to her at night for a few minutes only. I'm really afraid I shall be led into doing it, if she goes on persuading me much longer.'

I commended Maria for feeling scruples which proved her to be the best of good girls, and promised to relieve her from all fear of future temptation. This was easily done. Euneece kept the key of Philip's door in her pocket; and I kept the key of the dining-room in mine.

## CHAPTER LXI

### ATROCITY

On the next day, a Tuesday in the week, an event took place which Euneece and I viewed with distrust. Early in the afternoon, a young man called with a note for Helena. It was to be given to her immediately, and no answer was required.

Maria had just closed the house door, and was on her way upstairs with the letter, when she was called back by another ring at the bell. Our visitor was the doctor. He spoke to Maria in the hall:

'I think I see a note in your hand. Was it given to you by the young man who has just left the house?'

'Yes, sir.'

'If he's your sweetheart, my dear, I have nothing more to say.'

'Good gracious, doctor, how you do talk! I never saw the young man before in my life.'

'In that case, Maria, I will ask you to let me look at the address. Aha! Mischief!'

The moment I heard that I threw open the dining-room door. Curiosity is not easily satisfied. When it hears, it wants to see; when it sees, it wants to know. Every lady will agree with me in this observation.

'Pray come in,' I said.

'One minute, Miss Jillgall. My girl, when you give Miss Helena that note, try to get a sly look at her when she opens it, and come and tell me what you have seen.' He joined me in the dining-room, and closed the door. 'The other day,' he went on, 'when I told you what I had discovered in the chemist's shop, I think I mentioned a young man who was called to speak to a question of identity – an assistant who knew Miss Helena Gracedieu by sight.'

'Yes, yes!'

'That young man left the note which Maria has just taken upstairs.'

'Who wrote it, doctor, and what does it say?'

'Questions naturally asked, Miss Jillgall – and not easily answered. Where is Eunice? Her quick wit might help us.'

She had gone out to buy some fruit and flowers for Philip.

The doctor accepted his disappointment resignedly. 'Let us try what we can do without her,' he said. 'That young man's master has been in consultation (you may remember why) with his lawyer, and Helena may be threatened by an investigation before the magistrates. If this wild guess of mine turns out to have hit the mark, the poisoner upstairs has got a warning.'

I asked if the chemist had written the note. Foolish enough of me when I came to think of it. The chemist would scarcely act a friendly part towards Helena, when she was answerable for the awkward position in which he had placed himself. Perhaps the young man who had left the warning was also the writer of the warning. The doctor reminded me that he was all but a stranger to Helena. 'We are not usually interested,' he remarked, 'in a person whom we only know by sight.'

'Remember that he is a young man,' I ventured to say. This was a strong hint, but the doctor failed to see it. He had evidently forgotten his own youth. I made another attempt.

'And vile as Helena is,' I continued, 'we cannot deny that this disgrace to her sex is a handsome young lady.'

He saw it at last. 'Woman's wit!' he cried. 'You have hit it, Miss Jillgall. The young fool is smitten with her, and has given her a chance of making her escape.'

'Do you think she will take the chance?'

'For all our sakes, I pray God she may! But I don't feel sure about it.'

'Why?'

'Recollect what you and Eunice have done. You have shown your suspicion of her without an attempt to conceal it. If you had put her in prison you could not have more completely defeated her infernal design. Do you think she is a likely person to submit to that, without an effort to be even with you?'

Just as he said those terrifying words, Maria came back to us. He asked at once what had kept her so long upstairs.

The girl had evidently something to say, which had inflated her (if I may use such an expression) with a sense of her own importance.

'Please to let me tell it, sir,' she answered, 'in my own way.

Miss Helena turned as pale as ashes when she opened the letter, and then she took a turn in the room, and then she looked at me with a smile – well, Miss, I can only say that I felt that smile in the small of my back. I tried to get to the door. She stopped me. She says: "Where's Miss Eunice?" I says: "Gone out." She says: "Is there anybody in the drawing-room?" I says: "No, Miss." She says: "Tell Miss Jillgall I want to speak to her, and say I am waiting in the drawing-room." It's every word of it true! And if a poor servant may give an opinion, I don't like the look of it.'

The doctor dismissed Maria. 'Whatever it is,' he said to me, 'you must go and hear it.'

I am not a courageous woman; I expressed myself as being willing to go to her, if the doctor went with me. He said that was impossible; she would probably refuse to speak before any witness; and certainly before him. But he promised to look after Philip in my absence, and to wait below if it really so happened that I wanted him. I need only ring the bell, and he would come to me the moment he heard it. Such kindness as this roused my courage, I suppose. At any rate, I went upstairs.

She was standing by the fireplace, with her elbow on the chimney-piece, and her head resting on her hand. I stopped just inside the door, waiting to hear what she had to say. In this position her side-face only was presented to me. It was a ghastly face. The eye that I could see turned wickedly on me when I came in – then turned away again. Otherwise, she never moved. I confess I trembled, but I did my best to disguise it.

She broke out suddenly with what she had to say: 'I won't allow this state of things to go on any longer. My horror of an exposure which will disgrace the family has kept me silent, wrongly silent, so far. Philip's life is in danger. I am forgetting my duty to my affianced husband, if I allow myself to be kept away from him any longer. Open those locked doors, and relieve me from the sight of you. Open the doors, I say, or you will both of you – you the accomplice, she the wretch who directs you – repent it to the end of your lives.'

In my own mind, I asked myself if she had gone mad. But I only answered: 'I don't understand you.'

She said again: 'You are Eunice's accomplice.'

'Accomplice in what?' I asked.

She turned her head slowly, and faced me. I shrank from looking at her.

'All the circumstances prove it,' she went on. 'I have supplanted Eunice in Philip's affection. She was once engaged to marry him; I am engaged to marry him now. She is resolved that he shall never make me his wife. He will die if I delay any longer. He will die if I don't crush her, like the reptile she is. She comes here – and what does she do? Keeps him prisoner under her own superintendence. Who gets his medicine? She gets it. Who cooks his food? She cooks it. The doors are locked. I might be a witness of what goes on; and I am kept out. The servants who ought to wait on him are kept out. She can do what she likes with his medicine; she can do what she likes with his food: she is infuriated with him for deserting her, and promising to marry me. Give him back to my care, or, dreadful as it is to denounce my own sister, I shall claim protection from the magistrates.

I lost all fear of her: I stepped close up to the place at which she was standing; I cried out: 'Of what, in God's name, do you accuse your sister?'

She answered: 'I accuse her of poisoning Philip Dunboyne.'

I ran out of the room; I rushed headlong down the stairs. The doctor heard me, and came running into the hall. I caught hold of him like a madwoman. 'Euneece!' My breath was gone; I could only say: 'Euneece!'

He dragged me into the dining-room. There was wine on the side-board, which he had ordered medically for Philip. He forced me to drink some of it. It ran through me like fire; it helped me to speak. 'Now tell me,' he said, 'what has she done to Eunice?'

'She brings a horrible accusation against her,' I answered.

'What is the accusation?'

I told him.

He looked me through and through. 'Take care!' he said. 'No hysterics, no exaggeration. You may lead to dreadful consequences if you are not sure of yourself. If it's really true, say it again.'

I said it again – quietly, this time.

His face startled me; it was white with rage. He snatched his hat off the hall table.

'What are you going to do?' I asked.

'My duty.'

He was out of the house before I could speak to him again.

# THIRD PERIOD (concluded)

## *TROUBLES AND TRIUMPHS OF THE FAMILY, RELATED BY THE GOVERNOR*

### CHAPTER LXII

#### THE SENTENCE PRONOUNCED

Martyrs to gout know, by sad experience, that they suffer under one of the most capricious of maladies. An attack of this disease will shift, in the most unaccountable manner, from one part of the body to another; or, it will release the victim when there is every reason to fear that it is about to strengthen its hold on him; or, having shown the fairest promise of submitting to medical treatment, it will cruelly lay the patient prostrate again, in a state of relapse. Adverse fortune, in my case, subjected me to this last and worst trial of endurance. Two months passed – months of pain aggravated by anxiety – before I was able to help Eunice and Miss Jillgall personally with my sympathy and advice.

During this interval, I heard regularly from the friendly and faithful Selina.

Terror and suspense, courageously endured day after day, seem to have broken down her resistance, poor soul, when Eunice's good name and Eunice's tranquillity were threatened by the most infamous of false accusations. From that time, Miss Jillgall's method of expressing herself betrayed a gradual deterioration. I shall avoid presenting at a disadvantage a correspondent who has claims on my gratitude, if I give the substance only of what she wrote – assisted by the newspaper which she sent to me, while the legal proceedings were in progress.

Honest indignation does sometimes counsel us wisely. When

the doctor left Miss Jillgall, in anger and in haste, he had determined on taking the course from which, as a humane man and a faithful friend, he had hitherto recoiled. It was no time, now to shrink from the prospect of an exposure. The one hope of successfully encountering the vindictive wickedness of Helena lay in the resolution to be beforehand with her, in the appeal to the magistrates with which she had threatened Eunice and Miss Jillgall. The doctor's sworn information stated the whole terrible case of the poisoning, ranging from his first suspicions and their confirmation, to Helena's atrocious attempt to accuse her innocent sister of her own guilt. So firmly were the magistrates convinced of the serious nature of the case thus stated, that they did not hesitate to issue their warrant. Among the witnesses whose attendance was immediately secured, by the legal adviser to whom the doctor applied, were the farmer and his wife.

Helena was arrested while she was dressing to go out. Her composure was not for a moment disturbed. 'I was on my way,' she said coolly, 'to make a statement before the justices. The sooner they hear what I have to say the better.'

The attempt of this shameless wretch to 'turn the tables' on poor Eunice – suggested, as I afterwards discovered, by the record of family history which she had quoted in her journal – was defeated with ease. The farmer and his wife proved the date at which Eunice had left her place of residence under their roof. The doctor's evidence followed. He proved, by the production of his professional diary, that the discovery of the attempt to poison his patient had taken place before the day of Eunice's departure from the farm, and that the first improvement in Mr Philip Dunboyne's state of health had shown itself after that young lady's arrival to perform the duties of a nurse. To the wise precautions which she had taken – perverted by Helena to the purpose of a false accusation – the doctor attributed the preservation of the young man's life.

Having produced the worst possible impression on the minds of the magistrates, Helena was remanded. Her legal adviser had predicted this result; but the vindictive obstinacy of his client had set both experience and remonstrance at defiance.

At the renewed examination, the line of defence adopted by the prisoner's lawyer proved to be – mistaken identity.

It was asserted that she had never entered the chemist's shop; also, that the assistant had wrongly identified some other lady as Miss Helena Gracedieu; also, that there was not an atom of evidence to connect her with the stealing of the doctor's prescription-paper and the forgery of his writing. Other assertions to the same purpose followed, on which it is needless to dwell. The case for the prosecution was, happily, in competent hands. With the exception of one witness, cross-examination afforded no material help to the evidence for the defence.

The chemist swore positively to the personal appearance of Helena, as being the personal appearance of the lady who had presented the prescription. His assistant, pressed on the question of identity, broke down under cross-examination – purposely, as it was whispered, serving the interests of the prisoner. But the victory, so far gained by the defence, was successfully contested by the statement of the next witness, a respectable tradesman in the town. He had seen the newspaper report of the first examination, and had volunteered to present himself as a witnesses. A member of Mr Gracedieu's congregation, his pew in the chapel was so situated as to give him a view of the minister's daughters occupying their pew. He had seen the prisoner on every Sunday, for years past; and he swore that he was passing the door of the chemist's shop at the moment when she stepped out into the street, having a bottle covered with the customary white paper in her hand. The doctor and his servant were the next witnesses called. They were severely cross-examined. Some of their statements – questioned technically with success – received unexpected and powerful support, due to the discovery and production of the prisoner's diary. The entries, guardedly as some of them were written, revealed her motive for attempting to poison Philip Dunboyne; proved that she had purposely called on the doctor when she knew that he would be out, that she had entered the consulting-room, and examined the medical books, had found (to use her own written words) 'a volume that interested her', and had used the prescription-papers for the purpose of making notes. The notes themselves were not to be found; they had doubtless been destroyed. Enough, and more than enough, remained to make the case for the prosecution complete. The magistrates committed Helena Gracedieu for trial at the next assizes.

I arrived in the town, as well as I can remember, about a week after the trial had taken place.

Found guilty, the prisoner had been recommended to mercy by the jury – partly in consideration of her youth; partly as an expression of sympathy and respect for her unhappy father. The judge (a father himself) passed a lenient sentence. She was condemned to imprisonment for two years. The careful matron of the gaol had provided herself with a bottle of smelling-salts, in the fear that there might be need for it when Helena heard her sentence pronounced. Not the slightest sign of agitation appeared in her face or her manner. She lied to the last; asserting her innocence in a firm voice, and returning from the dock to the prison without requiring assistance from anybody.

Relating these particulars to me, in a state of ungovernable excitement, good Miss Jillgall ended with a little confession of her own, which operated as a relief to my overburdened mind after what I had just heard.

'I wouldn't own it,' she said, 'to anybody but a dear friend. One thing, in the dreadful disgrace that has fallen on us, I am quite at a loss to account for. Think of Mr Gracedieu's daughter being one of those criminal creatures, on whom it was once your terrible duty to turn the key! Why didn't she commit suicide?'

'My dear lady, no thoroughly wicked creature ever yet committed suicide. Self-destruction, when it is not an act of madness, implies some acuteness of feeling – sensibility to remorse or to shame, or perhaps a distorted idea of making atonement. There is no such thing as remorse, or shame, or hope of making atonement, in Helena's nature.'

'But when she comes out of prison, what will she do?'

'Don't alarm yourself, my good friend. She will do very well.'

'Oh, hush! hush! Poetical justice, Mr Governor!'

'Poetical fiddlesticks, Miss Jillgall.'

## CHAPTER LXIII

### THE OBSTACLE REMOVED

When the subject of the trial was happily dismissed, my first inquiry related to Eunice. The reply was made with an ominous accompaniment of sighs and sad looks. Eunice had gone back to her duties as governess at the farm. Hearing this, I asked naturally what had become of Philip.

Melancholy news, again, was the news that I now heard.

Mr Dunboyne the elder had died suddenly, at his house in Ireland, while Philip was on his way home. When the funeral ceremony had come to an end, the will was read. It had been made only a few days before the testator's death; and the clause which left all his property to his son was preceded by expressions of paternal affection, at a time when Philip was in sore need of consolation. After alluding to a letter, received from his son, the old man added: 'I always loved him, without caring to confess it; I detest scenes of sentiment, kissings, embracings, tears, and that sort of thing. But Philip has yielded to my wishes, and has broken off a marriage which would have made him, as well as me, wretched for life. After this, I may speak my mind from my grave, and may tell my boy that I loved him. If the wish is likely to be of any use, I will add (on the chance) – God bless him.'

'Does Philip submit to separation from Eunice?' I asked. 'Does he stay in Ireland?'

'Not he, poor fellow! He will be here to-morrow or next day. When I last wrote,' Miss Jillgall continued, 'I told him I hoped to see you again soon. If you can't help us (I mean with Eunice) that unlucky young man will do some desperate thing. He will join those madmen at large who disturb poor savages in Africa, or go nowhere to find nothing in the Arctic regions.'

'Whatever I can do, Miss Jillgall, shall be gladly done. Is it really possible that Eunice refuses to marry him, after having saved his life?'

'A little patience, please, Mr Governor; let Philip tell his own story. If I try to do it, I shall only cry – and we have had tears enough lately, in this house.'

Further consultation being thus deferred, I went upstairs to the Minister's room.

He was sitting by the window, in his favourite armchair, absorbed in knitting! The person who attended on him, a good-natured patient fellow, had been a sailor in his younger days, and had taught Mr Gracedieu how to use the needles. 'You see it amuses him,' the man said kindly. 'Don't notice his mistakes; he thinks there isn't such another in the world for knitting as himself. You can see, sir, how he sticks to it.' He was so absorbed over his employment that I had to speak to him twice, before I could induce him to look at me. The utter ruin of his intellect did not appear to have exercised any disastrous influence over his bodily health. On the contrary, he had grown fatter since I had last seen him; his complexion had lost the pallor that I remembered – there was colour in his cheeks.

'Don't you remember your old friend?' I said. He smiled, and nodded, and repeated the words: 'Yes, yes, my old friend.' It was only too plain that he had not the least recollection of me.

'His memory is gone,' the man said. 'When he puts away his knitting, at night, I have to find it for him in the morning. But, there! he's happy – enjoys his victuals, likes sitting out in the garden and watching the birds. There's been a deal of trouble in the family, sir; and it has all passed over him like a wet sponge over a slate.' The old sailor was right. If that wreck of a man had been capable of feeling and thinking, his daughter's disgrace would have broken his heart. In a world of sin and sorrow, is peaceable imbecility always to be pitied? I have known men who would have answered, without hesitation: 'It is to be envied.' And where (some persons might say) was the poor Minister's reward for the act of mercy which had saved Eunice in her infancy? Where it ought to be! A man who worthily performs a good action finds his reward in the action itself.

At breakfast, on the next day, the talk touched on those passages in Helena's diary, which had been produced in court as evidence against her.

I expressed a wish to see what revelation of a depraved nature the entries in the diary might present; and my curiosity was gratified. At a fitter time, I may find an opportunity of alluding to the impression produced on me by the diary. In the meanwhile, the event of Philip's return claims notice in the first place.

The poor fellow was so glad to see me that he shook hands as heartily as if we had known each other from the time when he was a boy.

'Do you remember how kindly you spoke to me, when I called on you in London?' he asked. 'If I have repeated those words once – but perhaps you don't remember them? You said: "If I was as young as you are, I should not despair." Well! I have said that to myself over and over again, for a hundred times at least. Eunice will listen to you, sir, when she will listen to nobody else. This is the first happy moment I have had for weeks past.'

I suppose I must have looked glad to hear that. Anyway, Philip shook hands with me again.

Miss Jillgall was present. The gentle-hearted old maid was so touched by our meeting that she abandoned herself to the genial impulse of the moment, and gave Philip a kiss. The outraged claims of propriety instantly seized on her. She blushed as if the long-lost days of her girlhood had been found again, and ran out of the room.

'Now, Mr Philip,' I said, 'I have been waiting, at Miss Jillgall's suggestion, to get my information from you. There is something wrong between Eunice and yourself. What is it? And who is to blame?'

'Her vile sister is to blame,' he answered. 'That reptile was determined to sting us. And she has done it!' he cried, starting to his feet, and walking up and down the room, urged into action by his own unendurable sense of wrong. 'I say, she has done it, after Eunice has saved me – done it, when Eunice was ready to be my wife.'

'How has she done it?'

Between grief and indignation his reply was involved in a confusion of vehemently-spoken words, which I shall not attempt to reproduce. Eunice had reminded him that her sister had been publicly convicted of an infamous crime, and publicly punished for it by imprisonment. 'If I consent to marry you,' she said, 'I stain you with my disgrace; that shall never be.' With this resolution she had left him. 'I have tried to convince her,' Philip said, 'that she will not be associated with her sister's disgrace when she bears my name; I have promised to take her far away from England, among people who have never even heard of her sister. Miss Jillgall has used her influence to help us. All in vain! There is no hope for us but in you. I am not thinking selfishly only of myself. She tries to conceal it – but, oh, she is broken-hearted! Ask the farmer's wife, if you don't believe me. Judge for yourself, sir. Go – for God's sake, go to the farm.'

I made him sit down and compose himself.

'You may depend on my going to the farm,' I answered. 'I shall write to Eunice to-day, and follow my letter to-morrow.' He tried to thank me; but I would not allow it. 'Before I consent to accept the expression of your gratitude,' I said, 'I must know a little more of you than I know now. This is only the second occasion on which we have met. Let us look back a little Mr Philip Dunboyne. You were Eunice's affianced husband; and you broke faith with her. That was a rascally action. How do you defend it?'

His head sank. 'I am ashamed to defend it,' he answered.

I pressed him without mercy. 'You own yourself,' I said, 'that it was a rascally action?'

'Use stronger language against me, even than that, sir – I deserve it.'

'In plain words,' I went on, 'you can find no excuse for your conduct?'

'In the past time,' he said, 'I might have found excuses.'

'But you can't find them now?'

'I must not even look for them now.'

'Why not?'

'I owe it to Eunice to leave my conduct at its worst; with nothing said – by me – to defend it.'

'What has Eunice done to have such a claim on you as that?'

'Eunice has forgiven me.'

It was gratefully and delicately said. Ought I to have allowed this circumstance to weigh with me? I ask, in return, had *I* never committed any faults? As a fellow mortal and fellow sinner, had I any right to harden my heart against an expression of penitence which I felt to be sincere in its motive?

But I was bound to think of Eunice. I did think of her, before I ventured to accept the position – the critical position, as I shall presently show – of Philip's friend.

After more than an hour of questions put without reserve, and of answers given without prevarication, I had travelled over the whole ground laid out by the narratives which appear in these pages, and had arrived at my conclusion – so far as Philip Dunboyne was concerned.

I found him to be a man with nothing absolutely wicked in him – but with a nature so perilously weak, in many respects, that it might drift into wickedness unless a stronger nature was at hand to hold it back. Married to a wife without force of character, the probabilities would point to him as likely to yield to examples which might make him a bad husband. Married to a wife with a will of her own, and with true love to sustain her – a wife who would know when to take the command and how to take the command – a wife who, finding him tempted to commit actions unworthy of his better self, would be far-sighted enough to perceive that her husband's sense of honour might sometimes lose its balance, without being on that account hopelessly depraved – then, and in these cases only, the probabilities would point to Philip as a man likely to be the better and the happier for his situation, when the bonds of wedlock had got him.

But the serious question was not answered yet.

Could I feel justified in placing Eunice in the position towards Philip which I have just endeavoured to describe? I dared not allow my mind to dwell on the generosity which had so nobly pardoned him, or on the force of character which had bravely endured the bitterest disappointment, the cruellest humiliation. The one consideration which I was bound to face, was the sacred consideration of her happiness in her life to come.

Leaving Philip, with a few words of sympathy which might help him to bear his suspense, I went to my room to think.

The time passed – and I could arrive at no positive conclusion. Either way – with or without Philip – the contemplation of Eunice's future harassed me with doubt. Even if I had conquered my own indecision, and had made up my mind to sanction the union of the two young people, the difficulties that now beset me would not have been dispersed. Knowing what I alone knew, I could certainly remove Eunice's one objection to the marriage. In other words, I had only to relate what had happened on the day when the Chaplain brought the Minister to the prison, and the obstacle to their union would be removed. But, without considering Philip, it was simply out of the question to do this, in mercy to Eunice herself. What was Helena's disgrace, compared with the infamy which stained the name of the poor girl's mother! The other alternative of telling her part of the truth only was before me, if I could persuade myself to adopt it. I failed to persuade myself; my morbid anxiety for her welfare made me hesitate again. Human patience could endure no more. Rashness prevailed, and prudence yielded – I left my decision to be influenced by the coming interview with Eunice.

The next day, I drove to the farm. Philip's entreaties persuaded me to let him be my companion, on one condition – that he waited in the carriage while I went into the house.

I had carefully arranged my ideas, and had decided on proceeding with the greatest caution, before I ventured on saying the all-important words which, once spoken, were not to be recalled. The worst of those anxieties, under which the delicate health of Mr Gracedieu had broken down, was my anxiety now. Could I reconcile it to my conscience to permit a man, innocent of all knowledge of the truth, to marry the daughter of a condemned murderess without honestly telling him what he was about to do? Did I deserve to be pitied? Did I deserve to be blamed? – my mind was still undecided when I entered the house.

She ran to meet me as if she had been my daughter; she kissed me as if she had been my daughter; she fondly looked up at me as if she had been my daughter. At the sight of that sweet young face, so sorrowful, and so patiently enduring sorrow, all my doubts and hesitations, everything artificial about me with which I had entered the room, vanished in an instant.

After she had thanked me for coming to see her, I saw her tremble a little. The uppermost interest in her heart was forcing its way outwards to expression, try as she might to keep it back. 'Have you seen Philip?' she asked. The tone in which she put that question decided me – I was resolved to let her marry him. Impulse! Yes, impulse, asserting itself inexcusably in a man at the end of his life. I ought to have known better than to have given way. Very likely. But am I the only mortal who ought to have known better – and did not?

When Eunice asked if I had seen Philip, I owned that he was outside in the carriage. Before she could reproach me, I went on with what I had to say: 'My child, I know what a sacrifice you have made; and I should honour your scruples, if you had any reason for feeling them.'

'Any reason for feeling them?' She turned pale as she repeated the words.

An idea came to me. I rang for the servant, and sent her to the carriage to tell Philip to come in. 'My dear, I am not putting you to any unfair trial,' I assured her; 'I am going to prove that I love you as truly as if you were my own child.'

When they were both present, I resolved that they should not suffer a moment of needless suspense. Standing between them, I took Eunice's hand, and laid my other hand on Philip's shoulder, and spoke out plainly.

'I am here to make you both happy,' I said. 'I can remove the only obstacle to your marriage, and I mean to do it. But I must insist on one condition. Give me your promise, Philip, that you will ask for no explanations, and that you will be satisfied with the one true statement, which is all that I can offer to you.'

He gave me his promise, without an instant's hesitation.

'Philip grants what I ask,' I said to Eunice. 'Do you grant it, too?'

Her hand turned cold in mine; but she spoke firmly when she said: 'Yes.'

I gave her into Philip's care. It was his privilege to console and support her. It was my duty to say the decisive words:

'Rouse your courage, dear Eunice; you are no more affected by Helena's disgrace than I am. You are not her sister. Her father is not your father; her mother was not your mother. I was present, in the time of your infancy, when Mr Gracedieu's fatherly kindness received you as his adopted child. This, I declare to you both, on my word of honour, is the truth.'

How she bore it, I am not able to say. My foolish old eyes were filling with tears. I could just see plainly enough to find my way to the door, and leave them together.

In my reckless state of mind, I never asked myself if Time would be my accomplice, and keep the part of the secret which I had not revealed – or be my enemy, and betray me. The chances, either way, were perhaps equal. The deed was done.


## CHAPTER LXIV

### THE TRUTH TRIUMPHANT

The marriage was deferred, at Eunice's request, as an expression of respect to the memory of Philip's father.

When the time of delay had passed, it was arranged that the wedding ceremony should be held – after due publication of Banns – at the parish church of the London suburb in which my house was situated. Miss Jillgall was bridesmaid, and I gave away the bride. Before we set out for the church, Eunice asked leave to speak with me for a moment in private.

'Don't think,' she said, 'that I am forgetting my promise to be content with what you have told me about myself. I am not so ungrateful as that. But I do want, before I consent to be Philip's wife, to feel sure that I am not quite unworthy of him. Is it because I am of mean birth that you told me I was Mr Gracedieu's adopted child – and told me no more?'

I could honestly satisfy her, so far. 'Certainly not!' I said.

She put her arms round my neck. 'Do you say that,' she asked, 'to make my mind easy? or do you say it on your word of honour?'

'On my word of honour.'

We arrived at the church. Let Miss Jillgall describe the marriage, in her own inimitable way.

'No wedding breakfast, when you don't want to eat it. No wedding speeches, when nobody wants to make them, and nobody wants to hear them. And no false sentiment, shedding tears and reddening noses, on the happiest day in the whole year. A model marriage! I could desire nothing better, if I had any prospect of being a bride myself.'

They went away for their honeymoon to a quiet place by the seaside, not very far from the town in which Eunice had passed some of the happiest and the wretchedest days in her life. She persisted in thinking it possible that Mr Gracedieu might recover the use of his faculties at the last, and might wish to see her on his death-bed. 'His adopted daughter,' she gently reminded me, 'is his only daughter now.' The doctor shook his head when I told him what Eunice had said to me – and, the sad truth must be told, the doctor was right.

Miss Jillgall returned, on the wedding-day, to take care of the good man who had befriended her in her hour of need.

Before the end of the week, I heard from her, and was disagreeably reminded of an incident which we had both forgotten, absorbed as we were in the other and greater interests, at the time.

Mrs Tenbruggen had again appeared on the scene! She had written to Miss Jillgall, from Paris, to say that she had heard of old Mr Dunboyne's death, and that she wished to have the letter returned, which she had left for delivery to Philip's father on the day when Philip and Eunice were married. I had my own suspicions of what that letter might contain; and I regretted that Miss Jillgall had sent it back without first waiting to consult me. My misgivings, thus excited, were increased by more news of no very welcome kind. Mrs Tenbruggen had decided on returning to her professional pursuits in England. Massage, now the fashion everywhere, had put money into her pocket among the foreigners; and her husband, finding that she persisted in keeping out of his reach, had consented to a compromise. He was ready to submit to a judicial separation; in consideration of a little income which his wife had consented to settle on him, under the advice of her lawyer.

Some days later, I received a delightful letter from Philip and Eunice, reminding me that I had engaged to pay them a visit at the seaside. My room was ready for me, and I was left to choose my own day. I had just begun to write my reply, gladly accepting the invitation, when an ominous circumstance occurred. My servant announced 'a lady' and I found myself face to face with – Mrs Tenbruggen!

She was as cheerful as ever, and as eminently agreeable as ever.

'I have heard it all from Selina,' she said. 'Philip's marriage to Eunice (I shall go and congratulate them, of course), and the catastrophe (how dramatic!) of Helena Gracedieu. I warned Selina that Miss Helena would end badly. To tell the truth, she frightened me. I don't deny that I am a mischievous woman when I find myself affronted, quite capable of taking my revenge in my own small spiteful way. But poison and murder – ah, the frightful subject! let us drop it, and talk of something that doesn't make my hair (it's really my own hair) stand on end. Has Selina told you that I have got rid of my charming husband, on easy pecuniary terms? Oh, you know that? Very well. I will tell you something that you don't know. Mr Governor, I have found you out.'

'May I venture to ask how?'

'When I guessed which was which of those two girls,' she answered, 'and guessed wrong, you deliberately encouraged the mistake. Very clever, but you overdid it. From that moment, though I kept it to myself, I began to fear I might be wrong. Do you remember Low Lanes, my dear sir? A charming old church. I have had another consultation with my lawyer. His questions led me into mentioning how it happened that I heard of Low Lanes. After looking again at his memorandum of the birth advertised in the newspaper – without naming the place – he proposed trying the church register at Low Lanes. Need I tell you the result? I know, as well as you do that Philip has married the adopted child. He has had a mother-in-law who was hanged, and, what is more, he has the honour, through his late father, of being otherwise connected with the murderess by marriage – as his aunt!'

Bewilderment and dismay deprived me of my presence of mind. 'How did you discover that?' I was foolish enough to ask.

'Do you remember when I brought the baby to the prison?' she said. 'The father – as I mentioned at the time – had been a dear and valued friend of mine. No person could be better qualified to tell me who had married his wife's sister. If that lady had been living, I should never have been troubled with the charge of the child. Any more questions?'

'Only one. Is Philip to hear of this?'

'Oh, for shame! I don't deny that Philip insulted me grossly, in one way; and that Philip's late father insulted me grossly, in another way. But Mamma Tenbruggen is a Christian. She returns good for evil, and wouldn't for the world disturb the connubial felicity of Mr and Mrs Philip Dunboyne.'

The moment the woman was out of my house, I sent a telegram to Philip to say that he might expect to see me that night. I caught the last train in the evening; and I sat down to supper with those two harmless young creatures, knowing I must prepare the husband for what threatened them, and weakly deferring it, when I found myself in their presence, until the next day. Eunice was, in some degree, answerable for this hesitation on my part. No one could look at her husband, and fail to see that he was a supremely happy man. But I detected signs of care in the wife's face.

Before breakfast the next morning I was out on the beach, trying to decide how the inevitable disclosure might be made. Eunice joined me. Now, when we were alone, I asked if she was really and completely happy. Quietly and sadly she answered: 'Not yet.'

I hardly knew what to say. My face must have expressed disappointment and surprise.

'I shall never be quite happy,' she resumed, 'till I know what it is that you kept from me on that memorable day. I don't like having a secret from my husband – though it is not *my* secret.'

'Remember your promise,' I said.

'I don't forget it,' she answered. 'I can only wish that my promise would keep back the thoughts that come to me in spite of myself.'

'What thoughts?'

'There is something, as I fear, in the story of my parents which you are afraid to confide to me. Why did Mr Gracedieu allow me to believe, and leave everybody to believe, that I was his own child?'

'My dear, I relieved your mind of those doubts, on the morning of your marriage.'

'No. I was only thinking of myself, at that time. My mother – the doubt of *her* is the doubt that torments me now.'

'What do you mean?'

She put her arm in mine, and held by it with both hands.

'The mock-mother!' she whispered. 'Do you remember that dreadful Vision, that horrid whispering temptation in the dead of night? *Was* it a mock-mother? Oh, pity me! I don't know who my mother was. One horrid thought about her is a burden on my mind. If she was a good woman, you who love me would surely have made me happy by speaking of her?'

Those words decided me at last. Could she suffer more than she had suffered already, if I trusted her with the truth? I ran the risk. There was a time of silence that filled me with terror. The interval passed. She took my hand, and put it to her heart. 'Does it beat as if I was frightened?' she asked.

No! It was beating clamly.

'Does it relieve your anxiety?'

It told me that I had not surprised her. That unforgotten Vision of the night had prepared her for the worst, after the time when I had told her that she was an adopted child. 'I know,' I said, 'that those whispered temptations overpowered you again, when you and Helena met on the stairs, and you forbade her to enter Philip's room. And I know that love had conquered once more, when you were next seen sitting by Philip's bedside. Tell me – have you any misgivings now? Is there fear in your heart of the return of that tempting spirit in you, in the time to come?'

'Not while Philip lives!'

There, where her love was – there her safety was. And she knew it! She suddenly left me. I asked where she was going.

'To tell Philip,' was the reply.

She was waiting for me at the door, when I followed her to the house.

'Is it done?' I said.

'It is done,' she answered.

'What did he say?'

'He said: "My darling, if I could be fonder of you than ever, I should be fonder of you now."'

I have been blamed for being too ready to confide to Philip the precious trust of Eunice's happiness. If that reply does not justify me, where is justification to be found?

## POSTSCRIPT

Later in the day, Mrs Tenbruggen arrived to offer her congratulations. She asked me for a few minutes with Philip alone. As a cat elaborates her preparations for killing a mouse, so the human cat elaborated her preparations for killing Philip's happiness. He remained uninjured by her teeth and her claws. 'Somebody,' she said, 'has told you of it already?' And Philip answered: 'Yes; my wife.'

For some months longer, Mr Gracedieu lingered. One morning, he said to Eunice: 'I want to teach you to knit. Sit by me, and see me do it.' His hands fell softly on his lap; his head sank little by little on her shoulder. She could just hear him whisper: 'How pleasant it is to sleep! Never was Death's dreadful work more gently done.

Our married pair live now on the paternal estate in Ireland; and Miss Jillgall reigns queen of domestic affairs. I am still strong enough to pass my autumn holidays in that pleasant house.

At times, my memory reverts to Helena Gracedieu, and to what I discovered when I had seen her diary.

How little I knew of that terrible creature when I first met with her, and fancied that she had inherited her mother's character! It was weak indeed to compare the mean vices of Mrs Gracedieu with the diabolical depravity of her daughter. Here, the doctrines of hereditary transmission of moral qualities must own that it has overlooked the fertility (for growth of good and for growth of evil equally) which is inherent in human nature. There are virtues that exalt us, and vices that degrade us, whose mysterious origin is, not in our parents, but in ourselves. When I think of Helena, I ask myself, where is the trace which reveals that the first murder in the world was the product of inherited crime?

The criminal left the prison, on the expiration of her sentence, so secretly that it was impossible to trace her. Some months later, Miss Jillgall received an illustrated newspaper published in the United States. She showed me one of the portraits in it.

'Do you recognize the illustrious original?' she asked, with indignant emphasis on the last two words. I recognized Helena. 'Now read her new title,' Miss Jillgall continued.

I read: 'The Reverend Miss Gracedieu'.

The biographical notice followed. Here is an extract: 'This eminent lady, the victim of a shocking miscarriage of justice in England, is now the distinguished leader of a new community in the United States. We hail in her the great intellect which asserts the superiority of woman over man. In the first French Revolution, the attempt made by men to found a rational religion met with only temporary success. It was reserved for the mightier spirit of woman to lay the foundations more firmly, and to dedicate one of the noblest edifices in this city to the Worship of Pure Reason. Readers who wish for further information will do well to provide themselves with the Reverend Miss Gracedieu's Orations – the tenth edition of which is advertised in our columns.'

'I once asked you,' Miss Jillgall reminded me, 'what Helena would do when she came out of prison, and you said she would do very well. Oh, Mr Governor, Solomon was nothing to You!'

THE END